Horde

Bryan Cassiday

Bryan Cassiday
Los Angeles
ISBN 9781732976368
Printed in the United States of America
First Edition: January 2021

BOOKS BY BRYAN CASSIDAY

Crime Blotter USA
Murder LLC (Scott Brody Thriller 2)
Bolt (Scott Brody Thriller 1)
Riptide of Fear
The Payout
Force of Impact (Ethan Carr Thriller 4)
Wipeout (Ethan Carr Thriller 3)
Dying to Breathe (Ethan Carr Thriller 2)
Countdown to Death (Ethan Carr Thriller 1)
The Bus Stops Here—and Other Zombie Tales
Two Moons Rising
Alien Assault
Comes a Chopper
Zombie Apocalypse: The Chad Halverson Series
Helter Skelter
The Anaconda Complex
The Kill Option
Blood Moon: Thrillers and Tales of Terror
Fete of Death

And Darkness and Decay and the Red Death held illimitable dominion over all.

—Edgar Allan Poe

Chapter 1

The man sitting on a knoll at the edge of the desert watched with washed-out grey eyes the setting sun. With his long, unkempt hair, tangled beard, tattered clothes, and sunburnt face, he looked like a wino that should be sleeping it off in a city gutter. From his slovenly appearance he could have been a sixty-year-old who would never see seventy. In reality, he was in his forties. Nothing but skin and bone, he hadn't eaten in weeks. Nevertheless, he didn't feel hungry.

He saw a man charging toward him. The man was on fire, flames shooting out of his scalp, smoke pluming from his head. Having charred his clothes, flames were now busy eating his flesh. On account of the flames the man's age was indeterminate.

The burning man had reached within fifteen feet of the begrimed wino when he slowed down, the flames eating him alive, his lungs filling with smoke on the inside and engulfed in flames on the outside. Suffocating, reeking of alcohol and smoke, he came to a halt, a statue of fire.

"I did this to myself," he cried in agony, coughing out a cloud of smoke, the flesh on his face melting like wax, beseeching the wino with his blackened hands clutching the air. "I'd rather be nothing but ashes than one of the . . . the . . ."

Unable to complete his sentence, continuing to burn, the man collapsed on his knees, took his last, dying breath, and pitched forward on what was left of his fire-ravaged face.

The desert rat stared at the corpse, unmoved, watching out of curiosity more than anything else the corpse burn, making no move to put out the flames.

Out of the corner of his eye, with little interest, he saw a car driving on a winding road toward him, kicking up dust behind it with its rear wheels.

He didn't know if the driver had seen him. He didn't care. He sat motionless, watching and waiting with indifference. He licked his chapped lips with what little saliva he had in his mouth with a tongue like a dry leather strap.

The rusted, beat-up Ford Taurus drew to a halt near the man's perch. On the dented front fenders the grey primer was exposed in splotches where the original black paint had worn off through years of neglect.

For a while nobody got out of the car.

The man didn't mind. He considered the car part of the scenery, as interesting and as dull as the knoll he sat on and the barren desert that stretched into the distance beyond the smoldering, charred corpse. He showed no curiosity.

Five minutes later, two jeans-clad men wearing black cotton bandanas with white paisley prints wrapped around their faces clambered out of the front seat of the car. The paunchy thirtyish guy with a boyish face who had been riding shotgun was gripping a baseball bat in his hand. Squinting, he wore his hair over his ears. The middle-aged bald driver with deep-set brown eyes and a furrowed brow wore a pistol in a holster on his hip.

They approached the foot of the knoll in no particular hurry, but they had a wariness about them and came to a halt seven feet away from the man. They took in the remains of the scorched corpse with horror.

"Jesus," said the paunchy guy, pulling a face at the stench of the corpse.

"I didn't even know that was a body till we got here," said the bald guy.

"What happened here, codger?"

The man said nothing, his face and eyes blank.

"What do you think, Danny?" said the bald guy.

"He looks like shit, Porter. I think he's got it."

"Old man," said Porter. "You heard Danny. Are you infected?"

The man gave him a blank look.

"You speak English, geezer?" said Danny.

The man gave Danny the same blank look.

"Want me to take this Louisville Slugger to your head?" said Danny, brandishing his bat. "I asked you a question. Where's your manners? Are you infected, scumbag?"

The man scratched his sunburnt, peeling forehead.

"What the hell's wrong with him?" Danny asked Porter.

"Maybe he's slamming skag. He's out of it."

6

"You think he's infected?"

"Can't tell. He could be just strung out."

"Where's he scoring skag around these parts? Nobody lives around here for miles and miles. I think he's infected. I need to bash his brains in," said Danny, thumping the sweet spot of the bat's barrel against his open left hand in anticipation.

"He could be drunk, I suppose. I dunno. He's got that dead, empty look in his eyes, like there's nothing alive inside his head."

"Exactly like one of the infected. I'm telling you he's got it."

"Are you infected?" Porter asked the man. "We don't have all day. Answer me."

The man stared at him with glassy eyes.

"I'm gonna bash your brains in," said Danny, "if you don't tell us right now if you're infected. Are you infected?"

The man continued staring, showing no fear—showing no emotion, for that matter.

"He doesn't care," said Porter. "Maybe he's retarded. He could've escaped from a loony bin."

"Yeah," said Danny. "They usually build bughouses in unpopulated areas like this." He surveyed the desolate surroundings. "Maybe there are more like him around here."

"He must be starving. Look at him."

"That's how the infected look. Like they're always hungry. Because no matter how much they eat, they're still hungry."

"He's skinny, but he doesn't look hungry. He looks like one of those skin-and-bone survivors from a concentration camp. He needs food in his belly. Maybe that'll wake him up."

"I say he's infected. We waste him here and now before he infects us."

"If he was infected, he'd be coming after the two of us right now trying to chow down our flesh."

"I don't like the way he's looking at me. I'm gonna brain him," said Danny, raising his bat and preparing to advance on the man.

"Leave him be. He looks harmless. Look at his face. It's all sunburnt. Maybe he came here through the desert. His brains could be fried from the sun."

"There's something wrong with him. I don't trust him. One bite from him, we're dead. And what about that burnt corpse? Did

7

the codger take a match to that poor guy?" Sniffing the air, Danny made a face. "I smell booze mixed with the smoke. Maybe that stiff was a wino."

"Keep your shirt on," said Porter. He turned to the man sitting calmly on the knoll. "Where's your mask?"

"What mask?" muttered the man.

"Did he say something?" said Danny.

"Knock it off," said Porter. "The guy's messed up in the head. Can't you see?"

"I don't want him near me if he's not wearing a mask."

"Put on a mask," Porter told the man.

"No mask," husked the man, barely audible.

"Did he say something?" said Danny.

Porter withdrew an unused white handkerchief from his rear trouser pocket and handed it to the man. "Use this."

The man folded the handkerchief into a triangle, wrapped it around his face, and tied a knot in it in back of his neck.

"Are you hungry?" said Porter. "We got food back at our camp."

The man's gaze was as dead as ever.

"He's dead inside because he's infected," said Danny, tightening his grip on his bat. "We gotta put down that whack job now."

"Take it easy."

"I don't like him. Why doesn't he tell us what he's doing here?"

"The sun did it. It scrambled his brains. Maybe that's why he's having trouble talking. And he's dehydrated. He's had a rough trip. That's all. He's not acting like the infected."

"He's not acting at all. That's the problem. He's like some cigar store dummy."

"Come back with us and we'll round you up some grub to eat," Porter told the man.

"Don't blame me if he starts eating *you* instead," said Danny.

"You're seeing infected under every rock."

"I didn't make the world the way it is. I'm just trying to stay alive another day in it."

Porter picked up on movement at the edge of the piney woods where they petered out into the desert. Grimacing, three figures lurched out of the woods and headed toward him. They growled at the sight of Porter and Danny.

Chapter 2

"We got ghouls coming this way," Porter told Danny.

"Buddies of this guy no doubt," said Danny. "Let 'em come. I'm ready for 'em."

He grabbed the handle of the bat with two hands and took practice swings with it, warming up for the main event.

"Your buddies are coming to rescue you," he told the man.

The man showed no reaction.

"Leave the old guy alone," said Porter. "He's harmless."

"Well, his buddies aren't."

Bat in hand, Danny strode toward the shambling trio to confront them.

The leader of the group was a beefy thirtyish guy in coveralls wearing a silver hardhat. Groaning, he grimaced at Danny, baring his teeth, streaked with blood, sticking his hands out toward him.

Clutching his bat, Danny swung it and clubbed the leader in the head, sending the silver hardhat flying. The leader's broad head jerked to the side, but, protected by the hardhat, he kept advancing on Danny.

"That was just a love tap," said Danny. "Eat this, slime bucket."

Danny swung at the leader's head again, smashing it with the bat's barrel, cracking the guy's jaw and temple, driving skull shards into the infected brain.

The ghoul staggered a little ways then toppled to the ground.

Danny let out a rebel yell, a war whoop that froze the blood, if you had any—and the ghouls didn't since they were already dead from the plague and had become flesh eaters. He swung the bat several times like he was taking batting practice.

Finishing warming up he angled toward the next infected.

"Don't get too close to them," said Porter, heading after Danny to help him.

"Don't worry about me. I can take care of myself. You take out the geezer."

"He doesn't have the plague," said Porter, striding toward Danny, gun in hand.

"Oh yeah? Then why can't he talk?"

"He talked. I heard him."

"You call that talking? He didn't answer any of my questions."

Danny advanced toward the second ghoul, a middle-aged woman with grey hair wearing wire-rimmed granny glasses, which sat askew on her bent nose. He swung and hit her with the bat upside her head, dashing her brains out, which splattered on the ground.

"Two down. One to go," he said.

The third ghoul, a teenager with a mullet, his T-shirt shredded and grime streaked, trudged toward Danny. Wearing ear pods and making gargling sounds with his throat, the teen reached for Danny's face.

Porter blew the teen's head apart with a bullet from his SIG P220. The teen collapsed in a heap.

"That gunshot'll bring more of them," said Porter. "We better beat it. You OK?"

"I'm fine," said Danny.

"I thought that thing took a bite out of you."

"No way. He didn't touch me. And that goes for his teeth, too."

"Let's take the old man back to camp."

"Lemme take a bat to his head before he starts biting people."

"Knock it off, Danny."

They returned to their Taurus.

"Let's go," Porter said to the man, who continued to sit on the knoll, his expression dull. "Don't you want something to eat?"

"He'll eat your flesh," said Danny.

"Shut up. He's not one of them."

"Sometimes I wish I could bash my own brains out with this bat. The way the world is, going from bad to worse every day. It's enough to drive me nuts—"

"There's no time for wallowing in self-pity. Let's get the old man and go."

"You get him. I'm not touching him. He's one of them."

"He's not one of them," said Porter. He turned to the man. "What's your name, mister?"

No words issued from the man's lips.

11

"Having fun talking to the infected?" said Danny, with a lopsided smile.

"I heard him talk before, I tell you."

"Ghouls can't talk."

"He's no more a ghoul than you or me." Porter eyed the man. "What's your name?"

No answer.

"*¿Habla español?*" said Porter. "*¿Cómo se llama? Me llamo* Porter."

"Your name, idiot," Danny told the man. "Mine's Danny."

The man shook his head, eyes blank.

"Maybe he's got some kind of brain damage," Porter told Danny. "PTSD or something. A lot of people can't cope with the plague."

"Are you saying the idiot doesn't even know his own name?"

"We need a name for him."

"I vote for Idiot."

"You're a big help." Porter turned to the man. "Your name is John Box."

"Box," mumbled the man. "John Box."

"He can talk," said Danny. "Whoopee. Give the dummy a cigar."

"Would you stop dissing him? He's sick in the head. He needs medical help."

"When are you gonna stop holding his hand?"

"When he gets his shit together."

Danny waved Porter off and returned to the Taurus.

Chapter 3

"Let's get something to eat," Porter told Box.

Box didn't move.

"Can't you stand?" said Porter.

Nothing.

Porter started to get miffed. "You wanna go on living and come with us, or do you wanna sit there until you die? Snap out of it, man."

Box shifted his legs under him. They were stiff and sore from being in the same position so long. He stood up and stretched, getting his circulation going. He was tall and lean. He stood hunched over like he was carrying the world on his back.

He walked stiffly down the knoll to Porter.

"That's better," said Porter, holstering his SIG. "Take a seat in the back."

Box climbed into the back of the Taurus.

"Keep all the windows open so we don't get infected," said Danny.

"He's not infected," said Porter, sliding into the driver's seat.

"You can't be sure of that. He could be asymptomatic."

"You can't be sure of anything in this world. Whoever thought the plague would hit ten years ago?"

"Why take chances with a stranger?"

"Because he's not infected. And he needs help. Can't you tell a sick man when you see one?"

"I can. And that's why I say he's infected."

Something exploded in the west.

"What was that?" said Danny.

"Sounded like mortar fire," said Porter, becoming wary.

"How do you know what a mortar sounds like? Were you in the military?"

"I was a sergeant in the marines for two years."

"Are you sure it was a mortar?"

"It sounded like it. It's too far away for me to be sure."

"Who would be firing mortars around here?"

"I dunno. And I don't want to find out. We're heading in the opposite direction."

"I thought we were the only ones still alive for miles."

"We run into nomadic tribes once in a while. You know that."

"None of them go around packing mortars. Even guns and ammo are hard to come by."

Porter fired the engine, shifted the Taurus into drive, and executed a U-turn.

"I hope I'm wrong," he said, glancing apprehensively in the rearview mirror.

"We got our hands full fending off the infected, let alone guys with mortars."

"Did you walk across the desert?" Porter asked Box.

"I . . . think so," Box managed to answer, his voice hoarse, his gaze vacant.

"You must be dying of thirst."

Porter snatched a plastic liter bottle of water that was rolling around in the driver's-side foot well and handed it over his shoulder to the backseat.

Box accepted the bottle, unscrewed the plastic cap, and took a gulp of the water. He immediately started coughing.

"Take it slow," said Porter, eying the rearview mirror. "Or you'll get sick. When was the last time you had a drink?"

"I can't remember," said Box between coughs, his face reddening.

"No wonder you couldn't talk. Your throat must be dry as a bone."

Box felt tired from coughing. He sipped water from the bottle.

"Where you from?" said Porter.

Box shook his head. He said nothing.

"How long were you in the Mojave?"

"I—I—can't remember."

"I hate the desert. The sun can fry your brains and drive you batshit nuts, I'm telling you."

Danny craned around in his seat and faced Box. "Maybe you know something about that mortar fire we heard. It came from the desert."

"No."

"Or maybe you don't want to tell us about it," said Danny, flaring up. "Maybe you're a scout for that bunch with the mortar."

Box looked blank.

Danny reached over the seat, grabbed Box's collar, and shook him. "Answer me."

"Lay off him," said Porter, shoving Danny in the rib cage with his elbow and pushing him back into his seat while holding onto the steering wheel with his left hand. "He's in shock from being in the desert."

"Or he's pretending to be. I don't trust the guy. Nobody's that stupid. It's an act. He could be in cahoots with that tribe that has mortars."

"The desert can do strange things to a man. I lost my mind in the desert once. Before the plague. My car broke down on the interstate, and I wandered around under the scorching sun for hours. It burned my mind into a blank space."

"This guy's putting on an act."

"First you say he's infected. Now you say he's putting on an act. Make up your mind."

"There's something hinky about him."

"He's stressed out." Porter paused. "I seen it before in the marines. PTSD. Shellshock. Guys get the same look in their eyes Box has. Like they're not there anymore. The lights may be on, but nobody's home."

"I'm getting hot," said Danny.

"Put up the windows and I'll turn on the AC."

"I'm not putting up the windows with that infected guy spreading germs in the car with us. The windows stay down. Or we throw him out."

"We're not throwing him anywhere. He stays."

Now that Box had some water in his system, he found himself sweating on account of the heat.

"Look, he's sweating," said Porter, eying the rearview mirror. "That's a good sign. He was pale as a ghost before. I thought he might have heat prostration."

"I'm not looking at that guy," said Danny. "He makes me nuts when I look into his crazed eyes."

"What's this infection you're talking about?" said Box.

15

"Oh sure," said Danny in exasperation. "The zombie plague killed just about everybody in the whole world in the last ten years, and you know nothing about it? You been living in a cave all your life? We're supposed to believe that?"

"His memory's shot because of shock," said Porter.

Chapter 4

"You mean to tell me you don't know what the ghouls are?" Danny asked Box, craning around to stare at him.

"Ghouls?" said Box, his head aching.

Back on the knoll he had felt nothing. Now, after drinking some water, he felt a throbbing headache.

Ghouls? he thought. Was this for real or was he having a nightmare?

"Did you see those three guys we busted up back where we picked you up?" said Danny.

"Yeah."

"They were infected. They're ghouls. They contracted the plague, died, and came back to life—if you wanna call it that—as ghouls, the living dead. They eat human flesh."

"Oh hell," said Porter, gazing through the windshield.

"What?" said Danny, turning to face forward. "Shit."

Scores of men and women in tattered clothes were shambling in the middle of the road a hundred yards ahead packed together in serried ranks.

"There's a bunch of them ahead," Porter told Box.

Box leaned to the middle of the Taurus and gazed through the windshield at the ghouls.

Plague? thought Box. Why couldn't he remember a plague? How could he forget something like ghouls and a plague? This had to be a nightmare. It couldn't be real.

"How can you tell they're infected?" he said.

"The way they move," said Porter. "They lurch around like klutzes. When you get closer, you can see their dead eyes staring out of their heads. If they bite you, you become infected, die, and become like them. There's no cure."

"If he doesn't know that by now, there's something wrong with him," said Danny. "This has been going on for ten years. How could he not know?"

"They used to believe the disease could only be passed by a ghouls' teeth. Now some believe the disease is airborne as well as bloodborne."

17

"Which means if you breathe their spores you can become infected."

The ghouls approached the Taurus in a throbbing mass of diseased, decomposing flesh. Their putrescent faces bobbed up and down like bobbleheads. Their limbs jerked awkwardly. They were human in form only, their movements out of sync.

"Not everyone believes that, though," said Porter. "There are skeptics."

"But not us," said Danny. "That's why we wear masks."

"I'm not totally convinced, but I advise you to wear one," Porter told Box.

"Isn't there a vaccine?" said Box.

"The dysfunctional government said ten years ago they'd have a vaccine ready in a year," scoffed Danny. "It never happened. All the vaccines they said they were working on failed to prevent infection. So much for government promises. Where have you been?"

Box scoured his memory, trying to remember something— *anything* about his past. A terrifying tabula rasa stretched out in front of him to infinity. It sent a frisson of fear down his spine.

"I'm trying to remember," he said, racking his brains.

Porter stopped the Taurus in the middle of the road and killed the engine.

"What are you doing?" said Danny.

"I can't go around those things without wrecking the car's chassis on the rocky ground on the sides of the road," said Porter.

"Who said anything about going around them? Let's plow straight through them."

"What if their body parts get stuck in the wheel wells and we get surrounded by the ghouls?"

"Going backward doesn't help us. We need to return to camp."

"Yeah. Let's mow 'em down."

"Now you're talkin'."

Porter fired the Taurus's engine. He stepped on the gas and drove straight at the mob of ghouls.

"Make a hole and make it wide," he said, his expression intent.

The ghouls made no effort to get out of the way.

Reaching sixty miles an hour with the Taurus, Porter rammed into the throng of plodding corpses. His plan was to plow through the wall of living corpses that was a dozen-odd rows deep stretching across the tarmac.

The front bumper smashed into the decaying ghouls. Bodies flailed on the hood and squirmed onto the windshield blocking Porter's vision.

Porter cursed. "I can't see."

"Just keep going," said Danny, watching the corpses writhe on the windshield with enthralled repulsion.

The car decelerated.

"Why are you slowing down?" said Danny, wide-eyed.

"It's not me. The tires are losing traction. There are too many of those things in front of us."

Porter floored the gas. The Taurus's six-cylinder engine roared. The tires shrieked on the tarmac.

"Power up the windows," said Danny, terrified, as a ghoul's arm reached toward him.

He powered up his window, trapping the groping hand between the glass pane and the steel window frame. Porter powered up the driver's-side window, and Box powered up his backseat window.

The car lurched forward and ripped four fingers out of the ghoul's hand trapped by the passenger's-side window glass. The fingers fell into the foot well beside Danny's feet.

He watched them with abject horror as they moved like inchworms across the polyester carpet. Face sweating, he stamped on them with his boot heels pulverizing them until they ceased moving.

"Get those things out of the car," said Porter.

"I'm not touching them. I'll get infected."

"They can't bite you and they can't breathe so they can't infect you."

"Why don't *you* get rid of them then?"

"I'm the one driving."

"Let's switch seats. I'll do the driving."

"We don't have time. This place could be swarming with the infected."

"I'm not touching those dead fingers, and that's final," said Danny, leering at the digits inching across the foot well.

The car made headway through the mass of traipsing bodies of the ghouls and over the ones flattened under the wheels.

Box started when he heard a thud on the car roof.

Chapter 5

A ghoul that had been crawling on a tree limb that spanned the road had dropped onto the Taurus's roof with a thud.

"What the hell was that?" said Danny.

"One of those things must be on the roof," said Porter, glancing up at the headliner.

Box saw an arm reach down from the roof, make a fist, and set to pounding the window on his right.

The Taurus broke free from the festering, growling infected bodies. In its wake, the best part of the ten ghouls that lay smashed on the tarmac continued to squirm even though their rib cages and limbs were flattened. Only the ones who had their skulls crushed by the Taurus's tires lay motionless.

Danny let loose a cheer and pumped his fist.

Box watched the ghoul's fist keep pounding the window, fracturing the safety glass. He powered down the window, snagged the fist, and yanked it down.

"What are you doing?" said Danny, hearing the ghoul's growl on the roof.

Danny craned around.

"It was breaking through the window," said Box, continuing to yank on the arm trying to dislodge the ghoul hitchhiking on the roof.

Gritting his teeth, grunting, Box yanked the ghoul's fist as hard as he could with both hands, planting his feet against the side of the door to gain purchase as he sat on the backseat with his legs extended across the vinyl seat.

His body launched backward as the ghoul's arm broke free from the shoulder socket.

"What are you trying to do?" said Danny, taken aback by the writhing dead arm in Box's hands.

"I'm trying to get the thing off the roof," said Box, and flung the fetid arm out the window.

"It's still up there," said Danny, scoping out the headliner as he heard movement on the roof.

21

Box slid toward the open window and stuck his torso out in order to see the ghoul. Wind rushed by his face as the Taurus sped forward, free of the churning throng of the infected. Clinging to the window frame's steel lintel, Box stuck his head over the roof, squinting in the wind, trying to locate the hitchhiking ghoul.

"Are you crazy?" said Danny's voice from inside the car.

The ghoul held onto the roof with its remaining arm and tried to kick Box in the face.

Box tried to grasp the creature's leg with his free hand. He didn't want to fall out of the car so he had to be careful to keep his balance as he reached for the leg. He managed to get ahold of the thing's foot and wrenched it toward him.

He dragged the ghoul across the roof. Sliding through the window into the car, he flung the creature onto the side of the road, where it landed on the dirt shoulder and lay, flailing its three limbs.

"Good work," said Porter.

"You looked like you knew what you were doing," Danny told Box in admiration. "Were you in the military?"

Box shook his head, eyes blank. He couldn't recall anything.

"We can use a guy like you," said Porter. "We need all the fighters we can get."

"We have to defend ourselves from their attacks at the camp every day," said Danny. "There are billions of those things out there. Way more of them than us. And the only thing they want to do is eat our flesh."

"Why is this happening?" said Box, trying to get his head around this new reality—if it *was* reality. He figured it could still be a nightmare.

"We don't know," said Porter. "This zombie plague spread all over the world in a matter of days. It's highly contagious."

"No cures?"

"A hundred grains of lead injected into their stinking brains with a gun cures them fine," said Danny. "Kill the brain, you kill the virus."

"Why don't you ask the government to send the military to help you?" said Box.

"Government?" said Porter. "We don't even know if there *is* a government. We don't got any commo. Nothing works. Internet, cell phones, landlines, forget it."

"A straggler told us the president nuked a lot of our cities, including New York and Vegas, trying to kill off the infected that are spreading the plague," said Danny.

"Can you imagine? Nuking our own country to save it?"

"Nuked Vegas?" said Box.

Box thought he was starting to remember something, but whatever it was faded out like a dream when you awake. He shook his head in frustration.

"What's wrong?" said Porter, eying him in the rearview mirror.

"Nothing."

"I'm no doctor, but I'd say you're still in shock. You'll come out of it sooner or later. Whatever it was that happened to you must've been pretty hairy to scramble your brains like that."

"Maybe you're better off not remembering," said Danny.

"Your mind could be protecting you by erasing your memories," said Porter. "Maybe it's a good thing."

"I want to remember," said Box, grimacing.

"Don't be too sure of that. Some memories are best forgotten," said Porter, wincing, as if recalling a painful moment in his past. "My mother . . . I had to . . . I had to—"

"You don't have to tell us," said Danny.

"I—I—I had to kill her with my own hands when she became infected," said Porter, his hands shaking on the steering wheel. "I"—he took a deep breath—"I blew her brains out with double aught buckshot from a twelve gauge."

"Jesus," said Danny, watching Porter with concern. "I never knew."

Porter lost control of the Taurus, which swerved off the road. Its shocks jouncing, the car bore for a culvert.

"What are you doing?" said Danny, and lunged to grab control of the steering wheel.

His hand on the wheel, Danny guided the Taurus back onto the tarmac.

"I'm all right," said Porter, brushing Danny's hand from the steering wheel and taking control.

Danny searched Porter's face. "Are you sure?"

"Do you ever feel like you're not in control of your life?"

"Can you control the car? That's all that matters here."

"Let's get back to camp," said Porter, shrugging it off, his face grim, refusing to talk about it any longer.

Box stared out the window at the pines and mesquites rushing past the car and hoped he wasn't harboring memories as painful as Porter's. Maybe amnesia was a good thing, he decided. Could it be that amnesia worked like novocaine for the mind, numbing it to pain? But novocaine didn't last forever. Apprehension gripped him. What horror was skulking in the cobwebs in the back of his mind awaiting him?

Who am I? What am I doing here?

"There's an abandoned car up ahead," said Porter.

Chapter 6

"Can you go around it?" said Danny.

"It's blocking both lanes, and there's no shoulder here," said Porter. "Probably ran out of gas." He spoke over his shoulder to Box. "Happens all the time. The gas stations are dry. We have to syphon gas from other cars."

He pulled to a halt behind the white Dodge Durango SUV, which was parked catercorner across the road.

He opened his door. "We need to push it out of the way."

"See any of the infected around?" Danny said, casting around the area.

"No," said Porter, doing the same.

Box opened the rear door, fixing to help move the Durango.

"Why'd they leave it blocking the road?" he said.

"To get a passerby to stop and help them," said Porter.

"So where are they?"

"Maybe the ghouls got them," said Danny, continuing to scan the area for the Durango's owners.

Box paused on the road, looking around. "I don't like it. Do you hear it?"

"I don't hear anything," said Porter.

"That's what I mean. Why aren't there any birds?"

"Where you been, Box?" said Danny. "A lot of the animals died out in the plague. It jumped species. But the animals stay dead. They don't come back to life as ghouls like humans."

"All species of birds were wiped out? Do you have any idea how many species of birds there are?"

"Carrion eaters actually multiplied," said Porter.

"I don't see any carrion around here, so why should there be any birds?" said Danny.

"Let's take a look inside the car," said Porter. "There might be someone inside we can't see because of the tinted glass."

Danny made a beeline toward the SUV. "Let's move this sucker."

Porter squinted through the Durango's windows, but couldn't see through their black-tinted glass. "Hello? Anybody there?"

He knocked on the windshield with his knuckles.

"Nobody must be in there," said Danny. "Where'd they go?"

"Maybe they decided they had a better chance on foot."

"I'll release the brake," said Danny, pulling on the front door's handle. "It's locked. How are we gonna move it?"

"Hold it right there," said a burly, bearded, six-two man pushing forty emerging from the pines in jeans and tan suede boots, training a pistol on the three of them.

A short, wiry man, ten years younger, and six inches shorter with a permanent sneer marring his face came out after him in black jeans and a polo with a twentysomething woman clad in jeans. Narrow-waisted with a toned figure, she was wearing a tight black T with I Brake for Squirrels printed on it in white block letters.

The short man produced a Ruger .357 Magnum revolver. "Do you see that, Hal? They're trying to jack our car."

"I see it, Zeke," said Hal.

"We're not jacking anything," said Porter. "We're trying to push your car out of our way. We can't get by. Put those guns away."

Hal laughed. "And I got swampland in Florida I wanna sell you."

"Let's get on with it," said the woman.

"Knock it off, Marta," said Hal.

"We've been waiting here for over an hour. Let's go."

"You heard the lady," Hal told Porter. "She's mad you tried to jack our car."

"We already got a car," said Porter. "Why would we want a car that's out of gas? Just move your car and we'll be on our way."

"I'm hungry," said Marta. "Let's beat it and get some food."

"We'll take care of them, Marta," said Zeke. "Don't you worry." He turned to Hal. "Let's do 'em, Hal. The whole thieving lot of 'em."

"You're forgetting one thing, Zeke," said Hal.

"Not that I can see."

"They got a piece."

"When did that ever stop us?"

"Who said we're stopped?"

"We don't want any drama here," said Porter. "Just move your car, and we'll go our separate ways. No harm, no foul."

"The problem is you tried to jack our car," said Zeke. "That calls for retribution."

"You're right about one thing, friend," Hal told Porter. "We *are* outa gas. Toss your gun down," said Hal, standing twenty-odd feet away from Porter with his pistol aimed at Porter's chest.

"After you do the same," said Porter.

"I'm not asking you, mister. Toss it down. And then I want your car keys."

"I got a syphon in my car. We can spare a gallon to help you guys out, and we'll be on our way."

"That's mighty white of you."

Hal fired at Porter. A bullet sparked on the tarmac a foot to the right of Porter's boot.

"Shut up and do it," said Hal. "The next one takes out your eye."

"You better do what he says," said Zeke, brandishing his piece.

Box felt a rush of adrenaline shooting through his system.

He started when he heard a commotion in the woods behind Hal and his gang.

A horse burst out of the pines and reared, whinnying.

Box could see the horse was in pain. He winced in shock at the sight that confronted him. A ghoul was hanging onto the horse by its teeth, which it had buried in the horse's stomach. The male, twentysomething bandy-legged ghoul had already ripped a hole in the horse's belly, and a pile of intestines had oozed out. The horse was dragging its unspooling intestines on the ground behind it. Riding on the length of dirt-dusted bloody entrails was a pack of red-eyed rats busily gnawing on them.

Marta screamed in anguish. "Ohmigod. The poor horse."

The ghoul's teeth wouldn't let go of the horse's belly, widening the hole and allowing more entrails to uncoil out onto the ground.

"Someone put him out of his misery," said Marta.

Porter started to reach for his holstered pistol to shoot the horse.

"Don't do it or I'll shoot you where you stand," said Hal, ignoring the horse.

"You better do what he says," Danny told Porter, taking stock of Hal and his piece apprehensively.

"Listen to your buddy," said Hal. "Take out your gun nice and easy and drop it. That gun stays pointed down as you drop it, and I'll let you live."

Of two minds, Porter grudgingly made a decision. He deliberately grasped his pistol's butt, withdrew the piece from his holster, and dropped it to the tarmac.

Zeke fired his .357 Magnum at Porter. The slug went wide of its mark. Porter froze.

Rearing, the horse let loose a strident neigh as the ghoul chewed its belly and the rats feasted on its innards. In agony the horse fell on its side. Craning its large, muscled neck, it struggled to right itself.

Box took the opportunity afforded by the distraction to dive for Porter's SIG P220 that lay discarded on the tarmac.

Jacked up, Zeke fired at him, gnashing his teeth and whipping his head back toward Box after glancing at the rearing horse.

Box was in the midst of snatching the SIG's stock, rolling over several times, coming to a halt on his chest, firing a bullet into Zeke's head, and then one into Hal's, as Zeke's bullet sang past him. Hal fired back as he was crumpling to the ground. His errant bullet hit his Durango's windshield, spiderwebbing it.

"Good shooting," said Porter. "I never seen shooting like that."

"Are you special forces or something?" said Danny.

Box looked blank. He gazed at the SIG he was gripping. It was obvious he knew how to handle a gun. His memory as yet yielded nothing.

Marta wept, muttering incoherently. "You bastards."

Box stalked toward the horse lying on its side fixing to shoot it, when he balked, nonplussed.

A rat a foot long coated with equine blood scampered out of the horse's wounded belly and bounded off the horse. Box shot the rat in revulsion. The rat somersaulted in the air and flopped on the ground dead, its mouth agape, exposing its jagged, bloody teeth with morsels of horse flesh wedged between them.

Ignoring Box the bandy-legged ghoul was still feeding on the horse's mutilated belly as the horse whickered in pain. Sickened by the ghoul's actions, Box shot it in the head, which caved in like a squash. The ghoul lay motionless on the horse. The rats perched on the horse's entrails scurried away into the woods, deciding they would return later to finish off the horse's remains.

Box approached the horse, which was still trying to right itself despite its traumatic injuries. His eyes morose, heaving a sigh, Box aimed the SIG between the horse's eyes and fired. The horse dropped its head and lay motionless.

Marta wept silently at the sight.

"Get the key to the Durango, Danny," said Porter.

Danny bolted over to Hal's corpse, searched its trouser pockets, fished out the car keys, and brought them back to Porter.

Porter approached Box.

"Gimme back my piece," said Porter in an even voice, no harm meant, just a man reclaiming his possession.

Box handed Porter the SIG.

"I'm glad you're on our side," said Porter.

Seeing no one was paying attention to her, Marta made a run for it.

Chapter 7

"Why's she running away?" said Porter. "We're not gonna hurt her."

"I'll get her," said Box, and sprinted after her.

"She must think we're gonna do something to her because her buddies tried to kill us," said Danny, watching Box chase her.

Box ran her down. Grabbing her wrist from behind, he held her under a pine.

"Come with us," he said, smelling pine scent.

"You think I'm an idiot? You're gonna kill me," said Marta, breathing hard and struggling to break free.

"Where are you gonna go all alone?"

"I'll take my chances," she said, not sounding convinced it was the right move.

"Come with us. We're going to their camp."

"*Their* camp? Aren't you one of them?"

"No. I met them out here. I was lost."

"Do you trust them?" she said, not struggling as hard.

"I'm trying to find out what's going on. They were telling me about some zombie plague that infected the world."

She stopped resisting him and looked at him in puzzlement. "Didn't you know?"

"I'm having trouble remembering things."

"We were trying to escape a pack of ghouls when we ran out of gas. Hal came up with the idea to block the road so we could jack a car."

"Are the ghouls coming here?"

"Thousands of them swarmed into the town where we were hiding. We took off."

"Where were you going?"

"I don't really know. We just wanted to get away from them. We don't want to get the disease."

"What do you plan on doing roaming around by yourself in the woods?"

"I thought you were gonna shoot me like you did Hal and Zeke."

"I did it to prevent them from shooting us. They started it. And they wanted to jack our car."

Marta bowed her head and clutched her forehead. "I don't know what to do. The infected ghouls are everywhere."

"Let's go to Porter's camp. It can't be any worse than wandering alone out here in the woods."

"You're not gonna shoot me?"

"Of course not."

"Then let go of my wrist. You're hurting me."

Box released his grasp on her wrist.

"What about your two pals?" she said, rubbing her wrist.

"Nobody's gonna hurt you. Let's go back to the car."

Now that Hal and Zeke were dead, she didn't know what to do with herself. She had to find a way to survive. She returned with Box to the Durango, where Porter and Danny were waiting for them.

"The filling stations are out of gas," she said. "Everything's going to pot."

"You shouldn't've attacked us," Danny told her.

"It was Hal's idea," she said, leering at his corpse, which had a bloody bullet hole in the forehead. "He didn't trust anyone. We're trying to escape the infected."

"Are they around here?" said Porter, scoping out the woods.

"We ran into mobs of them a couple hours ago," said Marta.

"That's not good. They could be heading toward our camp. We better get back ASAP."

Danny scooped up Hal's and Zeke's handguns. "We need guns."

"We also need ammo," said Porter.

"Where's your mask?" Danny asked Marta.

"I don't have one."

"None of you guys had one," said Danny, glancing at the two corpses on the ground.

"What good are they when those things attack?"

"Their spores can infect you."

"If you're that close to them, they'll bite you anyway."

She had a point, decided Box.

Danny ogled Marta's face. "You got a pretty face. It would be a shame for you to wear a mask. I guess you don't have to wear one, as long as you're not infected."

"If I was infected, I wouldn't be running away from those things. Would I?"

"Do you have any bites on your body?"

"No."

Danny ran his eyes up and down her figure. "We need to inspect your body before we let you join us. Take off your blouse."

"Knock it off, Danny," said Porter. "And put your eyes back in your head. Haven't you ever seen a woman before?"

"Ah. I was just having some fun. You're too serious."

"A plague is a serious situation. We all may be dead tomorrow. Is that serious enough for you? Or am I mistaken?"

Danny shrugged and looked sheepish.

The four of them headed to the Durango. Danny unlocked it with Hal's key fob, climbed inside, shifted the gears into neutral, and climbed out. He, Porter, and Box got behind the vehicle and shoved it off the road into a ditch.

"How did you hook up with those bad eggs?" Porter asked Marta.

"They were OK until we ran into a bunch of those ghouls. They're everywhere. Where are we supposed to go to get away from them? There's no escape from the plague."

Porter and Danny clambered into the front of the Taurus, Box and Marta into the back.

"The whole world's infested with the plague from the scuttlebutt we hear," said Danny.

Porter fired up the Taurus's engine and drove back to camp, putting on speed.

Chapter 8

The camp turned out to be an abandoned warehouse on the outskirts of a small town. A chain-link fence encompassed the warehouse and its parking lot in front of it. Various cars and pickups were parked in the lot.

Riding through town before they arrived at the warehouse, Box observed the charred, broken husks of small shops and restaurants that had been burned and looted along the sidewalk. A gutted barbershop had scorched plywood boards nailed to its window frame defaced with graffiti scrawled on them. The red, white, and blue barber pole stood intact beside the blackened doorjamb, the wooden door itself having been consumed in the flames.

He didn't see a single shop or restaurant that wasn't empty and in shambles, devastated by fire and looting.

At the warehouse, which remained untouched by fire, Box picked up on armed guards stationed on either side of the building and at two towers at the entrance gate in the chain-link fence.

When the guards saw Porter's car at the entrance, they opened the gate.

Porter parked the Taurus, and he and the other three piled out into the parking lot. Porter and Danny led the way into the warehouse, Box and Marta in tow.

Everyone milling around inside the warehouse wore a mask of some sort—bandanas, surgical masks, balaclavas, neck gaiters.

"We found two survivors," said Porter.

A stout blonde just this side of forty wearing jeans, a white blouse, brown leather hiking boots, and a backpack approached him with a no-nonsense look on her face. She wore wire-rim spectacles on her Roman nose. She jutted her chin at Porter like she was spoiling for a fight.

"How do you know they're not infected?" she said.

"They don't show any symptoms, Hilda," said Porter.

"You know as well as I they could be asymptomatic."

"The infected didn't bite them."

"They could be airborne infected."

"We're not 100 percent sure the plague is passed that way."

"Maybe you're not, but I am. We have overwhelming evidence people have become infected and turned into flesh-eating ghouls by inhaling the spores carried in the breath of the infected. We know they didn't get the plague by being bitten, so they must've got it from breathing spores."

"There are two schools of thought on that. I'm not convinced you can get the plague via the air. If the infected bite you, you are definitely infected. That's all we know for sure."

"We also know some people are asymptomatic."

"That's possible, but we have no proof of it."

"How do you know these two survivors aren't asymptomatic?"

"They told me they're not infected. They said none of the ghouls had bitten them. And they don't act infected. One guy has PTSD or something, that's all."

"Maybe that's a symptom he's coming down with the plague."

"Let's not panic. You're speculating. We don't know that PTSD is a symptom of the plague."

"You still haven't proven to me they're not asymptomatic."

"How the hell can I prove that, Hilda? We have no way of testing for the plague. If you turn into a ghoul, you're infected. That's all we know."

Hilda scrutinized Box and Marta. "We should quarantine both of them to be on the safe side. And where's your mask, what's your name?"

"Marta. I don't have one," said Marta, feeling her face.

"You're not coming in here without one."

"We got plenty of masks," said Porter. "Someone, give me a mask."

A frail, thin brown-haired woman approached him and handed him a red and black polka-dotted cotton bandana.

"Thanks," said Porter, and handed the bandana to Marta.

She folded it in a triangle and tied it around her face.

Other members of the camp gathered behind Hilda, looking concerned.

"Always err on the side of caution," said Gertie, a bony white-haired woman in her fifties with a club foot who halted up behind

Hilda. "We can't take chances with strangers. They need to be quarantined for two weeks."

"It's not necessary," said Porter. "They both look to be in good health. Box even saved our lives."

"Good health," said Gertie, looking aghast at Box. "He's bleeding."

Box realized blood was flowing down his arm and dripping onto the floor. He inspected his elbow.

"It's nothing," he said. "I skinned my elbow. I didn't even realize I'd done it. It must've happened when I dove for the gun on the road."

"If he's infected, his blood's infected."

"Where's Doc Epps?" said Porter, scoping out the crowd that was gathering.

Silence.

"Over here," said a baritone voice.

A five-nine, sixty-five-year-old florid-faced man wearing thick black-framed bifocals, an N95 surgical mask, and a charcoal grey blazer emerged from the gaggle of spectators carrying a black medical bag.

"Let's have a look at it," said Epps, approaching Box.

Box showed him his barked elbow.

Epps dug surgical gloves out of his bag and put them on. He applied Neosporin to a sterile bandage and compressed the wound with the bandage to stanch the bleeding. Using sterile cotton he wiped off the blood that was trickling down Box's forearm.

"Change the bandage a couple times a day and put more Neosporin on it," said Epps, handing Box some bandages and the tube of Neosporin.

"Do you think he's infected, Doctor?" said Gertie.

"He looks malnourished, but he seems alert."

"We found him in the desert," said Porter.

"I see. There's no way to be certain he's not infected. We don't have a reliable way of testing for the plague. Have someone mop up the drops of blood on the floor," said Epps, pointing to the blood at his feet.

"We're quarantining both of them," said Hilda.

"No ghouls bit me," said Marta. "I don't have it."

"I don't either," said Box.

35

"But you can't be sure," said Danny, "because you have amnesia. You couldn't even remember how you got across the desert, let alone your own name. Maybe a ghoul bit you in the desert before we met you."

"There aren't any bites on my body."

"You could've been infected by spores exhaled by one of the infected," said Hilda.

"We're not certain it can spread that way," said Porter. "Right, Doc?"

"I haven't seen it happen myself, but we can't rule it out," said Epps. "There's a lot about this disease we don't understand, and with civilization teetering on the brink of chaos we don't have the medical equipment and scientists to determine the truth."

"We're on our own," said Hilda. "We can't risk having these two new strangers infect us."

"Living in fear is not a viable lifestyle," said Porter. "We can't live the rest of our lives terrified of all strangers."

"It only takes one of them to infect and kill us. Being stupid isn't a viable lifestyle, either. Put them in quarantine right now."

Two tall well-built men in camo uniforms packing sidearms wended their way through the crowd, escorted Box and Marta to a room, and locked them inside.

"He saved our lives," said Porter. "Is this how we treat our friends?"

"It is if they're infected," said Gertie.

"We aren't sure they are."

"We're doing what's right," said Hilda. "And that's final. The lives of the camp members take pride of place. If those two are asymptomatic and we leave them free to intermingle with us, they could wipe out our entire population. It's my job to keep our community safe. They're not leaving the quarantine room without my say-so."

Chapter 9

The quarantine room contained five straight-backed wooden chairs and a wooden rectangular table in a windowless room. Against the side of three of the walls was a canvas cot, each with a pillow and a woolen blanket on it. Near one of the cots stood a portable wooden partition.

"It feels like we're in prison," said Marta, taking in the austere surroundings and taking a seat at the table.

"How did you wind up with Hal and Zeke?" asked Box, sitting beside her.

"I was trying to escape the infected. A pack of them killed my sister and mother. I ran for my life. Somehow I got out of the house without those things biting me. Blood-streaked teeth were snapping at me the entire time. I just kept running. I ran so fast I thought my heart would burst. I didn't stop till I couldn't breathe any more. Luckily I keep myself in good shape. I used to work out in the gym five days a week." Her voice broke. She tried to collect herself. "Mom and Jeanie didn't have a chance—"

Marta broke into tears, remembering their deaths, remembering the flesh-eating ghouls ripping their bodies apart and gorging on them, blood spurting out of her mom's throat, the ghouls lapping it up like it was nectar, practically singing with joy as they guzzled her blood and scarfed down her flesh.

"They ate Jeanie's ears and nose first," Marta went on. "She was still alive and begging for mercy as they chewed her flesh. I watched it all from a bedroom closet where I was hiding. I peeked through the louvered door at the slaughter. Blood spurting everywhere, the ghouls bathed in blood, humming with ecstasy. Oh, make the memories stop," she said, bowing her head and shutting her eyes.

"You don't have to tell me anything else," said Box.

"Why didn't I try to help them, you want to know."

"I don't want to know anything."

"I was terrified. I didn't want them to do the same thing to me. Mom and Jeanie were being eaten alive, screaming in agony.

'Make them stop, make them stop,' Jeanie kept crying, her face smothered in tears, as the ghouls chewed off her ears and nose. Was she talking to me? She had to be. Did she know I was hiding in the closet watching? She must have. She could have told the ghouls I was hiding in the closet, but she didn't. She saved my life, and . . . look how I repaid her. Mom was dead at that point. Jeanie was begging me to make them stop, and I failed her. I was too scared to go to her aid. I was literally shivering with fear, praying the ghouls wouldn't find me."

"What could you possibly have done? You would've ended up like your mother and sister."

"But I shoulda tried. I shoulda at least tried to save their lives. They were family, and I let them die in front of my very eyes," said Marta, coughing and sobbing. "I failed them."

"You didn't fail anyone. It's not your fault. There was nothing you could do."

"There were five of those things in the bedroom. How could I possibly have killed all of them?"

"You couldn't."

"Jeanie was still crying, 'Make them stop,' when I burst out of the closet and fled. The ghouls had no idea I was in the closet watching them tear Mom and Jeanie apart. 'Help,' Jeanie screamed at me. I didn't help. I didn't stop running. I was consumed with fear."

"Don't think about it anymore. It's over. Kicking yourself won't change a thing."

"You have no idea."

"I have no idea of anything. I don't even know who I am."

Marta stopped sobbing and looked at him. "You don't?"

"I can't remember anything. It's frustrating."

"I wish I could forget . . . horrible things. Maybe you're lucky you can't remember. It must've been something traumatic that happened to you."

"So awful my mind doesn't want to recall it."

"You have no memories at all?"

Box grimaced. "No." He paused, assembling his thoughts. "Apparently I'm pretty good with a gun, as you saw when Hal and Zeke tried to kill me. I have no idea how or where I learned to shoot like that."

"It just came natural to you?"

"I didn't even think about it. I just did it. I knew what I had to do, and I acted."

"It's good you did."

Box gave her a questioning look. "I thought they were your friends."

Marta heaved a sigh. "They helped me escape a passel of the infected. But . . ."

"But what?"

She didn't answer.

"You don't have to talk about it," said Box.

"Hal demanded sex in return. I refused. He has a mean streak. He had Zeke hold me down and . . ." Her voice trailed off, her eyes blank.

"You don't have to tell me."

"I need to. I need to tell someone."

"I get the picture. You don't need to go into the details—"

"Hal raped me." She paused, a faraway look in her eyes. "It was strange. He wouldn't let Zeke do it. Hal ordered Zeke to hold me down. Zeke wanted to take his turn with me, but Hal wouldn't let him. Hal said I was his, and nobody else could do it with me. Zeke got mad and tried to rape me. Hal pistol-whipped Zeke and threw him off me. Zeke never tried again. I could tell Zeke hated him, though. Whenever Hal forced me to have sex with him, Zeke would go on a walk somewhere, working off his bottled-up anger with exercise."

"I would've emptied my mag into Hal's head if I'd known."

She had horrible memories, and yet she could remember them, but he couldn't, Box decided. Was she stronger than he was? He couldn't cope with his memories, so he lost them. Her memories were horrendous and yet she retained them. How could his possibly be any worse than hers?

What the hell was wrong with him? he wondered. Did he know things that others didn't? Why would he think that?

"Why were you mad at me when I killed Hal?"

She shrugged. "A reflex, I guess. He *did* help me escape the infected. It's hard to explain. He was my savior, in a way, though I hated him for assaulting me. I wouldn't be alive without him.

When you killed him, it was automatic with me—my anger at you. I didn't think about it."

"Like the Stockholm syndrome," said Box, understanding.

"What's that?"

"Sometimes when people are kept hostage, they start having intimate feelings for their captors. They feel dependent on them. You felt dependent on Hal because he saved you from the ghouls."

"But then he assaulted me."

"Your anger at me for his death was a superficial reaction connected with the Stockholm syndrome. It was reflexive, like you said."

"Stockholm syndrome? I never heard of it. Are you some kind of psychiatrist?"

Box looked blank and shook his head in puzzlement. Was he? he wondered.

"A shrink who's good at shooting a gun?" he said. "I don't get it."

"If you're not a psychiatrist, how could you know about this syndrome?"

Box felt uncomfortable. He felt sweat pouring out of his armpits. "I get the feeling I don't want to ever find out."

"I used to work as a coder before the plague. Now all the computers are down. Nothing works around here. The world doesn't need coders anymore. I feel useless."

"The world doesn't need anyone."

"Don't say that. Not all jobs vanished."

"I don't know what my job was."

He racked his brains trying to remember. He saw the image of a blonde in a white dress walking along the shoreline, the surf frothing around her bare feet. Was it supposed to mean something to him?

"Do you think you can go on living without a past?" said Marta.

"I doubt it. The memories, I guess, will come back at some point," he said, not that he was looking forward to it, considering they must have traumatized him.

On the other hand, living without any idea who he was was driving him batty. He figured she was right—he couldn't go on living without memories. It wasn't normal. The mental block he had installed in his head as a psychological defense mechanism would lift and then . . . all hell would break loose.

Chapter 10

The quarantine door opened.

"You can come out and get some exercise," said Porter, appearing in the doorway.

"Just like prison," said Box, getting up from his seat.

"You're not prisoners. You're quarantined. There's a difference."

"Aren't you afraid you'll get infected if you're near us?"

"I don't believe the disease is spread via air. And even if it is, we're wearing masks to prevent the spread."

Porter led Box and Marta through the warehouse, now bustling with camp members carrying boxes filled with canned food. After Porter exited through the front door, he guided Box and Marta across the parking lot to an area enclosed by a chain-link fence containing weights and treadmills for exercise.

"Welcome to the exercise room," said Porter. "It's empty now. You have it all to yourselves."

He unlocked the padlock on the gate and let them inside.

Box and Marta entered the gym.

Porter locked them inside. "Sorry to do this. But Hilda doesn't want you wandering around and infecting people. I'll be back in an hour to let you out so you can have supper."

He departed.

"That Hilda's bad news," Marta told Box.

"Yeah. Porter seems OK."

Box stepped onto a treadmill and started jogging in place. He knew he was out of shape from malnourishment. But it made sense to exercise first, work up an appetite, then get something to eat.

Marta lifted a barbell above her head with both hands, supported it on the back of her neck, and did squats.

"You look like you know what you're doing," said Box.

"Gets my endorphins going and firms up my glutes. Nothing better than getting my endorphins going," she said, smiling, which lit up her eyes.

After he finished on the treadmill, Box figured he would get in some bench presses. He knew he was out of shape and needed to build himself up.

A strange sight caught his attention in the parking lot.

A vintage World War II–era Willys MB jeep manned by three men with a Browning .50 caliber machine gun mounted in the back careered across the parking lot toward the warehouse's front door, dragging a bloodied body in tattered clothes tethered by a chain to the rear bumper.

The driver, Rafael, pulled to a halt in front of the door and honked the jeep's horn. Another man sat with Rafael in the front, while a third man stood in the back aiming the machine gun over their heads. All of them in their twenties, they watched the warehouse door waiting for someone to come out.

A tattoo of Santa Muerte's face adorned Rafael's low forehead. Five eight, he had small ears, a pugnacious vulpine jaw, three-days'-growth of stubble, and suspicion-filled brown eyes that lurked under bushy brows.

When no one appeared at the warehouse door, Rafael honked the jeep's horn again.

"Come on, come on," he muttered.

Hilda walked out the door. "I heard you the first time."

"I don't have all day. We got a Big Eight of blow for you. Where's our food?" he said, holding up a translucent plastic bag filled with four ounces of white powder.

Hilda gazed with concern at the bloody man Rafael had dragged behind his jeep.

"Is that Bill Johnson?" she said, seething.

"Is that what you call him?" said Rafael with indifference. "I call him a rat."

Lying behind the jeep, Johnson groaned in pain, his flesh grated from being dragged across the road's tarmac and the parking lot's asphalt.

"You have no right to treat us like that," said Hilda. "We're dealing with you. What more do you want?"

"He came to my camp and told us you were refusing to deal with us anymore. He told me to leave here and never come back. Did you tell him to say that?"

"No, I didn't. I'm not reneging on our agreement. We're trading food for your product."

"So where's our food?"

She turned around and hollered into the warehouse. "Bring the boxes of food."

Two men and a woman emerged from the warehouse, each bearing a banker's box of canned goods. They loaded the goods into the back of the jeep.

"Where are the five other boxes?" said Rafael, holding onto the container of blow. "Our deal is a Big Eight for eight boxes of food."

"They'll get the rest," said Hilda, reaching for the blow.

Rafael drew it away from her. "Wait till we get the food."

The three loaders returned from the warehouse with three more filled boxes, which they stacked inside the jeep.

"That's only six," said Rafael.

"You had no right to treat Bill Johnson like that," said Hilda, gazing with concern at Johnson's writhing, bloodied body.

"Nobody tells me to get outa here. Not him. Not you. Not anybody. If they do, that's what happens to them."

Two loaders returned and packed two more boxes into the jeep.

"Now let him go," said Hilda.

"When I'm good and ready. He disrespected us. Nobody gets away with that."

Rafael handed her the plastic bag of blow. "That's zero zero zero. The purest blow on the market."

Hilda accepted the bag.

Rafael fired the jeep's engine, shifted into first, and drove off, dragging Johnson behind the jeep.

"Let him go," Hilda yelled, apoplectic. "You promised."

Before the jeep exited the parking lot, Rafael stopped. The guy manning the machine gun leapt out of the back of the jeep, released Johnson from the chain, and climbed back into the jeep. Rafael drove out of the parking lot through the open gate, the chain dragging behind him snaking and kicking up sparks on the tarmac.

Porter strode out of the warehouse. "What happened?"

"The cartel," said Hilda, her face grim. "They tortured Bill Johnson." She turned to the two loaders standing behind her. "Pablo and Tran, go help Bill."

The taller man Pablo and the wiry Tran dashed across the parking lot to retrieve Johnson, who was squirming on the asphalt, moaning, his grated flesh streaked with blood.

"Those bastards," said Porter. "I knew we should never have started dealing with them."

Hilda faced him.

"We need their product," she muttered, eying Rafael's bag in her hand. "And you know it. It's the only way we can stand living here under these godforsaken conditions. The plague is gonna kill us all sooner or later. We're all sick of this damn plague. We need an escape valve now and then."

"Snorting dope won't change anything."

"Nothing changes anything. That's the problem. We have to make do with what we have. We need relief from this endless, pointless misery."

"We can't trust the narcos."

"We're lucky they don't kill us all and take our food."

"Let 'em try it. We're not going down without a fight."

"You know they got more firepower than we do. Anyway, this stuff"—she glanced at the bag of nose candy—"helps us get through the day. We need it. Our people want it. The world's too awful to live in without drugs. If we don't get dope for them, they'll revolt."

"Maybe you're the one that needs it."

"What's that supposed to mean?" said Hilda, jutting her jaw at him.

"It's no secret you pack your nose."

"If it's not one drug, it's another. Everybody's taking some kind of drug. Wake up and smell the coffee, Porter. This is the end of the world. We're all gonna die. If you don't need some kind of release from the endless misery, you're not human."

"Maybe your habit is starting to cloud your judgment."

"You'd love to take over, wouldn't you? Well, not as long as I'm in charge, mister," she said, jabbing her forefinger into his chest.

Porter watched Pablo lift Johnson to his feet, drape Johnson's arm around his neck, and escort him back to the warehouse entrance. Tran took Johnson's other arm and did the same, supporting the other half of Johnson's weight. Johnson grimaced in pain.

"I can't believe it's come to this," said Porter. "We're all living on borrowed time." He became thoughtful. "Did you ever think maybe this is how the dinosaurs became extinct? Not from a comet striking the earth, but from a plague? Maybe this very same plague."

An explosion burst in the west.

"What was that?" said Hilda.

"Mortar fire," said Porter, disquieted, gazing westward. "It's getting closer. I heard it earlier when we found Box." He paused. "We may have trouble heading this way."

Chapter 11

Box had watched the whole thing from the makeshift gym.

At first he thought the three in the jeep were robbers, because he saw Hilda telling her men to load the jeep with food. But then he saw the driver of the jeep hand her something before he left. It could be a barter arrangement of some sort, decided Box.

On the other hand, if the trio in the jeep were bartering, why did they drag a bloody man on a chain through the warehouse parking lot? Box wondered. It looked more like extortion.

Porter angled toward the gym, unlocked the padlock on the chain-link door, and let Box out. Her face set in concentration, Marta kept doing squats.

"What was that all about?" said Box.

"They're from the cartel," said Porter. "We trade with them. Food for drugs."

"What kind of drugs?"

"Nose candy mostly. But they have everything. Murder 8, ice, weed, acid, ecstasy . . . You name it, they got it."

"What about the guy dragged on the chain?"

"He's one of ours," said Porter, dejected. "Bill Johnson. Apparently, he told the cartel we weren't gonna deal with them anymore, so they keelhauled him behind their jeep."

"You like cutting deals with cartel thugs?"

"Hilda thinks we need their dope to relieve the tension here. Several of our members have gone mad and had nervous breakdowns or committed suicide thanks to the plague. Our members think it's the apocalypse. And they're right. What kind of a future do we have with the infected running amok all over the world? It's only a matter of time . . . before we're all done for. Doing drugs takes the edge off. When you're locked up every day like a common criminal, you can easily go bonkers or commit suicide, if you don't have a release. So some of us do drugs."

"Far be it from me to tell you what to do—hell, I don't even know my own name—but I wouldn't trust cartel narcos."

"Who said anything about trusting them? They're a necessary evil. I told Hilda they're bad news, but she wants to keep dealing with them."

"Even after they tortured your man Bill Johnson?"

"Bill used to be a cop before the plague hit. He's a standup guy. Law and order mean everything to him. He's never gonna accept the chaos and anarchy brought on by the apocalypse. And he's never gonna accept our cutting deals with a cartel."

"Is he gonna make it?"

"I think so. Doc Epps is examining him. We're living in strange times. We're doing stuff we would never do under ordinary circumstances. We want to get on with our lives but we can't because of the plague. Some people are never gonna get used to it. Bill's one of those people."

A bleak expression crossed Box's face. "Cartels. They got *sicarios*. You gotta be careful around them. They don't mess around."

"*Sicarios*? What are they?"

"Hit men."

Porter gave him a puzzled look. "How do you know stuff like that?"

Good question, decided Box. "I wish I knew."

"Are you in law enforcement?"

Baffled, Box shook his head.

"You know how to handle a gun, and you know about these *sicarios*," said Porter. "Maybe you're a cop."

Box wasn't convinced. "Maybe I just watch a lot of cop shows on TV."

"TV . . . We don't even get TV anymore. Nobody's broadcasting. No news. No cop shows. No nothing. We have no idea what's going on in the world, except the stuff we learn from strangers like you and Marta."

"I'm no help at all."

"The hell with it. Let's get something to eat."

Marta finished doing squats, exited the gym, and caught up with them.

"What did I miss?" she said.

"Nothing," said Box. "You got your own drug."

"Huh?"

"Doing your exercises. Your endorphins make you feel good."

Marta shook her head in puzzlement. "Whatever."

"It's time to eat."

"I'm starving. I could eat a horse—" She caught herself, realizing what she was saying. Her face drained of blood. "That poor horse. I can't get him out of my mind."

"Don't think about it," said Porter. "We can't carry this stuff around with us. It'll cripple us. Put it out of your mind."

"I can't even remember the last time I had anything to eat," said Box.

"How about a can of Chef Boyardee beef ravioli?" said Porter. "We got tons of the stuff."

"Where's the dining room?" said Box.

"For you two it's the quarantine room."

"I get claustrophobic in there," said Marta. "Why can't we eat with the others?"

"It's only for two weeks. Then we'll know for sure if you have the zombie plague."

Chapter 12

Zodiac, aka "The Grim Reaper," stood in the middle of the road in a bright orange and blue floral print viscose aloha shirt with a sickle in his hand in front of his black Lincoln Navigator SUV in the Mojave Desert directing gunfire at a swarm of hundreds of infected who were blocking the road up ahead. He was sweating under the broiling sun.

He got his nickname "The Grim Reaper," or simply "Reaper," because of the sickle he carried around with him. Forty-seven years old, five ten with shoulder-length, thick, wavy black hair, he had No Fear tattooed on the inside of his right wrist and 666 tattooed on the inside of his left.

"This is the real helter-skelter," he said. "Not a race riot, like Manson said. It's this zombie plague. Manson was tuned in, but he didn't see this shit coming."

"Did you know Manson?" said a bare-chested rangy tanned guy in his late twenties, an AR-15 in his hands, his face sweaty, towy blond hair unkempt.

"My ma said she first met him in Haight-Ashbury and once belonged to his family at Spahn Ranch in the Valley, Tyler. They worshiped him like he was Jesus Christ."

"Heavy," said Tyler, impressed.

"Fire," said Zodiac.

Two guys manning an M327 120 mm rifle mortar ten feet to Zodiac's left lobbed a shell at the ghouls. The shell struck a knot of the infected and hurled them into the air as it exploded. Severed limbs, heads, and torsos catapulted through the smoke-clouded air. The rest of the infected kept shambling toward Zodiac and his entourage, which consisted of a dozen SUVs and a hundred-odd men.

"On target," he said, watching bomb-mangled corpses hurtled out of the writhing mob thud onto the ground.

Half a dozen men armed with AR-15s set on full auto fell to blasting the infected that were still on their feet with a hail of bullets.

Zodiac drank from a canteen of water that hung from a canvas strap around his neck and nodded watching the slugs tear apart the infected and fell them in their tracks.

Zodiac, whose real name was Zodiac Lancaster, had grown up in the Haight-Ashbury district of San Francisco, the son of two hippies. His father Vincent was a pothead who sold weed to support his habit. Zodiac's mother was named Janis. She, too, was a doper who tripped on weed and acid. She was fond of bragging she had once been a member of the Manson family before they had slaughtered Sharon Tate and her silk-stocking friends in an orgy of bloodshed in Benedict Canyon on a sultry night in August 1969.

Vincent and Janis's lifestyle consisted of taking drugs every day. The only way the Lancasters could support themselves and their habit was by hooking others on dope in order to accumulate more customers who bought their dope and provided them with a livable income.

Being hippies who were devout believers in astrology, they chose the name *Zodiac* for their one and only son. When he was young, Zodiac resented them for dumping on him such an oddball name, which earned him the derision and scorn of fellow children, who picked fistfights with him.

As he became older, he took a shine to the name when he realized he was different from other people and the uniqueness of his name separated him from the herd.

Growing up in Haight-Ashbury, spurned by his parents who were too busy getting stoned and preaching peace and love to pay attention to him, Zodiac grew up under the misconception that Haight-Ashbury was actually spelled Hate-Ashbury.

Vincent Lancaster died at the tender age of thirty, cut down by a burst of slugs from a rival drug dealer's MAC-10 machine pistol. Janis died two years later when she was tripping on Owsley Monterey Purple acid and, hallucinating that she was going for a swim in the ocean, walked in her nightgown into speeding traffic, which she got into her mind was breaking waves thanks to its whooshing sound, where she was promptly run over.

"Cut those dirty things to pieces," said Zodiac, watching his men pepper the infected with lead.

Bodies piled up across the road as bullet-riddled creatures crumpled, spasming and lurching.

"Drop another mortar shell on them," said Zodiac.

The gunners obliged and fired the mortar, whose shell struck the remaining ghouls that were still trudging and sent their necrotic bodies hurtling through the air like so much offal.

"Teach those stinking things a lesson. Nobody blocks the Reaper," said Zodiac, waving his sickle.

He picked up on a lone ghoul, a straggler, lurching toward them from their right. Clad in a postal uniform, it was a fortysomething Indian male with black-framed glasses askew on its nose. The thing was even carrying a navy blue canvas bag of letters over its shoulder like it was doing its rounds.

It was kind of funny, decided Zodiac.

"Look at that jerk," he said. "You got a letter for me, numb nuts?"

He didn't see any other ghouls anywhere near it. The thing was less than fifty feet from Zodiac, who could smell its putrescent flesh borne on the hot desert breeze.

The man to his right, clad in camos, turned his AR-15 on the straggler.

Zodiac snagged the AR-15's warm barrel and lowered it. "Leave this ugly mother to me."

Zodiac strode toward the postal ghoul as it shambled toward him extending its arms trying to grab him. Zodiac raised his sickle, sliced it through the air, and decapitated the ghoul, whose head flew through the air and landed on the ground six feet away, where it thumped, rolled two feet, and came to a halt. It opened and closed its mouth a few times, snapping at the air. The ghoul's body collapsed and lay motionless on its back.

Zodiac returned to his men.

"Want me to blow away the head to put it out of its misery, boss?" said the guy with the AR-15.

"Let it suffer," said Zodiac. "We don't want to waste ammo. The head can't hurt us without the ability to move. The sun will melt the skull's brains."

"I wanna see its head explode," said the guy, raising his AR-15.

Zodiac whirled around, wheeled the sickle through the air, and cut off the guy's head. Arterial blood fountained ten feet into the air, propelling the head ten feet away. Getting splashed with the blood, Zodiac stepped back, wiping the hot blood off his face.

"Anyone else don't wanna follow my orders?" he asked his men, the sickle in his hand dripping fresh blood.

They looked aghast at the dead man's bloody body that dropped to the ground, headless.

"When I give an order, you obey or else," said Zodiac. "Any questions?"

Silence.

"All right, then. Let's drive down to those dead ghouls in the road, drag them off the road, and be on our way."

"The mortar shells cratered the road, boss," said Tyler, nervous about speaking after he had watched the beheading.

"No problem. We'll drive around the craters. If we can't, we'll detour onto the desert."

Zodiac and his men returned to their vehicles, Zodiac to the lead Navigator, blood still streaming from his sickle, gleaming crimson under the bright sun.

The convoy of SUVs set out.

The penultimate SUV pulled the M327 mortar behind it. Not to be outdone, the last SUV hauled a catapult on a flatbed trailer.

Chapter 13

Box saw a blue-eyed blonde walking past him in a white dress that reached the ground. Caressed by a sea breeze that billowed her dress, she was walking along the shoreline in her bare feet. She seemed to be in a trance, as if sleepwalking. He recognized her, but he didn't recall her name. The surf rolled in, thrashing against the sand and frothing, then smoothing out as it licked her feet, damping the hem of her dress. She didn't care that her dress was getting wet.

As he looked down the shore, he realized a throng of ghouls was schlepping across the moist sand toward her, lurching and growling. She was headed straight for them, showing no reaction to their approach.

He wanted to scream to warn her to flee, but his scream curdled in his throat. He was lying on his back paralyzed, impotently watching her. They were closing in on her. She blithely walked toward them, her dress gliding along the wet sand at her feet. She could have been an apparition the way she moved.

Was he watching a ghost? he wondered. Was *he* a ghost? Was the reason he couldn't scream because he was already dead? None of it made any sense. How could he recognize her without knowing her name?

He started when he heard a scream. Was that him? Was he finally able to scream?

The piercing scream became louder. It wasn't him—

He jackknifed to a sitting position on his cot in the dark quarantine room. He had been dreaming, but the scream was real. He could still hear it emanating from beyond the door.

"What's happening?" said Marta.

He could hear her voice, but couldn't make her out in the darkness.

Senses alert, he scrambled off his cot, bolted to the door, and tried to open it. It was locked. He heard voices beyond the door. Gunfire erupted.

The door swung open.

Box backed away from the door in surprise, adrenaline surging through his body.

"Did you two leave your room?"

It was Porter, a pistol in his hand.

"No," said Box. "How could we? The door was locked. We heard screaming. What happened?"

"We got an infected out here. One of our members turned. Lynette. She started attacking people. I had to put her down."

Box could see a commotion in the warehouse. Harried members were scurrying around. Danny walked up to Porter, a baseball bat in his hands with blood and brains smeared on it.

"She bit Charlie before you shot her," said Danny. "I had to take him out."

"The question is, how did Lynette get infected?" said Porter.

"There's no question," said Hilda, striding toward them. "None of the ghouls bit her. She didn't have a mark on her. She contracted the plague from someone who's asymptomatic."

"You can't be sure of that," said Porter.

"It's the only explanation. There's no other way she could've got infected, since one of the ghouls didn't bite her. What about these two?" she said, nodding at Box and Marta.

"They said they were locked in the quarantine room."

"But they were among us earlier today. They must've got close to Lynette and infected her with their breath. You don't turn right away after you inhale the plague spores."

"You can't prove any of that. These two are fine. Look at them. Do they look infected?"

"That guy looks bony and malnourished to me. He could have a disease."

"It's because he hasn't eaten in a long time and he was walking through the desert."

"How can you be so sure? And it doesn't matter how he looks, anyway."

"Why not?"

"He could be asymptomatic."

"There you go with that again. I'm telling you, the plague doesn't spread that way. One of the infected has to bite you to infect you. That's the only way."

55

"It's not the only way. We can become infected by breathing spores exhaled by the infected."

"You're speculating."

"I am, am I? Then how do you explain Lynette's getting infected?"

Porter shook his head. "Your guess is as good as mine."

"Not a bite on her."

Gertie inserted herself into their presence.

"She's right. And we all know she's right," she said, addressing the crowd that had gathered around them. "It's these asymptomatic people we have to watch out for. To all appearances they look just like us. But they're the enemy. They have to be destroyed before they contaminate the rest of us." She glowered through the doorway at Box and Marta. "It's those two. They did it."

"They're quarantined," said Porter. "How could they contaminate anyone, even if they are infected. And they're not."

"Words," scoffed Gertie.

"We don't wanna get paranoid here or we'll be seeing infected everywhere we look," Porter told the crowd.

"If they're infected, they have to be destroyed," said Gertie, and set her jaw, glaring at Box and Marta.

Members in the crowd muttered in agreement.

"We're all gonna be at each other's throats," said Porter. "For no reason. Can't you see what's happening here? We can't be sure how Lynette got infected."

"Well, *I'm* sure," said Hilda. "Someone asymptomatic infected her."

"If that's true, how do you know it was Box and Marta that are asymptomatic? Maybe it's one of us."

Members in the crowd started looking at each other with suspicion.

"I see what you're doing," said Hilda. "You wanna fill us all with doubt and set us against each other so we can't make a decision. The fact is, Lynette became infected after these two strangers showed up."

The crowd grumbled their agreement and became fixated on Box and Marta.

"That doesn't prove anything," said Porter. "How long does it take for inhaled spores to infect someone? Maybe it takes several days or weeks. We just don't know. We don't know enough about this plague to be able to make sound deductions about it. We can't kill these two because of baseless suspicions."

"It's the only logical conclusion," said Hilda. "If we don't want to become infected, we have to execute these two strangers."

This was worse than the nightmare he was having about the woman in the white dress, decided Box.

"And what if someone else gets infected after you kill Box and Marta?" said Porter. "How will you feel then, finding out you were wrong about them?"

"It wouldn't mean I was wrong. It can take up to two weeks for symptoms to show."

"OK. Two weeks pass, and then somebody gets infected without being bitten. It would mean you killed two noncontagious people. Two innocent people."

Hilda thought about it. "I can see why you're so eager to protect them."

"What are you talking about?"

"If someone else gets infected two weeks after Box and Marta are dead, it would mean Box and Marta infected someone else while they were living, namely you and Danny because you were both in the car with them."

"What?" said Porter, taken aback. "Do you really believe that nonsense? Are you threatening to kill *me* now?"

"How do we know they didn't infect you while you were all in the car together?" said Gertie, putting in her two cents.

"Because they're not infected. Look at them. This is crazy."

"You were in the car with them. You breathed their air, their spores."

"Why are you singling them out? Because they're strangers? Any of us could be asymptomatic carriers, if you believe people can be infected with the zombie plague by spores. And we have no proof that ghoul spores can infect us. The only thing we know for sure is you become infected if a ghoul bites you."

"Then how do you explain Lynette getting infected?" said Hilda. "Where's the ghoul that bit her without leaving a mark on her?"

57

"Maybe you didn't examine her body close enough. Maybe there's a ghoul bite on it that you missed."

"Why do you refuse to believe in carriers? It's a medical fact that some people can be infected with a disease and are asymptomatic. These people are called carriers, and they spread the disease. They're just as deadly as infected people with symptoms."

"Do you want me and Marta to leave?" Box chimed in.

The others fell silent.

Chapter 14

"I don't want you to leave," said Porter.

"Are you sure?" said Box

"That might solve the problem," said Hilda. "I really don't want to give the order to kill anyone. That's not who we are."

"The two carriers should be executed," said Gertie. "It's the only way we can be sure of our safety."

"Stop calling them carriers when you have no way of knowing if they are," said Porter.

"All carriers need to be executed."

"Do you want to leave?" Hilda asked Box.

"I'd rather leave than be executed," answered Box.

"Nobody's being executed," said Porter. "And nobody's leaving. You and Marta need to remain in quarantine for two weeks. That's all."

"Then how many more of us are gonna die like Lynette?" said Gertie, raising her voice and addressing the crowd. "We can't allow the spores into our camp."

The crowd grumbled, disconcerted.

"How can we be sure everyone in here isn't a carrier?" said Porter.

"You're making things up," said Gertie.

"So are you. The point is, we have no proof that anyone here is a carrier. We can't even be 100 percent sure carriers of this plague exist."

"They exist," said Hilda.

"I don't understand any of this," said Danny. "Can't we all just calm down?"

"Nobody wants to turn," said a three-hundred-pound guy with jug ears wearing a navy blue T-shirt and a yellow hardhat, who was standing in the crowd.

"We don't have any proof that anyone's a carrier among us," said Porter. "Lynette might've gone outside at night without telling anyone and gotten bitten."

"There aren't any bites on her body," said Gertie.

"Let's examine her again. Is everyone OK with that? We need to be certain before we start executing anyone."

The crowd muttered, but nobody raised an objection—except Gertie.

"He who hesitates is lost," she said.

"*Festina lente*," said Porter. "Make haste slowly. What I'm saying is, let's not do anything rash."

"We'll all get infected if we take too long to make a decision."

Porter held up his hands to shush the crowd. "Lynette got infected somehow. If she was infected by spores, she could've been infected two weeks ago because that's how long it can take to start experiencing symptoms. Box and Marta just got here today."

The crowd became quiet.

"Which means we can't be positive Box and Marta infected her," Porter went on.

"Fancy words," said Gertie. "Fancy words is all. That's all you're good for, Howard Porter. Making pretty speeches."

"This solves nothing," said Hilda. "We still have to find out who infected Lynette, and we can't rest easy till we find that person or persons." She jabbed her forefinger at Box and Marta. "And these two haven't been exonerated. They could still be the carriers."

"Hear! Hear!" said a member of the crowd.

"So we keep them quarantined," said Porter.

"If only we had a test for the plague . . . ," said Danny.

"I'm telling you, Porter," said Hilda, "if we find out Box and Marta are the carriers, we'll need to quarantine you and Danny."

"We were wearing masks in the car," said Porter.

"Masks don't prevent the spread of all of the spores. Some of the spores can get through them."

"And what about social distancing? Look at us now. We're closer than six feet to each other."

Everyone in the crowd backed away apprehensively from their neighbors.

"You're changing the subject," said Hilda. "The question is, who infected Lynette? We need to find out to prevent more infections."

"Let's sleep on it," said Porter, stretching his arms and yawning. "We'll figure out what to do tomorrow."

Agitated but tired all the same, the crowd approved and dispersed.

"Meanwhile, Box and Marta stay quarantined," said Hilda.

Chapter 15

Porter ducked into the quarantine room with Box and Marta, closing the door behind him.

"I'll let you in on a little secret," said Porter.

"I hope it's good news," said Box. "I'm getting tired of all the bad."

"I thought they were gonna kill us," said Marta, widening her eyes.

"I told them I didn't believe the ghouls' breath could infect people with spores," said Porter. "Actually, I do believe the plague could be spread that way. I lied to stave off a lynch mob."

"Wait a minute," said Box. "Then you *do* believe Marta and me are infected?"

"No. I mean, I can't be sure. And none of them can be sure either. That's the point. They were rushing to judgment. They had to be stopped."

"I'm wondering if the best thing might be for us to leave."

"You're not going anywhere tonight. You need rest. I don't know what you've been through, but it must've been hell to mess up your mind the way it did. Is any of it coming back to you?"

Box sat down on his cot.

"No," he said, crestfallen, holding his head down.

"What we're going through now isn't exactly a love-in," said Marta.

"I apologize for their actions," said Porter, nodding toward the closed door. "People are scared of the unknown. When they don't understand why things are happening, they panic. Then it's only a matter of time before the killing starts."

"I don't want to be here when that happens."

"It's up to you two if you want to leave. We *do* have food here and we have electricity from a propane generator. I think you're better off here. Out there, on your own, you're gonna run into the infected—sooner or later. They're everywhere."

"Or we could end up at the end of a rope on a gibbet here," said Box, looking up at Porter.

"Our people will come to reason tomorrow after a good night's rest. I hope."

"You don't sound too sure of yourself."

Porter rubbed his eyes. "This plague is driving us all nuts."

A gunshot cracked in the warehouse.

Box heard a commotion. He bolted off the cot. A mob stampeded past the closed quarantine door. Yells cut through the warehouse.

"So much for sleep," said Porter, darting to the door.

Drawing his pistol, he opened the door to pandemonium.

Box sprang to the open doorway and watched.

"What happened?" said Porter, casting around for a shooter.

"I heard a gunshot," said Gertie, threading her way through the crowd trying to find the source of the report.

"It's Lucy," somebody cried. "She shot herself in the head."

Porter locked Box and Marta in the quarantine room.

Porter picked up on a hand waving above the crowd and made a beeline for it, elbowing bodies out of his way.

He reached the corpse of a twentysomething pale-complected woman with a brunette pageboy outstretched on the floor. A thin stream of blood trickled down the side of her striking if not beautiful face.

Hilda was kneeling beside the corpse reading a blood-splattered note in her hand.

"What's it say?" said Porter.

Hilda stood up and read the letter out loud. "'I'm the one who infected Lynette. We made love today. Lucy.'"

"They were lovers?"

"I guess."

"How did Lucy know she was infected?"

"She saw Lynette turn and figured it must've been her that infected her, since they were intimate."

Danny ran up, his eyes shining. "I heard that. It means Box and Marta aren't carriers, and Porter and me didn't get infected from them."

"If Lucy was a carrier, how do you know she didn't infect you or any of us?" said Hilda.

63

"This doesn't prove anything," said Porter. "All it means is that Lucy *thought* she was a carrier. But we can't be sure she was."

"Which means those two strangers aren't off the hook. Lucy could've been wrong about her being infected. She could've drawn the wrong conclusion from Lynette's turning. Lucy had a guilt complex because she thought it was her fault Lynette turned. She couldn't go on living with that knowledge and committed suicide."

"Why does everything have to be so complicated?" said Danny in frustration.

"We're in uncharted territory," said Porter. "We've never dealt with a zombie plague before. We're playing it by ear." He yawned. "I don't know about the rest of you, but I'm beat. Let's get some sleep and figure it out tomorrow."

"Every time I try to sleep you guys wake me up with all your running around and yelling."

"We gotta move Lucy's dead body out of here and cremate her," said Gertie, "or she'll infect us."

"We're not sure she *was* infected," said Porter, "but, you're right. There's no point in having a dead body in here." He turned to Danny. "Danny, get some help and haul her body outside."

Medical bag in hand, Dr. Epps wended his way through the mob. "What happened?"

Grim-faced, Porter pointed to Lucy's corpse.

"Are you sure she's dead?" said Epps, hunkering down beside her.

He withdrew his stethoscope from his bag and used it to listen for a heartbeat in Lucy's chest.

He stood up, shaking his head.

The crowd returned to their cots in different rooms of the warehouse.

Porter returned to the quarantine room.

Chapter 16

"We have to keep you two locked inside," Porter told Box at the doorway.

Box approached him. "Did I hear someone say 'suicide'?"

Porter nodded yes, his expression weary. "Lucy took her own life."

"Is this like one of those Jim Jones cults you have here with people committing suicide by drinking the Kool-Aid?" said Marta.

"We're not a cult," said Porter. "We don't teach religion here. We're just trying to survive one more day."

"Then why suicide?"

"We didn't tell Lucy to do it. She thought she infected her lover Lynette, who had to be destroyed. Lucy got it into her head that she was the one that infected Lynette."

"How did Lynette really get infected?" said Box.

"We don't know. Lucy was one of our members who believed the zombie plague can be transmitted by spores that when inhaled infect you. For a reason we don't know, she believed she was infected and spread the disease to Lynette."

"Then why—"

Porter held up his hand. "I know what you're gonna say. Let me explain. Lucy believed she didn't turn because she was asymptomatic." Porter paused. "There's so much about this plague we don't understand. Which gives rise to rumors and paranoia. Our worst enemies are the ones we can't see or understand. Because then our imaginations make up explanations that have no bearing in fact."

"And yet you can't rule out that Lucy's being close to Lynette was what infected Lynette."

"I can't rule anything out. We're too much in the dark to be able to make an accurate explanation of how the plague infects people. That's why we're quarantining you two, even though you may be free of the plague. We can't take any chances."

"Why aren't the scientists working day and night to discover a vaccine or cure?"

"What scientists?"

"What?" said Box, taken aback.

"Most everybody's dead in this country. If the plague didn't get them, the nukes did."

"Nukes?" said Box, trying to remember something but failing.

"We've heard info—and I think it's reliable—from travelers we've encountered that the president nuked all the major cities in America where the plague proliferated in order to wipe out the ghouls and the plague. I saw a mushroom cloud myself over Las Vegas."

"He nuked the whole country to save us?" said Marta. "That makes no kind of sense."

"Apparently, he thought the big cities were the major spreaders of the plague. Nuking big cities like New York, Chicago, and LA would eradicate the plague and make the rest of the country safe."

"But that hasn't happened. The infected ghouls are still roaming around at will."

"I didn't say his plan worked."

"Is he continuing to nuke the country?" said Box, frustrated that he couldn't remember something that had slipped his mind.

Porter shook his head. "We have no idea what's going on in Washington. Everybody could be dead there. We're cut off, like everybody else, and left to fend for ourselves. Now get some shuteye. Tomorrow's another day."

He locked Box and Marta in the room and departed.

Box killed the ceiling light. He and Marta returned to their cots.

"Death is following us around," said Box.

"How are we supposed to sleep under these conditions?"

Box didn't have an answer. He didn't even know his own name. How could he have an answer for anything?

He rolled over on his cot restlessly, his mind spinning questions.

A thud on the roof jerked him out of his thoughts.

He bolted up on his cot and stared at the ceiling in bewilderment.

"What was that?" said Marta.

Chapter 17

Five minutes later, Box heard knocking on the door.

Flicking on the light Porter entered the room, a pistol in his hand and one in his holster, a pair of night vision goggles suspended from his neck.

Box blinked his eyes in pain at the harsh brightness of the light. He shielded his eyes from the overhead light with his hand.

"Come with me," said Porter. "You're handy with a gun, and we got company."

His eyes adjusting to the light, Box lowered his hand, slid off his cot, and approached Porter.

"What's going on?" said Box.

Porter handed Box the pistol. "Someone's on our roof. Let's check it out."

Box and Porter left the quarantine room, cut through the warehouse, exited through the front door, walked around to the side of the building, located the fire escape, and climbed the clanking, zigzagging metal staircase to the thirty-foot-high flat roof in the darkness, Porter in the lead.

A quarter moon nestled in a cluster of stars smiled down at them from the indigo sky. It was a mild night in the upper sixties. Box could hear a multitude of crickets chirping in the distance serenading the moon.

"Did somebody sneak onto the compound?" he said.

"I heard a thud then some kind of movement on the roof," said Porter. "That's all I know."

"Somebody walking on it?"

"I couldn't tell."

"How did they get inside the gate?"

"Why are they on the roof? That's what I want to know."

They reached the landing directly below the roof and contemplated the final flight of steps.

"What do you think is up there?" said Box.

Gazing up at the eaves Porter drew his pistol from his holster. "I have no idea. But we better be ready for anything."

67

Box felt his heartbeat ratcheting up. SIG in hand, he followed Porter up the final flight of stairs.

Porter reached the roof and scoped it out.

"I can't see anything so far," he said. "Let's go up."

He climbed onto the roof, Box on his heels.

Box made out a silhouette lurching across the roof. The figure's arms and one leg were bent at unnatural angles. As a result, it walked in herky-jerky movements, if you could call it walking.

"His arms and leg are busted," said Porter with a wince.

"This doesn't look right."

Box raised his SIG at the figure. It was the first time he had looked at the piece closely. He recognized it. A SIG Sauer P226, a pistol favored by SEALS. How did he know that? he wondered. A frisson of anxiety ran down his spine. He didn't want to remember.

"Hold it," Porter told the intruder, training his pistol on him.

Instead of stopping, the figure turned and lurched toward Porter and Box, dragging his feet across the flat tar paper roof.

"It's one of them," said Box.

"How did it get up here?" said Porter.

"I'll take it out."

Box nailed the ghoul in the head with a slug from his SIG.

Box's concentration was interrupted by something flying through the air and landing with a thud on the rooftop some thirty feet from the ghoul with Box's bullet lodged in its head. Not thirty seconds later a third object landed ten feet from the second.

"Two more ghouls," said Porter in confusion.

"Those things can fly?" said Box, incredulous.

"How could they fly? They don't have wings."

The second ghoul advanced on them. It was a roly-poly thirtysomething brunette in a bus driver's tight grey uniform. Her black face grimaced at them in the darkness. Both her legs were bent askew with compound fractures in the tibia in her left leg and in the femur in her right one. Splintered bones protruded beneath her shorts from her emaciated skin. She could barely walk. She was flailing, making little progress.

"It makes me sick just looking at it," said Porter, pulling a face.

Box shot her in the head. She dropped with a thump.

The third intruder stood up with great difficulty, for it, too, had a broken leg and arm, and possibly a broken neck from the unnatural angle of its head.

It was too far away and too dark for Box to discern the intruder's face.

As the figure approached them in a plodding gait, Box could see it was another female ghoul, this one a blonde, a spray of freckles on her nose and cheeks, wearing a nurse's rumpled, besmirched white uniform. Slender, in her twenties, she halted toward them, her one good arm outstretched toward them as if in entreaty.

Porter leveled his pistol at her skew head and fired. Where once had sat her head the bullet saw to it that nothing remained but pulp and a jagged half of skull, minus the brain, which had fallen to the roof, perforated by the bullet.

She jerked, shuddered, and went down, spasming for a few seconds before she became motionless.

"I don't get it," said Porter. "Are they jumping up here?"

"I doubt they can jump thirty feet high," said Box.

"They can come back to life after they're dead, so why not jump onto a roof as well?"

"They can barely walk. How in the world can they jump that high?"

"And when they're landing, they're busting their legs and arms." Porter paused. "Do you think they have death wishes?"

"It's not a death wish. They're crazed with a ravenous hunger for human flesh. Breaking their own bones means nothing to them as long as they can get their hands on fresh food."

Box moseyed to the edge of the warehouse roof and scoped out the grounds as best he could under the star- and moonlit night sky. He didn't see any ghouls wandering around in the dim-lit parking lot. At the edge of the woods in the distance he made out what looked like a motor vehicle's pair of headlights shining in this direction.

He sensed Porter's presence behind him.

"Are those headlights?" said Box.

Porter squinted through the darkness. "Could be."

Box thought he saw movement behind the vehicle. He could have been imagining it. It was hard to tell from this distance.

He started when he heard a thud behind him on the warehouse roof.

Chapter 18

Box wheeled around, gun in hand, striving to locate the precise location of the thud. Out of the corner of his eye he picked up on movement. A heap on the roof rose to a standing position and morphed into a silhouette that commenced shambling, investigating the rooftop.

This one also held its head askew, like it had landed on its neck and broken it. One arm was broken and bent backward.

"I thought I saw movement near those headlights before that creature thudded on the roof," said Box. "Could there be a connection?"

Porter advanced toward the figure, scoping it out, his gun at the ready. It was a male teen, eyes glued on a cell phone in his hand. Since his neck was broken, he couldn't move his head. When the figure came within range, Porter shot him in the head. The creature dropped to its knees and flopped forward on its pimply face.

Porter returned to Box, holstered his pistol, put on his NVGs, and inspected the area around the headlights. The beams from the headlights interfered with his vision, causing the image to wash out with fluorescent green.

"Those lights are too bright for my NVGs," he said. "I can't make anything out."

He removed the NVGs.

"Too much light is always a problem with NVGs," said Box.

Porter gave Box a look. "And you know this how?"

"It's news to me."

"Are you in special forces? SEALS, Green Berets, Marine Raiders?"

Box's memory remained blank. He couldn't answer Porter's question.

"We need to figure out what's going on," said Box. "Why's that vehicle parked out there?"

"You shoot like a sharpshooter. If you can shoot out those headlights, I can use my NVGs on that vehicle."

71

"No way. Not with a pistol. We're too far away. I'd need a rifle. But it would alert them that we spotted them."

As if on cue, the headlights winked out.

"Look," said Box, nodding at the extinguished headlights.

Porter whipped his NVGs onto his head and glassed the now-darkened area.

"Maybe they killed their lights because they suspect we made them," said Box.

"It's an SUV," said Porter, the NVGs to his eyes. "And there's some kind of equipment behind it."

"What kind of equipment?"

"It looks . . . it looks . . . I'll be damned."

"What? What is it?"

"It looks like a catapult."

"A catapult?"

"And one of those ghouls is stuffed inside its payload basket."

The headlights flashed on again, washing out Porter's view with a swath of green light. Cursing, Porter looked away from the headlights.

Box caught sight of a dark, thrashing figure flying overhead blotting out the moonlight for a split second. He heard a thud behind him and craned around on the qui vive.

A dark heap the better part of twenty feet away from him rose to its feet.

A female teenage ghoul in a pink, torn T and jeans with holes ripped in the knees trudged toward Box and Porter, trailing her useless, broken left leg behind her.

Wanting to get a better look at the figure to make sure it was a ghoul, Box headed toward it, gun in hand. Its pale, sightless eyes, its grimace, and the putrescent flesh clinging to the creature's face like putty were all the proof he needed. He blew away the ghoul's head without a second thought and returned to Porter.

"They're catapulting ghouls onto our roof," said Porter, watching the headlights without his NVGs.

He saw a large white sign rise into view near the wash of the headlights. He couldn't make out the person holding it in the darkness.

Box spotted the sign and read the words on it out loud. "Do you surrender?"

"I can read. Who the hell do they think they are?"

"The Mongols did the same thing in the fourteenth century at the siege of Caffa. They catapulted carcasses of plague-infected victims into the Crimean city of Caffa and infected the residents with the Black Death to get them to capitulate."

"What are you? A history professor? You don't even know your own name, but you know about fourteenth-century Mongols."

Box couldn't explain. "Biological warfare is nothing new."

"If you say so, Professor. I oughta call you Mr. Peabody after that know-it-all dog on *Rocky and Bullwinkle* with his Wayback Machine. He knew all about history."

"The Mongols won the battle of Caffa. In other words, their tactics worked."

"Well, they're not gonna work here. We're not surrendering. This is terror tactics. That's all it is. If I had a sign I could hold up, it'd say Nuts. Like General Patton's answer to the Germans who demanded his surrender at the Battle of the Bulge. How's that, Mr. Peabody? I know a little history myself."

"It wasn't General Patton. It was General Anthony McAuliffe."

"Oh, phooey," said Porter, waving his hand dismissively.

The attackers doused the headlights.

"What? No more cadavers on our roof?" said Porter.

"They must figure we read the sign. They probably have NVGs so they can see us up here."

"Do you think they can see this?" said Porter, giving them the finger.

"Let's get out of here before they decide to start picking us off with snipers."

Box and Porter dashed for the fire escape.

Chapter 19

Box slept lousy. He wished he had some Halcion or, at least, Tylenol PM to knock him out. He tossed and turned most of the night on his uncomfortable cot.

During those rare times he managed to drift off, he saw the blonde in a white dress gliding along the sand on the shoreline, as combers crashed like cymbals around her. He didn't know who she was or why he kept dreaming about her. There was something tragic about her. Maybe it was her wooden, ashen visage, or her white dress, which could have been a shroud. Maybe it was her ghostlike gliding. Or maybe it was the desolate beach she walked on. Everything about her suggested death.

His eyes snapped open at the shrill sound of a whistle.

Through the darkness he saw movement on the other cot as Marta stirred.

"What was that?" she said, sitting up.

"Sounded like somebody blowing a whistle."

Box sprang off his cot when he heard furious knocking on the quarantine room door. Primed for an onslaught, he kept his eyes riveted on the door.

Marta leapt off her cot and stood at his side.

Box heard a key inserted into the door lock. The door swung open.

It was Porter, a Mossberg ATI Tactical 12 gauge pump-action shotgun in his hand.

"We're under attack," he said. "We need everyone who can fight at the fence."

Box and Marta whipped after Porter, who cut through the warehouse to the entrance.

"Who's attacking?" said Box.

"You'll see," said Porter, emerging outside and gazing at a portion of the chain-link fence that surrounded the parking lot. "Over there."

Fellow members of the camp, armed with everything from guns to pickaxes, were battling hordes of ghouls that were trying to break through the fence under the dawn's watery oyster light.

Many members had makeshift spears they were jabbing through the apertures in the fence into the heads of flesh eaters.

"Don't you have more guns?" said Box.

"We have to conserve ammo," said Porter. "I don't want to use it up repelling this one attack. This could be a vanguard for millions more of those things coming after us."

As camp members slaughtered ghouls, the ghouls' carcasses piled up outside the chain-link fence. The ghouls behind their fallen comrades stepped on the motionless cadavers and arrived at the fence, trying to pull it down or reach through it and grab the camp members who had gathered there to repel the attack, shooting ghouls and stabbing them with knives and spears.

Porter aimed his shotgun at a white-haired sixtysomething female ghoul that was trying to scale the chain-link fence with her withered hands and long, broken, dirty nails that curled like talons. Her brown dress hung in tatters on her scrawny body. She bared her yellow teeth at Porter and growled.

Porter blew her head apart with one shot from the Mossberg. Her head literally exploded and vanished from her neck. Her decomposing body collapsed on the prostrate corpse beneath it, providing an additional step for the ghouls to reach the summit of the fence and climb over it into the compound.

Porter withdrew a pistol from his holster and tossed it to Box.

"Aim carefully," said Porter. "We can't afford to waste ammo. We gotta make each shot count. We have no idea how many more of these things are approaching from the woods."

Off to Porter's left, Gertie aimed a crossbow at a redheaded ghoul dressed in a skintight fluorescent lime microskirt and carmine stiletto heels who looked like she used to be a porn star with her silicone-enhanced bust straining against her black leather tube top. Grimacing with jagged teeth, the porn queen was having trouble shambling in her stilettos, one of which had a broken heel. She was ten-odd feet from the fence when Gertie's bolt found its target—the porn queen's left eye. The ghoul spasmed and collapsed before she reached the mound of cadavers.

The ghouls were concentrating their attack on this portion of the chain-link fence and sparing the gate, which sentries continued to guard nevertheless, preparing for a second wave of ghouls that might be advancing through the woods.

Box spotted a short Japanese male ghoul with long white hair wearing a Nike ballcap backwards on his small head climbing corpses to scale the chain-link fence. Box drew a bead on the ghoul's snarling face and put a slug between the creature's eyes. The ghoul crumpled on the pile of dead meat, increasing the height of the fetid mound.

As the ghoul's corpse dropped, the chain-link fence buckled under the additional weight of another ghoul trying to scale it.

"I don't like the looks of this," said Porter, observing with concern the fence that was now sloping inward toward the warehouse. "If that fence goes down, we're goners."

He shot the teen ghoul with a crew cut climbing the fence in the forehead, felling the creature.

"Well, do something," said Gertie, approaching, crossbow in hand. "I have only so many bolts for my crossbow," she added, gesturing toward her half-empty quiver slung across her back.

"That's the problem. Bullets and bolts. We don't have enough of them."

"We have to shoot those things before they get close to the fence so they don't form a pile against it that they can climb," said Box.

"But we have to conserve ammo. We must not run out of bullets. Better to use spears, knives, and whatever else we can shove through the fence."

"We gotta watch our bolts, too," said Gertie. "My quiver has the last of them."

"CQB raises the pile of corpses that work as steps," said Box.

"CQB?" said Gertie.

"Close-quarters battle. If we kill them at a distance, they can't form a heap near the fence."

"Just how the hell do you know about CQB?" said Porter.

"I wish I knew," said Box, wondering himself.

The term had come to his mind unbidden.

"You been holding out on me?" said Porter. "I'm an ex-marine. You must be a military man yourself. *CQB* is not a term a layman would use."

Box shook his head in confusion. He had no memory of military experience.

He didn't have time to ponder it, with the ghouls pressing their attack. He shot a twentysomething male ghoul in surgical scrubs chewing on a pale blue mask used to cover his mouth. The flesh eater was shambling toward the fence a dozen feet away until Box's slug ripped into the creature's forehead and stopped him dead in his tracks.

"We put them down far enough away from the fence like that so they can't build a mound to climb over the fence," said Box.

"We haven't got the bullets," said Porter in exasperation. "We have to do our best with what we have."

"How about sending out a raiding party to confront the ghouls outside? We could draw them away from the fence and take them out."

"The raiders won't have any protection out there."

"They'll be exposed to the spores in the ghouls' breath out there if they get too close," said Gertie. "The fence prevents the ghouls from getting near us."

"A raiding party is our only option at this point, or we lose the protection of the fence when it collapses any moment now," said Box.

Porter gave him a look. "What makes you such an expert on military tactics? You think you're Karl von Clausewitz?"

"Maybe Sun Tzu," he said. "I'm using common sense, is all."

Porter hiked his eyebrows. "And you've read Sun Tzu's *Art of War*? Will wonders never cease? Your memory must be coming back."

"But it's not," said Box, frowning in vexation. "I can't remember anything about myself."

"Be that as it may, I'm not willing to risk letting my men attack the ghouls outside the safety of the perimeter."

"The perimeter isn't gonna exist much longer unless we change tactics."

Chapter 20

A middle-aged ghoul clad in khaki Bermudas and a grey linen newsboy cap listening to the static on a transistor radio he held in his hand like it was broadcasting an urgent news bulletin prepared to climb the chain-link fence.

Marta jammed a spear in the ghoul's throat.

The ghoul grimaced but kept coming, his throat impaled on the spear.

"You need to kill his brain," said Porter.

Marta yanked out the spear and thrust it into the ghoul's forehead, listening to his skull fracturing under the impact of the spear's point. Bermuda crumpled on the congeries of putrefaction. The chain-link fence bellied ever closer to the warehouse.

Hilda plunged a knife through the eye of a male longhaired twentyish ghoul wearing a grey sweatshirt and jeans. Hilda jerked away from the creature to avoid inhaling his dying, putrid breath and jogged backward the better part of two yards.

"Try to stay at least six feet away from them," she told Marta, who was standing close to the fence preparing to stab another approaching ghoul that was wearing a nun's black habit and white wimple.

Marta took two steps backward and thrust her spear through one of the apertures in the chain-link fence into the nun's nose. The ghoul's corpse fell onto the heap.

"We're not gonna be able to hold out much longer," said Porter, eying with apprehension the bending fence. "Their weight is piling against the fence collapsing it. We're gonna have to fall back to the warehouse."

"Just when did you become our leader?" said Hilda, stalking up to Porter and jutting her chin into his face.

"I'm in charge of defending the camp."

"But you're working for me."

"That fence isn't gonna hold much longer. We're gonna have ghouls running amok all over the parking lot."

"The final decision rests with me."

"We're a split second away from disaster."

"I know it's bad," said Hilda, scoping out that portion of the fence in question. "But the longer we can keep them out of here, the better. If they set foot on the parking lot, they'll have no trouble getting into the warehouse. We can't abandon the fence."

"We can station guards at the warehouse doors."

"But we won't be able to do any foraging if the infected control the parking lot and the warehouse doors."

"We can still go foraging. All we have to do is clear a path through the flesh eaters."

"Just like that, huh? A piece of cake."

"No piece of cake. We'll have to fight our way out of the warehouse when we go foraging. And we'll have to fight our way back in when we're done. It'll be a bitch—pardon my French. But what choice do we have? That fence is gonna come down."

A brunette ghoul with a walleye and an overbite and her hair done up with bugs crawling in it attempted to climb over the top of the chain-link fence, straddling it, one leg dangling over the parking lot. Marta charged up to her and shoved her spear into the brunette's face, cratering the ghoul's cheekbone and piercing her brain. Dead, the brunette continued to straddle the fence, frozen on it.

Marta yanked her spear free, its tip dripping brains.

"We can't leave her there," said Porter. "She's putting pressure on the fence by sitting on it."

Gertie snatched a shovel from the hands of a nearby camp member, approached the fence, and thrust the shovel into the brunette ghoul's face, knocking her backward off her perch. She tumbled down the ragged pile of corpses to the ground.

A mustachioed ghoul pushing forty dressed in a cop's uniform scrabbled up the mound of corpses to climb over the fence.

At the same time, another throng of ghouls emerged from the woods making their way toward the warehouse with their shambling gait, a swarm of flies hovering over them.

"We're backed into a corner," said Porter. "We don't have a whole lot of options left. We gotta pull back."

An explosion rocked the ground.

Chapter 21

The earth in the middle of the ghouls assembled in front of the fence exploded, flinging up ghouls among clods of dirt and billowing clouds of dust. Severed heads and limbs burst through the air like shrapnel. Some of the body parts hurtled over the chain-link fence and thudded onto the asphalt parking lot.

Box whipped his head around to scope out the source of the firing.

He saw a convoy of SUVs parked in front of the warehouse gate. In front of the lead SUV was a mortar.

"We got help," he said.

"I see that," said Porter, concern etching his face as he studied the newcomers.

"Are they yours?"

"Never saw them before."

A guy holding a sickle was standing in front of the gate talking to the sentries.

"What the hell do they want?" said Porter.

"Are they trying to get inside the compound?" said Box.

"The guards aren't allowed to let any strangers in without permission. We better get over there."

He and Box sprinted to the front gate.

"What's going on?" Porter asked the guards.

"That guy with the sickle wants to know if we surrender," said the tall guard with a dimpled chin in the booth on the south side of the gate. "I told him no."

Porter approached the gate and peered at Zodiac. "What's this all about?"

"It's a simple question," said Zodiac. "You don't need a college degree to figure out the answer."

"And we got a simple answer. The answer is no."

Zodiac chuckled. "You may want to reconsider your answer."

"We're not surrendering to anyone."

"Those ghouls swarming around your fence are gonna trample it to the ground and invade your compound—unless we help you. You obviously don't have the firepower to hold them at bay."

"If you wanna help us, help us. Don't gimme any of this 'surrender' crap."

"The price of our help is your surrender. Nothing's free in this world, or haven't you figured that out yet?"

"I figure we don't want you in our compound."

Hilda reached the gate, flushed from running.

"Fill me in," she told Porter.

"This guy says he'll help us kill the infected if we surrender to him."

Hilda approached the gate and peered through the diamond-shaped links at Zodiac. "We appreciate your help, mister, but nobody's surrendering here."

"Then I'll let the ghouls tear all of you apart. And when they're done, I'll move my men in here and take over. So you see," said Zodiac, swinging his sickle back and forth, "no matter what you do, whether you surrender or not, we're taking over your fort." He paused a beat. "If you surrender to me, at least some of you will remain alive when I take over. Otherwise, without my help you're all fodder for the ghouls."

He had a point, Box realized. The guy had superior firepower with the mortar.

"Why don't you just lob mortars at us and get us to surrender?" said Box.

"Because I don't wanna damage your warehouse. And I don't wanna blow your gate to pieces. I want this fortress intact, being that I'll be the new leader here. What good is a bombed-out fortress to me? You see what I'm saying?"

"You think you're some kind of big wheel, I guess," said Hilda. "A legend in your own mind."

"I got a mortar that can blow your head clear off, which means I got God on my side. That's all I need to become leader. You know what Voltaire said. *God is always on the side of the big battalions.*"

"You got a mouth on you. I'll say that for you. But your swelled head isn't gonna get us to surrender to you and open our gate."

"I'll let you in on a little secret. It may sound like an oxymoron, but the only way to empowerment is through submission. If you want power in this compound, you need to submit to me."

"That's the dumbest thing I ever heard. I'm the boss here, not you."

"But not for long. Those ghouls are gonna trample your fence, invade your compound, and have you for dinner." Zodiac turned to his men. "Saddle up, men. We're outa here."

A bloodcurdling scream rent the air.

Chapter 22

Box locked his gaze on a fat man in his fifties in an aloha shirt screaming for help among the flesh eaters a hop, skip, and a jump outside the fence. His blue eyes bugged out of his head behind his horn-rimmed spectacles. A throng of ghouls was converging on him, as two ghouls held his arms and gnawed on his wrists, their mouths dripping with fresh blood that glistened in the sunlight.

"Help," he screamed to Box and the others at the front gate, unable to yank his arms free from the ghouls' jaws.

"Afraid not," said Zodiac. "That guy's toast. He just doesn't know it yet. If I'm lying I'm dying. And I never tell a lie."

"We can't let this go on," said Hilda, watching the man's agony with consternation.

"The merciful thing would be to put a slug in his head," said Porter.

"Don't let me stop you," said Zodiac.

One of the ghouls, a male fortyish ghoul with a bullet head and only three fingers and a thumb on his hand, tore the man's arm out of his shoulder socket and took bites of flesh out of the forearm, as blood spewed onto the creature's face from the severed radial artery. The ghoul reveled in the shower of blood, alternately lapping it up and devouring the flesh on the severed arm.

"I can't stand watching this," said Hilda. "Somebody, do something."

"You can always shut your eyes," said Zodiac.

"Why don't you use your mortar on those ghouls?"

"I don't wanna waste my ammo on a lost cause."

The second ghoul, a tall, thin brunette in her late twenties, tore the man's remaining arm off and munched on it with ecstatic grunts, eyes cast upward with joy.

"Help," the man cried toward the front gate, his voice becoming weaker, blood gushing out of his shoulder wounds.

He staggered away from the ghouls and toward the gate, his torso crimson with blood.

"That guy doesn't know when to call it quits," said Zodiac with little interest.

"Nobody can save him now," said Box.

He trained his pistol on the suffering guy and shot him in the head. The guy crumpled, released from his agony.

"Nice shot," said Zodiac. "I want you on my team. How about it?"

"I'm staying here for the time being," said Box.

"For the time being?"

"I'm just visiting."

"Then you're siding with losers. Join me and you join an army of winners. Every compound we've encountered so far has surrendered to us or . . . ," Zodiac trailed off.

"Or what?"

"Or we conquered them. We're gonna conquer the whole country when we head to Washington to lay claim to the seat of government."

"Like I said, a legend in your own mind," said Hilda with a snigger.

"What do *you* know?" said Zodiac, stressing the *you* with contempt in his voice. "I conquered California and Nevada so far. Arizona ain't gonna be no kind of challenge."

"Why should we believe a word you say?"

"I was hoping you had something called a brain between your ears. It's difficult to get through to gibbering idiots."

Audrey, a chestnut-haired woman in her late twenties, seven months pregnant waddled out of the warehouse and approached them, wearing a mint green maternity dress and clutching a gooseneck carbon steel wrecking bar in her hand.

"I want to fight the ghouls, Hilda," she said.

"You need to take it easy in your condition, Audrey," said Hilda.

"I can't take it easy if the ghouls take over our camp."

"You don't want to lose your child, honey."

"All's lost if those things break in here," said Audrey, glancing apprehensively at the attacking ghouls.

Hilda couldn't argue with that. Reluctantly, she pointed out the portion of the fence that was under attack.

"Go over there and help out," she said. "But don't overexert yourself."

Audrey waddled toward the bent fence besieged by the ghouls.

"A brave girl," said Box.

"A knocked-up broad with a wrecking bar ain't gonna save your bacon," Zodiac told Hilda. "I'm the only chance you got. Submit to me and I'll empower you."

"I hate to admit it, but we need his firepower," Porter told Hilda under his breath. "We can't protect the fence by ourselves."

As if in response to Audrey's presence at the fence, a pregnant female ghoul with unkempt black hair shambled out of the throng toward Zodiac and his convoy.

"I don't even want to think about that," Zodiac said, watching her.

Porter leaned toward Hilda and whispered, "What if we pretend to surrender to him and throw him out after they get rid of the ghouls? We absolutely need his firepower to repel the infected."

With dismay Hilda watched Audrey jab her wrecking bar at a ghoul attacking the fence and almost fall over thanks to her unaccustomed excess weight. Hilda chewed over Porter's words.

"I don't like the idea of surrendering to anyone," she whispered back to Porter.

"I share your feelings. But in this case . . . those ghouls break through the fence, our lives will be horrible in the warehouse."

"I know," said Hilda, and compressed her lips.

The throng of ghouls from the forest were inching closer to the chain-link fence to reinforce the first wave of outliers.

The pregnant ghoul was making a beeline toward Zodiac.

"Looks like this red-hot mama doesn't wanna go on living anymore," he said.

He whipped a Glock 19 from the holster on his hip and drew a bead on the ghoul. He shot the plodding ghoul in the head. She collapsed and lay supine.

Then something bizarre and egregious happened.

Chapter 23

Box was shocked to see the belly bulging between the mother ghoul's legs. A baby's blood-soaked head chewed its way out of the mother's womb and through the maternity dress. The baby was unlike any Box had ever seen.

The baby had already cut its teeth, and he used them to rip easily through the dress's fabric.

The baby crawled out from between the mother's legs onto the dirt toward Zodiac and his men, baring its piranha-like teeth and grimacing, its body smeared with blood.

"Ohmigod," said Hilda, white-faced. "Shoot it . . . please."

Near the fence, Audrey watched the hideous spectacle in rapt revulsion.

"Let's see how long it takes to reach me," said Zodiac, amused at the grisly sight. He turned to his men. "Wanna place any bets, girls? Tyler? How many minutes will it take to reach me?"

Tyler barked a laugh. "An hour crawling on its hands and knees like that."

"I say an hour and a half."

"Kill it," said Hilda, aghast. "Kill it. It's an abomination. Don't let it live even one minute longer."

"That would wreck our bet," said Zodiac.

"For Christ's sake, put it down, man," said Porter.

Aroused by the commotion at the gate, a preacher wearing a black cassock emerged from the warehouse and headed toward Hilda. In his midthirties, he was Hispanic with a smooth complexion and only one arm. His large moist brown eyes followed the gazes of the others and set on the baby ghoul.

"I have seen the beast," he intoned. "And its number is 666."

"What's that you say, holy man?" said Zodiac.

Growling, the bloody baby ghoul kept crawling forward on its hands and knees, its mouth drooling.

"We surrender," Hilda told Zodiac, at her wit's end. "Just kill it. Kill that monstrosity."

"A one-armed preacher," said Zodiac. "What happened to your other arm?"

"A ghoul bit it," said Hilda. "We managed to amputate it before Diego became infected and turned."

"It was a miracle," said Diego, "and I am thankful." He gazed up at the sky with reverence.

"What are you looking at?" said Zodiac. "An empty sky is all I see up there."

Box could make out shards of decomposing flesh the infant creature had ripped out of its mother's womb impaled on its razor-sharp teeth and hanging out its gaping mouth along with a blood-soaked swatch of cotton it had torn from the maternity dress.

He couldn't stand the sight of it any longer.

He trained his pistol on the baby ghoul's head and fired. The baby's grimacing face exploded and disintegrated.

Hilda choked back sobs.

"You ruined our bet," Zodiac told Box with a stern expression. "I oughta shoot you on the spot," he said, drawing a bead on Box's head with his Glock.

"I said, we surrender," said Hilda. "What more do you want?"

"Then open the gate," said Zodiac.

"You said you'd kill the ghouls if we surrendered," said Porter.

"After you open the gate. How do I know you're not gonna renege on your promise?"

"Open it," Hilda told the guards in the tower.

The sentry in the guard tower unlocked the electronic gate and swung it open with the push of a button.

"Sammy, park your SUV in the middle of the gateway, in case these folks change their minds and try to close it on us," said Zodiac.

A five-eight, stocky, thirtysomething man with a shaved head wearing camos followed Zodiac's orders.

"Got it, boss," said Sammy from the SUV's driver's seat, and parked his vehicle in the gateway.

"Throw down your guns," Zodiac told Hilda and her men.

Box and Porter held onto their pistols.

"You didn't say anything about giving up our guns," said Hilda.

"That's what surrendering is all about," said Zodiac.

"I didn't agree to that."

"Those are my conditions. Or we don't help you defeat the infected."

Zodiac studied his fingernails with indifference.

Hilda considered the worsening condition of the beleaguered fence. She turned to her men.

"Throw down your weapons," she said.

His face sullen, Porter hesitated. "How do we fight the ghouls without weapons?"

"You don't," said Zodiac. "I'll take care of the infected."

Shrugging, Porter tossed down his pistol. Box and the others in the camp followed suit.

"Tyler, fire the mortar at that swarm of ghouls, but don't hit the fence," said Zodiac. "Get the ghouls coming out of the forest. Bomb the shit out of them."

Tyler and a wiry Korean guy with a flat top in his twenties wearing an olive drab tank top manned the mortar and fired it into the middle of the throng of ghouls that were the better part of a hundred feet from the besieged fence. The blast coughed up body parts into the air with pluming dust clouds.

Tyler fired again and again, lobbing shells into the thinning ranks of the attacking ghouls.

"All right, girls," said Zodiac, watching with approval. "The rest of you drive down there and clean up. Wipe those things off the face of the earth with your AR-15s. Blast their brains into Montezuma's revenge. Clear those stiffs away from the fence and straighten it when you're done."

The convoy tore off to the scene of the slaughter, where Zodiac's men clambered out of their vehicles and, with their automatic rifles firing on full auto, made short work of the remaining creatures massing near the fence.

"Our fence is saved," Zodiac told Hilda and Porter with a broad grin.

Hilda eyed Zodiac grim-faced, dreading she had cut a deal with the devil to save the compound.

Zodiac waved at Tyler, who was finishing off two ghouls with his AR-15.

Acknowledging Zodiac's signal, clutching his AR-15 at port arms, Tyler returned to Zodiac at a half run.

"Tyler, throw those stinking cadavers into a pile and torch it," said Zodiac.

Tyler jogged back to the dead ghouls, and, with his men, dragged the infected corpses into a heap in a clearing away from the fence.

"Burn, baby, burn," said Zodiac under his breath, watching them build a pyre with anticipation, his eyes gleaming. "We are cleansing the earth of pestilence."

Watching, he waited—

Till the massive pile of corpses burst into flames with a roar, discharging pillars of smoke into the mackerel sky.

Transfixed, he watched.

"What's your name?" he asked Hilda without taking his eyes off the conflagration.

"Hilda," she said. "What's yours?"

"You have the great honor of meeting Zodiac, the next president of these United States," he said, his eyes gleaming as he watched the flames leap skyward.

Hilda rolled her eyes.

Chapter 24

Audrey was sitting in her maternity dress at a table in the warehouse talking with Gertie.

"You were very brave today," said Gertie, "the way you fought the ghouls, despite your condition."

"I'm not brave. I'm scared."

"Scared of what? You're not scared of the ghouls. You killed them at the fence."

"I'm scared for my baby," said Audrey, glancing down at her belly.

"I don't understand."

"Did you see that pregnant ghoul that attacked us today?"

"It was horrible, but what does that have to do with *your* baby?"

"Didn't you see her baby?" said Audrey, appalled.

"That wasn't a baby. It was a monstrosity," said Gertie, remembering the horrific sight with repugnance.

"Exactly. What if my baby comes out like that? What if my baby is born infected? I couldn't stand the sight of it. I'd go insane."

"Why would *your* baby be born infected?"

"Maybe I'm infected."

"You don't have any symptoms."

"How can I know for sure I'm not infected and not asymptomatic?"

"Why would you think such a thing?" said Gertie, taken aback.

"What if I'm asymptomatic and I infected my baby in the womb?"

Gertie searched Audrey's face. "Is there something you're not telling me, child? Did you have contact with a ghoul?"

"No."

"Then why are you worried?"

"Because there may be asymptomatic people in the camp that have infected others, including me."

"You have no reason to make that assumption."

"You can't prove it's not true."

"The important thing is, we can't prove it *is* true. So don't worry about it."

"What if the two strangers are carriers? That Box guy and Marta."

"Stay away from those two."

Audrey clutched her face with her hands in anguish. "I couldn't deal with it, if my baby was born infected. The sight of that dreadful pregnant ghoul and her baby was unbearable. I'd— I'd—I'd"—her voice cracked—"I'd kill my own child."

She broke into tears.

"Settle down," said Gertie. "That's not gonna happen. You're a brave girl. I saw you fight the ghouls at the fence. Don't let your imagination run wild with you."

"How do you know *you're* not asymptomatic? You could be infected, too."

"Stop talking nonsense. You're going paranoid on me."

"We can't be 100 percent sure that no one's infected here."

"Maybe you should talk to Dr. Epps," said Gertie with concern. "You may be having a breakdown."

"I'm being realistic. And it's scaring the bejesus out of me."

"Have you discussed your concerns with Dr. Epps?"

"No. How's he gonna protect my baby? There's nothing he can do."

"He can give you something for your state of mind, perhaps."

"My state of mind is crystal clear."

Hilda approached the table carrying a tray of glasses and a pitcher of iced tea.

"We all need a glass of iced tea after that fight today," she said, setting down her tray.

She poured the three of them a glass of iced tea.

Audrey paid no attention to her.

"I'm thinking I should abort my child," she muttered, her eyes bleak.

"What?" said Hilda. "What are you talking about?"

"She thinks her baby could be born infected," said Gertie.

"Why in the world would that happen?"

"She thinks she could be asymptomatic."

"And . . . ," Audrey trailed off.

"And what?" said Hilda.

"Do I really want to have a baby in this plague-infested world?"

"Children are the one thing we do need—with so many of us being killed by the plague."

"The world is a nightmare. How can anyone want to bring a child into it under these wretched conditions?"

"You're depressed, is all. Stop thinking black thoughts. Drink your iced tea. Do you want lemon and sugar?"

"The world is chaos. It has no meaning. Why do we bother? Everywhere we go is more misery. More ghouls attacking us. More infections. More death and destruction. What's today's body count?"

"I think we should get Dr. Epps," Gertie told Hilda.

"She needs a psychologist," said Hilda. "He's only a GP."

"You're both in denial," said Audrey. "Neither one of you can accept the truth that life is endless, pointless suffering."

"We're still alive," said Hilda. "As long as we're alive, we need to keep going on living. We don't want to murder our own offspring. That's crazy talk."

"I'd be saving my baby from a life of abject misery, if I destroyed him—"

"Stop talking crazy ."

"What's crazy about it? Didn't you see that pregnant ghoul today? Didn't you see her—her"—Audrey sobbed—"her baby?"

"That wasn't a baby. It was a monster. A monster gave birth to another monster. That's all that was. And you need to put it out of your mind."

"Easy for you to say. You're not with child like I am. What's the point of all this suffering?"

Hilda paused. "The point is, to go on living."

"The point is, there is no point, if you ask me."

"This plague can't last forever. It's temporary. We just need to hang on a little longer."

Gertie took a pull on her iced tea. "Nobody's having infected babies. That includes you."

Audrey stared off into the distance, her face expressionless. "Dr. Epps can help me with the abortion."

Eyes full of determination, Hilda thrust to her feet. "No, he won't. I forbid it. There's nothing wrong with your baby."

"You're not in charge anymore," said Audrey in a quiet voice. "Zodiac is."

"He only *thinks* he is."

Audrey raised her voice. "And besides, it's my body. I'm the one in charge of it. Nobody but me. And if I decide not to bring a baby into this godawful world, so be it."

"Get out the coat hanger," said Gertie through the side of her mouth.

"Hush," said Hilda. "What's wrong with us? We're talking about a baby. A *baby*. Not some *thing*."

"You saw that thing that crawled out of that ghoul's womb today," said Audrey. "That was no baby. If something like that crawls out of my womb—"

"You're making yourself sick thinking about it. Maybe the doctor can give you some Valium or Soma to calm your nerves."

"Why don't I just get loaded?" Audrey became animated and spoke louder. "We all should. We're never gonna get out of this nightmare. Let's face it. Where's that dope we bought from the cartel?"

Chapter 25

"What's this about dope from a cartel?" said Zodiac, sickle in hand, looking annoyed as he approached Audrey.

"Nothing," said Hilda.

"Hippies use drugs. Is this a hippie commune? Is that what this is?"

"Not at all."

"Better not be, or I'll have to whack all of you. Hippies are bums and destroyers. If we let them live here, they will bring our camp down."

"Nobody's a hippie here. Didn't they all disappear in the sixties?"

"It was a counterculture for drug-addicted losers. It was DOA."

"Why should I care?"

"What kind of drugs are we talking about? Acid, weed, psilocybin, mescaline, ecstasy, blow?"

"Just a couple of recreational drugs to help some of us relax."

"Sedatives? Antidepressants?"

"Why is it your business?"

"Because I'm the man now. And what I say goes."

"What difference does the kind of drug make?"

"Nothing addictive. No smack. No psychedelics."

"Why not? Sometimes people need to escape this nightmare we're living. We could all become infected and die of the plague any minute."

"What's wrong with booze? It doesn't make you see things that aren't there. We need everyone in the moment. In case the infected attack again, we need to be ready. We always need to be on our toes. That's how we survive. We're not gonna survive with dope fucking up our systems."

"What's wrong with a little weed once in a while? Or some blow?" said Audrey.

"This isn't open for discussion. Why do you think you need drugs?"

Audrey said nothing.

"Audrey lost her husband Don to the infected," said Hilda. "He was out foraging with Porter. They were in the woods. Don was walking under a tree when one of those ghouls dropped down from a branch onto his head. The creature made mincemeat of Don's throat with its teeth. When Don turned, Porter had to shoot him in the head."

Audrey slipped into a gloomy trance as she listened to Hilda, recalling Don and the way he met his fate.

"Shit happens," said Zodiac. "Was he on dope in the woods?"

Audrey snapped out of her trance. "What are you? Some kind of prude?"

"Do you wanna die?"

"I'm not gonna die from dope," said Audrey.

"You're gonna die from my sickle," said Zodiac, lifting it.

"Let's not get into a fight about this," said Hilda.

"Where's the dope?"

"What difference does it make?"

"Don't give me any lip," said Zodiac, brandishing his sickle.

"Don't have a cow. It's in boxes in that room," said Hilda, pointing across the warehouse.

Box heard the commotion and wondered what was going on.

"That's all I wanted to know," said Zodiac, smiling and lowering his sickle. "Anybody got some marshmallows they wanna toast? We're gonna have ourselves a bonfire."

"What's up?" said Box.

"Who let you out here?" said Hilda. "You're quarantined."

"Not anymore," said Zodiac. "I let him out. As any fool can see, he's not infected."

"We won't know that for sure till he's been here two weeks."

"What's this bullshit about two weeks? He doesn't have a bite on him. If he wasn't bitten by one of the infected, he's not infected. Period."

"You don't know?"

"Don't know what?"

"The plague is airborne. If you breathe the spores, you become infected."

"Where'd you hear that old wives' tale?" said Zodiac with a scornful laugh.

"It's the truth."

"If he inhaled these so-called spores, why hasn't he turned?"

"Infection by the spores can take up to two weeks before the plague manifests itself."

"Are you shooting me a line?"

"It's the truth. And—"

"There's more?"

"Let me finish. And some people are asymptomatic. Box could be infected and not have any symptoms if he inhaled the spores."

Zodiac laughed. "That's the dumbest thing I ever heard. Why don't you just ask him if he's infected?"

"He can't remember anything. His memory's shot. The only way we can be sure he won't turn and start killing us is if we quarantine him for two weeks."

"I hate to tell you this, but you're nuts. The only way you get infected is if one of the ghouls bites you. End of story."

"I'm warning you—"

"You're a whack job, lady. The big boys are taking over. And we're not ruled by superstitious fear."

Chapter 26

Zodiac signaled to Tyler, who was striding through the warehouse with an AR-15 strapped to his shoulder.

"Tyler, take some men to that room over there," said Zodiac, pointing out the room. "Remove the boxes of dope and torch them in a bonfire outside the fence."

"Will do," said Tyler, who hollered to his men and angled for the room.

"You know why there aren't any hippies anymore?" Zodiac asked Hilda.

"No," answered Hilda without interest.

"Because potheads and acidheads can't make a living. The hippie lifestyle was stillborn."

"I know people who smoke weed, and they're not dead."

"They will be, if I catch 'em."

Everyone became somber.

Zodiac grinned. "What's wrong with a good ole can of ice-cold beer? Why so serious, everybody? This ain't the end of the world."

"You sure about that?" said Audrey.

Danny idled up to the table toking a joint, his eyes bloodshot. "What's all the ruckus?"

"You're not wearing your mask," said Hilda. "You're supposed to smoke outside if you want to smoke."

"I know that smell," said Zodiac.

He stalked up to Danny, lifted his sickle, and lopped off Danny's head, which landed on the table in front of Hilda and Audrey. Screaming, they both sprang to their feet. Arterial blood sprayed the table and everyone around it. Danny's bleeding torso, a scarlet splotch on the chest of his shirt, fell to the floor.

Porter dashed to the table, wild-eyed. "What the hell happened?"

"Danny said hello to the new boss," said Zodiac, holding up his sickle dripping with blood.

"You son of a bitch."

"Watch your mouth. Or do you wanna join him?"

"What did he do wrong?"

"He was taking drugs. No dope under my watch."

"But he didn't even know your rules."

"Ignorance is no excuse in the eyes of the law. He was found guilty and executed."

Porter seethed.

Box ushered him away from Zodiac, concerned Porter would say something that would provoke Zodiac to use his sickle again.

"He's burning all the drugs," Box told Porter.

"That doesn't give him the right to kill Danny," said Porter, resisting Box's escort but backing away from Zodiac with Box's help, nonetheless.

"Let's go outside and watch the bonfire," said Box.

"This is all wrong. We never shoulda let that whack job in here."

Zodiac glowered at Porter.

Holding Porter's elbow Box guided him outside, away from Zodiac, across the parking lot, and out the gate. They watched Zodiac's men wheel the pasteboard boxes of drugs out of the warehouse on dollies beyond the chain-link fence, pile the boxes together, douse them with lighter fluid, and fling wooden safety matches on the pile to ignite it. The boxes burst into flames.

Through the smoke Box saw buzzards swoop down on the warehouse roof.

"We got buzzards on the roof," he said.

"They're eating the dead ghouls up there," said Porter, watching the buzzards flutter down onto the roof with their massive black wings. "We gotta get rid of Zodiac."

"He's got the guns. You gave him the key to the armory."

"What choice did we have? Hilda surrendered."

"How do we get rid of him without guns?"

"We can't let him get away with killing Danny in cold blood."

Box started at the sound of a voice.

"Quite a bonfire," said Zodiac, appearing behind them, bloodstained sickle in hand. "You got vultures on your roof."

Box hoped Zodiac hadn't overheard what he and Porter had said about getting rid of the guy. Otherwise, the two of them might end up like Danny.

"And you know why," said Porter.

"There's dead meat up there," said Zodiac with a goofy grin. "Now how could dead meat get on top of the roof?"

The bonfire crackled, its glossy yellow flames tonguing the sky. A half dozen of Zodiac's men stood around the flames, faces sweaty, mesmerized by the blaze.

"Don't stand too close to the flames," said Zodiac. "I don't want you getting stoned from the weed smoke."

Grudgingly, the men stepped back from the bonfire.

"It's gonna be a hot day," said Box, wiping the sweat off his forehead.

"Are you following me around?" Porter asked Zodiac.

"No," answered Zodiac. "Should I be? I came out here to watch the bonfire."

"You shouldn't make rules without telling people what they are. A good leader tells his people the rules."

"What makes you think I'm good? I'm not simon-pure—if that's what you're expecting. A successful leader needs to know when to give his followers a taste of the whip. Are you a troublemaker?"

"What's the big deal about weed and dope?"

"I'll tell you a little story. My mom and dad were both drug-addicted hippies. Neither one of them could support themselves because they were stoned out of their minds all the time. They're both dead. I had to learn to survive by my wits. Dope fucks up your head so you can't think straight. No junkies allowed here. We need to have each other's back. I don't know about you, but I don't want a junkie on my six."

"I'm sorry about your mom and dad. It's a terrible thing to lose your parents when you're young."

"I'm better off without them. The only thing they ever cared about was dope."

"It doesn't give you the right to kill all dopers, though. Just because of your mom and dad."

"I have the right to do anything I see fit. Zodiac rules. Is that a problem?"

Porter decided to back off for the time being. "Just saying."

"They don't call me the Reaper for nothing," said Zodiac, scraping a swatch of coagulated blood off his sickle's blade with his fingernails.

"When can we have our guns back?" said Porter, glancing at the empty holster on his hip.

"Only my men are allowed to carry weapons. You know what happens if you disobey my orders," said Zodiac, raising his sickle.

"You're gonna make a lot of enemies ruling like that. Those that live by the sword—"

"What's wrong with having enemies? I'd rather be feared than liked. Friends are the ones that wind up knifing you in the back."

Straight out of Machiavelli's *Prince*, decided Box, and again wondered how he knew such things. He must have gone to college. He could remember stuff from college, but he couldn't remember his own name or how he got in the desert where Porter and Danny had found him. What college had he gone to? What was his job? He couldn't say. It was frustrating to have so many blanks in his memory.

Chapter 27

Audrey was lying alone on her back on her cot in her room, worrying about bearing an infected baby. Seeing Don's smiling face in her mind's eye put her at ease. But her calm didn't last.

She fretted about her baby. She couldn't stand the idea of an infected baby—like the one she had seen chew its way out of its dead mother's womb during the ghouls' onslaught. Would the same thing happen to her? she wondered. Why was she thinking such morbid thoughts? She wished she had some weed. It soothed her nerves. The only reason she smoked it. She didn't toke to hallucinate and see flying saucers.

She needed to think about something else. What would she call her baby? Don and her hadn't decided on a name before his untimely death. She thought Sam would be a good name. Samantha if it was a girl. Samuel if it was a boy. For some reason, she felt sure it would be a boy.

Wincing, she felt abdominal pangs. It felt like the baby was kicking, trying to get out. It was too early for that. She didn't want to have a premature birth. It would lessen the baby's chances for survival.

She had to admit sometimes she had horrible thoughts, like she wanted to rip the baby out of her womb when the fetus was acting up. She knew it was horrible of her to think such thoughts, but the baby's moving around inside her and kicking her caused her pain. It felt like the baby was feeding on her, a foreign entity consuming her internal organs. She glanced at a pair of scissors lying on the nightstand near her head.

Don't even think it, she told herself.

The baby was tearing her insides apart. She wanted to scream in pain. *Stop it, Sam. Stop it.*

The pain became so intense she thought she was going to pass out.

What if Don had been asymptomatic? she wondered. What if he had been infected by spores before the ghoul dropped out of the tree onto him? Don had killed a lot of the infected when he had gone on his foraging missions. What if one of the creatures had gotten too close to him and had infected him with the spores from its diseased breath, and Don had been asymptomatic while he impregnated her? She shuddered at the thought. If that was true, she might be infected even now, asymptomatic but contagious. Contagious to her baby?

She didn't know what to think. Nobody was safe in the plague.

She groaned in agony at the pain in her abdomen.

Was she experiencing a premature birth? she wondered. If so, it could be because the baby was infected.

She bent her knees as she lay on her back on the cot, preparing for a premature birth, just in case. She didn't alert the others, because she didn't want them to see her infected baby when she bore it. It would look like that monster the pregnant ghoul had. She felt nauseous at the memory of the baby ghoul.

The pain in her belly increased. Her face sweaty, she choked back her screams. She glanced at the pair of scissors on the nightstand. She knew what she must do if she bore a monster.

Pain racked her belly. Shutting her eyes she gritted her teeth. The baby was trying to come out. It felt like she was bleeding between her legs. She tried to sit up and look, but the pain was crippling. She lay back down, her whole body sweaty now.

Sam was coming out.

It took every ounce of her energy to suppress a scream. She mustn't let the others know. She mustn't let them see her infected baby.

She heard a thud on the floor.

The baby had crawled off the cot onto the floor.

Mustering all her strength she snagged the scissors from the nightstand. She had to be prepared in case the baby was infected. And it must be. Or why had it been born premature?

She raised herself to a sitting position on the cot and cast around for the baby. She saw it. It was crawling on the floor, leaving a bloody trail behind it, trying to escape. Sensing she was looking at it, it turned around to face her.

Its face covered with her blood, the baby bared its fangs, growled, and hissed at her.

She wanted to throw up. It was infected. She knew what she must do.

She must kill it.

Exhausted from giving birth, she could barely move. But she had to move. She had to catch up to it and stab it to death with the scissors.

Struggling to get up she fell off the cot onto the floor, the pair of scissors in her hand. She was still bleeding, she realized. She was losing strength by the second. The creature must have gnawed its way out of her belly as the monster born to the pregnant ghoul had.

Somehow the baby knew what she was going to do, and it crawled away from her toward the door. Because of its small size it moved slowly. She figured she could catch up to it before it reached the door. And so what if it reached the door? It couldn't reach the doorknob.

She crawled toward the baby and flopped on her face, her arms and legs feeble, her whole body feeble from loss of blood. She had to inch along the floor after the creature. She must kill it before it infected someone else.

If only her body would hold up long enough. She felt lightheaded. She felt like she would pass out any second. She shook her head so she wouldn't black out. If she blacked out, it was over. The creature would bite her. She may have been asymptomatic now, but nobody could withstand a bite by the infected and not turn. She must have been asymptomatic, or how else could her baby have contracted the plague? She might not even live long enough to be bitten what with all her hemorrhaging.

Since she was asymptomatic, it meant someone in the camp had infected her. Somebody was a carrier. How many more of them were infected? It didn't bear thinking about. The only thing that mattered now was killing her baby. The monster must die.

Flat on her bleeding belly, she could barely move. She wormed across the hardwood floor feeling her strength ebbing away with the steady loss of her blood. *Don't let me bleed out before I reach my baby.* Clasping the finger grips of the scissors in her hand, she stabbed the scissors' point into the floor and dragged her body forward.

The creature craned its head around and hissed at her.

"You think you can stop me?" said Audrey with determination, her face fierce.

The creature hissed at her again.

"Wait there," she said. "I'm gonna kill you, you little monster."

The baby continued crawling away, leaving a trail of blood in its wake.

Audrey yanked the scissors' point out of the floor, reached forward, and jabbed it into the floor ahead of her. She dragged her belly across the floor. She was going to catch the monster—if she could remain conscious long enough. She was catching up to it. The baby was tiny and couldn't make much headway by crawling.

"I'm gonna kill you," she told it. "You abomination from hell."

She was almost there. The baby was in reach.

Audrey tried to yank the scissors' tip out of the floor. It was stuck. She was becoming too weak.

"No," she said, grimacing, her voice pleading, sobbing. "Give me strength."

It was now or never. She felt her consciousness slipping away. If she didn't stab the creature now, she wouldn't have enough energy to do it later.

The baby turned around to face her, growled at her, baring its teeth, and swatted at her with its tiny hand.

"You killed me," said Audrey, who knew she was bleeding out from the baby's chewing through her womb. "Now I kill you."

Groaning, summoning her last reserve of energy, Audrey yanked the scissors' tip out of the floor, raised the scissors, and plunged the pointed tip into the baby's soft skull.

"Die, die," she gasped, and passed out, the baby's brain impaled on the scissors.

Chapter 28

Box and Porter were standing in the parking lot inside the perimeter and peering through the chain-link fence at the bonfire of dope that was winking out. The flames were diminishing now and would die out soon, leaving nothing but a pile of embers. Box could smell the sweet stink of the burning marijuana, which the wind was blowing toward the warehouse.

"I hate what Zodiac did to Danny just for toking a joint," said Porter. "I feel like I should have done something to save him."

"What could you do?" said Box.

"I dunno. I feel terrible about it. I feel like it was my fault it happened."

"You're better off than me. I can't feel much of anything."

"You don't care about Danny?"

"I didn't know him that well, but I'm not feeling much of anything. I don't even know who I am. How can I feel anything when I don't even know my own name?"

Porter scrutinized Box. "You can't feel anything?"

"I can feel fear. Otherwise, my feelings are gone or numb. Like my memory."

"It must be due to your PTSD or whatever it is you're suffering from. You need a shrink."

Box chewed it over. "Maybe I'm better off not remembering who I am."

"How can that be right?"

"Only a traumatic shock to my system could've triggered this amnesia."

Porter shrugged. "I'd rather know who I am than lose my memory and my emotions."

"It's like I'm a zombie in limbo."

"Do you think you're infected?" said Porter, searching Box's face with concern.

"No," said Box, quickly.

Box didn't think he was anyway. If he *was* infected, wouldn't he have turned by now? His problem was psychosomatic, not a symptom of the zombie plague. He decided to drop the subject.

He didn't want Porter to think he was infected. There was no telling what Porter would do if he thought that.

"I think we got bigger problems on our hands now, namely this Zodiac character," said Porter. "We might all end up like Danny, if we don't take action against him."

"He controls the guns."

"For now." Porter paused in thought, furrowing his brow. "I need to do something to make up for letting Danny get killed. It's really bugging me."

"Why do you think it's your fault?"

"I feel responsible for him. I was like his mentor trying to help him adapt to the plague. We have to learn to adapt to it because it's not going away. I should've warned him about Zodiac."

"How could you? You had no idea what he was going to do to Danny."

"I should've had an idea. That's the point. Anybody who catapults infected corpses at a warehouse has to be sick in the head and capable of any atrocity."

"Kicking yourself won't do any good."

"I was responsible for Danny, and I blew it. I blew it big-time," said Porter, clutching his forehead.

"You can't let your guilt eat you apart."

"The only way to stop feeling guilt is to do something about Danny," said Porter, dropping his hand from his forehead.

Nerve-shattering screams erupted from the warehouse.

Box wheeled around at the commotion and saw a woman running out of the warehouse entrance, her face wild with fright.

Box and Porter bolted to the warehouse door.

Chapter 29

Dashing into the warehouse Box spotted Hilda, who was standing white-faced in front of Audrey's room.

"What happened?" said Box.

"It's Audrey—" Overcome, Hilda couldn't continue.

Box darted toward Audrey's room.

"Don't go in there," said Hilda, wide-eyed. "It's . . . it's . . . a scene from hell."

Box entered the room. He saw a bloodbath. Audrey's cot and the floor were covered with a pool of blood. Audrey's prostrate figure in her blood-drenched maternity dress, which had once been mint green, was lying in the pool. Her blood-soaked arm was extended, a pair of scissors clutched in her hand, a tiny figure's head impaled on them.

The blood drained from Box's face. He suppressed the urge to wretch. He backed out of the room, shutting the door behind him.

"What?" said Porter.

"She—she—she killed her baby," said Hilda, managing to collect herself enough to speak.

"No," said Porter, grimacing with disbelief. "Why in the name of all that's holy would she—"

"It looks like she had a premature birth. The baby . . . tried to crawl away so Audrey . . . so Audrey," said Hilda, putting her hand to her chest, "wouldn't be able to kill him with a pair of scissors."

"Premature birth? How is that possible?"

"Audrey died from hemorrhaging because of it."

"Is that possible?"

"What other explanation is there?"

"Did anyone see this?"

"She was in the room alone."

"Did you see that baby's face?" Box asked Hilda.

"I didn't take a good look at it," she answered. "I couldn't stand the sight of . . ."

"The baby had teeth."

"What? You're seeing things. Babies aren't born with teeth."

"They're more like fangs."

"What are you saying?" said Porter, his face livid.

"It must've been born infected with the plague," said Box.

"Impossible. Audrey wasn't infected."

A pall of silence fell over them.

"She could have been asymptomatic," said Hilda, her voice barely audible.

"That's crazy," said Porter.

"How else can you explain her having an infected baby?"

"That would mean there's a carrier among us," said Box.

"I don't believe it," said Porter.

"It could've been Lucy," said Hilda. "She believed she was infected and asymptomatic. It drove her to suicide."

"Lucy *thought* she was asymptomatic. That doesn't mean she really was."

"Then how do you explain Audrey's baby?" Hilda looked around the warehouse, gripped with apprehension. "We must have a carrier among us."

Zodiac stormed through the warehouse up to Hilda. "What's the ruckus?"

"Audrey," said Hilda, nodding to Audrey's bedroom.

Zodiac flung open the bedroom door and took in the ghastly sight.

Pulling away he shut the door and, nonplussed, leaned back against it like he was about to collapse.

"Jesus," he said.

"Her own child," said Hilda.

"My wife Emmy died giving birth to a stillborn child," said Zodiac, a faraway gaze in his eyes.

"She knew her baby was infected, and she killed it. Can you imagine? She killed her own child," said Hilda, an expression of horror on her face.

"Emmy was only twenty-five when she died. She had her whole life before her. How do you think I felt?"

"Is this the new normal? Somebody dying here every day from the plague?"

"This isn't normal," said Porter. "No way is this normal. We're living through a plague, a catastrophe. Catastrophes aren't normal. We're living in a catastrophic event."

"A catastrophe that never ends," said Hilda.

"We'll go down as a footnote in a history book."

"What makes you think there are gonna be any history books written after this is over?" said Box. "Who's gonna be left to write them?"

"And we have another problem," said Hilda.

"What?" said Zodiac, snapping out of his grief for his lost wife.

"We have a carrier among us. If we don't find them, we may all become infected."

"A ghoul? We have a ghoul here?"

"An infected member who's asymptomatic. They look just like you and me. Not putrescent creatures."

"That's impossible. The only way you get infected is from a bite from one of the ghouls."

"A lot you know. Anyone can become infected from breathing spores the ghouls emit."

"Who told you this BS?"

"We found it out through experience. And Audrey's baby is proof. She was *not* a ghoul, and yet she gave birth to a ghoul. How do you explain that? The only way you can explain it is that she was asymptomatic and she passed the plague on to her child."

"Not necessarily. Maybe her husband was a ghoul when he impregnated her, passing on the plague to their child."

"Her husband Don wasn't a ghoul seven months ago when she conceived, I can assure you. Audrey wouldn't have gone to bed with a ghoul. Are you crazy?"

Zodiac advanced on Hilda, his face menacing. "Where do you get off calling me crazy? You're the one that's crazy with all this nonsense you're spouting about the disease."

"How do you explain Audrey's infected child?"

"He was a freak. Some kind of monster. These things happen."

"The fact is—and you don't want to admit it—there's a carrier among us and we're all in line to get infected, unless we find them first and kill them."

"Listen to you," said Porter. "You sound scarier than Zodiac. Hunting down people and killing them? Come on. We're better than that."

"It's the only way to save us from being infected," said Hilda. "Or banish them." She paused. "Or do you have a better idea?"

"How do we prove someone is infected, if they don't turn into a ghoul?"

Hilda looked glum. "I wish I knew. There must be some way."

"There isn't a way," said Zodiac, "because if you're not a ghoul, you're not infected."

"I wish you were right," said Hilda, shaking her head.

"I am right. I don't believe what I can't see with my own two eyes. None of this asymptomatic hogwash. Audrey gave birth to a freak. Horrified and ashamed of what she had done, she hunted her baby down and executed it. I'm sure many of us would have done the same thing in her shoes."

"God help us, if that's true."

"You know I'm right, but you're afraid to admit it."

Chapter 30

"If we don't expose the carrier and deal with them ASAP, they'll end up infecting and killing all of us," said Hilda.

"Stop spreading fear and paranoia in my camp. I won't have it," said Zodiac, raising his sickle.

"Killing me isn't gonna change the truth."

"You're the one that wants to hunt somebody down and kill them."

"We don't have to kill them. We do have to get them out of our camp, or they will infect us with the plague."

"You're a whacko," said Zodiac, making a circular motion with his finger at the side of his ear. "Don't make me lock you up for going around spreading lies and panic."

"Where's the science about airborne plague?" Box asked Hilda.

"I don't know anything about science. I'm not a scientist. But I have eyes. And I can see what's happening." Hilda stared at Box. "What are you doing out of quarantine, anyway? You should be locked in your room for two weeks."

"I let him out," said Zodiac. "What's this about quarantine?" He turned to Box. "Were you bitten by a ghoul?"

"No," said Box.

"Then why are you quarantined?"

"He could've inhaled plague spores from the ghouls while he was in the desert," said Hilda. "He has no memory so he can't tell us what happened."

"That's ridiculous." Zodiac turned to Box. "You're not quarantined anymore."

"You're putting the rest of us at risk, if we don't keep him quarantined," said Hilda. "I'm in charge—"

"You are *not* in charge. You surrendered to me."

"You're making a big mistake, and we're all gonna pay for it."

"How can ghouls exhale plague spores when the creatures can't even breathe? They're dead. They're resurrected corpses. There's only a tiny portion of their brain that is alive generating electrical impulses to their bodies telling them to eat human flesh. They can't breathe."

"Then how can they walk? How can they eat? How can they do anything?"

"Electrical impulses. Their nerves work and are reanimating them. I don't know the science."

"Then why is your explanation any better than mine?"

"Because I've never seen a human turn into a ghoul simply by being close to a ghoul. The plague is spread by a ghoul's bite. That's what I've seen, and that's all. I know what I see. Nothing else."

"Then how do they pass the plague spores without biting?"

"They don't."

"They do. And some people after they breathe the spores are asymptomatic—like Audrey. The only reason we know she's infected is because she gave birth to an infected baby."

"You're making this stuff up out of whole cloth. The ghouls don't breathe. If they don't breathe, they can't exhale."

"Maybe the spores are sloughed off from their putrescent skin when they're in close contact with humans. The spores get on a person's hand. The person touches his eye or mouth or nose and the spores spread infection into the body."

Zodiac shook his head no. "All you're giving me is speculation."

"How do you explain Audrey's infected baby?"

"A ghoul bit her, and she didn't tell anyone—because she was scared we'd kill her. It's the logical explanation. If we examine her body, we'll find a ghoul's bite on it."

"If a ghoul bit her, why didn't she show any symptoms? Why didn't she turn into a ghoul?"

"All I know is what I see with my own two eyes. Maybe it takes longer for some people to turn than others after getting bitten."

"Or she was asymptomatic. A carrier. Carriers can infect the rest of us. There could be more like her among us. We have to find them and quarantine them."

"There you go again spreading panic."

"The truth can be scary. We're living in scary times."

Chapter 31

Zodiac eyed Hilda with suspicion. "Did you ever work for the government?"

"No," said Hilda. "What's that got to do with anything?"

"They're the ones that spread panic to get power."

"I have nothing to do with the government."

"The people in government are the ones that got us into this catastrophe. They've got some explaining to do."

"The government doesn't even exist anymore, not in these parts anyway."

"They could be in hiding, for all we know. Like those clowns in Washington. I bet they're hiding somewhere. They got themselves a hidey-hole, you know it. Some bombproof bunker with six-foot-thick concrete walls able to withstand a nuclear blast. If I'm lying, I'm dying."

"I don't care. What matters is here and now."

"It matters to me. I'm going to Washington to conquer it and save our country. Their leadership—or lack of it—is bringing our great country to its knees. We're a shadow of what we used to be."

"Because of the plague."

"And the corrupt government. They carpet-bombed the country with nukes to eradicate the plague by killing the ghouls."

"What about the rest of us? How are we supposed to survive being nuked?"

"That's my point. I don't think we were meant to survive. Collateral damage, acceptable losses, and all that. They can't get away with it. We're marching on Washington, and we're gonna take back our country."

"Then why are you still here?"

Zodiac stalked up to her. "We're not ready to leave yet. You got a problem with that?"

Hilda backed off.

"I got a problem with getting infected with plague," she said, sotto voce.

"Join the club. But don't spread rumors that are gonna panic everyone. You're gonna incite riots and who knows what else."

"Covering up the truth won't change it."

"You're not telling them the truth. You're spreading unsubstantiated rumors. It's time for you to shut up."

Hilda glared at him, but kept her own counsel.

Zodiac turned to Porter. "Are you a government worker?"

"What government?" said Porter. "What used to be the government is a shambles."

"There's only one way to find out if that's true—going to the capital."

"What's the point? Whoever's left there isn't doing us any favors. Like you said, they tried to nuke us."

"So we can take over, of course. Why else would we go there? Now what about you?"

"What?" said Box, realizing Zodiac was addressing him.

"Do you work for the government?"

"No," said Box, having no idea what his job used to be, his amnesia going strong. "Not that I know of."

Zodiac cocked an eyebrow. "What's that supposed to mean?"

"I lost my memory."

"We already told you all that," Porter told Zodiac. "He's got PTSD or something. What difference does it make if he worked for the government?"

"It makes plenty of difference."

Zodiac addressed the crowd that had gathered in the warehouse. "What about the rest of you? Do any of you work for the government?"

A six-three guy with a shaving-brush, salt-and-pepper mustache and wire-rimmed spectacles, clad in black slacks and a white button-down shirt, raised his large mitt. "I did. I used to work at the IRS before the plague hit."

"What's your name?"

"Nordstrom. Hal Nordstrom."

"Anybody else? Don't be shy." Zodiac scanned the crowd and saw no other hands raised. "Step forward and be recognized."

Nobody made a move.

Zodiac withdrew his pistol from his holster at his waist. He trained the barrel on Nordstrom's head and fired, his slug hitting its mark. Screams rent the air, as the back of Nordstrom's skull hurtled across the room like a bat on the wing and struck a short, middle-aged, pear-shaped woman in the face. Wiping the bloody brains from her face in consternation, she felt her knees go weak and crumpled to the floor.

"What the hell are you doing?" said Porter.

"Anyone who works for the government is the enemy," said Zodiac, holding his pistol above his head and brandishing it. "If I find out anyone else here works for the government, they'll meet the same fate."

Steamed, Porter gritted his teeth. "You're insane."

"Just perceptive and well oriented."

Porter glowered at him.

Zodiac laughed gaily. "Hey, everyone, the rest of you should be happy as clams Norberg—whatever his name is—is gone. He worked for the IRS. I'm sure most of you wanted to kill an IRS agent at one time or another in your life. Dirty revenuers. Remember those times you got audited?"

The crowd swallowed their screams, terrified of Zodiac and what he might do next, his moods unpredictable.

"Insane," muttered Porter. "Off-the-wall whacko."

"I didn't catch that," said Zodiac, his merriment vanishing. "What'd you say?"

"Nothing."

Zodiac nodded. "Good." He turned to Tyler, who had started threading his way through the crowd toward Zodiac after the shot had been fired. "Tyler, drag the government informant's dead body out of here."

"Got it, boss," said Tyler, and changed direction toward Nordstrom's corpse, which the crowd had moved away from.

"He said he worked for the IRS," said Porter. "Where do you get government informant out of that?"

"Anyone who works for the government is an informant. The government tried to kill us—all of us"—Zodiac gestured toward the crowd—"with nukes. The government is the enemy. They have informants everywhere."

Chapter 32

Box opened the door to the quarantine room and saw Marta sitting on her cot inside.

"Come on," he said. "Let's go to the gym and get some exercise."

"We're under quarantine. They won't let us out of here without some kind of escort. Or have you forgot?" She looked at him with unease. "Is your memory getting worse?"

"Change in orders. Zodiac says we're not infected and don't need to be quarantined."

Marta got to her feet. "I guess we should be thankful. But that guy bothers me. I don't trust him."

"He's a control freak, all right. And like most of them, he's paranoid."

"And he's a murderer. Don't forget that one."

"How can I forget?"

"Maybe we should leave this place."

"I was thinking the same thing. But where would we go?"

"I haven't given it much thought."

As they left the quarantine room, Zodiac picked up on them and told them to hang up the wash. He pointed to plastic laundry baskets full of wet clothes sitting near the laundry room.

Box and Marta each grabbed a basket with both their hands, struck out for the warehouse front door, entered the parking lot, and made for the clotheslines that were strung from the chain-link fence to the sides of two parked stake trucks.

Box and Marta set their laundry baskets down on the asphalt. Box withdrew a wet bedsheet from his laundry basket, took it to one of the clotheslines, and draped it over the line. He found a leather pouch of clothespins hanging from one of the clotheslines, scooped out several grey weathered wooden clothespins, and used two on the sheet. Hanging from the line the sheet flapped in the wind.

"You should squeeze the water out of the sheet first," said Marta.

"The sun'll dry it out in no time."

"I can see you never did the wash in your family."

Marta retrieved two white bras from her laundry basket and fastened them to the clothesline with two clothespins.

Box stepped back from the flapping sheet and felt his heel slip on the asphalt. He looked down at his shoe's heel, which looked crooked. He leaned over, untied his shoe, and took it off to get a better look at the heel. Twisting the heel he picked up on a hollowed-out compartment between the heel and the sole of his shoe. He found an electronic device in the compartment.

He removed the device to inspect it. Some kind of battery-operated transmitter, it looked like. Puzzled, he deposited the transmitter in his trouser pocket, straightened the crooked heel on his shoe, tossed his shoe on the asphalt, stepped back into it, and, hunkering down, tied the laces.

"A rock in your shoe?" said Marta, watching him.

He didn't know if he should tell her the truth. He had no idea what was going on. Was somebody tracking him? If so, why?

"Yeah," he said. "It was bugging me."

"I hate it when that happens."

"Do you think we're being watched?"

Marta glanced at Zodiac's armed guards standing at the locked gate. "I don't think they want us to leave, if that's what you mean."

"I mean, is someone watching our every move?"

"They *did* have us locked in that quarantine room to make sure we didn't go anywhere. I suppose they did it so they could watch where we were. You think they have a video camera in the room watching us? You're creeping me out."

Box hadn't thought of that. "I didn't notice one."

"They can make video cameras really tiny nowadays."

Whoever had installed the transmitter in his shoe must have done it before he arrived at the compound, decided Box. These were the same shoes he had been wearing in the desert when Porter and Danny found him and brought him here. This was some kind of trick heel on his shoe. It hadn't been added after he arrived here.

He removed the shoe and inspected it more closely. The bottom of the heel looked as worn as the scuffed sole, proving it wasn't a new heel installed by someone in the compound.

"What's wrong?" said Marta, a couple of wet socks in her hands. "Another rock in your shoe?"

"Yeah," he lied, finishing inspecting the shoe, putting it back on, and tying it.

Why didn't he want to tell her about the transmitter? he wondered. He instinctively wanted to keep it to himself, like it was part of his past to keep certain things to himself. What was his past? What kind of past would make him want to keep quiet about finding a transmitter in his shoe? Or was he overthinking this and making things up about himself and his reactions because he was so desperate to regain his memory?

"A penny for them," said Marta.

"What?" he said.

"You looked deep in thought."

"I was just feeling my foot to see if there were any more rocks in my shoe," he said, taking a few steps, as though trying on a new pair of shoes.

Marta attached the wet socks to the clothesline with clothespins.

"Too bad there aren't any washing machines and driers here," she said. "They have to do everything by hand."

Who the hell was he? wondered Box. And who was tracking him? Why would anyone want to track him?

A shot rang out, jerking him out of his thoughts.

A bullet tore a hole through the sheet flapping on the clothesline.

Chapter 33

"Get down," said Box, diving to the asphalt.

"Where'd that shot come from?" said Marta, lying on her belly.

"Outside the chain-link fence."

He peered toward the gate.

Alerted by the report of the gunshot, the guards held their AR-15s at the ready and scoped out the clearing before the woods in search of the shooter.

A jeep with a .50 caliber machine gun mounted on the back of it drove down the road toward the gate. Three black SUVs drove behind it Indian file.

One of the guards at the gate keyed his walkie-talkie to summon Zodiac. The rest of the guards trained their AR-15s on the approaching jeep.

The cartel, realized Box. Why did they try to kill him? Or was this their usual way of making a dramatic entrance to instill fear in their customers? He remembered the previous time they had paid the camp a visit dragging someone on a chain behind their vehicle. It was all part of the same strategy: keep customers terrified so they won't put up any resistance.

Zodiac strutted out of the warehouse, sickle in hand, and made a beeline for the front gate, Tyler at his side bearing an AR-15.

Rafael's driver parked the jeep twenty feet in front of the gate. Geraldo, a twentysomething guy with a shaved head and wearing a black T with Lamborghini printed on it in fluorescent lime letters was manning the machine gun. He brought the muzzle to bear on the guards at the gate.

"Where's Hilda?" demanded Rafael. "What's all this bullshit with the guards with their guns on us?"

"Start talking," said Zodiac, reaching the front gate.

"I ain't talking to no one but Hilda. Not one of her flunkies."

Zodiac glanced at his wristwatch. "You're running out of time."

"*Vete a la chingada.* Get Hilda out here."

"I suggest you start talking or take a hike."

"Do you have any idea what a .50 caliber bullet can do to your head, *puta*? Well, I'll tell you. It can atomize your head. It will turn you into—into—an airhead. Do you want to be known as an airhead for the rest of your short life?"

Baring his crooked teeth the machine-gunner giggled at Rafael's joke.

"I wouldn't want to be in your shoes," said Zodiac.

"Do you want me to make an example out of you?" said Rafael, livid at the delay. "Get Hilda out here now."

"Why do you need Hilda?"

"I'm not talking to one of her bottom feeders. Lower your weapons and get her."

Zodiac said nothing. He stared at Rafael.

Masked, Hilda emerged from the warehouse and stalked to the front gate.

"Hilda," said Rafael. "Tell your men to lower their guns and let me in. I have new supplies."

"We don't need your supplies," said Hilda.

"What? You crazy? I got good stuff."

"What supplies?" said Zodiac.

"All good stuff. I got ice, blow, weed, murder 8, you name it."

"We don't want any dope. Good-bye."

"Hilda, tell him what's what."

"You tell him," said Hilda.

Rafael bridled. "What's wrong, lady boss? Tell him who's in charge."

"I'm in charge," said Zodiac. "Hilda works for me."

"Zodiac's in charge," said Hilda, her expression wooden.

"I'm disappointed in you, Hilda. Oh well, it doesn't matter to me. Zorro, or whatever your name is, open the gate or we'll have to teach you a lesson."

"Why are you still here?" said Zodiac.

"Lemme blast 'em, *patrón*," said Geraldo, pivoting the machine gun back and forth, including Zodiac in the barrel's arc, his finger on the trigger aching to fire.

Zodiac slowly raised his hand above his head.

"Are you surrendering, Zorro?" said Rafael with amusement.

At the sight of Zodiac's signal that they had prearranged on their walkie-talkies, Tyler, who was standing near the mortar out of sight of the gate watching Zodiac, fired the mortar.

The last SUV in Rafael's convoy exploded into a fireball.

"You're next," said Zodiac. "Beat it or die."

Bowled over by the blast, Rafael realized he was under attack, thought better of counterattacking due to Zodiac's superior firepower, and ordered his driver to split. Its tires shrieking, Rafael's jeep peeled away, the cartel's remaining two SUVs tailgating it.

Tyler lobbed another mortar shell at the convoy. The blast cratered the road's shoulder, missing the convoy, which sped into the woods and disappeared.

"That's what I'm talking about," said Zodiac with a crocodile grin. "Three blind mice. See how they run."

Tyler drove a black BMW sedan across the parking lot to Zodiac.

"Want me to inspect the wreck for survivors, boss?" said Tyler, sticking his elbow and head out the window, as he brought the BMW to a halt the better part of three feet from Zodiac.

Zodiac eyed the flaming crumpled steel that was once an SUV as it expelled a column of black smoke that drifted across the sky.

"Nobody could've survived that hit," he said.

"I'm not so sure," said Tyler, eying the burning wreckage. "Cartel SUVs are usually bulletproof."

"Bulletproof, maybe, but not bombproof. Nobody's still alive in that mess. If anyone is, the fire will take care of them."

"Want me to go after the leader?"

"I doubt he'll be back now that he knows we got more firepower than him."

Box pricked up his ears at a scream emanating from the flaming SUV wreckage.

"I'll take care of it," said Tyler.

He got out of his car and exited the front gate with one of his men.

They inspected the wreckage and emptied their AR-15 magazines into the conflagration where a charred head was sticking out twisting like a turtle's head and screaming in pain. The head stopped screaming and hung motionless.

"You can't let thugs push you around like that, Hilda," said Zodiac. "Otherwise, they'll keep coming back."

"They didn't push me around," said Hilda. "We did business with them. In a fair trade there is no theft. Food in exchange for drugs."

"What they traded you was worthless crap. They got the better of you. If it wasn't for me, they'd still be taking you to the cleaner's."

"You don't understand what we're going through. The people here are fed up with the plague. They want to get their lives back to normal. But they can't. They take out their frustration doing drugs. It's either that or they'll start killing each other."

"They can kill for me. I need killing machines for my march on Washington. But I don't want any dopers. Dope messes up your perceptions and reactions."

The chugging of a motorcycle drowned out the crackling of the flames engulfing the decimated SUV.

Chapter 34

Box watched a motorcycle mounted by a guy wearing a black leather jacket with slash zipper pockets and zippers running down its sleeves approach the gate. He wore stone-washed blue jeans and black leather boots to complete his outfit.

Tyler, who was standing near the burning SUV, raised his AR-15 and drew a bead on the motorcyclist.

"Hold it right there," Zodiac told the motorcyclist, raising his voice above the motorcycle's clatter.

"Want me to blow him away, boss?" asked Tyler.

"Not yet," answered Zodiac. "Take it easy."

The motorcyclist parked his machine a few inches in front of the gate, remaining mounted. "Hello."

"We just sent the rest of your gang running for their lives," said Zodiac. "I suggest you do the same."

In his thirties, the motorcyclist had three days' growth of black stubble on his face. He was wearing a black carbon fiber motorcycle helmet.

"I don't know what you're talking about," he said, adjusting his helmet.

"Your buddies in the drug cartel. They just left." Zodiac nodded at the burning wreckage. "That's their SUV."

The motorcyclist shook his head. "I don't have anything to do with them."

"Then why are you here?"

"I'm running low on gas. I need a place to stay. The flesh eaters are massing in the forest. Thousands of 'em. Never seen so many. It's like they're sending signals to each other where to meet."

"They're too stupid to send signals. They're so stupid they can barely walk. How could they possibly send signals?"

The motorcyclist shrugged. "Regardless, they're massing in a clearing in the middle of the woods."

"What's your name?"

"Dean. Dean Pataki."

"Zodiac here. Do you mind giving me the Glock in your holster?"

Pataki couldn't help but notice that Tyler was training an AR-15 on his head.

"I'm running low on bullets," said Pataki.

"Who isn't?" said Zodiac, holding his hand out for Pataki's handgun.

"Is this necessary?"

"If you're not part of the cartel, why do you need it?"

"For the infected. They can tear a man from limb to limb in a matter of minutes."

"You're preaching to the converted. There aren't any infected in our camp, so you don't need it here. You do want to come inside, don't you?"

"I do."

"We'll give your piece back when you leave."

"All right," said Pataki, and reached for his Glock.

"Whoa. Take the butt out with your finger and thumb and toss the piece over the gate."

Tyler hoisted his AR-15 to his shoulder and peered through the sight at Pataki's head.

Pataki gingerly withdrew his Glock from its holster and tossed it over the gate into the parking lot.

"Where you headed?" said Zodiac, retrieving the Glock and hefting it in his hand.

"I'm running from those things and trying to find more people. I haven't seen a living person in a couple of days, and I've driven a long ways. I was beginning to think I was the last man standing."

"Nice Harley."

"Thanks." Pataki glanced at Tyler. "I don't like guns pointed at my head. Do you mind?"

Tyler grinned back at him, keeping his gun leveled at Pataki's head.

Zodiac signaled to Tyler to lower his automatic rifle. Tyler complied.

"A lot of the country is a nuclear wasteland," said Pataki.

"You can thank our government for that," said Zodiac.

"I'm sure they had a reason for it."

124

"They did. To save their own necks. It would've been nice if they had warned us in advance that they were gonna start nuking us, so we could've found shelter."

"Communications are out everywhere, the way I understand it."

"No excuse if you're gonna nuke your own people."

"Does anyone know what's really going on with this plague?"

"Drive your machine inside and rest a while. Have a can of ravioli."

"Much obliged."

"Open the gate," Zodiac told the guard.

Pataki drove through the open gate, parked his bike next to an old, rusted pickup in the lot, toed the kickstand, and dismounted. He removed his helmet and hung its strap on his Harley's handlebars. He hobbled around with stiff legs, getting his circulation going.

"We wasted a bunch of ghouls and torched them when they attacked our fence," said Zodiac, nodding at the burnt corpses in front of the chain-link fence about a hundred yards from the gate. "I thought we got most of them."

Pataki shook his head no. "There are thousands more in the woods."

"Not good."

"Did you see the cartel's camp when you were in the woods?" Box asked Pataki.

"No," said Pataki, eying Box. "No sign of life. Just the flesh eaters."

"How can we be sure you're not with the cartel?" said Zodiac.

"You'll have to take my word for it," said Pataki.

"It's hard to believe you'd come along right after the cartel takes a hike and have nothing to do with them."

"It's true I have nothing to do with them."

"You're not a mole they want to plant in my camp so they can destroy us from within?" said Zodiac, arching an eyebrow.

"I got nothing to do with them."

Pataki eyed Box again.

Box thought he caught Pataki nodding at him. Box wondered what that was all about. Or was he imagining it? Maybe it was a trick of the light. Or maybe his mind was playing tricks on him.

After all, his memory hadn't come back. Did he have other things wrong with his mind? Like seeing things?

"We *do* need people, if the infected are massing to attack like you say," Zodiac told Pataki, and fetched a sigh. "I guess it's possible you could arrive right after the cartel left and have no connection to them. Let's go into the warehouse and tuck into some ravioli."

"Sounds good," said Pataki.

"Nothing better than a can of Chef Boyardee beef ravioli, huh? Hits the spot I'm telling you," said Zodiac, rubbing his stomach and smiling.

"We need to give him a mask and quarantine him first," said Hilda, adjusting her mask, which was slipping down her nose as she spoke.

"Don't you ever take that thing off?" said Zodiac, who wasn't wearing one.

"When I sleep and eat."

"Nobody's infected in the camp so you don't need it. You only need it when you're around infected people."

"Like this guy. How do we know he's not infected?"

"Look at him. Does he look infected?"

Hilda stuck to her guns. "We don't know where he's been."

"What difference does it make?"

"We can't take the chance of his being infected."

"Have you been bitten by a ghoul, Pataki?" asked Zodiac.

"No," answered Pataki.

"There," Zodiac told Hilda. "Enough said."

"Why aren't you wearing a mask?" Hilda asked Pataki.

"Why should I?" said Pataki. "I'm here alone on my Harley."

"Makes sense to me," said Zodiac.

"He could've breathed spores from the infected," said Hilda.

"I told you before, it doesn't spread that way."

"We can't take that chance. He needs to be quarantined."

"You're full of shit. Do you want me to teach you a lesson?" said Zodiac, raising his voice in anger.

Somebody screamed in the warehouse.

"Not again," said Zodiac.

Alarmed, everyone charged inside.

126

Chapter 35

A plump twentysomething redhead wearing jeans and a lime green viscose blouse was writhing on her back on the floor in front of the cafeteria, her face turning blue, frothing at the mouth. She had wavy red hair and a fleshy face with narrow, finely chiseled lips, which were chapped and flaky with carmine lipstick.

"What's wrong with her?" said Pataki.

"It's Frieda," said Hilda.

"Get Doc Epps," Box heard someone cry.

"She's OD'ing," said Zodiac, staring at the woman.

"She's not OD'ing," said Hilda. "She's infected."

Thrashing around on the floor, Frieda clutched her throat.

"Maybe she's choking," said Marta.

"She's OD'ing on smack," said Zodiac. He surveyed the crowd that was gathering around Frieda. "How did she get drugs? We burned all the drugs. Who gave her smack?"

Frieda stopped thrashing and lay motionless.

Black medical bag in hand, Dr. Epps barged through the crowd. "Let me through. Let me through."

"It's too late," said Zodiac, eying Frieda.

"She's gonna turn," said Hilda. "Somebody, shoot her in the head."

"Wait a minute," said Epps. "I'm here."

Face hectic, he elbowed his way through the last of the crowd and spotted Frieda.

"Get away from her, Doc," said Hilda. "She's gonna turn."

"What happened to her?" said Epps.

"We don't know. We were outside when we heard her scream."

Epps knelt down beside Frieda, withdrew his stethoscope from his bag, applied it to Frieda's chest, and listened for a heartbeat.

Alarmed, he straddled her and started CPR.

"Is she dead, Doc?" said Hilda.

"Her heart's stopped," said Epps, continuing CPR chest compressions on Frieda.

"Get away from her. She's gonna turn."

127

"Who gave her the H?" demanded Zodiac.

Frieda growled. She snapped her mouth at Epps. Terrified, Epps leapt off her.

"Gimme a gun," said Hilda.

Frieda writhed on the floor, snapping her jaws at the air, her eyes milky.

Zodiac withdrew his pistol from his holster and shot her in the head.

"I hate junkies," he said. "Who gave her the smack?"

"She was clinically dead," said Epps.

"Obviously not. Her heart stopped then it restarted."

"She's infected," said Hilda, "and she turned into a ghoul."

"She OD'd," said Zodiac.

"How could she try to bite Doc Epps if she OD'd?"

"She wasn't dead. She saw him on her chest, thought he was trying to strangle her, and tried to bite him."

"Then why'd you shoot her?"

"I knew she was in her death throes and I didn't want her to suffer. She was beyond saving. I seen junkies die before. It's not a pretty sight. My mom and dad were dope addicts and they hung out with junkies. They were always jonesing and strung out. Pathetic, really, with track marks up and down their arms and legs. A lot of 'em OD'd." Brooding, Zodiac pointed at the vein inside Frieda's elbow, which was showing now because her long-sleeve blouse had bunched up her arm as she was squirming on the floor. "Look at the tracks on her arm."

"OK. Maybe she was a heroin addict. But she didn't OD. She's infected with the plague and she turned into a ghoul. Somebody infected her. You saw her turn right before your eyes. You can't deny it."

"If she was infected, show me the bite on her body."

"Frieda never left the compound. I don't see how a ghoul could've bitten her."

"You proved my point. She wasn't infected."

"Correction. She wasn't *bitten*. She was infected by inhaling spores from a carrier in our compound."

The crowd that had gathered around Frieda started muttering to themselves.

"Stop scaring everyone with your lies," said Zodiac.

"We've seen it before in our community. Everyone knows what I'm saying is true."

"Are you some kind of witch spreading fear and paranoia?"

"I'm trying to save us all from the plague."

"They oughta burn you at the stake."

"Who's the carrier, Hilda?" said someone in the crowd.

"That's what we have to find out," said Hilda.

"She's gonna have us all at each other's throats, if we listen to her," Zodiac told the assembly. "Can't you see what she's doing? Don't listen to her."

"We just want to know the truth," said Gertie. "We have a right to know the truth."

"I'm telling you what you need to know to stay alive. That's all that matters. This woman lying here"—Zodiac gestured to Frieda—"was a junkie hooked on smack. She OD'd. Unless someone can show me a ghoul bite on her body, end of story."

"Not finding a bite on her body doesn't prove anything, if a carrier infected her," said Hilda.

"Will somebody inspect Frieda's body so we can clear this matter up?"

"Nobody touch her. She might have contagious plague spores on her body. The cadaver needs to be burned immediately."

Zodiac glowered at Hilda. "Stop countermanding my orders."

"I'm looking out for the good of the community."

"I'll inspect her," said Epps, withdrawing a powder blue surgical mask from his medical bag and attaching it to his face.

He slipped on a pair of purple surgical gloves.

"Be careful," said Hilda.

"I'll take her to the quarantine room and inspect her. Does anyone want to help me lift the body?"

The crowd drew back as one.

"Nobody wants to get infected," said Hilda.

Epps shrugged. "We don't know if she *is* infected."

"I'll help you," said Zodiac. "You grab her arms, and I'll grab her feet."

He and Epps lifted Frieda's corpse and carried it to the quarantine room. They laid the corpse on a cot. Zodiac left the room shutting the door behind him to allow Epps to undress and inspect the corpse in private.

"This is a waste of time," said Hilda. "You're allowing the carrier to remain loose and infect others. We need to ID the carrier and isolate them."

"You need to stop spreading disinformation and panic," said Zodiac.

They waited for Epps to finish his examination.

Epps opened the door to the quarantine room and appeared in the doorway.

Chapter 36

"I couldn't find any bites on her body," said Epps, "and I even inspected her scalp. One of the infected didn't bite her."

"Then she became infected from inhaling spores spread by a carrier," said Hilda. "I told you so."

"She OD'd," said Zodiac. To Epps he said, "What did she die of, Doc? Tell Hilda so she stops making up stuff about carriers."

Epps knitted his brows. "I can't be sure without doing lab tests. I don't have the facilities here. And even if I did, I'm not a trained ME. I'm a GP. With lab tests I would be able to find out if Frieda had a toxic level of drugs in her system. I can't tell for sure what she died from without bloodwork."

Epps held up his hand, which contained a vial filled with blood.

"What's that in your hand?" said Zodiac.

"Her blood. I can do some simple tests on it in my office. It may give me some idea what happened to her."

"What's your best guess?"

"I'd say she died from cardiac arrest. I can't tell you with any certainty what caused it," said Epps.

"That bullet to her head didn't help any," said Box.

"She was dead before she was shot," said Hilda. "The plague resurrected her."

"What about it, Doc?" said Zodiac. "Was she dead before I shot her?"

"She didn't have a heartbeat," said Epps.

"Meaning she was dead."

"She probably had a stroke."

"Could a drug overdose have caused it?"

"Yes."

"What about the plague?" said Hilda.

"It could have. However, I didn't find any bites on her body."

"That doesn't rule out infection by plague spores."

"This is true," said Epps, nodding. "There is much we don't understand about this so-called zombie plague and how it spreads."

"Don't encourage her, Doc," said Zodiac. "We'll never hear the end of it."

"Well, I'm not taking off my mask," said Hilda. She addressed the crowd, half of which were wearing face coverings while the other half weren't. "And I advise all of you to do the same."

"The federal government must know more about this plague and how it's transmitted than we do," said Epps. "But I have no way of contacting them, and my laptop can't connect to the Internet."

"Good luck to anyone trying to get on the Internet," said Zodiac. "That baby's down. Cell towers are down. Wasted by nuclear blasts and fires. No TV. No radio. The broadcasting antennas were taken out with everything else. Which is no great loss because most mainstream news is fake, anyway. If anyone's left in power, we can't communicate with them. There's only one way left."

"What's that?"

"We go to Washington in person. Which is where I'm headed once we leave here."

"That's not gonna help me with my diagnosis of Frieda."

"I don't care about Frieda. She's a junkie. Junkies are trash. They don't care about themselves enough to go on living, so why should we give a damn about them when they croak?"

"I'm gonna analyze her blood as best I can—"

"Why bother? It's an open and shut case. I know a junkie that OD'd when I see one. I have experience. One less junkie in the world isn't worth losing any sleep over."

"I'm a doctor, and I don't look at it that way. Every human life is important."

"Except drug addicts'. They're good for nothing. Like my parents. Good riddance to bad trash."

"I'm sorry you feel like that. And I'm sorry about your parents. We'd all like to have good parents, but it's not our fault if we're not lucky in that regard."

"I don't want your pity, Doc. My parents got what they deserved—an early death. It's what happens to most junkies." Zodiac nodded toward the quarantine room. "Like Frieda in there."

132

"Maybe your parents had a tough life. Did you ever think of that?"

"A lot of people have a tough life and they don't take refuge in drugs. You think we got it easy living during a plague that has a 100 percent kill ratio?"

"What I'm saying, I guess—what I'm trying to say—is there's no shame in feeling sorrow for your parents' deaths."

"I don't feel nothing for them. And I don't feel any shame. So stop slobbering over dead junkies and stop feeding me your psychobabble because you ain't even a shrink."

"It's OK to shed a few tears for your mom and dad."

"Shed tears for those junkie bums? You couldn't pay me to shed tears for those two."

Epps heaved a long sigh. "I've said my piece." He held up the vial of blood. "I'll see if I can find anything abnormal in Frieda's blood that might tell us how she died."

Epps left for his office.

"Tyler, take that dead junkie Frieda from the quarantine room, toss her outside the perimeter, and torch her," said Zodiac.

"Sacha, help me take the stiff outside," said Tyler.

Scratching the dry, itchy skin on his cheek, Sacha, a thirty-seven-year-old, pale-complected, white-haired, brawny ex–hockey player missing his two front teeth, nodded and ducked into the quarantine room after Tyler.

"Don't forget to wear your masks," said Hilda. "She's contagious."

Tyler and Sacha ignored her.

"They don't take orders from you," said Zodiac, his face smug.

"That's their loss," said Hilda.

"I'll let you in on a secret to being a good leader." Zodiac lowered his voice. "Keep your followers ignorant while pretending to keep them well informed."

"Is that your way of saying you really believe Frieda died of the plague?"

"She died of being a junkie."

Tyler and Sacha hauled Frieda's corpse out of the room and across the warehouse. The crowd cleared a path for the two to allow them to exit. Tyler and Sacha carried the corpse out the front door.

Chapter 37

Box felt cut off from everybody. He didn't even have his memories to comfort him in his solitude. He wished he knew how he fit into this world. What was his job before the plague hit? The more he thought about it, the more frustrated and alienated he felt.

The one most alone is the one without memories.

Where do I fit in in this messed-up world? Maybe I don't fit in. What am I doing here?

"Can I count on you?" Hilda said, buttonholing him, drawing him away from Zodiac and his crew.

"Count on me for what?" said Box.

"To bear out what I said about how the plague is spread by spores."

"I'm not an expert on the subject."

"I don't care. What I need is as many people as possible backing me so we can change Zodiac's mind about the spreading of the plague."

"He doesn't care about how much support you have in the compound. All he cares about is being in power. He'll never back your theory because he doesn't want you to look better than him."

"He'll change his mind if I have the support of the community."

"Why should I support *you*? You're the one that wants to keep me locked up in quarantine."

When she had quarantined him, he had felt even more isolated than now. The only thing that made it bearable was Marta's presence in the quarantine room.

"Being quarantined is for your own good and for the good of the community," said Hilda. "What's best for the community is best for you. You don't want to infect the others, do you?"

"I don't necessarily believe what's best for the community is best for me. And I don't believe I'm infected, either."

"But you can't be certain because you have no memory of what happened to you in the desert. In two weeks if you show no symptoms, we'll let you out of quarantine. I'm not picking on just you. Marta needs to be quarantined, too."

135

"If I don't have symptoms in two weeks, it means I'm not infected?"

Hilda hedged. "Yes and no."

"What does that mean?"

"It means you could be asymptomatic, in which case you are infected but have no symptoms. Which means, you can still infect others." Hilda paused. "In that case, we'd have to banish you from the camp."

"But there's no way you can prove someone is asymptomatic. You have no idea how to prove it."

"Not at the moment. We're hoping Doc Epps will find a way in the near future."

"So you're gonna keep me locked up after two weeks. Probably forever, because you're panic-stricken, terrified you'll be infected by me because you think I *might* be asymptomatic. I don't want to be locked up. So I'm not gonna back you against Zodiac."

"You're making the wrong decision. Zodiac is wrong about how the plague spreads. He refuses to accept the truth that spores from the ghouls can cause infection. It is what it is, and you can't change it."

Box kept his voice down. "Look, I don't like Zodiac any more than you do, but he let me out of quarantine, so I'm not gonna take sides against him."

Not yet, anyway, decided Box.

"You'll be sorry," said Hilda.

Box started when he heard the crack of a gunshot outside.

He bolted to the door, following Zodiac and a knot of Zodiac's crew, who had already run to the door.

Zodiac barreled through the door and tore across the parking lot to the front gate.

"What happened?" he asked Tyler, who was standing outside the gate with a pistol in his hand.

Frieda's corpse lay on the ground at Tyler's feet.

"Was she turning?" said Zodiac, eying Frieda. "It's impossible. I put a slug in her brain."

"I caught a dweeb out here lurching around," said Tyler, nodding at the corpse of a fat guy wearing a bespoke suit, who was lying on his back staring at the sky, a bullet hole between his eyes. "I put him down," he said, brandishing his pistol.

"That guy looks familiar. Isn't that the senator from Arizona—what's his name? Clemens?"

"I hope so. I didn't vote for that lying crook. Didn't they get him on a graft charge?"

"Politicians are corrupt? Say it ain't so."

Tyler sniggered.

"Are there more of those things out here?" said Zodiac, scoping out the perimeter. "They're like cockroaches. Where there's one in view, there's a million out of sight."

"I didn't see any others. Maybe this dweeb got separated from the pack and got lost."

"Why do you call 'em dweebs?"

"Because they're retards. They don't know how to walk."

"I don't see any others around here. Pataki says they're massing for an attack. They could show up any minute. Keep your eyes peeled. We need to prepare our defenses. Right now, torch the ghoul and Frieda."

"Will do," said Tyler.

Sacha was standing next to Frieda's cadaver, a can of lighter fluid in his hand.

"Here's as good a place as any," said Tyler.

He dragged the dead ghoul over to Frieda. Sacha doused the two corpses with lighter fluid. Tyler lit a match from his matchbook, flicked it onto Frieda's drenched hair, and stepped back to watch her head burst into flames, which spread to the ghoul and engulfed him.

"A junkie and a party hack going up in flames," said Zodiac. "My day is made."

"I guess he didn't make it to the bunker for fat cats," said Tyler.

"Get back inside. We need to figure out how to defend this place from an army of ghouls."

Tyler and Sacha returned inside the gate, which the guards in the watch tower closed and locked.

"This chain-link fence isn't gonna hold if thousands of those things attack at the same time," said Zodiac, scanning the perimeter.

"We need to fortify it somehow," said Box.
"Got any bright ideas?"

Chapter 38

"What if we run an electric current through the fence?" said Box.

Zodiac nodded, pleased. "I like the way you think, Box. The ghouls don't like fire. Some primal fear inside them, I suppose. All living things are terrified of fire. The ghouls aren't living exactly, but their bred-in-the-bone instincts tell them to stay away from fire, which can burn their rotten flesh."

Was it instinct, or was it memory? What if even the ghouls had memories, but he didn't? Box wondered with annoyance and something akin to envy.

"They may not be living, but they're not dead either," said Tyler. "Anything that moves is alive, if you ask me."

"I'm not asking you," said Zodiac, annoyed at the interruption. He resumed forming his plans of defense. "A shot of electricity should fry their brains and kill them."

Chastened, Tyler kept his mouth shut and stared at the ground in a brown study.

"If the lead ghouls get electrocuted and hung up on the fence as they go up in flames, it should deter the others behind them," said Zodiac.

"The question is, do we have enough electricity here?" said Box.

"We have a spare propane generator," said Porter, running his gaze along the fence. "We could run a cable to the fence and juice it."

"How many volts are we talking about?" said Zodiac.

"About 480 volts. Enough to fry a ghoul. Those things go up like kindling, did you ever notice? They're bone-dry. Their decrepit flesh is like parchment. They get hit with an electric charge, they'll flare up good. Only their bones will be left."

"The ghouls could climb a stack of bones over the fence."

"It would take a whole bunch of bones to form a stack as high as one of cadavers. It would take much longer to form such a pile."

"All right. It'll buy us time, if nothing else."

"It'll give us time to shoot 'em and send a gang armed with baseball bats out there to bash their brains before they reach the fence."

Zodiac nodded yes. "Run a cable to the fence, and warn everyone not to go near the fence. I wanna see those babies burn and light up the sky," he said, widening his eyes.

"You're worrying too much about the dangers from without when it's the dangers from within that will wipe us out," said Hilda.

"Are you harping on that infection-by-spores shit again?"

"One carrier in our midst can infect all of us, if we don't quarantine or kick them out of here."

"Tell them to leave, why don't you?"

"They don't know they're infected. How could they, since they don't have any symptoms? Which means nobody knows their infected. How can I tell them to leave if I don't even know who they are?"

"So what's the answer?"

"How should I know?"

"Then shut up."

Hilda puffed up her chest and glowered at him.

"I oughta make you stand guard outside the fence all by yourself," said Zodiac.

"If you're gonna fuck me up the ass, at least give me some lubricant."

Zodiac ignored her. "Tyler, get the propane genny, house it in a car near the fence to protect it from the elements, and hook up a cable from the genny to the fence."

"You got it, boss," said Tyler. "Where's the genny?" he asked Porter.

"Never mind," said Porter. "I'll take Box and get it."

"Whatever," said Zodiac. "Just do it."

"I'll go with you," said Pataki, joining Porter and Box as they set out for the warehouse.

"What do you want me to do?" Tyler asked Zodiac.

"Sit tight," answered Zodiac.

"You're condemning everyone in our commune to death by not dealing with the carrier," Hilda told Zodiac.

140

"This ain't a commune," said Zodiac. "The extinct, useless hippies had communes. This is a community or, better yet, camp. No hippies allowed."

"Quibbling over semantics won't solve our problems."

Fed up with Hilda, Zodiac raised his sickle. "Do you know why they call me the Reaper?"

"You don't scare me. We all could be dead soon."

"You don't want to find out. Believe me."

The hot dry wind freshened.

"We may have other worries," said Hilda, feeling the wind gust against her.

"What?"

Hilda looked in the direction the wind was blowing from and saw looming in the distance a dark cloud that stretched all the way from the ground high into the sky.

"Five dweebs headed this way," said Tyler.

"And that's not all," said Hilda, her voice apprehensive, her eyes on the ominous cloud.

Chapter 39

"Do you ever ask yourself why you go on?" Porter asked Box on their way to the warehouse.

"There isn't any why," answered Box. "You're either alive or you're not. That's all. I'm alive so I'm gonna keep fighting to stay that way."

"I keep thinking about Danny. I blew it. I let him down."

"What's up?" said Pataki, catching up to them.

"He's got the plague blues," said Box.

Pataki shrugged. "Life goes on."

"You guys stay here," said Porter. "I'll call you when I find the genny. I can't remember exactly where I stored it. This may take a while. No sense in your coming with me."

They entered the warehouse. Porter broke away from them.

Pataki drew Box aside and searched Box's face. "Halverson?"

"What?" said Box.

"Halverson. Is that you? It's hard to tell with that thick beard on your face and all that hair."

Halverson? wondered Box. Why was Pataki calling him Halverson? Was Halverson his real name?

"You know me?" said Box.

"I know Halverson. You look like him."

"Halverson?"

"Are you saying you're not Halverson? Why are they calling you Box? Is that your cover name here?"

"My memory's gone. I forgot my name."

"You're Halverson. Chad Halverson. It has to be you. The CIA transponder secreted in your heel led me here, and you're the only one I've seen so far that looks like him. Your long hair and beard threw me off, but I'd know your eyes anywhere."

"CIA?" said Halverson, squinting, trying to remember. "I don't think so."

"You're a CIA black-ops agent."

"What was I doing in the Mojave Desert?"

"I don't know what you've been doing. We haven't been able to contact you. There was a time when we were trying to take you out."

"The CIA trying to kill me?" said Box, taken aback.

"That's right. Terminate with extreme prejudice."

"Why would they want to do that?"

"I don't know the specifics, but it's history. You know the agency. They never tell us working grunts anything. We had a regime change in the agency. We need you back in Mount Weather, where the government is holed up. The government is on the verge of collapse. They're under siege by thousands of ghouls."

"Mount Weather?"

"It has bunkers where the president and his cabinet and security agencies are taking refuge. The bunkers can withstand nuclear blasts and mass assaults by the ghouls, but nobody knows for how long. Meanwhile, the number of ghouls keeps increasing. We need you to return to the agency and help us."

"Help you do what?"

"We think President Cole is going mad. He's drunk with power. He declared a national emergency and proclaimed himself president for life because we can't hold elections in the country thanks to the plague. He wants to nuke more of the country to clear it of the plague. We're worried the entire country will be left uninhabitable because of radiation if he continues to nuke it."

"Can't Congress remove him from office with the Twenty-fifth Amendment because of mental illness and replace him with the vice president?"

"The Senate and the House are both in shambles. Too many of their members are dead. They've ceased to function."

"I don't see what I can do. What do you want from me?"

"You're well respected in DC. A faction in the CIA tried to take you out, but they've been removed. We want you back to help us remove Cole from office and restore the government."

"I'm just one guy."

"The reason Cole is so dangerous is because he chained the nuclear football to his arm and has surrounded himself with his praetorian guards of Secret Service agents and US marshals. They guard him wherever he goes. With the football he can fire nukes at will. He can invoke the Insurrection Act of 1807 and obliterate any part of the country that resists him. We believe he'll rain down nukes on the rest of the country to wipe out the plague, despite the massive loss of lives that will result."

Box thought about it. "That football is heavy. It's a metal Zero Halliburton briefcase that weighs forty-five pounds. I wouldn't want to lug it around with me all the time."

"Cole's paranoid," said Pataki. "He believes everyone is out to get him. I hate to admit it, but he's not wrong. A lot of people want him out of office. He believes the football is the only thing that keeps him in power. Plus he keeps himself surrounded with his praetorian guards. And . . ."

"And what?"

"And how would you know how much the football weighs unless you really are the CIA black-ops agent Halverson?"

Box found all of this bewildering. He must be Halverson, even though he couldn't remember it. Pataki had identified him.

"Whatever you do, don't tell Zodiac you work for the CIA," said Box, lowering his voice. "He hates everyone in the government."

"OK. I'll keep my mouth shut about you, too. We can't stay here, anyway. We have to go back east to the Mount Weather Emergency Operations Center at the Blue Ridge Mountains in Virginia." Pataki hung fire. "I have to admit I've been running into lots of people across the country that hate the government thanks to the nukes the president dropped on them."

"Can you blame them?"

"You have to look at it from his point of view. He's nuking the plague hot spots to save the entire country."

"He's cutting off his nose to spite his face."

"He knows he's not popular for his actions, but he believes a few must be sacrificed for the greater good of the many."

"You sound like you still support him."

"I did until he declared himself president for life and started carrying the football around with him wherever he goes." Pataki shook his head, face grim. "He's losing it."

Chad Halverson, decided Box. That was his name. But all it was was a name. He still couldn't remember anything about himself. Memories weren't flooding back to him. It was good to know his name, but he continued to be identityless without any memories.

But was it really *his* name? If it was his name, why couldn't he remember anything about his life? Maybe Pataki was mistaken about him.

If it *was* his name, he didn't think he should tell it to anyone. Nor should he tell anyone Pataki had told him it. People would ask how he knew Pataki. If Pataki explained that they both worked for the government, Zodiac would take out the two of them. It was best for Box's and Pataki's survival to not use Halverson's name in public. Box would continue to answer to the name Box.

In truth, whatever name Box went by made no difference to him since there were no memories attached to any of the names. Memories made you who you were, not a name.

Porter came into view. "Hey, you guys. I found the genny. Give me a hand."

"Remember, not a word to anyone that we work for the government," Box whispered to Pataki.

Pataki nodded yes. "I have a cover story."

Could Pataki be mistaken about him? wondered Box.

They strode toward Porter, who headed away from them and motioned for them to follow him to the genny in the storage room.

Chapter 40

"We got bogeys outside," said Sacha who was armed and listening to his walkie-talkie in the warehouse. "We need you guys to juice the fence."

Box was wheeling the genny, which was packed in a pasteboard box, on a dolly alongside Porter and Pataki when he heard Sacha.

"We're heading outside now," said Porter.

"Get moving," said Sacha, brandishing his AR-15.

"We love you, too."

"Are these the thousands you were talking about massing in the clearing in the forest?" Box asked Pataki.

"I don't see how they could've gotten here this fast."

"Maybe they sent a vanguard."

"We need to get the fenced juiced ASAP," said Porter.

"What's that sound?" said Box, as they reached the warehouse front door.

Box could hear what sounded like raindrops impinging against the walls.

"It sounds like rain," said Pataki.

"There wasn't a cloud in the sky a few minutes ago," said Box.

An Alsatian started barking inside the warehouse.

"Something's got him spooked," said Pataki.

"I hope it's not what I think it is," said Porter, his face anxious.

He opened the front door.

A furious gust of wind flung the door open so hard it sent Porter stumbling backwards. Sand and debris, including snapped tree branches, burst into the warehouse, scattered, and skidded across the floor.

"Shit," said Porter.

"What?" said Pataki, grimacing in the wind.

"Haboob."

Squinting, Pataki shook his head incomprehensibly.

"Dust storm," said Porter. "We get 'em here in Arizona. We're gonna have to fight our way through the storm to the fence. The biggest problem is we won't be able to see a foot in front of us."

"Plowing through that wind won't be a piece of cake either," said Box.

"Follow me."

Putting on his mask, hunching his shoulders, bowing forward, Porter fought his way through the gusting wind and the encompassing darkness that obliterated the sky, Pataki in tow.

Box wheeled the dolly into the violent storm, which bore down on him like a bellowing freight train.

He had trouble maintaining his balance and steering the dolly as the wind buffeted him.

"What about the fence?" said Pataki. "Will it hold?"

"That's a cyclone fence," said Porter. "No sandstorm's gonna knock it down."

"What about the gate?"

"Same deal with the gate. The problem's the ghouls. The wind's blowing them toward the fence, and it'll help push them over it when they climb it."

"We need to get this genny to the fence," said Box, sand flying into his mouth as he spoke.

He coughed, clearing his throat, and spat dirt out.

"Put on your mask," said Porter.

Box could barely see or hear him in the storm. He thought he caught Porter's last word and raised his mask to his face.

"Don't go so fast," said Box. "I can hardly see you. My sense of direction's screwed up by the storm."

"We need to stick together," said Porter. "It's impossible to see in this stuff. You could walk around in circles for hours without knowing it. If we keep bearing straight, we'll hit the fence."

"How can we tell if we're going straight?" said Pataki.

"We head into the wind. As long as it doesn't change direction, we should be OK."

"How can I see where we're going? I can't even open my eyes without getting dirt in them."

"Listen to my voice. We need to keep talking all the way to the fence. You there, Box?"

"Here," said Box. "Blind back here, but following your voice as best I can through the screaming wind."

"You got that right," said Pataki.

"You got the genny?" said Porter.

"I got it," said Box. "I can't see either one of you, though."

"That's OK. Keep keying on my voice."

Box thought he heard a gunshot through the cacophonous wind.

"Shot fired," said Pataki.

"How can anyone see to shoot in this storm?" said Box.

"Ghouls must be at the fence."

A gust of wind toppled the genny off Box's dolly onto the asphalt parking lot.

"Damn," he said.

"What?"

"Hold on."

"What's the problem?" said Porter.

"The genny fell off the dolly," said Box. "Pataki, help me lift the genny back onto the dolly."

"No problem—if I can find you," said Pataki, reaching out his hands and feeling for Box in the blizzard of sand.

"Over here," said Box. "Do you see me yet?"

"Keep talking."

"I'm right here," said Box, waving his hand to gain Pataki's attention.

Pataki bumped into Box's shoulder. "Gotcha. Where's the genny?"

"At your feet. Bend down and we'll lift it onto the dolly together."

They both bent down, gripped the bottom of the pasteboard box containing the genny, and lifted it onto the dolly.

"Everything OK?" said Porter.

"Good to go," said Box, and took hold of the dolly's red plastic handgrips. "Start walking."

"Follow my voice," said Porter, hunching over and fighting his way through the gales of sand.

Another shot rang out.

"More ghouls must be at the fence," said Pataki.

"That's where we're heading," said Porter. "We should be there soon. That gunshot sounded louder."

Chapter 41

The gusting sand excoriated the exposed portions of Box's face, which he felt might start bleeding any minute—if they weren't doing so already. It felt like hundreds of tiny needles pricking his skin.

"Who's there?" said Zodiac's voice.

"It's us," said Porter.

"Good. We need you guys to go outside the gate and kill those ghouls out there."

"Why can't you shoot them from here?"

"We can't see them."

"Then how do you know they're out there?"

"We saw them approaching just before the dust storm hit."

"I thought you wanted us to hook up the genny to the fence."

"In due time. Right now I want those ghouls outside clubbed to death by you three. We got baseball bats for all of you here in the guardhouse."

"Why are you sending us to do it?"

"Because you're here. And you made it here through this frigging dust storm. So you must know what you're doing. Go out there and bash brains for me."

Box parked the dolly near an SUV and, fighting the wind, accompanied Porter and Pataki to Zodiac. Zodiac distributed three baseball bats among them.

"We can't see those things out there any better than you can," Porter told Zodiac.

"Go out there and waste those things before they reach the fence."

"Let's juice the fence and save ourselves the trouble."

"The sand pelting the fence and sparking it might dilute a charge running through the steel enough to make it useless against the ghouls. Whack those things before they reach the fence. That's our best shot at dealing with them. We absolutely can't allow them inside the perimeter."

"What's the big deal with letting them inside?" said Pataki.

"We wouldn't be able to see them in here with all that sand blowing around. Nobody would be safe. You're wasting time. Get moving," said Zodiac, pointing his AR-15 at them.

Clutching their bats, Box, Porter, and Pataki made for the front gate, which Zodiac told the guard to open.

Box, Porter, and Pataki hunched over and carved out a path through the howling sandstorm.

The guard closed the gate behind them.

"How are we supposed to get back in?" yelled Porter.

"Tell us when you're done whacking them," said Zodiac. "Then we'll open the gate."

"How many of them are out here?"

"I counted five before the storm hit."

Box couldn't even see Zodiac. Instead, he heard a disembodied voice squeaking like a rusty door hinge in the din.

"Why'd he pick us?" said Pataki.

"He wants me dead," said Porter, lowering his voice as he moved farther away from the gate. "He sees me as a threat to him. And he's right. As far as I'm concerned, his leadership sucks. He wants Hilda gone, too."

"How are we supposed to find those stinking things out here?"

"Maybe we can smell 'em," said Box, though he doubted it with all the sand blowing into his face. "One good thing about these masks we're wearing is they keep the sand out of our nostrils."

"But not our eyes," said Pataki. "And I can't smell much, anyway."

"You smell the stench of death and you'll know it. It's not a stink you forget."

"You sound like an expert on the subject."

Why would he be an expert? wondered Box. Had he been around a lot of corpses in his life? More so than the average joe? Even with his amnesia, he recognized the stink of a putrid corpse whether it was inanimate or walking. Did his job have something to do with corpses—as in making them? Was he a CIA hit man? Pataki had said Halverson worked for the CIA. Box decided not to pursue the thought.

"We need to stick together," said Porter. "I don't want to lose any of you in the storm. We might end up bashing in each other's brains if we split up."

"I smell one near," said Box, wincing at the sickening reek of death as sand pelted his face.

"All right. Be on your guard."

Box tightened his grip on his bat and held it in front of him so he could swing it at a moment's notice.

"Don't swing unless you're sure it's a ghoul," said Porter.

"How can we be sure of anything out here in this muck?" said Pataki. "I can't see shit."

"Take it easy. Remember, if we can't see them, they can't see us."

"I bet those things can smell living human flesh. It's the only thing they care about."

"What's that sound?" said Box, tensing. "Did you hear something?"

"All I hear is the storm screaming in my ears," said Pataki, hunched over.

With a start Box saw a wizened hand thrust out of the storm toward him. He batted it away.

"There's one over here," he said. "I'm going in for the kill."

Raising his bat shoulder-high, he stepped toward the decomposing hand and swung with all his might at a blurred sphere at the level of his face a yard away. The bat's barrel connected with a loud thwack, crunching bone. The creature was still standing, but it had dropped its hand to its hip.

Box didn't think he had killed it. Maybe he had clouted the jaw and missed the brain. He reared the bat back and swung again at the spherical blur in front of him, aiming a little higher trying to score a direct hit on the brain. He felt the bat's barrel thud on impact and heard muffled shattering. The creature's skull, he hoped. The silhouette collapsed to the ground.

"One down," he said. "Four to go."

"That was close," said Pataki. "Didn't you see me?"

"What? No."

"I saw the tip of your bat cut through the air. That ghoul you took out must've been standing next to me."

"Give a holler next time if you see my bat to let me know you're near. For all intents and purposes I'm swinging blind."

"I didn't have time to do much of anything."

"The things tend to hunt in packs. The others must be near. Is Porter there?"

"Over here," said Porter. "If anything, this sandstorm's getting worse."

"There must be gravity because the world sucks," said Pataki, squinting in the thrashing gusts of sand. "Hold on. I think I can smell one of them."

Out of the corner of his eye, sand swirling about him, Box caught sight of the tip of a bat cutting a swath through the vortex of wind inches away from his face. Jerking his head back, he heard the bat thump something that cracked. A ghoul's skull, Box hoped.

"I got him," said Pataki.

"Make sure I'm not in your line of fire next time," said Box.

"I didn't see you."

"I can't see you, either, but I saw your bat swing a few inches from my face."

"You know what's scary?"

"What?"

"I had no idea you were there."

"This would be a lot easier with guns instead of these bats. Why didn't he give us guns?"

"He's afraid we'll use them on him," said Porter. "I know how this guy thinks. He's paranoid, like all petty tyrants."

"And don't forget," said Pataki. "Loud noises attract the ghouls. We don't want more of those things coming here when they hear gun reports."

"I can smell one," said Porter. "Watch your six."

Chapter 42

Pataki glimpsed Porter's bat slicing through the lashing sand toward his head and pulled away in the nick of time to avoid getting struck.

"Hey, that's me," said Pataki, all but falling over as he dodged the bat and was buffeted by the wind.

"You need a shower, man."

"I've been on the road for a couple of days. I haven't had time."

"You smell like something dead."

"Three more to go," said Box. "Keep your eyes peeled."

"They must be near us," said Porter. "It's hard to smell anything in this storm. Whoa. There it is."

"Porter, what happened?" said Box. "Did you get it?" Box paused, listening. All he heard was the raging sandstorm. "Pataki, do you see Porter?"

"Negative. I'm blind here."

"We have to find him. He may be in trouble."

"Porter?" said Pataki.

"I got her," said Porter. "I had to hit her twice. The first time I hit her I got her in the shoulder with a glancing blow. She kept coming at me like she was on a mission. She got too close for me to take a swing at her with my bat. I had to poke her with the end cap to keep her away from me. Then I stepped back so I could take a swing. That's when I clobbered her in the head. I connected. Boy, did I connect. I hit a home run to deep center field. Kaboom! She dropped like a sack of potatoes."

"Thanks for the play-by-play," said Box. "Only two left."

"She was uglier than Medusa, I'm telling you."

"We get the message," said Pataki.

"Aren't you a baseball fan?" said Porter.

"Some other time."

"I could've sworn I saw two of them near me."

"Where's the other one?" said Box.

"He must be around here. Ow."

"What happened? Porter?"

"Something grabbed my arm," said Porter, his voice agitated. "I shook him off. Can't talk now."

At that moment Box picked up on two hands groping through the sandstorm toward him. The hands were too close for him to club the head with the bat. Instead, he made a fist and threw a right hook into the ghoul's grimacing face. Box knew he could fend off the ghoul with his fist, but he couldn't kill it with a punch to the head.

Grappling with the creature he tried to shove it away so he could bash its brains in with his Louisville Slugger. It was a thirtyish female ghoul with an egg-shaped shaved head. She kept clawing her way toward him, trying to get a grip on his head so she could take a bite out of his cheek. Every time he tried to push her away she clung to his arm hanging onto him.

He kicked her in the knee to get her to let go of him. She paid no attention to his kicks, even when he smashed his heel into her kneecap dislocating her knee. With one leg crippled she continued to hang onto him, as if she instinctively knew if she let go of him it would mean her death.

He jabbed his bat into her stomach to get her to release his arm. She held him fast. He jabbed her rib cage and heard a rib crack. She wouldn't let go.

He couldn't figure out how to get her to release him without getting bitten. There had to be a way. One bite from her decomposing teeth would infect him with the plague.

She decided not to go for his cheek anymore. Growling, she took aim at one of his hands with her gaping mouth primed to take a bite out of it. Terrified, he jabbed at her face with the tip of the baseball bat to keep her teeth away from his hand that she refused to release. He broke her nose, listening to the bone crack. It did not deter her. She kept snapping at his hand with her jaws. If it wasn't for his constant jabbing of the baseball bat to her face, she would have bitten his hand.

He couldn't get enough force into his jabbing that he could fracture her skull and destroy her brain.

Desperate, he stuck his leg behind her good leg, pushed her backward, and tripped her. She fell to the ground on her back, pulling his hand after her, all but hauling him to the ground with her. Managing to keep his balance he stamped on her throat to keep her pinned to the ground so he could yank his arm free from her clutches.

He pulled free and commenced stomping on her grimacing face to smash her skull and brain. Concerned she might bite his foot, he changed tactics. He clenched the bat handle with both hands, raised it high, and brought the barrel's blunt cap crashing straight down on her skull like a pile driver, crushing her frontal bone.

She stopped moving, her pulverized brain a puddle of mush trapped in her shattered skull.

"Porter, are you OK?"

Chapter 43

Maybe Porter couldn't hear him thanks to the howling, flailing sandstorm.

"Porter, are you OK?" Box yelled into the slashing sand.

The heat inside the sandstorm was brutal, he decided. The eddying sand blasting him made the air seem hotter. It felt like he was suffocating ensconced in the whipping, churning sand. His mask only made things worse. It restricted his breathing, turning his hot breath back onto his face.

"Over here," said Porter. "I got it. The ghoul was a little nine-year-old boy, and I didn't want to hurt him. But he wouldn't stop trying to bite my hand. I put it off as long as I could, but, in the end, I had to pound his brains into applesauce."

"You have to keep telling yourself they're not human," said Pataki. "It's the only way to deal with them. Even though they look like us, they're ghouls."

"I kept thinking of my son when the thing was trying to bite me. Every time I went to club it, I saw my son Eric's face looking back at me. And I couldn't kill it."

"Is Eric here with you at the camp?"

Porter's voice caught in his throat.

"Porter?" said Pataki.

"Eric's dead. A ghoul bit him."

"I'm sorry to hear that."

"These are the times we live in."

"Could that have been Eric you clubbed?"

"It looked like him." Porter's face clouded. "I don't want to think about it."

"We killed five," said Box. "Zodiac said there were five out here. Let's go back to the compound."

"I'll drink to that," said Pataki. "My face is getting sandblasted."

"Let's go," said Porter.

Box felt a hand on his shoulder. "Is that you, Porter?"

"It's me talking. Let's go."

"I mean, is your hand on my shoulder?"

157

"No."

Box became anxious. His heartbeat accelerated.

"Pataki? What about you?"

"No."

Box wheeled around, slapping the hand off his shoulder. He confronted a male sixtysomething ghoul a head taller than him baring its scraggy teeth at him. It had long grizzled hair that enclosed its head like a helmet. The ghoul closed in on him and tried to bite Box's face. Box landed a roundhouse on the creature's chin, sending it stumbling to its right. Box grabbed his bat's handle with both hands and swung at the ghoul's head, listening to the head implode under the impact of the blow. The ghoul dropped to the ground, quivered its hands, and died.

"What's going on?" said Pataki.

"Another ghoul," said Halverson.

"Why'd Zodiac lie to us?" said Porter. "He said there were only five."

"Yeah," said Pataki. "How many more of those things are out here?"

Mauled by the sand and wind, they fought their way back to the gate.

"Why's it taking us so long to reach the gate?" said Box.

"Are you sure this is the right direction?" said Pataki.

"I'm positive," said Porter. "We must be close by now."

They took a few more steps.

"There it is," said Porter. He raised his voice. "Open the gate. We killed six of them."

Nothing happened.

Pataki reached toward the gate to shake it and get Zodiac's attention.

"Don't," said Box, grabbing Pataki's arm.

"Why not?"

"I thought I saw sparks on the chain-link fence as the sand struck it."

"So what? It's called friction."

"They might've hooked up the genny to the fence while we were gone."

Pataki withdrew his hand from the fence. "Why would they do it after we left?"

"Ask Zodiac."

"I don't trust that guy."

"We're here, Zodiac," said Porter. "Are you there? We killed six of them. Did you hear me? *Six*. You told us there were only five out here."

"Don't get your knickers in a twist," said Zodiac, his voice issuing from the guard tower. "We saw five just before the sandstorm hit. Maybe another one was blown here by the storm."

"What about the fence?" said Box.

"What about it?"

"You juiced it."

"What of it? We did your job for you."

"At least you could've told us," said Pataki. "I almost touched it."

"I was gonna tell you when we let you back in. We don't want any ghouls in here. Attaching the genny's cable to the fence ain't rocket science. Alligator clips and a cable. Big deal. We did it fine. What are you bitchin' for?"

"Because nobody told us, and we could've been electrocuted," said Porter.

"I just told you. Don't touch the fence."

Porter smothered his anger. "So let us back in."

"Are you sure you killed all those things out there? We can't see a thing in this dust storm."

"What makes you think *we* can? We're in the same boat."

"I don't want any of the ghouls coming in here and infecting us."

"Neither do we. Just let us in."

"Did they bite any of you?"

"No."

"How can I be sure you're not infected?"

"Stop playing games."

"This isn't a game. This is serious. Nobody wants the plague. If any of you got bit, let me know."

"Nobody got bit," said Porter, his patience wearing thin. "Some of the infected might be headed this way under the cover of the storm. Let us the hell in."

"That's why we should leave you out there. To prevent the ghouls from reaching the fence."

"We have no idea what's going on three feet away from us," said Box. "It serves no purpose for us to be out here in this blinding sandstorm."

"Just hold on a few more minutes," said Zodiac. "I think the storm is dying down."

"We don't have much choice," Porter told Pataki and Box, fit to be tied.

"Somebody needs to beat the crap out of that guy," said Pataki.

"He's got the guns," said Porter. "He's right about one thing. Getting infected. Nobody wants to go through that."

"Including us," said Box.

Chapter 44

"I saw Eric, my son, turn," said Porter into the blowing curtain of sand. "Buboes sprouted up all over his face, swelled with blood and burst open, leaving putrid scars. His irises lost their pigment and turned milky. The stench of his decomposing flesh was stomach-turning. I wanted to throw up. His teeth turned into rotting yellow fangs. I knew then he would bite me as soon as look at me and I would have to kill him. My son the monster. I thought I was gonna have a heart attack looking at that abomination."

The blood drained from Porter's face.

"Best not to talk about it," said Pataki. "Memories can mess you up bad."

Box wondered if that was true. It would explain why his unconscious was suppressing his memories of what had happened to him in the desert. His memories must be the stuff of nightmares. The suppression was a self-defense mechanism to prevent the memories from surfacing and traumatizing him. However, his amnesia intensified his feelings of isolation and alienation, which depressed him.

"The pestilence is wiping out the world," said Porter. "We can't let ourselves get infected. We may be all that's left of the human race."

The wind died down as abruptly as it had started.

Box could discern his surroundings as the dust storm subsided. He saw crumpled ghouls lying on the road in front of the gate. He didn't see additional ones advancing on the compound. He noticed something else. The storm had strewn assorted types of birds on the ground among the corpses. Some of the birds were dead. Others were walking about, uselessly flapping their wings broken by the buffeting winds, unable to fly.

"There aren't any more living ghouls out here," Porter told Zodiac. "Let us in."

"All righty," said Zodiac, scanning the perimeter from his perch in the guard tower. "That's all I wanted to know." He paused for effect. "One more thing. Don't ever question my orders. Do you understand?"

"Do you understand we want to come in?"

Zodiac laughed.

"Some people," muttered Porter.

The guard in the tower with Zodiac pressed the button that swung open the gate.

Box, Porter, and Pataki entered the compound.

"What say we beat the crap out of that guy right now?" whispered Pataki.

Box couldn't tell if Pataki was kidding. Box smiled briefly, but said nothing.

"I hate to be the bearer of bad tidings, but he happens to have a gun on him—as do his men," whispered Porter.

A blonde pushing forty wearing jeans, an orange cream bandana wrapped arounder her face, and a cerise crepe tube top charged up to Halverson, jabbed her forefinger at his face, and cried, "Murderer."

Box started. He had no idea who she was.

"What's this about, Box?" said Zodiac.

"I have no idea," said Box. "I never saw her before."

"Don't try to pull that stunt with me," said the blonde. "You're Earl James. You killed my brother Cole Younger in a barroom brawl in Abilene over a waitress you were both flirting with."

"I don't know what you're talking about."

"You clubbed his head with a full bottle of whisky and cut his throat with the jagged glass bottle that remained in your hand after the bottle broke on his head."

Earl James, decided Box. Could he possibly be Earl James? Pataki had told him he was Chad Halverson. Pataki or this woman must be mistaken. But which one?

Pataki leaned confidentially toward Box. "Want me to set her straight and tell her your true identity?"

"No," said Box under his breath. "We'll both end up dead if Zodiac finds out we work for the government."

"If I don't say anything, they'll think you're this murderer Earl James."

Pataki had a point, decided Box. But Zodiac might not mind if Box was a murderer like Earl James, whoever he was. Zodiac with his twisted mind might approve of murderers, whereas Box knew for certain that Zodiac hated government employees and had no compunction about blowing them away—the way he had done ex–IRS agent Hal Nordstrom.

"I want to hear your side of the story, Box," said Zodiac. "Or should I call you Earl James?"

"I can't tell you what I don't know," said Box. "I never saw this woman before."

"What about her brother Cole Younger?"

"Never heard of him."

"And what about this bar in Abilene she's talking about?"

"I have no idea."

"But you admit you lost your memory?"

"Right."

"So maybe you *did* kill Cole Younger, and you forgot about it because of your amnesia."

Box shook his head. "I would remember something like that."

Zodiac turned to the blonde. "What's your name, young lady?"

"Kate Younger."

"Are you sure you're not mistaken about knowing Box?"

"I don't know anyone named Box." She pointed at Box. "That man is called Earl James, the murderer of my brother."

"Does anyone know what this man's real name is? Is it Box or Earl James?" said Zodiac, looking at everybody in the immediate vicinity.

"I gave him the name Box because he couldn't remember his own name," said Porter.

"Do you know what your real name is, Box?"

"No," said Box.

He didn't want to implicate Pataki by saying Pataki had identified him as the CIA spook Halverson. In any case, maybe Pataki was as mistaken about Box's identity as Kate Younger was, decided Box.

"So your name could be Earl James," said Zodiac.

"I don't believe it."

"Then what is your real name?"

"I dunno."

"You're not helping your cause any."

"I can't remember."

"Kate, how can you recognize this man even though he's wearing a mask?"

"It's his eyes," said Kate. "I'll never forget his eyes. He has murderous eyes. You can see them dripping blood."

"I just got through killing ghouls," said Box.

"You murdered my brother. I'm sure of it. It's you, Earl James. You can't deny it."

Box couldn't figure out why this woman had it in for him. He didn't recognize her. Was he really a murderer? Was that why he was suppressing his memory with amnesia? But Pataki had told him he was Halverson. Who was telling the truth? Why would Pataki lie? For that matter, why would Kate Younger lie? Was one of them mistaken? Which one?

"Do you have any witnesses to the murder, Kate?" said Zodiac.

Kate became sullen. "None of them are alive. They all got infected in the bar by a swarm of ghouls. But *I* saw the murder. *I'm* the witness."

"So it's your word against Box's."

"He did it, I tell you."

"Take off your mask so Box can see the face of his accuser."

Kate lowered her bandana under her chin.

Box looked at her. Her face didn't ring any bells.

"I don't know her," he said. "I never saw her before."

"Liar," said Kate, and put her mask back on.

"Box, remove your mask and show your face to Kate," said Zodiac.

Box lowered his mask.

"That's him," said Kate. "I knew it."

Box put his mask on.

Zodiac chuckled. "It looks like what we got here is one of those he said, she said things. I'll have to think about this."

Box walked away.

"Don't think you can hide from me, Earl James," said Kate. "I'll hunt you down wherever you go."

Box kept walking.

Chapter 45

Box went to the outdoor gymnasium and saw Marta running on a treadmill. He opened the gate in the chain-link fence and entered.

"You missed the excitement," he said.

"The storm? I was inside the warehouse."

"No. I mean, a woman just accused me of being a guy called Earl James, the man who murdered her brother."

Marta slowed her pace on the treadmill. "So now you know who you are?"

"The name Earl James doesn't ring any bells. I think she's mistaken."

"You don't want to find your memory and discover you're a murderer."

"I have no memory of killing her brother in a barroom brawl."

Marta switched off the treadmill, came to a halt, and wiped sweat from her face with a towel draped around her neck.

"You think your real name is Box?" she said.

"My name isn't Box. Porter made that name up. I'm pretty sure this woman Kate Younger has mistaken me for somebody else."

"You're pretty sure, or you don't want to admit you're a murderer?"

"If Earl James is my real name, why aren't any memories coming back to me?"

On the other hand, if his name was Chad Halverson, where were the memories connected to that name? wondered Box. It boiled down to who did he believe? Kate Younger or Dean Pataki.

Box climbed onto a treadmill and fell to jogging.

He couldn't tell her that Pataki had told him he was Halverson. If Box *was* a CIA agent, like Pataki had said, he had to keep it secret.

"Maybe you don't want to remember you're Earl James because then you would remember you're a murderer," said Marta.

"The thought crossed my mind."

"Murdering someone must be a traumatic experience. Something you would want to forget."

"Do you think I'm a murderer?" said Box, looking at her.

"I want to say no, but I've never met a murderer. I don't know what a murderer looks like. Maybe they look like the rest of us."

She stopped drying her face, wrapped her towel back around her neck, switched on the treadmill, and picked up her pace.

"I never saw this woman Kate Younger before," said Box.

"That could be part of your amnesia." She paused. "Maybe you have dementia."

"Dementia? I thought only old people got dementia."

"A lot of people think that, but it's not true. My uncle Bob had it in his thirties."

"How could I have gotten it?"

"A blow to your head could have triggered it. The damaged brain cells could cause you to lose your memory."

"What's the cure for it?"

"There isn't any."

Nonplussed, Box didn't like what he was hearing.

At last, he said, "How do you know all this?"

"Uncle Bob told me."

"You don't have a medical degree?"

"No. Not me. I'm a coder. I'm just trying to help you figure out why you lost your memory. Are you starting to remember anything?"

"No."

Box couldn't say anything about himself with any certainty thanks to his memory loss. He had to feel his way, groping in the darkness for the truth. His gut told him he wasn't Earl James. He believed Pataki over Kate Younger. Of course, it was more romantic to believe he was a CIA black-ops agent rather than a murderer. Was that the real reason he chose to believe Pataki?

"Why is your memory so important to you?" said Marta. "Maybe you're better off without it."

"You don't know what it feels like to not know who you are. I feel alienated."

"*I* feel alienated, and my memory's intact. My name's Marta Costello. I grew up in a middle-class suburb in Connecticut, daughter of two school administrators, moved to California, graduated from UCI, and became a coder. Having my memories doesn't make me feel like I belong anywhere."

"But your memories can keep you company when you're alone."

"They can also make me feel sad for someone I lost."

Box couldn't stay here. He believed Pataki. He had to get out of here and get back to Mount Weather with Pataki to save the crumbling government. If Box stayed, he might end up in Zodiac's kangaroo court facing a murder charge for killing Cole Younger. If convicted, he would never be able to leave.

"I need a haircut," he said, feeling the hair hanging over his ear.

"I'm getting tired of this plague. Will it never end?"

A scream emanating from the warehouse demanded their attention.

Box and Marta dashed out of the gym toward the warehouse front door.

Chapter 46

Box and Marta burst into the warehouse and cast around for the screamer, uncertain where to initiate their search.

They spotted a huddle of onlookers staring at something in fear and awe in the middle of them.

Box and Marta hurried over to them to find out what was happening.

A seventyish man was lying on his back holding his throat in agony, gasping, his face covered with buboes that were swollen with blood and bursting.

"He's infected," said Hilda. "Stay away from him."

"Who is it?" said Zodiac, attracted by the ruckus and barreling toward the rubberneckers.

"Old man Audziewicz."

"How did he get it?"

"The carrier must have given it to him."

"Impossible. The plague isn't spread by carriers."

"Then who infected him?"

"He must have gone outside the perimeter, and ghouls attacked him."

"Your guards would have seen him if he went out the gate."

"How else could he get infected?"

"It's time for you to wake up and smell the coffee. We have a carrier among us."

"And they're going around biting people?" Zodiac said with sarcastic disbelief.

"They're asymptomatic. They don't have to bite anyone to pass it. If you get too close to them and breathe their spores, you become infected."

"Breathe their spores? Are you joking? You're the one that's infecting people. You're infecting them with panic and paranoia."

Dr. Epps jostled through the crowd, drawing looks of annoyance. "Let me pass. Let me pass. Dammit, I'm a doctor."

"Don't get too near him, Doc," said Hilda. "He's infected with the zombie plague."

"How do you know he's infected?"

"Look at his face. It's got bleeding pustules on it."

"Those are buboes," said Epps.

"Whatever they are, they're symptoms of the plague."

"You got that right. Did a ghoul bite him?"

"We think he must have gone outside the gate and was attacked by a ghoul," said Zodiac.

"I see."

"That's not what I think," said Hilda. "He never left the compound. He's been here in the warehouse the whole time."

"Is there a ghoul in here?" Epps asked with concern, swiveling his head to take in his surroundings.

"A carrier infected Audziewicz."

"And who is this carrier?"

"We don't know yet. But he has to be kept away from the rest of us, or he'll infect everyone."

"She doesn't know what she's talking about," said Zodiac.

"I've lived long enough," said Audziewicz in agony, barely able to speak. "I'm seventy-five. That's long enough to live."

"Did one of the ghouls bite you?" asked Epps.

"Oh, it hurts. It hurts bad. But I'm old. I've lived a long time. Seventy-five—that's old enough, isn't it? Does it matter how long we live? I don't feel like I have to live till I'm eighty. Do you get a reward if you live till eighty? How about a hundred bucks? And what am I supposed to do with it if I'm a basket case? Are you kidding me? Are things supposed to get better the older you get? Horsefeathers. I got news for you. They don't get better. They get worse. I feel like a sack of shit when I wake up in the morning. You know what that's like? It doesn't make me want to live till I'm eighty, I can tell you that—"

"Shut up and answer me. How did you get infected?"

"Do they hand out medals if you reach eighty? Phooey. That's what I say to that. Is life some kind of competition where the oldest guy wins all the marbles? What good is winning if your body feels like a junker headed for the town dump? I'm telling you, I don't feel like a loser if I only reach seventy-five. Am I supposed to feel like a loser if I don't reach—what's the age they say is average nowadays? Eighty-three, is it? Do I get demerits if I only live to be seventy-five? Hogwash, I say. Hogwash. Do you hear me?"

"Would you stop babbling for a second and answer me? How did you get infected?"

"I can't breathe. My face—it's—it's on fire."

Audziewicz gasped for breath. His body spasmed. Blood oozed out of the buboes on his face.

"Do something, Doctor," said Hilda, overwrought.

"I could give him a tracheotomy to help him breathe," said Epps. "But I fear it's too late. The disease is too advanced."

"Hurry, Doctor."

"Everybody, back," said Epps, backing away from Audziewicz. "Don't let his blood get on you."

Two women in the crowd screamed, appalled by the erupting buboes spurting blood.

Audziewicz lay still, his face a grotesque mask of blood and scarred flesh.

"He inhaled spores from the carrier," said Hilda.

"Hilda, we need to talk," said Zodiac. "Spreading disinformation and fear isn't the way to handle this."

"How many times does this have to happen before you accept the truth?"

"Did anyone see the codger get bitten by a ghoul?" Zodiac asked the crowd.

Nobody answered.

"You see," said Hilda. "A ghoul didn't bite him. Just like a ghoul didn't bite Audrey. This isn't the first time, and it won't be the last until we identify the carrier and isolate them."

"All you're doing is scaring the bejesus out of everybody," said Zodiac.

"The truth is a scary thing. We can't shy away from it because it's scary." Hilda turned to Epps. "Doc, did you get a chance to test Audrey's blood to see if it had something in it that could prove she was infected with the zombie plague?"

"I did. I tested both Audrey's and Frieda's blood," said Epps.

"Frieda the junkie?" said Zodiac.

Hilda rolled her eyes. "What is it with you and junkies?"

"Don't roll your eyes at me."

"I did find one interesting thing in both samples," said Epps.

"Yes?" said Hilda.

"The leukocyte cell count in each blood sample was huge. I've never seen anything like it in my medical career, nor have I ever read about such a high count in any of my medical books."

"In layman's language, Doc," said Zodiac. "No technobabble. What's a leukocyte?"

"A white blood cell. They counteract foreign substances and diseases in the blood."

"Maybe there were so many white blood cells in Audrey's and Frieda's blood because they were fighting off the plague," said Hilda.

"I haven't been able to prove that, but it's a definite possibility. Whatever the leukocytes were fighting they were in a losing battle. They weren't able to kill off the invaders. Hence the bodies of the two women kept creating more leukocytes, more than I've ever seen in a human blood sample."

"What was the invader?" said Zodiac.

"My hands are tied. My antiquated microscope isn't powerful enough to identify it. You need state-of-the-art medical equipment to do that."

Gun in hand, Zodiac approached Audziewicz and shot him in the head. "I'm not taking any chances with this guy. I don't want him turning into a ghoul."

Clad in a taupe dress, a middle-aged brunette with a perm in the crowd started weeping.

"Is there no end to the dying?" she said.

Chapter 47

Marta felt ill gazing at Audziewicz's motionless body. She was full of questions. How had he become infected while he was in the warehouse? Was nobody safe here? Were they all living with the illusion that they were safe inside the warehouse? Were they in reality in as much danger here as beyond the perimeter where they had no protection from the ghouls? How could they find out the truth?

"You finally admit he had the plague," Hilda told Zodiac. "He was going to turn, and you know it. Or why did you shoot him?"

"He had it," said Zodiac. "I'm not disputing that. The question is, how did he get it?"

"The carrier gave it to him," said Hilda, her visage determined. "We're never gonna be safe until we identify the carrier."

"So who is it, Hilda? Tell us. You're the one that knows everything."

"Maybe we could use the doctor's information to ID the carrier," chimed in Box. "The doctor could test everyone's blood to see if anyone has a massive number of white blood cells. If anyone does, maybe that person is the carrier."

"What do you say, Doc?" said Hilda.

"It wouldn't be an infallible method of identification," said Epps. "All it would tell us is that the person with a high leukocyte count was infected with something. It wouldn't tell us exactly what. It could be cancer or something else altogether."

"Do asymptomatic people have high counts of white blood cells?" asked Box.

"Depends. They could be high, or, in some cases, they could be low, indicating a lot of the leukocytes had died fighting off the invasive cells."

"But carriers don't have a normal count. They would definitely have an unusual number of white blood cells?"

"I can't say *definitely*, especially with some newfangled disease we know nothing about, but my answer to your question is yes. In all likelihood the white blood cell count would be abnormal. And since this is a virus we're dealing with—I think it is, anyway—the lymphocyte count would be very high."

"Lymphocyte?"

"There are five types of white blood cells. Lymphocytes, monocytes, neutrophils, basophils, and eosinophils. The lymphocytes are the ones that deal with viruses—"

"Man, I don't want a biology lesson, Doc," said Zodiac. "Let's cut to the chase. Will a carrier have a high white blood cell count?"

"If this zombie plague is like any other disease, I would say yes. The insanely high leukocyte count in Audrey's and Frieda's blood could be explained by the plague."

"Wouldn't being a junkie give Frieda a high white blood cell count?" said Zodiac.

Epps nodded yes. "That's a possible explanation. But her white blood cell count was off-the-charts high, as was Audrey's."

"There, you see, Hilda. Frieda could've died from an overdose, not necessarily plague."

"Why can't you accept the truth?" said Hilda. "What's your explanation for Audrey's high leukocyte count? Audrey wasn't a junkie."

Zodiac stared at her and said nothing.

"And Audrey's blood infected her baby," Hilda told Epps. "Right, Doctor?"

"That's right. Her baby's blood had a similarly high count of white blood cells."

"If you take a sample of everybody's blood, and you find anyone with a lot of white blood cells, it would indicate they're a carrier. Right?"

"Not so fast," said Epps. "It would indicate they have a serious disease, not necessarily the zombie plague."

"If the white blood cell count was 'insanely high,' like you said before about Audrey's blood, a level you've never seen, then it would mean they have the plague."

Epps didn't answer. He didn't want to commit himself.

"Give her the straight skinny, Doc," said Zodiac.

"I couldn't say with absolute certainty that such a person had the zombie plague," said Epps.

"We can't be absolutely certain about much of anything in this world," said Hilda. "What's your best guess?"

"There's a good chance if their leukocyte count was astronomically high, like Frieda's and Audrey's, that person could be infected with the zombie plague."

"A really good chance."

Zodiac stroked his chin, pondering.

"I have to admit what she says makes sense to me," he said. "I guess there's a first time for everything, since this is the first time anything she has said has made any kind of sense—*if* we accept the conclusion that we have a carrier among us."

"We do have one," said Hilda. "And there's no harm in the doc's taking blood samples from everyone to determine their white blood cell count."

"Unless we falsely identify a person as a carrier in the process," said Epps.

"It sounds like a foolproof method to me," said Zodiac. "I'm all for it. Doc, get to work taking blood samples from everyone."

"I thought you didn't believe there's a carrier here," said Hilda, puzzled at Zodiac's about-face.

"If the doc's bloodwork shows nobody with a high leukocyte count, will that prove to you there isn't a carrier?"

"The fact is, I know there's a carrier among us. Nothing will change my mind on that," said Hilda, folding her arms across her chest.

"I'm beginning to believe you might be right."

Hilda couldn't believe her ears. Zodiac admitting he was wrong? Could it be possible?

"We need to be very careful about what we do," said Epps. "We don't want to falsely single out anyone as being infected. The stigma would cause egregious harm to that person if they got blamed for spreading the plague."

"Harm to the carrier is the least of my worries," said Zodiac. "I'm concerned about the rest of us. The carrier has to be dealt with."

"I'm not talking about the carrier. I'm talking about someone *falsely* identified as a carrier."

"If you're as good a doctor as you say you are, you won't make a false ID."

"I'm in uncharted territory. This zombie plague is a new disease. How can you expect me to be 100 percent certain of my ID?"

"Let me worry about that, Doc," said Zodiac. "I'm in charge. I make the decisions. Your conscience is clear, no matter what happens with the test results."

"I wish we had better equipment."

"You know what my wise old gramma used to say. If wishes were horses, beggars would ride. You get to work and start drawing blood."

Chapter 48

"I have a question, Doctor," said Marta, stepping forward from the throng.

"Yes?" said Epps.

"If a person is a carrier, do they know they are?"

"I would say no, since they are asymptomatic by definition."

"So they can't confess they're carriers."

Epps mulled it over, knitting his brows over his close-set eyes. "Not unless they figured it out somehow."

"Is that possible?"

"For instance, if the carrier's friends all died from the plague, the carrier might suspect he had infected them, though he could never be sure."

"A lot of the people here, including me, have had friends die from the plague," said Porter. "We can't all be carriers."

"Granted. Which means it would be next to impossible for the carrier to know for certain that they're a carrier."

Marta wondered if she was a carrier. She had thrown up this morning for no reason she could think of. She didn't remember any food disagreeing with her. The Chef Boyardee beef ravioli went down fine last night. Did she have other symptoms? Did she have a fever? She felt her forehead. She didn't feel hot.

Did carriers have symptoms of other diseases or ailments instead of symptoms for the plague? It seemed possible to her because of all the white blood cells that might be in her body. What if the doctor found out she was a carrier? Would the others lock her up? Why was she jumping to conclusions? She wasn't sure she *was* a carrier. Vomiting by itself didn't make her a carrier. But why did she throw up? She couldn't be the carrier. Could she? Her head was beginning to ache. Another symptom experienced by a carrier? But carriers were asymptomatic. She was giving herself a headache thinking about it.

She told herself to think about something else.

She would worry about it if the doctor found too many leukocytes in her blood. But then it would be too late. Then the others would know, too, and they would hunt her down and lock her up to prevent her from infecting anyone else.

Somehow she would have to find out the results of her bloodwork before anyone else in the compound did, except for the doctor, of course. He would know right away, and there was nothing she could do to prevent it.

"Look what I found," said Tyler, striding up to Zodiac, his chest puffed out, a flamethrower in his hands.

"You been holding out on me, Porter? Why didn't you tell me we have a flamethrower here? We're gonna light up some ghouls with this baby," said Zodiac, snatching the flamethrower from Tyler, a broad grin lighting up his face.

Zodiac's walkie-talkie squawked. Zodiac answered.

"We got about a dozen bogeys at the front gate. Over," said the guard over the walkie-talkie.

"Roger, hold your fire," said Zodiac. "I repeat. Hold your fire. I'm coming out there. Over and out." Patting the flamethrower he told Tyler, "I wanna try this baby out. Time to light 'em up."

"The only good dweeb is a dead dweeb," said Tyler.

"How about a fried dweeb?"

Chapter 49

"What will they do to the carrier?" Marta asked Box, as Zodiac and his men made for the front door.

"With Zodiac in charge they'll probably kill the guy," answered Box.

"Kill them?"

Box shrugged. "I call 'em like I see 'em."

"What if some people don't allow the doctor to draw their blood?"

"Interesting question. If you *do* refuse, Zodiac will probably think you're the carrier."

"In which case he'll kill you."

Box gave a wry half smile. "I wouldn't bet against it."

"But didn't you hear what the doctor said? He said the carrier doesn't know they're a carrier."

"Then why would someone refuse to give a blood sample?"

"Maybe they don't like needles."

"Even if they have a legitimate reason, Zodiac will assume they're trying to hide from everybody that they're carriers."

Marta fetched a sigh. "Giving blood always makes me feel tired afterward. Did you ever think about escaping from here?"

"Don't let anyone overhear you saying that."

"Look, the doctor is already drawing blood samples."

"The sooner he gets started the better. There must be over a hundred people here in the compound. And then there are Zodiac's men."

Epps and two nurses were drawing blood from a three-hundred-pound thirtyish man wearing navy blue galluses in a queue of fifty-odd camp members.

"I wonder how long it will take," said Marta.

"Everyone, line up to give a blood sample to the doctor," announced Zodiac.

Box heard grumbling, but most of the people he could see were heading toward Epps, albeit slowly.

"No need to fear," said Zodiac. "A little needle won't hurt you."

"It's not the needle they're worried about," said Box under his breath to Marta.

"It's the results of the test," said Marta. "And I don't blame them."

"Box, you're with me," said Zodiac from the front door. "I want you at the gate to help us fight the ghouls. Everyone else, see the doctor to give blood."

Box set off for the front door.

Marta followed him.

"I'm not in any rush to give blood," she told him.

"No one is. Nobody wants to find out they're the carrier. How would you feel if you found out it was you?"

"Terrified."

"I'm sure Zodiac will have a list of those who don't cooperate and don't give blood. You're better off not being on it," said Box, going through the front door.

"I suppose." She paused. "What a terrible time to be alive."

At the gate, Box saw a knot of ghouls milling toward the compound.

"Nobody shoot till I say so," said Zodiac. "Loud noises attract those things. If there are more ghouls in the woods, they'll head here at the sounds of gunshots."

"The more the merrier is what I say," said Tyler. "I love whacking those things."

Zodiac held up his sickle to Tyler. "Tyler, you're the only one I trust to hold Suzie Q for me."

"Thanks, boss. I'll take good care of her."

Zodiac handed him the sickle.

Chapter 50

Zodiac carried the flamethrower up the guard tower, which jutted above the chain-link fence. In position, he hoisted the forty-five-pound flamethrower's backpack, which Tyler had already deposited in the observation post, onto his back. The backpack contained napalm in the fuel canister.

"The good thing about flamethrowers is they don't make a lot of noise," he told Tyler, who was standing at the base of the guard tower gazing up at him.

Zodiac trained the barrel on the nearest ghoul, a sixteen-year-old zaftig brunette wearing skintight jeans and a bright tie-dye blouse, who was the better part of twenty feet from the gate.

"Time to give this baby a test run and light up a ghoul," he said, and pulled the trigger.

A streak of yellow flame shot out of the barrel toward the teen ghoul. She waved at the thrusting flame like she was trying to push it away from her face. Her hands and arms caught fire. Her clothes burned. Her head and long hair flared. Engulfed in flames, she twisted back and forth, flailing her arms.

"She's trying to fly," he said with amusement.

His men guffawed, watching the ghoul burn to death.

"This works good," said Zodiac. He gazed down at Porter, who stood on the ground near the gate. "What kind of fuel does this thing use?"

"Napalm," said Porter.

"Beautiful. That stuff leveled Nam. Did everyone see *Apocalypse Now*?"

"Yeah, boss," said Tyler. "A great flick."

"We don't have much napalm left," said Porter.

Zodiac's face registered disappointment. "How many gallons?"

Porter mulled it over. "Ten gallons max, I'd say."

"What's the tank on my back hold?"

"Three and a half gallons."

Zodiac shrugged. "We'll have to make do."

"The ghouls are attracted to bright lights. They'll see your fires."

"Yeah, well, they're in the woods. They can't see what's going on here with all those trees between us blocking their vision. They *will* hear a gunshot, though. We're better off using the flamethrower." He paused for effect. "Plus, it's fun."

The charred, smoking teen brunette fell to the ground. Zodiac's men whooped with delight.

"The hottie is incinerated," said Tyler, grinning.

"Time for another crispy critter," said Zodiac. "I'm gonna burn that hippo coming at us."

Zodiac pulled the flamethrower's trigger and torched a fat twentysomething male ghoul wearing a Yankees baseball cap backwards. The ghoul burst into flames. His face and double chin melted and dripped down his throat like burning wax and continued down his belly, which sizzled like rashers of bacon on a hot griddle.

"Meet Godzilla," Zodiac told a seventyish henna-haired woman, who was shaking her head and arms like she had Parkinson's disease as she lumbered toward the gate.

He squeezed the flamethrower's trigger.

"They go up like scarecrows," he said, smiling with approval, as the woman shivered with flaming flesh.

Her flesh burning, she slogged toward the gate, but tripped over her own feet before she could reach it.

"That looks like fun, boss," said Tyler on the ground a few feet from Porter, peering up at Zodiac. "When's my turn?"

"We gotta take this nut bag out," Porter whispered to Box.

"What's that?" said Zodiac. "No secrets here, Porter. What'd you say?"

"I said, how come you get to have all the fun?" said Porter.

"'Cause I'm the man."

Zodiac's men clapped, hooted, and cheered for him.

"Anyone here ever eat fried ghoul flesh?" said Zodiac, as he fired the flamethrower again and set another ghoul aflame.

"I wouldn't eat any kind of dweeb meat, raw or cooked, if you paid me," said Tyler.

"Only got two of 'em left. What am I gonna do with 'em?"

"Toast 'em," cried his men.

"Up in smoke," said Tyler, waving Zodiac's sickle.

"Be careful with Suzie Q," said Zodiac.

"Oh, sorry, boss," said Tyler, carefully lowering the sickle.

"You know how women are. You gotta treat him nice and gentle before you fuck their brains out and they scream with delight."

"You got it, boss."

"Now ghouls are another matter entirely."

Zodiac squeezed the flamethrower's trigger. A blue-tinged golden streak of fire whooshed from the hot muzzle, arced thirty yards across the ground, and landed at the feet of two bedraggled, winolike ghouls shambling after their burning companions. Zodiac raised the flamethrower's barrel so the arcing fire rose and connected with the winos' feet. By degrees, he kept raising the barrel so the blaze consumed the winos' legs, torsos, and, at last, their disheveled heads, which popped like balloons under the blistering heat, their brains boiling out of their burst skulls.

What was left of the smoldering, blackened corpses of the twelve ghouls littered the ground, mixed with the carcasses of birds strewn by the dust storm.

"Maybe any other ghouls marching on our compound will get the message when they get a load of that carnage," said Zodiac, letting up on the trigger and lowering the flamethrower.

"Even if they're dweebs, they should understand," said Tyler.

"Wait a minute. Looky, looky. What have we here?" said Zodiac, spying a ghoul staggering out of the woods toward the camp. "We got another one that wants to meet Godzilla."

Zodiac raised the flamethrower then lowered it.

"What's wrong, boss?" said Tyler.

"I just thought of something. I wanna see if our electrified fence works on those things. Let him reach the fence. Everybody, hold your fire," said Zodiac, raising his hand above his head.

"It better work," Pataki told Box. "If it doesn't, we're not gonna be able to keep out the swarms of them gathering in the forest to attack. They'll trample the fence into the ground because they're gonna keep coming and coming no matter how many of them you kill. They'll climb over all the dead bodies in their way and crush the fence."

It was a six-five, wide-hipped black male ghoul with greying temples in his fifties that approached the front gate, dragging his feet across the ground. He was wearing jeans, suede tan boots, and a brown leather vest.

"Come and get us," said Zodiac.

Growling, the ghoul neared the gate. He balked three steps away from it.

"What's the matter, big guy?" said Zodiac. "Getting cold feet?"

The ghoul sniffed the air and smelled fresh human flesh near him.

He hobbled toward the gate, grabbed it, and tried to yank it out of his way. An electric shock coursed through his system as the decomposing flesh on his hands touched the steel links. Grimacing, his body stiff, he held onto the fence that shook and hissed at him with electric sparks. His hair commenced smoking. He slumped forward against the fence, still grasping it. His face smashed the fence and sizzled and smoked. The red-hot chain links branded his face with a pattern of diamond shapes.

He hung frozen on the fence like he was trying to push it down. He didn't know his pushing days were over.

"Eureka," said Zodiac. "It works."

"Like a charm," said Tyler, strutting up to the ghoul and staring him in the face.

"Porter, I want you and your buddies to go inside and get your blood tested ASAP. The bunch of you."

Chapter 51

"Danny would be here with us if it wasn't for me," Porter told Box as they entered the warehouse.

"You had nothing to do with his death," said Box.

They made for the queue that extended from Dr. Epps and his nurses.

"I should've been watching him more carefully," said Porter.

"How were you supposed to know he'd smoke a joint in front of Zodiac?"

"And how were you supposed to know Zodiac would kill him for it?" said Marta.

"If I was with Danny, I could've talked Zodiac out of killing him," said Porter.

"Don't be too sure of that," said Box. "I doubt that guy listens to anyone."

"Does anyone else *not* want to find out if they're a carrier?" said Marta.

"It's not your fault if you are," said Box.

"Something tells me the guy with the sickle doesn't think like that. Everything with him is kill, kill, kill."

"What can we do about it?" said Porter. "He's got the firepower."

"You heard the doc," said Box. "His test isn't infallible. It just shows if someone has an abnormal amount of white blood cells."

"Do you really think Zodiac cares if it's infallible?"

"He couldn't care less," said Pataki. "If someone has too many white blood cells, Zodiac will take action against him."

"Let's get out of here and forget about all of this," said Marta.

"Don't you want to know who the carrier is?" said Porter.

"If I leave I don't care. I say let's leave."

"Zodiac's not gonna let us up and leave," said Box. "If he catches you leaving, he'll assume you're the carrier."

"Then he should be happy I'm leaving."

"He doesn't think like that. He's a control freak. If we try to leave without his permission, we're the enemy, in his eyes, and he'll take action against us."

Pataki drew Box aside and whispered, "Halverson, it's imperative we get out of here and back to Mount Weather. The future of our country depends on it. The government is collapsing. We don't have to tell Zodiac we're leaving. We can sneak out of here without his ever knowing."

"How?"

"We overpower the guards at the gate and split on my Harley."

"When?"

"Tonight's as good a time as any."

"What are you two talking about?" said Marta, closing in on them.

"Uh, uh—we're wondering what to do if one of us tests positive for the zombie plague," said Pataki.

"Well, don't keep it a secret. I want to know, too."

"So do I," said Zodiac, swaggering toward them, sickle in hand, Tyler and Sammy with him.

"We're—uh—we're wondering what you're gonna do to the carrier if you ID them," said Pataki.

"I'll take care of it. Don't worry about it. Did you give blood yet?"

"We're at the end of the line."

"Ah, that's no good. Go to the front of the line."

Pataki gave him a look. "You want me to cut in front of everyone?"

"That's right. You, Box, Marta, and uh"—Zodiac snapped his fingers—"and Porter. You people are the new kids on the block, so we need to make sure you're clean."

"I'm not any new kid," said Porter. "I've been here longer than any of you."

"But you were exposed to Box and Marta in your car, is how I hear it from Hilda."

"You're newer than us," Box told Zodiac.

"But I'm the one calling the shots, don't you know?"

"I should point out another of these unexplained plague infections happened before Box and Marta arrived here," said Porter.

"That doesn't clear them," said Zodiac, raising his sickle. "They could still be carriers. Nobody is cleared until the doc checks everybody's blood. The truth is, I think it's one of you. Now go to the head of the line."

Box, Marta, Porter, and Pataki cut in front of everyone. Nobody seemed to care. They weren't eager to get their blood tested, either.

A thirtysomething brown-haired Hispanic nurse with friendly brown eyes wrote down their names, applied a tourniquet to their arms, told them to make a fist, swabbed the site of the upcoming puncture on their arms with alcohol, and used a hypodermic needle to draw their blood, one at a time. For each of them she pressed gauze against the puncture wound and then applied a tiny red Band-Aid to it after withdrawing the hypo from the median cubital vein.

"When will you know the results, Doc?" said Box.

"As long as it takes me to go through hundreds of tests," said Epps. "Testing for white blood cells doesn't take that long. Once I get everybody's blood sample, it should go pretty quickly."

"Have you ID'd a carrier yet?" said Zodiac.

"I haven't performed any bloodwork yet. I'm still taking samples. I want to get all of the samples before I start testing."

"I don't want you to dick around on this. I want the results fast."

"I'm not going to rush the job and make mistakes. This has to be done hygienically and accurately."

"Of course. You're the doctor."

Chapter 52

Hilda interrupted Zodiac with annoyance. "I saw what happened here."

"What?" said Zodiac.

"These people with you cut in front of everybody else in line."

"Hilda, I told them to. Don't worry about these things. You're not in charge."

"If it wasn't for me, you wouldn't know there's a carrier among us."

"And I'm grateful to you for that. We can all learn things if we open our minds. I'm even thinking about giving you a promotion. Remember, submission is the road to empowerment."

"A promotion?" said Hilda, indignant. "This is *my* camp. How can *you* promote anyone?"

"Your memory deceives you," said Zodiac with a smile. "Remember, you surrendered to me."

"It's still my camp."

"No, it's not. But I'm not gonna hold it against you. In fact, I want you to be part of my team. There's room for smart people like you on my team."

"Is this your way of saying you want to join forces?"

"With all due respect, you have no forces. You are a single person I'm talking to. You don't represent anybody or any group. When you surrendered to me, you were stripped of your leadership."

"You don't understand the power dynamics here."

"Don't talk to me about power. You have none. I'm giving you a good deal. Are you refusing to accept it?"

"I want to see the doctor take blood in an orderly fashion, not with anyone cutting in front of people to get to the front of the line. We have to have order here. Otherwise, we're left with anarchy. No cutting in line."

"Don't make me lose patience with you. I'm the one that told them to go to the head of the line. I want to know whether any of them is the carrier. I suspect one of them is."

187

"Really?" said Hilda, taken aback. "Which one?"

"That's the question. That's why I want them tested ASAP."

"I guess that makes sense. Why do you think it's one of them?"

"I have my reasons." Zodiac leaned closer to Hilda and lowered his voice. "There's something about that Pataki guy that rubs me the wrong way. I have a built-in bullshit detector that lights up when I'm with him."

"He's a newcomer. I doubt he's the carrier. We had infections before he arrived."

"Are you certain all of those infections were caused by a carrier? Maybe they were caused by ghoul bites."

"It's hard to be sure of anything without scientific examination."

Zodiac grinned. "That's why I like you, Hilda. You got a head on your shoulders. We need people like you on our leadership team."

"It's obvious you need me," she said with self-satisfaction, folding her arms over her chest.

"We always need good people."

"I have to think about it."

"You're playing footsie with me. It's time to fish or cut bait."

Hilda thought about it. "I'll make you a counteroffer."

"What?"

"I'll let you share equal power with me over the camp. Do you agree?"

Zodiac cocked an eyebrow. "Is that your way of saying yes?"

"I said what I said."

"Your wording leaves something to be desired. You're gonna have to rephrase your acceptance of my offer."

"I've said my piece."

"We'll discuss this later. Right now I want you to get your bloodwork done."

"Where's Gertie?"

"I have no idea."

"I want to talk to her."

"Talk to her after you give blood."

"Fine. I have no problem with getting my blood tested."

"Good, because you're next," said Zodiac, holding back the rest of the line so Hilda could approach Dr. Epps and his nurses.

Chapter 53

Folding wooden chairs had been placed in the middle of the warehouse for the members of the compound where they could sit after giving blood and wait for the results of the tests.

Box and Marta took seats next to Pataki and Porter.

"This is the part I hate," said Marta. "The waiting game."

"Don't think about it, or you'll go nuts," said Box.

"What are we supposed to do here?"

"Read a book. Don't they have books in this place?"

Porter overheard them. "We have books, but Zodiac took all of them and locked them in a room."

"I suppose it could be worse," said Box. "He could've burned them."

"Don't give him any ideas."

"I wonder how long we'll have to wait," said Marta.

Box scanned the seats. "The seats are filling up. With any luck, maybe not too long."

"A lot of you have forgotten something," said Pataki.

"What's that?" said Porter.

"You got thousands of those ghouls massing for an attack in the forest. They could get here any time now."

"That's why we electrified the fence."

"Do you think that fence will kill thousands of bloodthirsty ghouls?"

"We'll kill the rest of them with baseball bats, clubs, crossbows, bullets, and whatever else we got."

"How much ammo do you have here?"

Porter shrugged. "Not thousands of rounds, that's for sure."

"That's what I thought."

"What do you suggest?"

"It's time to abandon ship, if you get my drift."

"Zodiac said he's planning to head to DC. He's not gonna stay here forever."

"What's he gonna do there?"

"Take over the country, he said."

"Let's get there before him," said Pataki, lowering his voice. "Let's go there now."

He exchanged looks with Box.

Box could follow Pataki's line of thought. Pataki was saying he and Box had to get to Mount Weather pronto, even though Pataki hadn't said it in so many words. Pataki wanted Porter to go with him, but didn't want Zodiac or his men to overhear them.

"I keep hoping things will get better," said Marta, "but there's no sign of it. We keep going from bad to worse."

"You're thinking too much again," said Box.

"She's right," said Pataki. "If we stay here, we're screwed."

Box caught sight of Zodiac, flanked by armed guards, strutting toward the lectern set up on a dais in front of the rows of seats. Zodiac mounted the dais.

"I got an announcement to make," he said behind the lectern facing the compound's members seated before him, his two bodyguards standing behind him, their AR-15s at port arms. "We're almost done with the bloodwork of all the members. We'll know the results and determine who the carrier is soon. I know all of you are champing at the bit to find out the carrier's name."

"I have a question," said a middle-aged construction worker, his face a broad slab of raw meat with stubble on it, clad in jeans and a white T, sitting on the end seat in the fifth row of the audience, an aluminum construction hat perched on his head, his T straining against his potbelly.

"This isn't a democracy. I'm not taking questions from the audience."

"Hilda used to take questions from us. Why don't you?"

"Hilda works for me now."

"This isn't right."

"It is what I say it is."

"This is still a free country. We can all have our say."

"What's your name?"

"Harvey. Harvey Kolchak."

"Is this how you talk to your foreman in his trailer at your construction site, Harvey? You tell him you're gonna have your say about a construction project you're working on?"

"Uh, why—no. He's the boss. I do what he tells me."

"Exactly. Think of me as your boss."

"But you're not my boss. You're not paying me every other week like he used to."

"I'm protecting you from getting infected."

"You're running a protection racket?"

"I wouldn't put it that way."

"Well, I didn't vote for you."

"I told you, this isn't a democracy. Are you hard of hearing?"

"I wanna talk to Hilda."

"You're overthinking this, Harvey. Let it die. Let me do the thinking. Then you won't have to bother. Look at it this way: I'm the brain, and you're one of my feet. When I say walk, you walk."

"I'm nobody's foot. I'm a free man. I have my rights."

"Harvey, come up here."

"Why?"

"I want to show you something."

"I can see fine from here."

Zodiac did a slow burn. "Harvey, don't make me come down there and get you."

"What's the big deal?"

His face glum, Harvey got up and walked toward Zodiac's lectern.

Zodiac strutted out from behind the lectern, raised his sickle, swung it, and sliced off Harvey's head. Blood fountained out of Harvey's shredded throat, propelling his head ten feet across the floor. Several camp members in the audience screamed in terror. Harvey's torso dropped to the floor, spilling blood onto the floor through his open throat.

A twentysomething blonde sitting in the second row screamed in terror, clutching her blood-splattered head in her hands.

Some of Harvey's blood had gushed onto Zodiac's face. Zodiac wiped the blood away with a handkerchief that he withdrew from his trouser pocket. Aghast, members of the audience sitting in the first row also wiped Harvey's blood from their faces and hands.

"Don't be alarmed," Zodiac told the audience. "Harvey's blood isn't contaminated. We got his bloodwork results back. He isn't one of the carriers. You don't have to worry if some of his blood splashed onto you."

"This is an outrage," cried Porter, bolting to his feet.

"Calm down, Porter, and be seated."

"You just murdered a man in cold blood. Have you no decency?"

"He defied me. I had to teach him a lesson. The punishment for mutiny is death."

Zodiac fell to wiping off his sickle's blood-soaked blade.

"You can't go around beheading people," said Porter.

"Not to put too fine a point on it, if you mutiny against me, you will get a visit from Suzie Q," said Zodiac, brandishing his sickle above his head.

"We don't want a murderer leading us."

"Earl James is the murderer," said Kate Younger from a seat in one of the back rows.

Box craned around and spotted her staring at him.

"Hold it down back there," said Zodiac.

Box looked back toward Zodiac.

"Sit down, Porter," said Zodiac. "Or do you wanna come up here like good ole Harvey?"

Pataki snatched Porter's wrist and yanked Porter down into his seat.

"He's a homicidal maniac," whispered Pataki.

"We can't stand by and watch him murder us," said Porter, seething.

"Now's not the time. We're surrounded by armed guards, if you haven't noticed."

"Where was I?" said Zodiac, returning to the lectern and addressing the audience. "We have identified possible carriers. These people have higher-than-average counts of white blood cells."

Several in the audience gasped in surprise.

"I know what you're thinking," said Zodiac. "It's the same thing we all thought. Everyone but me, that is," he went on, his face smug. "You thought that there was just one carrier. I suspected otherwise, and my suspicions have been confirmed."

Chapter 54

"Do you think we should believe him?" Marta asked Box, leaning toward him, keeping her voice low.

"We can't believe anything he says," answered Box, still annoyed at Kate Younger for calling him out.

Could she possibly be right that he was Earl James? he wondered. He didn't believe her. He believed Pataki, and Pataki had told him he was Chad Halverson.

"We have to deal with these carriers," said Zodiac. "We can't let them infect the rest of us."

"You said they're *possible* carriers," said Box.

"The doc doesn't want to commit to anything. You know how he is with his scientific method and all that technobabble. But he's not the one making decisions. That's the job of your great leader, the man you are looking at. Does anyone have a problem with that?"

Zodiac surveyed the members in the audience.

"We can't let this carnage continue," muttered Porter.

"Keep it down," said Pataki. "Sweetcakes will hear you."

"Did I hear someone say something?" said Zodiac. "Porter? Was that you?"

Managing to hold his temper in check, Porter kept his own counsel.

"He didn't say anything," said Pataki.

"All right, then," said Zodiac. "Kate Younger, would you sit down?"

"I can't hear anything back here," said Kate. "I want a seat closer up."

She edged sideways past the members sitting in her row and reached the aisle. She headed down the aisle, turned left, and entered Box's row. Marta stood up so Kate could fit past her. Box, who was sitting beside Marta, followed suit. Kate whipped a knife out of her purse and thrust the four-inch blade toward him.

"Die, Earl James, die," said Kate through clenched teeth.

Catching sight of the knife out of the corner of his eye, Box felt adrenaline course through his body, sharpening his senses. He burst into action, shooting out his hand and snagging Kate's forearm, deflecting the blow from his flank.

"She's got a knife," cried Marta.

"Drag her out of there," Zodiac told the guard standing the best part of ten feet away from Kate.

Wearing a nose ring a musclebound five-ten guy pushing forty with a full head of hair and fetid armpits shoved his way past Marta, seized Kate's arm whose hand was holding the knife, and dragged Kate out of the row. Fighting and squirming, Kate refused to release the knife and tried to break free. But the guard was too strong. He overpowered her, shoved her to the nearest wall, and slammed her hand against it again and again, causing her to yelp in pain as he banged her knuckles against the sheetrock, fracturing them and cratering the sheetrock. Howling, she dropped the knife to the floor, her knuckles bloody and misshapen.

Pinning Kate's arms behind her back, digging his knee into her spine, pressing her chest to the wall, the guard whipped a black plastic zip tie out of his trouser pocket and bound her wrists behind her back. As he pulled back from her, she craned her head around and tried to bite his throat. Furious, he slammed his fist into her jaw and decked her. She lay prostrate on the floor, motionless.

"Is there anyone else who has something to say?" said Zodiac.

Nobody said anything.

Zodiac cleared his throat. "Good. I'm tired of these interruptions. I'm the one who will decide who is the murderer. I haven't decided yet if Box's real name is Earl James. That's not important now. What's important is, who are the carriers? Does everyone agree?"

Several in the audience said, "Yeah."

Others nodded yes.

"Is everyone prepared to listen to the list of the carriers' names the doc gave me to read aloud?"

"I'm not," said Marta sotto voce to Box. "Why's he keep looking over here?"

"He's trying to intimidate us," said Box out of the side of his mouth.

"He's doing a good job. If he reads out my name, I'm gonna pass out."

"Take it easy."

"You know he's gonna kill the carriers. Look what he did to Harvey, and all the poor guy did was complain. Everybody's scared of getting infected. They'll want Zodiac to kill the carriers. Can you hear my heart beating? It's beating so loud I can hardly hear anything else. Why didn't you grab Kate's knife?"

"I tried to. I thumbed a pressure point on her wrist, but I couldn't do it long enough to get her to release the shiv because the guard shoved me out of the way."

"Pressure point? How do you know about pressure points?"

Good question, decided Box. His knowledge of pressure points must have had something to do with his CIA black-ops training. Which lent further proof to Pataki's claim that Box was indeed the CIA agent Chad Halverson. In any case, the fog had not yet lifted from Box's memories, leaving them obscured even with Pataki's intel.

"Is everyone ready for me to read out loud the list of carriers?" said Zodiac.

"Hell, no," whispered Marta.

"Then let me begin."

"We who are about to die salute you," muttered Marta.

Absolute silence, as Zodiac placed the list on the lectern before him.

Chapter 55

"The first name on the list of carriers is"—Zodiac paused for effect.

"Get on with it," said Marta under her breath.

"He knows everyone's scared to death their name will be called," said Box, his voice barely audible.

"Gertrude," said Zodiac, and looked up. "Gertrude is a suspected carrier."

"He never did like Gertie," said Porter, keeping his voice down.

Gertrude sat silent next to Hilda in the audience.

"The other names are, as follows: Porter . . . , Pataki . . . , Box . . . . , and Marta."

"I knew it," said Marta, her worst fears confirmed, her face blanching.

"How convenient he can't stand any of us," said Porter.

"Yeah, what a surprise," said Box.

"Is this rigged or what?" said Pataki.

"Zodiac's version of a coup."

"I wonder why he didn't name Hilda," said Porter.

"I overheard her and him talking about cutting a deal," said Marta.

"I can't believe Hilda would side with that guy."

"So what happens now?" said Marta, her palms sweaty.

As if on cue, Zodiac said, "I need you folks to step up here."

The audience cast sidelong glances at Box, Porter, Marta, Pataki, and Gertrude as the five made their way to the front of the assemblage.

Zodiac put on his mask.

"There must be some mistake," said Gertie, approaching the lectern. "I feel healthy as an ox."

"Of course you do," said Zodiac. "You're a carrier. You don't experience any symptoms of the plague even though you're infected and can infect others. Don't get any closer to me and keep your mask on."

Gertie halted six feet from Zodiac.

"That goes for the rest of you carriers, too," said Zodiac.

Box and the others stopped next to Gertie.

"How can we prove we're not carriers?" Box asked Zodiac.

"You can't. Unless you can explain why your blood has so many white blood cells in it," answered Zodiac.

"I just got here," said Pataki. "How could I have caused any of these infections you've had here before I arrived?"

"Your blood indicates you're a carrier. Whether or not you infected anybody in this compound is immaterial."

"Me and Box are both latecomers," said Marta.

"So am I, for that matter," said Zodiac. "But that doesn't let you off the hook. Hilda told me about the unexplained infections they had here before my arrival. The fact is—and the science doesn't lie—ask the doc—the fact is, we have more than one carrier in our midst. The proof's in the blood. Blood doesn't lie. Science doesn't lie. You are all carriers."

"Could we at least see the test results of our bloodwork?" said Box.

"I'm not sharing anybody's personal information. That would be an invasion of privacy. Privacy is something we respect in my community."

"Then how can we tell if the results haven't been fudged?"

"Who would dare do such a thing?"

"Somebody who was out to get certain people."

"Are you making an accusation against me? Out with it," said Zodiac, hacked off.

"I'm just saying the bloodwork results should be reexamined to make sure there are no errors. What's the harm in double-checking? You don't want to charge innocent people with being carriers."

"There are no mistakes in the bloodwork. This isn't about politics. It's about science. The people I have named are carriers."

"Who said anything about politics?"

"You said somebody messed with the test results."

"So what happens next?" said Marta.

"You're all going to the quarantine room for the time being," said Zodiac.

He withdrew his pistol from the holster on his hip and shot Gertie in the head. Droplets of her blood sprayed Zodiac's mask. She crumpled on the floor.

"Except Gertie," said Zodiac.

"What the hell did you do that for?" said Porter, incensed.

"The number of her white blood cells was off the charts. The infection was ravaging her system, making her highly infectious. It's best for the community she be removed."

Hilda screamed, bolted out of her seat, and sprang toward Gertie, weeping.

"Gertie," said Hilda, kneeling down beside Gertie's motionless body. "Oh, Jesus, what have you done to her?"

Chapter 56

"You've had it in for us from the start," Porter told Zodiac.

"What's that supposed to mean?" said Zodiac.

"You rigged the tests so you could lock us up."

"That's not the way science works."

"You call this science? You call murdering people science?"

Zodiac trained his Glock 19 on Porter's forehead. "Do you want to follow Gertie?"

Hilda got to her feet and confronted Zodiac, her face flushed and streaked with tears. "Why did you have to kill Gertie?"

"If I didn't, she would've infected everybody here with the zombie plague," said Zodiac, keeping his Glock's muzzle trained on Porter.

Zodiac's guards raised their AR-15s and leveled them at the accused carriers.

"I've been with Gertie for years," said Hilda. "How come she didn't infect me?"

"How should I know? I'm not a doctor. Ask him."

"This is barbaric. We quarantine carriers. We don't murder them."

Zodiac sniggered. "Yeah, that's what you say now when we find out one of your friends is a carrier. You were all for whacking out carriers not too long ago."

"Gertie wasn't afraid of you. That's the real reason you killed her."

"The science says the most effective way to deal with carriers is to eliminate them. I obeyed the science and took care of the supercarrier Gertie. We'll cremate her body and she'll never infect anyone again. That's how you eradicate a highly infectious disease like this zombie plague."

"Science? What kind of science says to commit murder?"

"The disease must be eradicated in order to save the community."

"You're using pseudoscience to prop up your dictatorship."

"You need to watch what you say, Hilda. You're a smart lady, and I want you to be one of my top lieutenants, but you gotta watch your mouth."

Hilda started sobbing. "Gertie was my best friend. How could you?"

"It wasn't me. It was the disease. The plague took her from us. These are horrible times we're living in. The plague is wiping us out. We have to do everything we can to stop it from spreading."

"The plague didn't shoot her. You did."

"The science told me it had to be done. I do what the science says. The science is always right." Zodiac paused. "You should be happy."

"Happy?" she said, taken aback.

"You were the one that told me we had carriers in the warehouse. If it wasn't for you and the doc, we never would've known who the carriers are."

"You don't have to *murder* carriers to prevent them from infecting others."

"It's the only sure way. But, I have to admit, Gertie was an extreme case. Her blood was saturated with white blood cells. I don't know how she was even alive with all that plague in her system poisoning her."

"Don't tell me you're gonna line up all the other carriers in front of a firing squad."

"I'm quarantining them. Haven't you been listening?"

"All I can hear is that gunshot that killed Gertie," said Hilda, staring at Gertie's corpse and sobbing.

"Take the other carriers to the quarantine room, Tyler," said Zodiac. "Except for Pataki."

"Will do, boss," said Tyler.

"Don't get too close to me," Pataki told Zodiac dryly, "or you'll get infected."

"I'm wearing my mask," said Zodiac, adjusting his blood-mottled mask.

"Aren't you worried about getting infected from that blood on your mask?"

"I believe I'm immune to the contagious spores."

"Oh, yeah? Then why wear the mask in the first place?"

"Your concern for me is touching."

Zodiac ripped off his mask and flung it in Pataki's face.

"There," said Zodiac. "Happy now?"

"You bastard. I oughta . . ."

"I'm taking you to a special room."

"Great. I like being special."

"You're gonna change your mind about that PDQ," said Zodiac with a caustic laugh.

He ordered a guard to bind Pataki's wrists behind his back. "Keep your eye on him."

What was that all about? wondered Box. A special room? Not good.

A rifle's muzzle jabbed into his ribs cut short his ruminations. He groaned.

"Get your ass in gear," said Tyler, prodding Box in the ribs again.

Tyler and Sammy ushered Box, Marta, and Porter at gunpoint to the quarantine room.

Box was concerned about Pataki. Why had Zodiac singled Pataki out and hived him off from the others? Box had a bad feeling about it. Pataki was the newest member of the camp, but why treat him differently? Was Zodiac going to quarantine Pataki separately? But why? It made no sense. If all of them were carriers, why isolate Pataki in his own room? Carriers couldn't infect each other because they were already infected.

If Zodiac wasn't going to quarantine Pataki, what was Zodiac going to do with him? Would Pataki end up like Gertie? What if Zodiac found out Pataki was working for the CIA? Had Zodiac already found out somehow?

No matter how Box analyzed it, Pataki's treatment filled him with dread. No good could come from it, Box knew. And poor Gertie. What did she do to deserve getting her head blown off? If Zodiac shot her for just being a carrier, what would prevent him from meting out the same fate to Box and the other carriers?

Chapter 57

"Divide and conquer," said Porter inside the quarantine room with Box and Marta. "He wants to separate us from the others so we won't unite against him."

"You don't believe we're carriers?" said Marta.

"Not at all. It was an excuse to prevent us from organizing the others against him. He's afraid of us. He sees us as the ringleaders of the resistance."

"How can you be sure? Maybe we really are carriers."

"It's too pat."

"I'm inclined to agree with you," said Box.

"It's just too damn convenient having only his antagonists ID'd as carriers," said Porter. "Science doesn't work that way. Politics does."

"The problem is, what do the others think?" said Box. "If Zodiac has convinced them we're carriers, they might decide to kill us."

"Kill us?" said Porter, raising his eyebrows. "I don't think they will. I know most of them. They're good people."

"It was good people who put Hitler into power."

"The people here didn't put Zodiac in charge. He took over without their permission."

"Hilda surrendered to him. Didn't she represent the people?"

Porter became worked up. "Hilda made a mistake about Zodiac. After Gertie's brutal murder, I'm sure she realizes that she made a pact with the devil when she surrendered."

"That's all well and good, but we have to realize our lives are in danger now that we've been singled out as carriers."

"We're quarantined. That's it. He won't do anything to us beyond that."

"He just took out Gertie in front of our very eyes. How can you trust him?"

"I don't trust him. But the people will rise up against him if he tries to waste us."

"They didn't rise up after he took out Gertie."

"To tell you the truth, Gertie didn't have a lot of friends here, other than Hilda. They hit it off for some reason. Gertie turned people off."

"I don't like it. He's setting us up."

"Setting us up for what? He's got us locked up so we can't rebel against him. What more does he want?"

Shaking his head Box paced around the room. "We need to make our move. We need to plan our escape. Don't you see what he's doing? He's making us scapegoats by branding us as carriers."

"The people are on our side. They'll help us."

"I was tired of this place a long time ago," said Marta. "I'm for escaping."

Porter thought about it. "What if we get the others to rebel against Zodiac and throw him out?"

"It's too late," said Box. "He's consolidated his power and aligned them against us by declaring us personae non gratae— carriers. How can you rally them to our side now? They're afraid of getting infected by us."

"I refuse to believe they'll turn against us."

"Are you willing to stake your life on it?"

"What's *your* suggestion?"

"We need to escape the warehouse before they whack us."

"Easier said than done. He's got us locked in this room, if you haven't noticed. He's also got armed guards manning the perimeter."

"I still say it's our best bet. If we elect to stay here, our days are numbered."

"You can do what you want, but I'm not onboard. I don't want to desert my people. There's no stigma to being quarantined."

"There is, if they did it because you're a carrier. Carriers are a threat to them."

Porter confronted Box. "Who are you? You don't sound like just anyone. You sound like you know something. What aren't you telling us?"

Porter had caught Box off guard with his last questions. Box wasn't prepared for a confrontation over his identity. Willy-nilly, he couldn't tell Porter his real name and what Pataki had told him about his profession at the CIA. The fewer who knew about it, the better—for their sakes as well as his, decided Box. If Zodiac found out the truth about Box's ID, it would imperil Box's life. Box had to keep his mouth shut.

"I haven't regained my memory," he said. "I don't know what my real name is. Or the nature of my job."

"Hmm. I wonder . . . I think you're holding back on us."

"We can't turn against each other," said Marta, put out. "That's what they want us to do."

"He's in special forces or something."

"What difference does it make?"

At his wits' end, Porter clutched his forehead. "I dunno. Something's not right about him."

"I'm not the one causing our problems," said Box. "It's Zodiac. He's the one in control."

Chapter 58

"I know this isn't a democracy, but I want to know your opinions on what we should do with the carriers," said Zodiac to the audience sitting in front of him, as he stood behind the lectern on the dais.

"And then what?" said Hilda. "You'll kill us, like you killed Gertie?"

"That was a mercy killing," said Zodiac, his voice sincere. "I did it for her own good and for the good of the rest of us. She was a supercarrier. Nobody was safe from infection with her around. None of you need fear giving me your honest opinion."

Hilda harrumphed and crossed her arms over her chest, unconvinced as she sat in the audience looking up at Zodiac, her jaw set, her mouth a compressed white line.

A thin, seventysomething grey-haired woman sitting two rows behind Hilda raised her hand.

"Yes," said Zodiac, pointing to her.

The woman stood up. "I think the carriers need to be kept away from the rest of us. We can't let them near us."

"I agree," said Zodiac. "But what is the best way to isolate them? Do we keep them in the quarantine room? Do we banish them from the compound? What are our options?"

"We can't allow them to get anywhere near us."

The woman took her seat.

A tall, sixtyish guy with a shock of white hair raised his shaking hand dappled with liver spots.

"You, sir," said Zodiac, nodding at the man.

The man got to his feet. "We need to banish them from the camp. It's the only sure way to keep them away from us."

Several members of the audience muttered their agreement.

"What is your name?" said Zodiac.

"Henry."

"Thanks, Henry. The problem is, what if the carriers decide to come back here?"

"Why would they?"

Zodiac pulled a face. "Revenge? Who knows? Maybe to see some friends they left behind."

"I doubt they would come back. They'd know we wouldn't let them back inside."

"If they wanted revenge, nothing would stop them, I'm afraid."

A suet-faced, sixteen-year-old boy wearing thick, black-framed glasses raised his pudgy hand. Zodiac pointed at him.

"What's your name, young man?"

Henry sat down.

The teen stood up. "Arnold."

"Have your say, Arnold," said Zodiac.

"What if we build a special cage for them and keep them locked inside it?" said Arnold, shifting nervously on his feet.

Two whoops of agreement burst from the audience.

Arnold sat down, acknowledging the whoops with a smile, his nerves calmer now.

"We shouldn't treat them like animals in a zoo," said Hilda. "These are human beings we're talking about."

"Arnold's concerned about our welfare, the welfare of the community," said Zodiac. "The community is more important than the carriers. We must do whatever it takes to keep the community safe. What's best for all is best for each of us. Everybody, repeat after me. What's best for all is best for each of us."

"What's best for all is best for each of us," chanted the audience.

"And who decides that?" said Hilda.

"I do," said Zodiac. "I am your leader. I get things done."

"Who elected you?"

"That's irrelevant. What matters is, I'm in charge. Like I said, this isn't a democracy. That said, I want to know your honest opinions about the carriers."

"We don't have the right to treat anyone like animals."

Zodiac ignored Hilda. "The problem is, what if the carriers escaped from their jail cell?"

"They would infect us," said Henry.

"That's right," said Zodiac, pointing at Henry with approval. "Our camp wouldn't be 100 percent safe, if we locked the carriers in a cell. We need the safest option to deal with the carriers. That rules out the quarantine room and a jail cell. The carriers' escape would put us all at risk."

"Then how do we protect ourselves from them?"

"Good question. We've ruled out quarantine, banishment, and permanent incarceration. What's that leave us with?"

"A cure," said Hilda. "What if we cure them?"

"That could be years away. Or it may never happen. Look at cancer. There's no cure for it, and they've been looking for one for lo these many years. Why do you think they'll be able to find a cure for the zombie plague?"

"Why not? They can cure just about everything else."

"You forget. Most of the country was destroyed by nukes and the ensuing fires, not to mention marauding ghouls. All of our science and virology labs have been destroyed and most of our leading scientists have been killed—"

"How do you know?"

"I've been around the country. It's nothing but a wasteland."

"Why should we believe you?"

"Because I'm your leader. That's all that need concern you. The point is, with the country in ruins, who's left to find the cure for the plague?"

"Somebody will come along. Somebody always does. It's not over till every one of us is dead."

"You're living in a dream, Hilda. Dreams can't protect us. We need real answers in the real world. Our decisions now will affect the future, or lack of it, of the human race. We can't wait for a scientist to come along and cure the plague. We might be wiped out by then. We need real answers for real time."

"How do we know the country is as bad off as you say it is? How do we know all the scientists are dead? How—"

"That's enough out of you, Hilda," said Zodiac, chopping the air with his hand. "Let somebody else have a chance to speak."

Diego raised his hand in the audience.

"Holy man, you are recognized," said Zodiac. "Say your piece."

"We have to do the humane thing," said Diego, rising to his feet. "It's the right thing to do."

"Isn't saving our community the right thing to do? How is that not right?"

"Not if it means saving it at the expense of the carriers."

"The well-being of the many is more important than the well-being of the few."

"I disagree. Each man and woman is important, including the carriers. Each one of the carriers is as important as the rest of us. *Any man's death diminishes me.*"

"The whole is more important than the sum of its parts."

"*No man is an island, entire of itself . . . Never send to know for whom the bell tolls—*"

"Preachers," scoffed Zodiac. "I ask you a question, and I get a sermon from John Donne. I'm surrounded by preachers. Preachers and monks. That's all this country is. A nation of preachers and monks. They're all over the place. They have all the answers. They're in government. They're in academia. They tell everyone what to do and what to think and take everybody's money in the bargain. We need to round up the preachers and monks that control the country. You guys hate being alive. So you foist your hate on the rest of us. You're all antilife while you pretend to be prolife. What are we supposed to do, holy man?"

"We quarantine the carriers until we have a cure for them."

"Haven't you been listening? Who's left to find this magical cure? The country's a nuked-out shambles. Where are all the scientists working on these vaccines and cures? Where are they? Hiding in the rubble? Hiding on the moon? Where are their labs? I'll tell you where. They're gone. Destroyed when the government's nukes rained down destruction from the sky," said Zodiac, his voice rising in fervor, his eyes upward.

"You must have faith. God's ways are mysterious. Even if you can't understand them, you must believe. It's not about understanding. It's about believing."

"No matter how big a lie it is, believe it, and everything will be fine. Is that what you're saying, holy man?"

"You don't need to understand to believe and have faith."

"I believe and have faith in what I see with my own eyes, holy man. Why should I believe anything you've dreamed up that nobody else can see?"

"Because it's right. If it's right, it's true."

"Doubletalk. Because you're a preacher, that makes everything you say true?" said Zodiac, his voice dripping with sarcasm. "*J'accuse* Jesuit," he said, pointing his forefinger at Diego. "Monks and preachers everywhere I look." He flourished his sickle over his head. "Your kind are taking over the world ordering people what to do. You can't order me around with your bullshit, holy man. I don't take orders from lying monks and preachers. We can't let the lying preachers and monks take over. We don't believe in your fairy tales and silly dreams, holy man."

"I'm not telling fairy tales. The truth will set you free."

"And you're the only one that knows the truth? What makes you so special? That black cassock you wear? It's just a piece of cloth. You expect me to believe you're better than the rest of us?"

"This has nothing to do with me. It has to do with faith. You must have faith."

"I have faith in *me*," said Zodiac, pointing to himself.

"That's not enough."

"Why am I surrounded by monks?" said Zodiac in exasperation.

"You know I'm right. That's why you're so angry. Your anger comes from frustration at your inability, or your refusal, to accept the truth and do the right thing."

"Meaningless gibberish. You're filling the community with lies. We will not accept lies here. If you can't say anything constructive, you need to sit down."

"Take the log out of your eye that you may see."

"Holy man, you're the one that's blind. You can't even see the nose in front of your face. There's no log in my eye." Zodiac raised his sickle. "I oughta chop you down."

"Chop him down. Chop him down," chanted several in the audience.

"You see, holy man. They agree with me."

"Chop him down. Chop him down."

Diego was going to object, but thought better of it, sensing the mood of the audience, and decided to sit down, becoming anxious thanks to their ominous chanting.

"Then what's *your* answer?" Hilda asked Zodiac.

As one the audience became silent and waited with bated breath for Zodiac's response.

Chapter 59

"My answer is the only answer," said Zodiac. "The only thing that will keep us all 100 percent safe from infection by the carriers." He paused. "The final solution."

All ears, the restless audience became still.

"You heard me right, my friends," he said. "The. Final. Solution."

Nobody rustled in their seats. Quiet prevailed.

"You're not saying what I think you're saying," said Hilda, shattering the silence.

"There's no way around it," said Zodiac. "We have to execute them and burn their corpses into ashes."

The audience hung on every word.

"It's the only sure way to prevent the carriers from infecting anybody else," went on Zodiac. "Do any of you want to suffer the misery of becoming infected and turning into a ghoul? Can you imagine the agony you would have to endure?"

"Mass executions aren't the answer," said Hilda.

"They are if they're the only way to secure the safety of the community."

"I agree," said somebody in the audience.

"Our lives are at stake," said another.

"We have no choice. It's them or us," said another.

"They'll kill all of us without blinking an eye if we let them," said yet another.

Zodiac nodded with approval and raised his fist above his head. "The carriers must be executed."

The audience clapped.

A big guy in his thirties wearing jeans and a red and black tartan lumberjack shirt, sporting a short, dark beard, leapt out of his seat, pumping his fist. "Let's get 'em now. Let's get 'em."

"String 'em up," cried a petite, narrow-shouldered woman with brown eyes, her brown hair in a bun.

"Settle down," said Zodiac, motioning for everyone to hold it down. "This is gonna be an execution, not a lynch mob. We will do it in an orderly fashion."

"What's gotten into you people?" said Hilda, standing up and facing the audience. "Porter's in quarantine. Did you hear me? *Porter*. He's one of us. He's been with us from the get-go when things were hopeless. And now you want to kill him? Where would we be without him?"

"He's a carrier," said Arnold. "He's gonna infect us with plague."

"Hang 'em from the highest tree," said Lumberjack.

"Hilda, I'm warning you, keep your mouth shut or we'll take care of you as a collaborator," said Zodiac.

"Yeah," came a yell from the back row. "Death to collaborators."

"Quisling bitch," cried a woman.

Somebody in the audience hurled a full plastic water bottle at Hilda's head. Hilda ducked in the nick of time. Taken aback by the behavior of her fellow members in the compound, she sat down, visibly rattled.

"Kill the carriers," hollered Arnold.

"And death to murderers," cried Kate Younger. "Death to Earl James."

"Not yet," said Zodiac, raising his fist. "But I promise you, good people," he said, surveying the audience with electric, approving eyes, "the sentence is death, and the carriers will be executed by firing squad." He hammered the air with a violent downward thrust of his fist.

The boisterous sounds of cheers, whistles, applause, and the stamping of feet erupted from the audience, shaking the very foundation of the warehouse.

Groaning, Hilda bowed her head, burying her face in her hands with despair.

Chapter 60

"You're coming with me," Zodiac told Pataki, bounding off the dais.

"Kill the carrier," somebody in the boisterous audience yelled at Pataki.

"Chop him down," came another voice.

A guard frog-marched Pataki behind Zodiac, who stalked across the warehouse into a private room. Two other guards followed them, closing the door behind them.

An operating table with an inch-thick cushion with a long sheet of white paper unrolled on top of it stood in the corner of the room. This particular operating table had leather restraints on either side of it for the patient's arms and similar restraints at one end of the table for the patient's ankles.

"Strap him down," said Zodiac.

Pataki struggled in vain to free himself from the guards' grasps.

"Are you nuts?" said Pataki, grimacing and writhing as the guards restrained him. "Is this how you treat carriers?"

"This is how I treat spies," said Zodiac.

"What are you talking about?"

"One of my men overheard you talking to Box. You told him you worked for our enemy, the CIA."

Pataki felt his heart stop beating, his blood freeze. His face broke into a cold sweat.

"He's lying," he said, remembering Halverson had told him Zodiac hated the government.

"Why would he lie?"

"He wants a promotion. How should I know? Ask him."

"I'm asking you."

"All I can tell you is he's lying."

Zodiac angled across the room, picked up a white towel that lay folded on a bureau, and returned to Pataki.

"Do you know what this is?" said Zodiac.

"A towel."

"Do you need to dry your hands?"

"No."

"Do you work for the government?"

"No."

"Do you work for the CIA?"

"No."

"How do you know Box?"

Pataki shook his head, puzzled. "I met him here."

"That's not what I asked. How do you know him? My guard said you recognized Box."

Pataki's heartbeat shifted into high gear. How much did Zodiac know? he wondered, palms sweaty.

"Do you want to dry your hands?" said Zodiac, raising the towel in his hand.

"No."

"How do you know Box?"

"As usual, your guard is wrong," said Pataki. "I never saw Box before in my life."

"How am I gonna get you to tell me the truth?" said Zodiac, unfolding the towel.

"I am telling you the truth."

One of the guards carried a plastic Sparkletts jug containing a gallon of water to Zodiac.

"Do you want a glass of water?" said Zodiac.

"No."

"Doesn't your throat feel dry?"

"No."

"Good. Because you're not getting one."

Pataki snickered.

"Are you familiar with waterboarding?" said Zodiac.

"I've heard of it," said Pataki, his heartbeat ratcheting up yet again.

As a CIA black-ops agent, he had been trained to expect to be tortured by waterboarding and had been subjected to it. As a member of special forces he had taken SERE training at Fort Bragg to resist torture. Survival, Evasion, Resistance, and Escape. What he really needed to do now was escape.

"Nobody can endure it without talking," said Zodiac. "That's why the CIA uses it on people that lie. In the end, they see the error of their ways and tell the truth."

"The CIA doesn't use waterboarding anymore."

"How would you know that unless you work for them?"

"Like everybody else, I saw it on the news on TV. Back when we had news and TV."

"Then you know what waterboarding is."

"Everybody does. So what?"

Pataki knew what to expect with waterboarding, but he also knew he would not be able to withstand it for long. The suffering was too great. It broke everybody. The terrifying sensations of drowning and helplessness induced by waterboarding could not be withstood. The victim would do anything, say anything, to prevent the torture from continuing.

"The beautiful thing about waterboarding is its simplicity," said Zodiac. "All you need is a towel and a gallon bottle of water. Anybody can do it in their own home. You don't have to go to a hardware store and buy a generator, cables, electrodes, and alligator clips to hook to someone's balls. I understand those alligator clips hurt bad enough by themselves when you clamp 'em onto a guy's gonads, even without the electric charge. Did you ever wonder if a tortured guy could have babies after his balls got fried with electricity? It makes you wonder." He held up the towel, admiring it. "It's amazing. A simple thing like this towel, available in everybody's home, can become a weapon of torture worse than a rack."

"You're wasting your time," said Pataki. "I'm telling you the truth."

He tried to appear relaxed without revealing his anxiety, even as he feared his heart would burst from the gallons of adrenaline shooting through his body. He needed to maintain his bluff. It was his only defense left. Lie.

"Do you know Box?" said Zodiac.

"No."

"What's Box's real name?"

"I have no idea."

"You're lying."

Zodiac laid the towel over Pataki's face.

Dear god, thought Pataki.

The guard lifted the water bottle over Pataki's head.

Chapter 61

Kate stole toward the quarantine room. She didn't see any guards posted near the door. She didn't want anyone to see her there. She had a new knife with her, a steak knife she had commandeered in the cafeteria utensils drawer. She would not let anyone deter her from her mission.

She grasped the doorknob and turned it.

It wouldn't turn. It was locked.

She should have known. She rapped gently on the door.

"Hello," she said, keeping her voice low and looking behind her to make sure no one was watching.

"Hello," said a voice from within the room.

"I have bad news for you."

"What?"

"They're gonna kill all of you."

Silence.

"Why?" said Porter. "That's crazy."

"They're scared of you. They think killing you is the only way to be sure they can save themselves from getting infected."

"It's not the only way. Tell them we'll volunteer to leave the camp."

"They won't listen to what I have to say."

"Why not?"

"Zodiac has roused them to a fever pitch. They want blood."

"Why are you telling us this?" said Porter.

"I want to help you."

"Can you open the door?"

"No. It's locked. Do you know where I can get a key?"

Kate didn't think she was talking to Earl James, her brother's murderer. It sounded somewhat like Porter's voice. But she couldn't be certain. She had heard James's voice only a few times. Plus the door was muting the voice of the guy doing the talking, making it difficult to recognize.

"Hilda should have a key," said the voice.

"OK. When I get the key, I'll let you guys out."

"Who are you?"

Kate decided not to answer. She stole away from the door and set off to find Hilda.

She found Hilda moping in one of the seats in the all but empty makeshift auditorium. She took a seat beside Hilda.

"We need to save the carriers before Zodiac kills them," Kate told Hilda.

Hilda looked up at Kate. "I thought you were one of the bloodthirsty ones that want them executed."

"They can't help it if they're carriers. It's not their fault. Why should they be punished for it?"

"I'm glad you see the light. Everybody else here"—Hilda shook her head in despair—"why, they're turning into animals. I don't recognize them anymore. I can't understand it."

"Do you have the key to the quarantine room?"

"I gave my key to Zodiac."

Kate slumped her shoulders in disappointment.

"However, I have a spare," said Hilda.

Kate perked up. "That's what I want to hear."

"If only I can remember what I did with it," said Hilda, frowning in thought.

"You must have put it in a safe place," said Kate, trying to jog Hilda's memory.

"I don't think I'd put it in my purse, because that's where I kept the original. I would've put it somewhere else, in case I lost my purse." Hilda paused. "I'm not sure we should let the carriers out, though. After all, they are carriers and can infect the rest of us."

"If we don't let them out, Zodiac will kill them."

"You have a point. We have to get them out of there. We should help them escape the camp. That's what we should do. That way they can't infect any of us, and Zodiac can't murder them."

"Right. All we need is the key."

So I can kill the murderer Earl James, thought Kate.

Diego greeted them, darting his eyes back and forth uneasily. "I thought he was gonna kill me for a second."

"Nobody's safe with Zodiac in charge," said Hilda.

"The worst thing is, he's got everyone on his side."

Hilda nodded grimly. "He knows how to work a crowd."

217

"He's a natural-born showman."

"He's a rabble-rouser, is what he is."

"What can we do? If we don't do something, he'll kill all the carriers."

"When you figure it out, let me know. Come, Kate, let's go to my room. I think I know where it is."

"Where what is?" said Diego.

Hilda and Kate departed, leaving Diego standing, a baffled expression on his face.

"I'm glad you didn't tell him about the key," Kate told Hilda.

"I don't trust anyone anymore," said Hilda. "Not after Zodiac got everybody on his side. We have to do this on the qt."

"Agreed."

Kate didn't want anyone getting in the way of her killing Earl James. The preacher might try to knock her plans into a cocked hat if she told him. Even Hilda might try to stop her from accomplishing her mission, if she found out its true nature. *If only Hilda can find that key.*

Hilda entered her room, found her bureau, opened its top drawer, and withdrew her sewing box. Opening the box she rummaged through it and dredged out a key.

"Here it is," she said, holding up the key to the quarantine room, elated. "I knew I had the spare in my room. I'm glad you reminded me," she said, turning to face Kate, who, standing behind her, scoffed up a lamp on the bureau and brought the lamp's base down on the back of Hilda's head with a sickening thud.

Groaning, blacking out, Hilda felt her knees buckle and collapsed to the floor.

Kate hunkered down over Hilda, pried the key loose from Hilda's fingers, clutched it, and left the room, easing the door shut behind her to prevent anyone from seeing Hilda's unconscious figure. About to leave, she balked. She hoped she hadn't killed Hilda. She had nothing against Hilda, but she couldn't let Hilda know what she was really going to do after she unlocked the quarantine room. Hilda, no doubt, would have tried to stop her.

Nobody seemed to understand that the murderer Earl James must die. Her blouse was hanging untucked over her jeans to hide the knife snugged inside her waistband behind the small of her back.

She had to get going. She had more important things to worry about than Hilda.

Chapter 62

Kate reached the quarantine room door without incident. She decided she had better alert the carriers that she, not Zodiac, was the one unlocking their door. Otherwise, they might try to jump her.

She rapped softly on the door.

"It's me again," she said.

She couldn't let Earl James get away with murdering her brother. It broke her heart every time she thought of poor Cole dying at the hands of the murderer Earl James. She couldn't shed any more tears over Cole's premature death now. She had to steel her heart to seek vengeance against his killer.

"Do you have the key?" said the voice behind the door.

If it was Earl James, she could stab him as soon as she unlocked and opened the door. No way would he expect to be attacked from someone who had come pretending to help him escape, she decided. A surprise attack was always the best kind of offense. If it *was* James, she needed to get out her knife so she would be ready to stab him as soon as she set eyes on him. She peeked over her shoulder to make sure nobody was watching her.

On the other hand, if it wasn't the murderer Earl James who opened the door, she would expose her hand by letting the guy see the shiv, and James could be lurking in the back of the room out of striking distance. Maybe it was best to wait till she saw who opened the door before she got out her shiv.

She inserted Hilda's key into the door lock. She twisted the key. She was so filled with hatred for Earl James that she wanted to shove open the door in a burst of fury, lunge into the room, and cut his throat. She needed to put a lid on her hatred. If she flew into the room like a deranged maenad brandishing a knife, she would alert the carriers and put them on guard.

If she stole inside the room, without a weapon in her hand, the carriers would welcome her with open arms. And then she could shove her knife into Earl James's spine.

She nudged open the door, pricking up her ears for any sounds inside the room.

She started when she felt a hand on her shoulder.

"Kate, what are you doing?" said Zodiac, standing behind her.

"Uh—uh—I—uh—one of the carriers said he needed medical attention," Kate managed to croak through a hoarse throat, a shiver running down her spine. "I—uh—I wanted to check on him and see if I should get the doctor."

"Nobody's supposed to enter this room without my permission. You're putting your life at risk by entering here. These people are contagious."

"He—uh—he sounded like he was in pain."

"How do you know it's not a trick to get you to open the door so the carriers can escape and infect us?"

"He sounded like he was dying."

Zodiac eyed the key in the door lock. "Where did you get that key?"

"From Hilda."

"She didn't tell me she had another key to this room. Maybe . . ." Zodiac paused in thought, his face expressionless.

"Maybe what?"

"Maybe I should let you join them. How would you like being quarantined with the carriers?"

"I don't want to get infected."

"I have a good mind to throw you in there with them."

Zodiac's walkie-talkie squawked. He answered it.

"The ghouls are attacking, boss," said the guard at the gate. "Do you copy? Over."

"Roger. How many?"

"A shitload of 'em."

"I want numbers."

"Hundreds that I can see. There may be lots more inside the woods headed this way."

"Make sure the fence is juiced."

"We checked. The genny's on. The alligator clips on the fence are secure."

"Roger. I'm on my way. Over and out." Zodiac turned to Tyler, who was standing behind him with Pataki and several armed guards. "We got company. We need soldiers at the fence."

"Got it, boss."

"The carriers are good fighters. I want them at the fence with us."

"They'll infect us," said Tyler with concern.

"Not if we're outside. The wind will blow away their spores."

Zodiac withdrew his pistol from its holster on his belt and flung open the quarantine room door to confront the carriers.

"Aren't you afraid we'll infect you?" said Porter, sarcastically.

"Just keep your distance. We need you guys at the fence. Swarms of ghouls are attacking."

"We're gonna need guns," said Box.

"You'll get what I give you."

Chapter 63

Box could make out Pataki standing with Zodiac's men behind Zodiac. Wan, Pataki could barely stand. He looked like he had gotten the shit kicked out of him. And yet Box didn't see a bruise on him. Pataki's hands were shivering at his sides, his eyes blank. Box tried to catch Pataki's eye without success. Pataki's mind was elsewhere, unfocused and wandering.

"What are you looking at?" said Zodiac.

"Nothing," said Box.

Box caught Kate Younger glowering at him.

"Gather the members of the camp together," Zodiac told Tyler. "I need to speak to them."

"You got it, boss," said Tyler, and left to get the others.

"Come out of there to the meeting hall," Zodiac told Porter, Box, and Marta.

Box made his way toward Pataki, eager to speak to him.

"What happened?" Box asked Pataki, keeping his voice low.

His hair bedraggled, his eyes wandering, Pataki muttered gibberish, as they walked toward the meeting hall.

"What did he do to you?" said Box.

More gibberish from Pataki.

Box could reach no other conclusion than that Zodiac had tortured Pataki, even though he didn't see any bruises on him. From the drawn looks of Pataki, Box was concerned that Pataki might have confessed he was a CIA agent for the government. Did that mean Pataki had told Zodiac Box's real name was Halverson and that he, too, worked for the CIA? If that was the case, Box's life was in jeopardy. Zodiac detested the government and anybody who worked for it.

Box wondered if he should make a run for it. Armed guards were marching on his flanks. He didn't like his chances. Not now. He didn't doubt Pataki's ability as a CIA agent, but he had to assume Pataki had spilled the beans about him.

Box reached the meeting hall, where the camp members were taking their seats and Zodiac was mounting the podium.

"Good people, we are under attack," said Zodiac behind the lectern. "The infected are at the gates."

The crowd murmured apprehensively.

"But it is not only from without that we are under attack," went on Zodiac. "We are being attacked from within. Yes, that's right. We have a government spy in our midst. A CIA agent sent to destroy us." Zodiac pointed to Pataki, who was standing beside Tyler. "The newcomer Dean Pataki is a CIA spy." Zodiac paused for effect. He heard oohs and aahs from the audience. "We welcomed him to our camp with open arms, and look what we got. A government informer. The government hates us. They tried to nuke us, and they killed millions of good law-abiding Americans. But we are some of the few that survived their attack. When they found out we're still alive, they sent one of their secret agents to destroy us." Zodiac waved his sickle toward Pataki. "The spy has confessed everything to me."

Box felt his pulse race. *Everything*? Did that mean Pataki had revealed Box's true identity to Zodiac? Was Zodiac going to torture him next?

"He must be punished for his crimes, of course," said Zodiac. "If anyone else knows of any other government spies here, let me know. Their nukes couldn't kill us. Now they're sending their spies. We will not let them destroy us."

"Chop him down," chanted several members of the audience. "Chop him down."

"Don't worry. I have a different kind of punishment awaiting the treacherous spy. He'll wish he never spied on us. His death won't be pleasant, I assure you."

"Death to spies," came the chant. "Death to spies."

His palms sweaty, Box had to figure out a way to save Pataki's neck. They needed to get back to Mount Weather and save the government from collapsing.

"We need to help Pataki," Box whispered to Marta.

"What happened to him?" she said. "He looks like a zombie."

"They tortured him."

"Because he's a carrier?"

"I don't know why," said Box, even though he suspected the reason had to do with Pataki's being a CIA agent, though how Zodiac had tumbled to Pataki's secret was beyond him.

"Does that mean they're gonna torture us, too? They're gonna turn us all into vegetables like Pataki."

They might torture him, decided Box. He doubted they would torture Marta or Porter.

"Not unless Zodiac thinks we're hiding something from him," said Box.

Box didn't like his chances. If Pataki had talked, Zodiac knew Box was really Halverson, a CIA agent, and would want to interrogate him, or, to put it bluntly, torture him. It depended on how much Pataki had told Zodiac and what Zodiac had specifically asked him. Box had taken CIA courses on torture at the Farm and also had undergone SERE training at Fort Bragg. He knew it was impossible to withstand torture indefinitely. Especially waterboarding. Which didn't leave a trace on the victim's body. Pataki without a mark on him, but with his brains scrambled. They had waterboarded Pataki, decided Box.

"Spies work for the government that's trying to kill us," said Zodiac from the podium. "The government and its agents are enemies of the people. What do we do to spies, good people?"

"Death to spies," the audience chanted. "Death to spies."

Zodiac nodded yes. "The spy Pataki will die a gruesome death. Right now we are under attack by the infected. We must defend the gates. We will fight the ghouls to the death."

Zodiac leapt off the podium and barreled toward the front door, ever-present sickle in hand.

Chapter 64

As soon as Zodiac emerged from the warehouse and set foot in the parking lot, he beheld hordes of ghouls converging on the gate in the chain-link fence.

"Bring me the catapult, Tyler," he said.

Tyler darted across the parking lot to retrieve the SUV that had the catapult hooked up to its tailgate.

Zodiac raised his walkie-talkie to his lips. "Jackman? Over."

"Jackman here, boss. I copy. Over."

"Tell your men at the gate to open fire. Over."

"Roger."

The guards at the gate fell to blasting the invading ghouls with their AR-15s. The ghouls kept coming, trampling the bullet-riddled bodies of their dead comrades underfoot.

With the diversion of the ghouls' attack, this might be a good time to escape, decided Box. On the other hand, how far could he hope to get through the swarms of invaders assaulting the camp? There were hundreds of them out there. And thousands more headed this way, if Pataki could be believed. Box decided to be patient and wait for a better opportunity.

Tyler drove a black Chevy Suburban at speed to Zodiac and screeched to a halt. He clambered out of the driver's seat.

"What's the range of the catapult?" asked Zodiac, amid the cracks of gunfire at the gate.

"Three hundred feet, more or less," answered Tyler.

"That'll do it. Aim the catapult at the road in front of the gate where the ghouls are."

Nodding, Tyler got Sammy to help him unhook the catapult from the back of the Suburban and turn it toward the gate.

"She's all set, boss," said Tyler.

"Prime the arm."

Tyler and Sammy strained to pull back the catapult's arm preparing it for firing.

"What payload do we use in the basket?" said Tyler.

"Not what. Who."

"Huh?"

"The spy Pataki," said Zodiac.

"What?"

"Bind his wrists so he doesn't try to escape. Then dump him in the basket."

Tyler produced a plastic zip tie and bound Pataki's wrists. Pataki was still out of it, and didn't know what was going on. Tyler frog-marched him to the catapult and with Sammy's help hauled Pataki into the basket. Pataki ended up sitting crammed awkwardly into the basket, which had a rope net for its bottom, his legs sticking out.

Even though his mind was addled, Pataki sensed his danger and tried to extricate himself from the basket, but because of his awkward position and bound wrists he didn't make any headway.

With the intention of helping Pataki out of his predicament, Box bolted toward the catapult basket.

Zodiac whipped out his Glock 19 from his holster and trained it on Box. "Don't move, Halverson."

Box froze at the sight of the Glock's barrel directed at him, chilled to the bone. It wasn't just the sight of the gun but the sound of his real name that gave him a turn. He pretended otherwise.

"What did you call me?" he said.

"I called you by your real name. Chad Halverson, black-ops agent and hit man for the CIA."

Box exchanged glances with Pataki. Box saw a look of regret mixed with fear in Pataki's eyes.

"You're mistaken," Box told Zodiac.

"I'm not mistaken, and you know it. I have plans for you. Do you want to end up like your buddy Pataki?"

"I don't know anything about the CIA or this Halverson, whoever he is."

"Don't you get it? Your buddy talked. He confessed. I know everything. Lying isn't gonna do you a bit of good."

"He's mistaking me for someone else. I'm Earl James."

"I told you he was," said Kate, scowling at Box. "He murdered my brother."

"He's lying to save his skin," said Zodiac with a mordant laugh. "He's not Earl James. We'll talk about this later." His face grave, he turned to Tyler. "Fire the catapult."

The blood drained from Pataki's face at Zodiac's words.

Tyler obeyed.

The catapult hurled a squirming Pataki over the chain-link fence into the scrum of ghouls congregating in front of the gate. Pataki landed on two of the ghouls, knocking them to the ground. A half dozen ghouls in the vicinity converged on Pataki and commenced tearing his flesh with their decomposing snaggleteeth. One of the ghouls went for Pataki's throat. Pataki screamed in agony, blood jetting out of his carotid artery and arcing fifteen feet through the air.

"Death to spies," said Zodiac, relishing the spectacle of Pataki's mutilation at the hands of the flesh eaters.

Bastard, thought Box, seething. He struggled to bridle his desire to rip Zodiac's face off with his bare hands.

Chapter 65

Box picked up on Kate making her way toward him, her eyes burning with animosity. She lunged at his side with a shiv in her hand. He parried her thrust with a swipe of his arm.

"Earl James must die," she said, taking another swipe at him with her shiv.

"That's not Earl James, you idiot," said Zodiac. "Shut up, bitch, and die."

He shot her in the chest. She groaned. He shot her in the forehead. She dropped.

Box was surprised Zodiac had saved his life, but he didn't trust the man and wanted him dead, burning to avenge Pataki's brutal and senseless murder.

Kate lay motionless on her belly on the asphalt.

"Crazy woman," said Zodiac, leering at her corpse.

He used his foot to flip her onto her back so he could make sure she was dead.

Box saw her knife lying next to her limp hand.

"Not a good idea," said Zodiac, aiming his Glock at Box. "A knife against a gun."

Box said nothing, thinking of the miserable end Pataki had met courtesy of Zodiac.

"Anyway, you should be thanking me, instead of trying to waste me," said Zodiac. "You'd be dead with Kate's shiv sticking in your belly if it wasn't for me."

He ordered one of his men to retrieve Kate's knife.

"I know what you're thinking, Halverson," said Zodiac. "You're thinking I'm gonna put you next in the catapult's basket and cast you to the ghouls."

"I'm not Halverson."

"You can stop with that fake amnesia routine. It's getting old. Was that the cover story the CIA gave you—a guy pretending to be an amnesiac? Is that the best they could do? What is your mission? Did they send you here to whack me?"

"Nobody sent me anywhere."

Box still couldn't recall how he got into the desert or why. He kept glimpsing a ghostlike blonde wearing a white dress walking on the sand as if she was gliding across it. He didn't know who she was or why he kept seeing her in his dreams and in his mind while he was awake. *She must have a name.*

"Give me one good reason I shouldn't put you in the catapult next?" said Zodiac.

"I'm not Halverson."

"Don't you get tired of lying?"

Box said nothing.

"You do know I can torture the truth out of you if you refuse to talk," said Zodiac, twirling his sickle in his hand.

Box said nothing.

"You'll end up a vegetable like Pataki. In which case I'll have to feed you to the ghouls because you'll be useless to me."

Box said nothing.

He wondered if torture would succeed in getting the truth out of him, even though he had amnesia. Could torture break through the blockade in his mind that was preventing him from remembering what had happened to him in the desert?

"Tell me the truth," said Zodiac. "Did the CIA send you here to whack me?"

"No."

"Does the CIA know about me?"

"How should I know?"

"How did they find out about me?"

"I don't know anything about the CIA."

"You're not worried I'll put you in the catapult?"

"I can't tell you what I can't remember. I can't remember how I got in the desert."

"No matter. I got different plans for you. I need your knowledge. I need you to tell me the way to Mount Weather so I can bring down the corrupt government that's blowing apart our great country. Tyler?"

"Here, boss," said Tyler.

"Put Kate in the catapult and throw her to the ghouls."

"Won't she turn into one of those things if they get to her?"

"Not with a bullet in her brain." Zodiac trained his Glock on Kate's head, which already had a bullet hole in it, and put a slug between her eyes. Her head jerked on impact with the lead. "Maybe if we feed them, they'll leave the rest of us alone."

"Gimme a hand, Sammy," said Tyler.

Tyler and Sammy hauled Kate's corpse to the catapult and tossed her into its basket. They catapulted her into the ghouls massing in front of the gate. She landed on a sixtysomething grey-haired female ghoul in an electric wheelchair. Stunned at first by the impact of Kate's body hitting her head, the ghoul noshed on the fresh meat bestowed on her lap. The surrounding ghouls converged on Kate and commenced tearing her flesh to shreds in a feeding frenzy.

Box eyed the gate with concern. The problem was, there were many hundreds more of the things shambling out of the woods toward the chain-link fence, dragging their feet on the ground raising clouds of dust, almost as thick as the sandstorm that had blown through earlier.

One or two fresh corpses wasn't going to feed all of them, he knew. They would finish picking Kate's bones in no time.

Zodiac noticed the same thing.

Several of the flesh eaters grabbed the chain-link fence and shivered as electricity shot through their deceased bodies, igniting their decrepit flesh.

"I'm not liking the looks of this," said Zodiac, scoping out the hordes of attacking creatures. He turned to Tyler. "Lob some mortar shells into the bogeys."

"We only got three shells left," said Tyler, his face sweaty from his having hauled Kate to the catapult. He wiped away the sweat under his nose with the back of his hand.

"That all? Hmm. Fire all of them."

Two female ghouls clutched the chain-link fence and fried on the electrified metal links, their mouths rictuses of agony, their hair standing on end. The mephitic stench of their burning flesh was overpowering.

"And get me the flamethrower," he said. "We're heading to the front lines, boys. We're gonna barbecue us some ghouls."

Chapter 66

Tyler and Sammy fired the first shell from the mortar into the marauding ghouls. The explosion flung mutilated ghouls and their severed body parts into the air in a fountain of dirt.

"You can't help but hit those things. There are so many of them," said Zodiac, eyes beaming with delight at the sight of the carnage inflicted by the blast. "Fire two."

Tyler and Sammy unleashed the second mortar shell at the invaders.

A dozen ghouls erupted into the air as the shell detonated in their midst. They arced like fireworks from the center of the blast.

"It's raining ghouls, huh, girls," said Zodiac with approval. "Shove the third shell down their throats."

The shell whistled through the air. Several of the ghouls looked up at it wondering what it was. It landed among a congested scrum of the shambling flesh eaters and blew them apart. Body parts and clods of dirt showered down on the remaining mass of ghouls swarming toward the fence.

A tall male ghoul wearing a toupee that didn't fit properly grabbed the fence and got a shot of electricity for his troubles turning his face into a mask of smoking pain, his body quivering like a sheet on a clothesline in a stiff gust of wind.

"Get the flamethrower, Tyler," said Zodiac.

Tyler sprinted across the parking lot into the warehouse, retrieved the flamethrower, and returned to Zodiac.

"Ah," said Zodiac, gripping the flamethrower, "let's lay down the law to those suckers."

He stalked to the front gate, where the guards were strafing the ghouls with their AR-15s set on full auto. A writhing mass of decomposing bodies undulated toward the perimeter, the ghouls packed together with barely enough room to move, holding their dead comrades up by their very proximity to the bullet-riddled, lifeless bodies and bearing them forward with them toward the fence in a writhing mass of death and destruction bent on the single-minded purpose of consuming living human flesh.

The guards at the gate carpeted the mob with AR-15 slugs. But the swarm kept undulating toward the fence as a juggernaut of death.

"Take care of Suzie Q," Zodiac told Tyler, handing him the sickle. "And don't let Halverson out of your sight."

"Where's he gonna go, boss?" said Tyler. "We're surrounded by dweebs."

"Just keep your eyes on him. These CIA guys are tricky."

Zodiac carried the flamethrower up the tower and trained it on the army of ghouls.

"Time to get torched," he said.

Grinning with a kind of mad glee, he raked the creatures with a blast from the flamethrower. Putrescent heads burst in the heat of the flame. Hair and clothes ignited and smoked. Yet the unstoppable mass churned forward. As long as some of the reanimated dead were living they kept grinding forward.

"Say hello to Godzilla," said Zodiac.

He squeezed the trigger and unleashed another blast of flame at the creatures, welding some of them together in their death throes, as the nauseating and suffocating reek of their burning rotting flesh charged the air.

The members of the camp defending the fence coughed on the sickening stench, but held their positions. Those without guns carried baseball bats, shovels, pickaxes, or whatever tool they could find in the warehouse. They were ready if the ghouls trampled over the fence.

Still the fence held. The ghouls that managed to reach it and clasp it died as sparking electricity grilled their bodies. They hung like slabs of gangrenous meat on the fence, memento mori to the continuing onslaught of ghouls.

Zodiac picked up on a male ghoul in his twenties with long curly black hair and a mustache crawling over the carcasses of two rows of smoking ghouls hanging on the chain-link fence. To Zodiac's annoyance and surprise, the ghoul wasn't frying from an electric shock. The ghoul hadn't touched the fence thanks to the insulation provided by the dead ghouls he was crawling over. Since the ghouls' carcasses weren't conductors of electricity, the living ghoul kept on climbing and was heading toward the top of the fence.

Zodiac drew a bead on the ghoul with his flamethrower and squeezed the trigger. A golden flame spat out of the muzzle at the ghoul and licked the ghoul's head, igniting his face and hair. Zodiac ran the flame down the rest of the ghoul's body, engulfing it in flames. Writhing, the ghoul burned to death.

"Shit," said Zodiac, squeezing the trigger without effect as the flame died out. "I'm out of napalm."

Chapter 67

Zodiac carried the flamethrower down the guard tower.

"We got a problem," he told Tyler.

"You need more napalm?"

"It's not just that. There are too many carcasses hanging on the fence. They're acting as insulation preventing the new attackers from being electrocuted. The attackers are climbing over the bodies without frying because they're not touching the fence."

"What can we do?"

"We need to launch a sortie out of the gate to clear the stiffs off the fence."

"The members of the sortie will get slaughtered by the ghouls."

"Not if they defend themselves. I'm not sending them out unarmed."

Standing a dozen-odd feet from Zodiac, Hilda shot a bolt from her crossbow into a female fortysomething ghoul in a grime-streaked yellow dress who was shambling toward the gate, her head tilted to the side like she was trying to look at the sky, bite marks on her face, half of her nose missing. Hilda's bolt struck the ghoul in the forehead, felling the creature, who stumbled two steps forward and plunged to the ground on its belly.

"You're pretty handy with that bow, huh, Hilda?" said Zodiac.

"I wasn't born yesterday," said Hilda.

Zodiac approached her. "I need someone to lead a sortie out the gate to clear the dead ghouls that got fried on the fence. The other ghouls are climbing over the bodies without getting electrocuted. They're gonna climb over the fence into our camp any minute if we don't clear the fence. How does that sound to you?"

"You want me to commit suicide."

"No, no. I'll give you help. I'm not sending you out there alone. Halverson and Porter will go with you. Halverson and Porter, come over here. And Marta, you too."

"Are you talking to me?" said Box.

"You're the only Halverson here."

"I'm not Halverson."

"Knock off the I'm-not-Halverson routine and get over here."

Box, Porter, and Marta angled toward Zodiac, not eager to find out why they were summoned.

"I want Hilda to lead a sortie out the gate and clear the bodies off the fence," said Zodiac. "I want you three to go with her."

"Why can't we clear off the bodies from here?" said Box. "We can poke them off with garden tools and pry bars."

"Because I want you to drag the stiffs away from the fence so the ghouls can't use them as steps to get over the fence."

"We'll need guns."

"Do you think I'm an idiot? I'm not giving you a piece, Halverson. You're a government agent, an enemy of the people. A CIA hit man, for Chrissake."

"You expect me to go out there with just my bare hands?"

"No. Take a baseball bat with you or any tool." Zodiac snatched a pickaxe from a camp member standing nearby and tossed it to Box. "Here, take this."

"How about that flamethrower for me?" said Porter.

"That's mine," said Zodiac.

"Then I'll take a gun."

"No pieces. I don't want you guys trying to make a run for it. Especially you, Halverson."

"Why would we try to run away into an army of ghouls?" said Porter.

"Because you're carriers, and you know we're gonna have to deal with you when this is over."

"Then why should we help you at all?"

Zodiac whipped out his Glock from his holster. "Because if you don't, I'll shoot you where you stand."

"You're gonna shoot us anyway as carriers."

"I'm giving you a chance to save yourselves. If you succeed in your mission, I might decide to spare your lives." Zodiac eyed Marta. "Marta, you go with them, and I might spare your life, too."

"There are hundreds of those things out there," said Marta.

"That's why we need you to clear the fence." Zodiac surveyed the camp members who were constellated around him and carrying tools for weapons. "You there, give Marta your cold chisel."

A fiftyish woman with short brown hair with scarlet highlights, who was wearing tortoiseshell-framed glasses, was holding a cold chisel. She handed it to Marta.

Porter found an old toxic lead pipe lying on the ground where a camp member had dropped it. He picked up the pipe and hammered it against his open palm a few times.

"This'll do," he said. "If a blow from this pipe doesn't kill the thing, the lead will."

He inspected his palm and wiped it off on his trousers to make sure it didn't have any lead on it.

"That crossbow isn't gonna work in CQB," Box told Hilda. "You're not gonna have time to reload with ghouls jam-packed around you."

"He's right," said Zodiac. He scanned the knot of members around him again. "Holy man, give Hilda your screwdriver."

"I don't think this mission is a good idea," said Diego.

"You don't, huh? Maybe you wanna go with them?"

"I'm not a carrier."

"Why does that exclude you from a sortie?"

"The others you chose are carriers."

"Hilda isn't."

"You're forcing them to commit suicide."

"Shut up with that nonsense. Are you handy with any kind of weapon?"

"No. I'm a man of peace. The endless killing won't solve anything."

"The ghouls are already dead. How can you kill something that's already dead?"

"Then why are we killing them?"

"Because they'll infect us and kill us if we don't. Understand?"

"Peace is the answer, not endless war."

"Peace doesn't work against a bloodthirsty mob of ghouls. Give Hilda your screwdriver or you're elected to take her place in the sortie."

Diego offered his screwdriver to Hilda, who accepted it.

"The killing must stop," Diego told Zodiac.

"Tell that to the ghouls," said Zodiac. "And see where it gets you."

"Killing isn't the answer."

"Are you forgetting who took your arm, holy man?"

"I want it on record I'm against the endless killing."

"On record, huh? You think they're gonna hold Nuremberg trials after the apocalypse and you don't want the judges to convict you of murder? Dream on, holy man."

Zodiac looked up at the fence, saw a ghoul climbing over dead bodies strung on it, and with his Glock plugged the ghoul between the eyes before it had a chance to get over the fence into the compound. The dead ghoul slid down the layer of corpses welded to the fence.

"Hilda, gather your group together and make your sortie," he said. "We don't have any time to waste. Pluck those Kentucky fried ghouls off the fence."

Chapter 68

A bloodred sun was setting peeking out behind ragged clouds that were skating across the icy blue sky when Hilda and her squad ventured out of the gate. Guards laid down cover fire raking the ghouls with AR-15 slugs carving a path of corpses in the attacking swarm. Box took point, marching over the multitude of corpses, their twisted bodies and shattered heads strewn on the ground, flies buzzing over them.

His lips chewed off, a heavyset forty-two-year-old three-hundred-pound guy with a cropped haircut and tattoo sleeves on bulky arms that emerged from a torn blood-smeared white T lumbered over the carpet of corpses toward Box, slobbering on himself.

Box raised his pickaxe above his head and brought it down hard on the heavyset guy's head, cleaving his skull and brain in half, his skull sounding like a watermelon cracking open. The point of the pickaxe kept going till it penetrated the creature's throat and down into the trachea. Box yanked out the pickaxe, tearing out the trachea with it. He leered at the trachea. Lowering the pickaxe he stepped on the trachea and toed it off the pick end.

"Halverson," yelled Zodiac from the guard tower.

Box craned around and looked up behind him.

Zodiac pointed his forefinger and middle finger at his eyes then pointed them at Box's face.

Zodiac's meaning was clear, decided Box. It would be foolhardy to attempt to escape at this time with Zodiac watching his every move.

Box trudged on the path of corpses to the perimeter of the chain-link fence. Scores of ghouls were shambling across the road toward him, extending their arms in front of them as though they could already feel Box in their clutches so certain were they of consuming his flesh.

A scrawny teenage girl in skintight jeans staggered toward him, growling and salivating, her mouth watering for the taste of raw human flesh. A limpid string of saliva depended from the

239

corner of her lips all the way down to her chest like a spider's silk strand.

Box heaved the pickaxe above his head and slammed it down into the girl's skull. As the girl dropped to her knees with a broken head leaking brains, Box worked his way past her over two layers of fresh cadavers that lay supine on the ground, their white eyes staring eerily up at him.

Hilda took out an eightysomething, swarthy, white-haired codger wearing a Sikh's burnt orange turban and round, wire-rimmed spectacles whose lenses were so filthy she wondered how he could see anything through them. She plunged her screwdriver through one of the creature's glass lenses, fracturing the safety glass and penetrating his eye. She buried the screwdriver up to its hilt into the codger's white eye, penetrating his brain and dropping him where he stood. She jerked out her screwdriver dripping with brain matter.

Standing before her, Box snagged the leg of one of the ghouls on the second layer of ghouls welded to the fence, gave it a good yank, and hauled its burnt-to-a-crisp body off the fence, its charred fingers breaking off and remaining hanging like talons on two of the chain links. Box dragged the corpse away from the fence. He was surprised at its lightness, the only thing left of its fire-ravaged body its skeleton, which tipped the scales at less than thirty pounds. If nothing else, it would make his job of clearing the fence easier. If only the sortie squad could keep fending off the attacking ghouls and give him enough time to work on the fence.

Careful not to touch the live links of the fence, he pried another charred ghoul corpse from the fence, which hissed and sparked, and heaved it five feet away. He wondered if the so-called spores sloughed off by the skin or exhaled by the breath of the ghouls could infect him after the corpse had been consumed in fire. He doubted it. The burned ghouls weren't breathing and their skin had burned into ashes in the fire. Whatever spores had been on the ghouls had been cremated along with their festering flesh. He wasn't going to worry about being infected by the torched ghouls.

Porter came up behind him, brandishing his lead pipe.

Box saw the reason.

A male ghoul almost seven feet tall with one ear chewed off wearing tattered green surgeon's scrubs was slogging toward Box, aiming to grab Box's head in its mitt, its mouth gaping, exposing its jagged, broken teeth.

Porter closed in on the creature swinging. He clobbered the ghoul's head with the lead pipe, rearranging the surgeon's face. But the pipe hadn't penetrated to the ghoul's brain. The ghoul kept coming.

Marta leapt into action, kicking the ghoul in the kneecap, slowing its progress, forcing it to hobble.

Porter cursed and swung his pipe again, putting all of his weight into the blow. The pipe crashed down on the surgeon's head splitting its massive skull. Porter felt the pipe meet mushy brain matter. He drove the pipe deeper into the mush and knew he had dealt a mortal blow to the creature. The ghoul crumpled to the ground, landing on a bed of corpses.

Box flashed a thumbs up to Porter and Marta. He heard voices inside the compound.

"We're running out of ammo," yelled Tyler.

"Cease fire," cried Zodiac from the guard tower.

Chapter 69

Box eyed the horde of ghouls plodding toward the fence, his apprehension mounting.

"Zodiac's throwing us to the dogs," said Porter. "Without cover fire, we're as good as dead."

"There are too many of these things for us to handle by ourselves," said Marta, driving her cold chisel through the temple of a cockeyed blonde middle-aged ghoul.

She yanked out her brain-smeared cold chisel from the creature's cracked skull and fought her way toward Box, dispatching a scraggy teenage male ghoul by thrusting her cold chisel through its ear canal and into its brain. Surprising her the ghoul jerked its arms toward her in a reflex movement, not knowing it was dead. She dodged the arms, but the creature was already dead as it dropped to the carpet of ghouls that littered the ground.

"Does he want us to die out here?" said Hilda.

"He could care less what happens to us," said Porter, wielding his lead pipe to bust a ten-year-old male ghoul's head sporting a beanie.

"We need to pry more stiffs off the fence," said Box.

"How can we do anything while these things keep coming at us from behind?" said Porter, felling a fat bald fiftysomething ghoul, its filthy pants hanging halfway down its butt, with a blow to its head from his pipe.

Box grabbed a foot of one of the corpses burned on the fence and gave it a good yank. He tossed the charred ghoul six feet from the fence, hitting an approaching thirtyish male ghoul in a tattered Hugo Boss bespoke navy blue suit in his thighs, slowing his advance.

Marta bolted toward the stunned besuited creature and jammed her cold chisel into his eye, driving the shank through the ghoul's brain, terminating him. She whipped the cold chisel out from his head as he toppled forward on his face, the shank dripping gouts of brains.

Box and Hilda each hauled ghoul corpses from the fence.

"Whatever you do don't touch the fence," said Hilda.

Box felt one of the ghouls breathing down the back of his neck. A frisson of fear ran down his spine. He knew he had only seconds to act. A thirtyish bearded one-eyed ghoul was standing inches behind him.

Box wheeled around, grabbed the ghoul by the arm, and flung it into the electrified fence. Sparks jumped from the fence as the ghoul sizzled on it, its body spasming and smoking. Box coughed on the reek that emanated from the ghoul's frying flesh.

He heard a whoosh overhead, looked up, and saw a streak of fire arcing into the middle of the ghouls. Zodiac had reloaded the flamethrower and was throwing down cover fire. The flamethrower checked the ghouls' advance for the moment.

"I guess he found the rest of the napalm," said Porter.

"Let's pry these bodies off the fence," said Hilda, grimacing at the burnt creatures welded to the chain links.

Porter and Marta pitched in, as well as Box, dragging the burnt remains of the ghouls from the fence. It was a time-consuming job.

Box heard whirring above. He peered into the dusky sky and watched it resolve into blackness as a conspiracy of ravens eddied overhead, cloaking the sky. They started cawing at the carnage on the ground, eager to get started consuming the fresh carrion but wary of the throng of living ghouls storming the chain-link fence. The ravens retreated higher into the sky, fanning out, revealing patches of azure sky, awaiting their opportunity to dive in and commence their feast.

Zodiac let loose another streak of fire from the flamethrower. The blaze ignited a half dozen ghouls, who went up in smoke and flames. The fires helped Box see in the twilight enough to locate and remove dead ghouls suspended on the fence.

"Wait till the buzzards come," said Porter, taking a break to watch the swooping, clamorous ravens filling the sky.

"Let's get cracking," said Hilda. "We got more stiffs to remove from the fence."

"It looks like the swarms of ghouls are thinning out," said Marta, who couldn't make out any additional creatures emerging from the forest.

"I think you're right," said Box, checking out the perimeter of the woods.

"Why worry about newcomers when you got plenty of the ghouls attacking here to deal with?" said Hilda. "Let's clear this section of fence then go back inside."

"Sounds good to me," said Porter, turning around in time to see a creature lunging at his throat.

Pipe in hand, Porter slewed around swinging and caught a fortyish female ghoul dressed in a cop's uniform on the side of her face, caving in her cheekbone and temple. The pipe ripped through her temporal and sphenoid bones pulverizing her brain, downing her.

Box dragged two electrocuted ghouls from the fence at the same time. He swung the stiffs into the remainder of the ghouls that continued to assault the warehouse perimeter.

"Let's wrap this up," said Hilda, finding another corpse hanging on the fence and jerking it free. "I don't wanna be out here in the dark. We won't be able to see those things attacking."

"It's dark enough with those ravens overhead," said Box.

"I see only about twenty more of them left alive, if you want to call them alive," said Marta.

"OK. Porter, you brain the rest of those things, and we'll clear the fence."

"My pleasure," said Porter, wading into the mob of invading ghouls, swinging his pipe left and right, taking out anything that crossed his path, grunting and cursing with his efforts.

Box, Hilda, and Marta cleared the remaining carcasses from the section of the fence that had the heaviest buildup of ghouls with two or more layers of them dangling from the chain links, which was where the ghouls had focused their assault near the gate. The rest of the fence had scattered ghouls stuck on it that wouldn't provide enough insulation to aid attackers scaling it.

"Let's get out of here before more of the things launch an attack from the woods," said Hilda, satisfied with the results of her squad's labor.

Still swinging his pipe Porter had dashed the brains of ten of the ghouls, leaving only ten living.

"Box, help Porter," said Hilda.

Box laid into the ghouls with his pickaxe, aiming at and cleaving skulls with fierce abandon, despite his weariness and aching muscles from clearing the fence.

Glancing at the forest he wondered if he could make a mad dash for it before Zodiac spotted him. Box wielded his pickaxe, cracked another ghoul's skull, and glanced up at Zodiac, catching him staring back at him, flamethrower in hand. Box decided he would never make the woods in one piece. Maybe if it was darker, which would conceal his flight . . . but, even then, Zodiac could light up the area with a blast from his flamethrower.

Box would have to bide his time, waiting for a better chance. If he stayed here with Zodiac, his days were numbered.

Hilda and Marta returned to the gate.

After wiping out the last of the assailing ghouls, Box and Porter followed them.

Chapter 70

"Looks like we cleaned their clocks," said Zodiac, standing in the guard tower gripping the flamethrower and surveying the battlefield of fallen ghouls, some of which were still smoldering from the blasts of napalm he had incinerated them with.

"There may be more of them out there," said Box, standing outside the gate. "You heard what Pataki said about thousands of them massing in the forest."

"If they try again, we'll beat them back again."

"We're really low on ammo, boss," said Tyler, standing below the tower and gazing up at Zodiac, his AR-15 in one hand, Zodiac's sickle in the other.

"What about the mortar?"

"We're out of shells."

"We'll think of something."

"Do you mind letting us in?" said Hilda, who was standing with Box, Porter, and Marta outside the gate.

"You better believe it," said Zodiac. "I don't want any of you getting any funny ideas out there—like making a run for the woods. Huh, Box? I mean, Halverson."

"I'm not Halverson," said Box.

"That's all you spooks ever do in the CIA, huh? Lie like rugs."

"Can we come in?" said Porter. "I need to take a leak. I got a prostate the size of an orange."

"Open the gate," Zodiac told the guards.

Hilda and her squad entered the compound, haggard from exhaustion.

Porter discarded his pipe and made a beeline for the warehouse.

Played out, Box yawned.

"Time for dinner," said Zodiac. "What's on the menu tonight?"

"How about some Chef Boyardee beef ravioli?" said Hilda.

"Is that all you have in this joint?"

"Afraid so."

Zodiac expressed his displeasure with a drawn-out sigh. "Is this plague never gonna end?"

Hilda, Box, and Marta made to depart for the warehouse.

"Wait a minute," said Zodiac. "Aren't you forgetting something?"

"Forgetting what?" said Hilda.

"Drop your weapons here. You don't need them inside."

Shrugging, Hilda dropped her screwdriver. Box and Marta dropped their weapons and followed Hilda back to the warehouse.

Zodiac gestured to Tyler to approach him.

"I got an assignment for you," said Zodiac.

"Want me to waterboard Halverson?" said Tyler with a shit-eating grin.

"No. We can't afford to turn him into a vegetable like Pataki. Halverson's the only one who knows the way to Mount Weather."

"What's my assignment, then?" said Tyler, puzzled.

"First, give me back Suzie Q."

Tyler handed the sickle back to Zodiac. "Thanks for entrusting her to me, boss."

"There are some loose ends that need to be tied up," said Zodiac, gazing at the warehouse.

He heard a multitude of ravens cawing behind him. He turned around and saw them dive-bomb out of the sky down on the corpses that strewed the smoking battlefield, eager to peck their beaks into a raft of carrion, pluck out eyes, and eat like kings tonight.

"Friggin' ravens give me the creeps," said Zodiac.

Chapter 71

Box, Marta, and Porter were locked in the quarantine room after eating dinner.

Porter lay on his back on his cot and was asleep seconds after his head hit the pillow.

Box couldn't blame him. He could do with some z's himself. He sat down on a cot.

"Who are you really?" said Marta, watching him.

"Earl James."

"You murdered Kate's brother with a broken whisky bottle?"

"No, I didn't. I have no memory of it. I don't remember ever meeting someone name Cole Younger."

"Do you remember meeting Kate?"

"No."

"Then what makes you think you're Earl James?"

"Who else could I be?"

"Zodiac called you Halverson, a CIA agent."

Box decided he couldn't tell her who he really was. If Zodiac knew she knew Box's real identity, he might waterboard her to find out how much else she knew about Box.

"He's mistaken," said Box. "He sees spies under his bed."

"How can you be so sure you're not Halverson?"

Box rubbed his forehead in frustration. "My memory hasn't come back. I'm still not positive who I am."

He wished he knew who he really was. He figured Pataki was probably right about his being Chad Halverson, but his own memory hadn't confirmed it yet. There was room for doubt. Yet Pataki seemed certain Box was Halverson. On the other hand, Kate Younger had been certain he was Earl James. Box didn't see himself as a murderer.

If he wasn't Chad Halverson, how did he know the way to Mount Weather in Bluemont, Virginia, where the president was holed up? And he *did* know the way there. Which was why Zodiac wanted to keep him alive so he could guide Zodiac there to oust the president and take over the country.

If he was Chad Halverson, as he suspected, where were his memories? What had he been doing in the desert when Porter and Danny first encountered him? Why were there so many gaps in his memory?

My name is Halverson. Chad Halverson. But I still can't remember anything about how I got here. Am I really Chad Halverson?

"Are you afraid of telling me the truth?" said Marta.

"No," said Box. "Why should I be?"

"I dunno. But what made you like this?"

"An amnesiac, you mean?"

"I guess. Your mind's definitely messed up." She paused, crestfallen, shoulders drooping. "In the end it doesn't matter, since Zodiac is planning to execute all of us carriers."

"We need to find a way out of here."

"Are we carriers for the rest of our lives, or just for a short time?"

"I don't think we're contagious for the rest of our lives."

"Then, for how long? How long can we infect others?"

"Maybe the doctor knows."

"If it's only temporary, why does Zodiac have to kill us? Why can't he just quarantine us till we get better?"

Box wondered how much he should tell her. "That's not the real reason he wants us dead."

"What, then?"

"He feels we're a threat to his power."

Marta shook her head in dismay. "I hope we're not carriers for the rest of our lives. I don't think I could go on living like that. Everybody would fear us and hate us for as long as we lived."

"They wouldn't have any way of knowing unless somebody told them. After all, we look as healthy as them."

"As long as somebody knows we're carriers, they can finger us and brand us as outcasts."

"It's hard to imagine we'll be carriers for the rest of our lives. On the other hand, this plague is unique. There's never been a zombie plague before in history. We've had a bubonic plague, the Black Death, a catastrophe that wiped out half of the population in Europe, but never a zombie one. We can't predict what it's gonna do."

"So we have to stay away from everyone forever?" she said, not looking forward to the prospect. "We'll be detested pariahs for the rest of our lives?"

"Nobody knows."

Marta sat down on her cot, bowed her head, and buried her face in her hands.

Muttering, Porter rolled onto his side on his cot. "I'm glad I'm asleep and can't hear a word you're saying, because it's depressing as hell listening to you two."

"If you got any answers, feel free," said Box.

"Not a one. Now let me catch up on my beauty sleep."

"You are a dog."

"You know what they say. Let sleeping dogs lie."

Box pulled a face.

He lay down on his cot. He couldn't keep his eyes open any longer.

Chapter 72

Dr. Epps was lying in bed with his nurse Rachel in his dark bedroom. He was wearing green plaid boxers. She was wearing a diaphanous lemon chiffon negligee. Their blanket was down at their waists. He was staring at the ceiling.

"I can't sleep," said Epps.

"Why not, Leon?" said Rachel.

"A guilty conscience, I'm afraid."

"About what?" said Rachel, propping herself up with her elbow to look at him.

"I have to tell someone and get it off my chest."

"I'm listening."

Epps demurred.

"Tell me, Leon."

He puckered his lips with tension. "Zodiac told me to rig the blood tests."

"What?" said Rachel, with surprise. "Why?"

"I don't know his reasons. He didn't tell me. He just told me who he wanted to be identified as carriers."

"What about the real carriers?"

"I found only one who might be a carrier because of the large amount of white blood cells in his blood."

"Did you give his name to Zodiac to announce?"

"I gave it to him, but he didn't announce it. He announced the ones who aren't carriers, at least according to the leukocyte count in their blood. And I'm not sure that's a reliable indicator that they have the plague. They could easily have some other disease that's triggering the increase in their number of leukocytes."

"Why would he rig the results?"

"I'll let you in on a secret."

"Yeah?"

"I don't think he cares about the science. He doesn't believe it. He's just using it as a pretext to quarantine the alleged carriers."

"Why are you going along with it?"

"I didn't have much of a choice."

"You're a doctor. He can't boss you around."

He paused, debating whether to tell her the truth. "He said he would accuse me of being a child molester in front of the community. He says he talked to a ten-year-old girl who accused me of raping her."

Rachel sat up in bed. "I don't believe it. It can't be true."

"It's not."

"You can't let him get away with it."

"The mere accusation would ruin my career."

Rachel flopped back on the bed and stared at the ceiling, hangdog. "The horrible thing is, you're probably right."

Epps nodded yes, his face morose.

After a while he said, "I hate the idea that innocent people have been accused of being carriers when their bloodwork doesn't bear it out. I'm thinking about telling the others the truth."

"And risk being stigmatized as a pedo for the rest of your life? That's something nobody will ever forget."

"I know, but . . . I feel compelled to do the right thing."

"The right thing for the accused carriers won't be the right thing for you if Zodiac carries through on his threat."

"It's been hanging over me all day. The guilt."

"Forget about it. Get some sleep."

"Did you ever think the world would end like this?"

"Like what, dear?"

"Like . . . like . . . nothing."

"What do you mean?"

"We all die for no reason from a plague," said Epps, staring upward with glassy eyes. "I keep thinking of that T. S. Eliot poem:

This is the way the world ends.
This is the way the world ends.
This is the way the world ends.
Not with a bang but a whimper.

"It's so anticlimactic."

"You think too much," said Rachel. "You're bumming me out. Go to sleep."

She put her fingers on his eyelids and closed them over his eyes.

"I'll sing you a lullaby if you want," she said.

"I'll banish you from my bed if you do."

They shared a laugh and felt more relaxed.

But Epps knew nothing had changed. He would wake up tomorrow and put on his mask and face another day of plague and death with no end in sight.

Chapter 73

The man standing in the dark slipped on purple latex surgical gloves and put his ear to Epps's door, listening for any sound inside. The man heard none.

He tried the doorknob.

It was locked, as he had expected.

He dug his lock pick gun out of his trouser pocket and, as quietly as he could, went to work on the lock in the doorknob. He picked it in less than a minute. It was the dead bolt lock above it that would be problematic, he knew. On the off chance the dead bolt might be unlocked he twisted the doorknob. The knob turned because he had defeated its lock, but, when he pushed against the door to open it, it didn't yield. It could mean only one thing. The dead bolt was engaged.

He went to work on the dead bolt. It was more difficult than the lock in the door, but not impossible. The lock pick gun did its job.

He looked behind him to make sure nobody was watching, twisted the doorknob, and nudged the door, which gave this time. He opened the door gingerly so its hinges wouldn't squeak. He stole inside the dark room, closing the door behind him. He eased the door bolt into the strike plate to avoid making any noise.

He turned to inspect the dark room.

His eyes were already accustomed to the dark, since the hallway outside Epps's door had been poorly lit. It didn't take his eyes long to become accustomed to the total lack of light. It wasn't quite total, since he could make out the green-lit numerals on the clock sitting on Epps's nightstand.

The man could discern Epps's face lying on the pillow next to Rachel's face.

The man didn't know they were lovers, nor did he care. If she didn't wake up, he might let her live.

He took a step on the hardwood floor toward the bed. He was dismayed it was a hardwood floor. He had been a carpenter before the apocalypse struck and knew some of them creaked like crazy when you stepped on them either because of moisture in the air or because the subfloor had become separated from the joists.

In an attempt to reduce the creaking he balanced his weight so he didn't put too much of it on one foot causing the floorboards to creak. If he could keep his weight equally distributed he figured the floorboards would make less noise. Still the boards creaked. The sound wasn't deafening, but in the absolute silence of nighttime the creaking could be heard distinctly.

Watching the sleepers anxiously, he hoped they wouldn't wake.

They stirred, but didn't open their eyes.

He continued walking, reached the bed, and with relief saw that neither Epps nor his nurse lover had awoken. He sidled along the bed and reached Epps's head.

Epps was an ugly man, decided Tyler, looking down at him. Even in his sleep, the guy was ugly. It must have been a case of beauty and the beast, he decided, as he eyed the thirty-five-year-old Rachel's pretty face a few feet from Epps's.

It was amazing how helpless people looked when they were asleep, decided Tyler.

He placed his hands around Epps's neck, almost lovingly, not wishing to arouse the guy from his sleep and commenced strangling him.

The son of a bitch thrashed around under the covers and woke up Rachel with a kick of his leg that struck her in the knee. She opened her eyes and glimpsed Tyler looming over Epps and throttling him. She was about to scream when Tyler let go of Epps's throat and slammed his right fist into Rachel's jaw throwing his entire weight into the blow as he lunged across the mattress to deliver it.

Gasping, she went limp, her face tilted away from Epps, her jaw dislocated, her mouth ajar.

Tyler felt Epps struggling to break out of his grasp now that Tyler had only one hand on Epps's throat. Tyler thrust his other hand around Epps's throat and squeezed with both of them, crushing Epps's Adam's apple under his two thumbs. Epps made a horrible wheezing sound. Or was that the guy's windpipe cracking under his thumbs? Tyler wondered. Whatever it was it sounded bad.

In any case, he kept squeezing, unconcerned if he cracked Epps's windpipe while strangling him. If only the guy would stop thrashing about, decided Tyler. He kept one eye on Rachel, making sure she didn't regain consciousness and start screaming for help. Being the recipient of another one of Epps's kicks could easily bring her to her senses.

Why was it taking this geezer so long to die? wondered Tyler. *Christ. Die you old bastard, die.*

As if on cue, Epps heaved a death rattle and went limp in Tyler's hands.

Tyler felt for a pulse in Epps's neck. Tyler's gloves desensitized his fingertips. He wondered if he couldn't feel the pulse because of the layer of latex sheathing his fingers or because there wasn't any pulse to feel. To quell his doubts he lifted Epps's eyelids with his fingers and inspected Epps's eyes, which were staring blankly. Tyler figured the guy was dead.

He heard Rachel moan.

Adrenaline shot through his body. Reacting on a dime he reached over to the other side of the bed, collared Rachel's throat in his hands, and dragged her across the mattress closer to him beside Epps so he could throttle her without having to reach to the other side of the bed and strain his back in the process.

Chapter 74

Early the next day, Box awoke in the quarantine room to screams outside his room. He jackknifed up in bed. Marta and Porter also awoke.

A woman was tearing through the hallway outside their locked room screaming.

"Dr. Epps is dead," she cried.

Box leapt off his cot, pressed his ear to the door, and listened. He heard footfalls tramping by the door and people muttering as they passed.

"What's that all about?" said Porter.

"Something's up," said Box.

He and Porter threw on their clothes. Marta dressed behind the folding partition set up beside her cot.

Twenty minutes later, the door opened.

Standing in the hallway with his guards, Zodiac confronted the three carriers.

"Come with me," he said.

Box stepped toward Zodiac.

"Put your masks on first," said Zodiac. "I don't want your damn disease."

Box put on a mask, as did Marta and Porter. They may not have had much at the camp, but they had plenty of masks.

As soon as Box, Porter, and Marta entered the hall, armed guards surrounded them.

"Is this how you invite people to breakfast?" said Box.

"This isn't about breakfast," said Zodiac.

They reached a crowd of rubberneckers that had gathered in front of Dr. Epps's room.

"Make a hole," said Zodiac.

His guards shoved the rubberneckers out of the way so Zodiac could enter the doctor's room. Box, Porter, and Marta followed Zodiac to the doctor's bed, where Epps and Rachel lay on their backs motionless.

"Epps died last night," said Zodiac.

Box approached the bed and scoped out Epps. "There are ligature marks around his neck."

"Exactly. He didn't die naturally. Somebody strangled him. His girlfriend, too."

"Looks that way."

"Somebody could've done it with their hands," said Porter.

"Like maybe one of you," said Zodiac. "What about you, Halverson? Where were you last night?"

"You can't pin this on me," said Box.

"Just answer the question. Where were you?"

"I was locked inside the quarantine room last night."

"Can you prove that?"

"How could I get out?"

"You tell me. You CIA black-ops thugs are full of tricks. You can pick locks, hotwire cars, hack computers, hack cell phones, infect computers with viruses, you name it. The Stuxnet worm—was that you guys or Mossad? What can't you do? They teach you to be top-drawer crooks in the Agency."

"I don't know what you're talking about."

"Answer the question. Did you strangle the good doctor?"

"No. Why would I?"

"Maybe you were mad at him for identifying you as a carrier. You decided to get your revenge by taking him out."

"That's ridiculous. Why would I blame him if my blood had too many white blood cells?"

"Because it marked you as an outcast leading to your imprisonment, for one thing. For another, it means you and your friends will be executed. All of which can't make you very happy."

"How did I get out of my locked room?"

"The same way you got into the doctor's locked room."

"Which is?"

"You picked the lock."

"With what? I don't have a lock pick. Go ahead and search me, if you don't believe me."

"Why bother? You dumped it. You three are the only ones with motives to kill Epps. Who else would want to kill a doctor?"

"Somebody who wanted to shut him up,"

"Shut him up about what?" said Zodiac.

"That's what we need to find out."

"Why don't you just admit you strangled him? After all, you're gonna be executed anyway."

"Because I didn't strangle him."

"We were all locked in the quarantine room last night," said Porter. "We had nothing to do with this."

"Maybe you were in on this, too, huh, Porter," said Zodiac. "Like maybe you're the one that strangled Rachel while your buddy Halverson did Epps."

"That's insane. Why are you trying to frame us for this? You already got us locked up like criminals for something that's not even a crime."

"I'm getting tired of your lip. And what about you, Marta? Did you help murder the doctor?"

"Yeah, sure. They call me Marta the Murderer back home."

Zodiac fumed. "You're gonna regret talking back to me like that. I had plans for you. I was gonna help you go places. You got potential to be one of my top warriors."

"Then why am I locked up?"

"It's only temporary. You have to learn to trust me. That's the most important trait of my men. Trust. They trust me implicitly. If you don't have that trait, you're not gonna cut it as one of my elite warriors."

"I'm supposed to believe this bill of goods you're trying to sell me?"

Zodiac shook his head with disapproval. "I can see I'm gonna have to teach you three a lesson. You haven't got it through your heads who the boss of this outfit is."

"Maybe you're the one that killed the doctor," said Box. "That's why you're so eager to pin it on us."

"You've earned yourself pride of place in the march of shame, Halverson, with that flat-out lie. Didn't you ever learn how to keep your trap shut in the CIA?"

"Only when I'm with important people."

"You're gonna wish you never said that." Zodiac turned to Tyler. "Tell Sammy to call everyone to the lecture room."

"Sammy, you heard the boss," said Tyler.

"Will do," said Sammy, and took off to notify the others.

"Tyler, take Halverson and Porter out of here to the lecture room."

Tyler jammed his AR-15 into Box's ribs. "You heard the man. Let's go."

"I need to talk to Marta alone," said Zodiac.

Chapter 75

Zodiac closed the door behind Tyler so he was alone with Marta with the two corpses that lay on the bed.

"I could make life easy for you, Marta," said Zodiac.

Marta looked at him, but said nothing.

"Tell me what you know about Halverson."

"I don't know anyone named Halverson," said Marta.

"Did he tell you to say that?"

"Who?"

"Halverson, who pretends his name is Box."

"I don't know why you call him Halverson. He told me his name is Box."

"He must have told you something. I've seen you two talking together."

"He told me he has amnesia."

Zodiac stepped closer to Marta. "I like you, Marta. You got a head on your shoulders, and I like the way you're put together." He ogled her weightlifter's toned arms and trim figure. "You know how to keep yourself in shape by lifting weights. You're my kind of woman."

Marta said nothing.

"Just tell me what Halverson told you about himself and we can get along fine," said Zodiac, invading her space.

"I don't think so."

"Don't you understand? I could treat you like royalty."

"He told me he lost his memory. That's all he told me."

"What was he doing in the desert when Porter found him?"

"He doesn't remember."

"You can level with me. I won't tell him you told me. You don't have to worry about his retaliating against you."

"I can't help you."

"Can't or won't?"

"Can't."

"What's his real name?"

"He can't recall it."

"Did he admit to you he works for the CIA?"

"No."

"Pataki told me Halverson works for the CIA."

"Box didn't tell me anything about Halverson."

"Don't you want to share some quality time with me?" said Zodiac, lowering his voice as he pressed against her.

"Aren't you afraid I'll infect you?"

"Actually, no, I'm not."

"Why not? You think you have antibodies in your blood that will kill the zombie plague spores?"

"Antibodies can't kill the plague. Nothing can. There's no known cure."

"Then you should be afraid of getting too close to me."

Zodiac pressed harder against her. "I fear nothing. That's why you should join me and my army. Did the CIA send Halverson here to kill me?"

"I don't know anyone name Halverson."

Feeling uncomfortable with Zodiac pressing against her chest, she took a step backward.

Zodiac eyed her with suspicion. "Are you working with him for the CIA?"

"I don't know anything about the CIA."

"Then why are you afraid of joining me?"

"I'm not afraid."

Zodiac's eyes widened. "Then you want to be my girlfriend," he said with a leer. "Is that it? I knew you did."

"I didn't say that."

"If you don't fear me, you want to be my girlfriend," he said, putting his arm around her narrow waist.

"How do you figure that?" she said, pulling away from him.

"There's only one requirement for you to become my girlfriend. You tell the others that Halverson murdered Dr. Epps out of revenge for exposing him as a carrier."

"I have no idea who murdered Epps."

"Idiot," said Zodiac in a burst of frustration, whipping out his Glock. "You'd rather side with the loser Halverson and be a loser like him than join me. You'll regret this. You could've had a good life at my side." He shoved her toward the door and trained his pistol on her. "Get moving."

Marta's eyes blazed. But she knew there was nothing she could do against a gun.

She made for the door.

Chapter 76

Standing near the dais in front of the lecture room, Box and
Porter, guarded by Tyler with his AR-15, watched Marta prodded
toward the dais by the Glock's muzzle Zodiac was sticking in the
small of her back.

Box could tell she was fit to be tied. The room was SRO with
camp members sitting in the audience and standing in the aisles.
He smelled the pungent odor of patchouli emanating from a fat
twentysomething woman wearing jeans and a yellow and black
polka-dotted blouse in the front row scarfing down popcorn out of
a plastic bag on her lap.

Zodiac deposited Marta with Box and Porter.

The patchouli was making Box's eyes water. The lady must
have poured a whole bottle of the perfume on her body, he
decided. It was even overpowering the smell of the popcorn.

"I've discovered the murderers," Zodiac told the audience,
bounding onto the dais and taking position behind the lectern.

The audience listened enthralled.

"It was the carriers that murdered the good doctor out of
revenge for his revealing them as carriers," said Zodiac.

The audience grumbled, expressing their displeasure.

Zodiac descended from the dais.

"Strip," he told the carriers.

Box didn't respond. Neither did Porter nor Marta.

Zodiac pressed his Glock's muzzle against Box's temple. "Do
it."

Grudgingly, Box started taking off his shirt.

"You and Marta, too," Zodiac told Porter.

Marta and Porter obeyed, grim-faced.

Box stood in his briefs, Porter in boxers, Marta in bra and
panties.

"Take off everything," said Zodiac.

"What's the point of this farce?" said Box.

"Figure it out," said Zodiac, gloating at the half-naked
carriers.

Box balked.

"Or do you want to die now?" said Zodiac, training his Glock on Box's head.

Box removed his boxers. Porter and Marta removed their remaining undergarments.

"Tyler, bind the carriers' wrists behind their backs," said Zodiac.

Tyler roughly jerked Box's hands behind his back and fastened a black plastic zip tie around his wrists. He did the same with Porter and Marta, not before ogling Marta's naked body.

"March onto the dais in front of the audience," said Zodiac. "Go ahead, Halverson. You're the ringleader of the murderers."

Box climbed the dais, marched to the far side of it, and stood facing the audience.

The audience booed. Some held their noses, others flashed their thumbs down or their middle fingers up. Porter and Marta joined Halverson on the dais. Jeers rang out.

"The three carriers are murderers," cried Zodiac, pointing at them. "They murdered our good doctor in his sleep. They didn't even give him a chance to defend himself."

"Boo," yelled the audience. "Murderers."

Someone bolted to their feet and flung a rotten tomato at Box, striking him in the cheek. Box winced.

Emboldened, others in the audience pelted Box, Marta, and Porter with tomatoes. Humiliated, the three of them withstood a barrage of rotten tomatoes and offal hurled at them. Their hands bound behind them, they couldn't defend themselves from the missiles. All they could do was try to dodge projectiles.

Box tried to dodge them by anticipating where they would strike him, but he found this strategy ultimately useless thanks to the many different members who were trying to pelt him. He could only dodge one missile at a time. When he dodged one incoming tomato, he opened himself up to another one slung by someone else in a different row of the assembly.

Marta and Porter had the same problem as they tried to run away from the projectiles, exposing themselves to multiple blows.

"Stand still on the dais and face the audience," said Zodiac, waving his Glock's barrel back and forth between the carriers to keep them in check.

Box, Marta, and Porter stood still, pelted again and again by whatever the audience hurled at them.

Zodiac waved his sickle above his head, egging on the audience.

"Chop them down," said the audience when they saw the sickle. "Chop them down."

"Whore," cried a wizen-lipped middle-aged woman wearing a yellow scrunchie in her black hair and khaki Bermuda shorts, a green nylon backpack strapped to her back with Velcro snaps, her face twisted with fury, shaking her fist at the dais. "Whore. Chop down the whore."

She flung a rotten tomato at Marta, striking one of Marta's breasts, which reddened.

Humiliated, her body smarting, Marta stood in front of the audience wondering if her degradation would never end. A flying egg splattered in her hair. She wanted to scream.

"Chop them down," came the chant. "Chop them down."

Box ducked a UFO directed at his head, his body smeared with gunk from scores of missiles launched at him that had hit their mark. Some jerk in the third row peppered him with walnuts, bruising his body when they hit.

Marta stood, white-faced, enduring trash slung against her body, syrup and juice from rotten fruit and vegetables oozing down her flesh. Someone pitched a rotten banana at her face, which struck her forehead with a thud. The dais was littered with debris.

"Don't let Zodiac tell you what to do," Porter told the audience.

In response they unleashed a barrage of offal at his body. An egg smashed and cracked against his lips, the albumen oozing into his mouth, the yolk sliding down his naked chest.

"Chop them down," roared the crowd.

"Chop them down," cried Patchouli, and eagerly jammed more popcorn into her mouth, rapt with the show.

"All right," said Zodiac. "Settle down. Now's not the time for that. We showed the carriers for what they are. Murderers."

"Murderers," agreed the crowd.

"Murderers and whores," cried Yellow Scrunchie. "Murderers and whores."

"Settle down, settle down," said Zodiac, waving his sickle. "For now we'll lock them up."

"Lock them up," chanted the crowd. "Lock them up."

At the same time, tomatoes struck Box and Marta in their faces. Box spat the tomato skin and juice off his mouth. Marta wobbled, almost passing out from the furious blow, her hair gnarled and sticky with tomato juice, egg yolk, albumen, and banana juice. Porter rolled his eyes, groaned, and doubled over in agony when a tomato slammed into his groin. A grapefruit smashed into Box's groin. Blanching, he gasped and doubled over.

"Beg for forgiveness," Zodiac told the carriers.

"Beg, beg, beg," chanted the crowd.

Box, Marta, and Porter said nothing.

"Criminals," Zodiac told them.

"Beg, beg, beg," roared the crowd.

Box and Porter straightened up by degrees, wincing, saying nothing.

"That's enough," said Zodiac, motioning for the audience to be silent. "You three losers, get down from there."

"Shame," Patchouli cried at the carriers. "Shame on you."

Degraded, their naked bodies mired in filth, Box, Marta, and Porter exited the dais, as jeers rained down on them.

Marta choked back sobs, refusing to show her mortification for the bloodthirsty mob to see.

Animals, decided Box, glowering at the audience, who responded with more taunts.

"Take them to their cell," Zodiac told Tyler. "Before our people tear them limb from limb," he added under his breath.

Nodding, his jaw set, Tyler took several of his men and ushered the carriers out of the auditorium at gunpoint. Boos and catcalls swarmed after them like enraged hornets.

"I don't want their stinking clothes," Zodiac told Sammy, who was standing near the three puddles of clothes abandoned near the dais. "Sammy, take their clothes back to them,"

"We don't want no stinking clothes," crooned the mob.

"All right already," muttered Zodiac.

Chapter 77

Over two thousand miles away from Zodiac's Arizona
compound, President Cole was hunkered down in the bunker, aka
Area B, at the Mount Weather Emergency Operations Center in
Bluemont, Virginia, forty-eight miles northwest of Washington,
DC. The 564-acre high-security government complex was
surrounded with a fifteen-foot-high chain-link fence crowned with
barbed wire canted outward and inward.

Area B occupied six hundred thousand square feet and could
withstand a direct hit from a nuclear missile. There was enough
room for two thousand federal officials, though only a select few
had their own bedrooms, namely the president and his cabinet.

Congress had been decimated by the zombie plague. Not
more than 40 percent of them had survived.

Both masked in the president's office, General Pabst,
chairman of the Joint Chiefs of Staff, and President Cole discussed
the sorry state of affairs. Pabst didn't mince words.

"We're surrounded by the ghouls," he said, wearing his dress
uniform, showing off his fruit salad.

Despite the horrors of the pestilence and its devastation
wreaked on the country, fifty-seven-year-old Pabst maintained an
erect bearing, his jaw set, his grizzled black hair combed back
neatly.

The amount of worry lines had multiplied on Cole's forehead
due to the country's permanent state of crisis. Sometimes he
wished his mask covered his brow. Looking healthy was part and
parcel of his job of being president and commander in chief. As
president he was a cheerleader. How could you cheer anybody on
if you looked like hell? he wondered.

He couldn't let the public down, even if he had little idea if
there was any public left living in these United States. And even if
there *was* anyone out there alive, they never saw him and maybe
never would. Still, he had to keep up appearances, even if it was
only for his cabinet and the finite number of persons he met in
Area B.

"But they can't get inside the bunker," said Cole, sitting behind his massive oak desk, his arms hanging down at his sides. "Correct?"

Pabst hedged. "We don't think so. But they're causing problems in the air ducts."

"Explain, General."

"They're trying to crawl through the HVAC air ducts into the bunker."

"Don't the ducts have grates or wire screens to protect them?"

"They do, but the ghouls have managed to break down the exterior grates. They haven't gotten through the interior ones. We're not gonna let that happen."

"Then kill them while they're trapped in the ducts."

"That's what we're doing. And none of them have been able to reach the interior of the bunker."

"Then what's the problem?"

"Their corpses are piling up and clogging the ducts, cutting off our air. This is a big complex, but we're slowly running out of air, Mr. President, and if we don't find a solution, we're going to suffocate."

Cole pounded his desktop with his left fist. "Clear the damn things out of the ducts."

If he was startled by the president's access of rage, Pabst didn't show it. "That's what we plan to do. The problem is there are millions of those things out there. It makes it difficult to venture out of the bunker."

"How do they even know we're in here?"

Pabst shook his head in puzzlement. "Maybe they can smell us. Somehow they know."

"Cut them down with bullets. We're the best-armed country in the world. Don't tell me we can't blow away a bunch of ghouls that can't even figure out how to walk."

"The ghouls are jammed so close together they can hardly move out there."

"Which makes them easier to kill. How can you miss?"

"No matter how many we kill, there are always more of them to take their place."

"Throw grenades at them," said Cole in frustration. "That'll separate them."

269

"We're in the process of staging a sortie now, Mr. President, and we plan on using flamethrowers as well as grenades."

"Good. Blow the suckers up and burn them alive. The best news I've heard all day."

"I'm not gonna candy-coat this for you, Mr. President. Whenever we kill a hundred of them, a hundred more take their place."

"Then blow *them* up, too. Keep blowing them up till you can get outside and clear out the air ducts."

"As soon as we clear out the air ducts, more ghouls crawl into them and block them. It's a never-ending battle."

"Keep killing them and removing them."

"Right, Mr. President," said Pabst, snapping to attention and saluting.

"If we have to, we'll nuke them."

"Sir?" said Pabst, his face falling, not sure he had heard correctly.

"Area B is built to withstand a nuclear blast, isn't it?"

"Yes, Mr. President."

Cole used both hands to lift the football that was chained to his wrist and set it on his desktop with a thud. "I can nuke this place in the blink of an eye."

Pabst wiped sweat off his forehead with his palm. "I wouldn't suggest doing that, Mr. President, unless you want to commit suicide. The nuclear blast would poison the air with toxic radioactivity."

"If it's a choice between either breathing radioactive air or suffocating thanks to clogged HVAC ducts, which do you prefer, General?"

"Neither."

"If you do your job right, I won't have to resort to nukes."

"Correct, Mr. President."

"Go get 'em, General. You're our pit bull. I have full faith in you. If you can't clear the air ducts, nobody can."

Chapter 78

"I'm gonna kill that guy," said Marta in the quarantine room, seething as she buttoned her blouse.

"No, you're not," said Box, sitting on his cot tying his shoes.

"You watch me."

"Listen to me," he said, looking up at her. "You're not gonna kill him."

"What makes you so sure?"

"Because *I'm* gonna kill him."

"Not if I get to him first," said Porter, standing in front of the door, fastening his belt buckle.

"If he hates us so much, why doesn't he just kill us and be done with it?" said Marta.

"He needs me," said Box. "Maybe he'll whack you two."

"Oh, thanks a bunch."

"I don't think he will," said Porter. "He needs fighters, and he knows we're all good fighters in this room."

"I hope you're right," said Marta.

"I am. Who's he gonna get to clear off the fence when the ghouls return? And they *will* return. Mark my words. This ain't over by a long shot. It's not about killing hundreds of those things. It's about killing billions of them."

"Billions? Are you crazy?"

"I wish I was."

"He's right," said Box. "They'll launch another attack. Pataki said he saw thousands of those things massing in the woods. We killed hundreds when they attacked, not thousands. There's more where they came from."

"Poor Pataki," said Porter. "He looked like they lobotomized him. Did you see his glassy eyes? And then they catapulted—"

"Don't," said Marta, holding up her hand, looking squeamish. "I'm trying to get it out of my mind."

"Another good reason to kill Zodiac," said Box, gritting his teeth. "But we have to wait. He's our ticket out of here."

"How do you figure?"

271

"He needs me to lead him to Mount Weather. He doesn't plan on staying here."

"I don't think I have that kind of patience," said Marta. "I'll probably try to kill him the next time I see his ugly face."

"No, don't," said Box. "We need to bide our time."

Marta grumbled. "I don't know if I can control myself."

"He's asking for it," said Porter. "And he's gonna get it."

Chapter 79

"There's only one way to get rid of the ghouls," said Diego, who was standing with Zodiac in the lecture room that had emptied out after the guards had carted off the carriers to quarantine.

"What would that be, holy man?" said Zodiac, polishing his sickle with his handkerchief and only half listening.

"A sacrifice. We must make a sacrifice to appease our maker," said Diego, flinging his eyes toward heaven.

"Who should we sacrifice?" said Zodiac, putting his polishing on hold.

"Hmm. Maybe a pet. Like a dog."

Zodiac couldn't help but laugh. "And that will make the ghouls leave us alone?"

"I believe so. If the sacrifice is accepted."

"I don't think a dead dog is enough of a sacrifice. What about you?"

"I think it might be."

"That's not what I meant. I meant, what about you as a sacrifice?"

"Me?" said Diego in shock. "You want to sacrifice me?"

"I want you to sacrifice yourself. You're the holy man. The sacrifice must come from you."

"It's against my religion."

"Sacrifice is a part of Christianity. Jesus Christ himself was sacrificed."

"Christians are not allowed to commit suicide."

"Where does it say that?"

"The Ten Commandments. Thou shalt not kill."

"Even if your sacrifice will save the rest of us?"

"Even so."

Zodiac approached the dais. "Then the community means nothing to you."

"That's not what I said. I want to save all of us from the ghouls. That's why I suggested a sacrifice."

"As long as the sacrifice isn't you," said Zodiac with a chuckle. "What makes you so special? How come you're willing to sacrifice everybody else but yourself?"

"You're twisting my words."

Zodiac laid down his sickle on a chair, withdrew his Glock from his holster, ejected the magazine, and commenced dispensing bullets from it.

"If I give you my gun with one bullet in the magazine, will you shoot yourself as a sacrifice?" he said.

Diego broke into a sweat.

Zodiac handed him the Glock. "Take it."

"I can't commit blasphemy."

"It was your idea to make a sacrifice. Sacrifice yourself and save us. Think of Jesus's sacrifice for mankind when you kill yourself."

Diego accepted the Glock with a sweaty palm. Deliberately, he put the gun to his temple. He closed his eyes for thirty seconds. He opened his eyes. He turned the Glock on Zodiac and squeezed the trigger.

Zodiac snatched the Glock out of Diego's hand. "You didn't really think I'd give you a loaded gun, did you? I oughta blow you away for that."

He loaded the Glock's magazine with the bullets he had removed and slapped the magazine back into the Glock's butt. He racked the slide and drew a bead on Diego's head.

Diego widened his eyes in fear.

"No," said Zodiac. "A waste of ammo, I'm afraid."

He holstered his Glock. He smiled.

"I had you going, though, didn't I, holy man?"

Diego eyed him with resentment.

Chapter 80

An AR-15 strapped to his shoulder, the lanky thirtyish guard with a prominent Adam's apple standing in the tower at the camp's front gate idly watched a bluebottle buzz around his head. A few minutes later, the fly landed on his nose. He brushed it off with his hand.

Additional flies congregated around the guard's head, buzzing, swooping, and circling. He waved his hand in front of his face in disgust.

"Where are all these flies coming from?" he said.

"All those dead ghouls down there," said the twentysomething guard sporting a man bun in the tower at the other side of the gate, waving his hand in front of his face to ward off the flies.

Through the dark cloud of flies around his head, Lanky picked up on movement at the edge of the forest. Several ghouls were shambling out of the woods.

"We got more bogeys coming," he said.

Swatting with his hand at the multitude of flies swarming around his head, he held his walkie-talkie up to his face, keyed the mic, and said, "Boss, this is the front gate. Do you copy, over?"

"I copy. Go ahead," said Zodiac.

"The ghouls are mounting another attack. Over."

"Roger. Hold your fire till I get there. Over and out."

"Holy crap," said Man Bun, gazing at the woods in awe.

"What?" said Lanky, spitting flies out of his mouth and following Man Bun's gaze.

Thousands of ghouls were emerging from the woods slogging toward the chain-link fence.

Sickle in hand, Zodiac dashed out of the warehouse.

"Looks like they mean business this time, girls," he said, arriving at the gate and surveying the ghouls marching en masse toward them, flies hovering over them. "The main force is here."

Tyler scurried over to him and locked eyes on the army of advancing ghouls. "Hello."

"We're already low on ammo," said Zodiac. "We can't hold them off much longer."

275

"What do we do, boss?"

"They'll trample the fence this time around. There are too many of them. We won't be able to clear all the corpses off the fence, and they'll walk right over it, insulated from the electricity by all the fried stiffs welded onto it."

"The flamethrower?" said Tyler.

"We're running out of napalm." Zodiac paused. "Looks like they're forcing our hand."

"Boss?"

"It's time for us to load up, amscray, and attack Mount Weather. Get the SUVs ready. I want us out of here before the ghouls reach the gate."

"Are we taking anyone with us?"

"The carriers. They're good fighters. And we need Halverson. He's the only one that knows the way to the bunker."

"What about members of the camp?"

"They're mostly idiots. Who needs them? I might take some of them with us. Maybe Hilda. Round up our men and drive the SUVs up here."

Nodding, Tyler took off. Sammy was about to go after him, when Zodiac stopped him.

"Sammy, you get Halverson and the other carriers," said Zodiac.

"Right, boss," said Sammy, and bugged out for the warehouse door.

Chapter 81

Five minutes later, Sammy ushered Box, Marta, and Porter to the gate at gunpoint.

"Ohmigod," said Marta, setting eyes on the myriad of ghouls shambling toward the chain-link fence.

"I need you three to go outside and clear the corpses off the road," Zodiac told the carriers.

"What's the point?" said Box, not eager to get into a mano a mano with thousands of ghouls. "When we start killing the newcomer ghouls, the bodies will pile up in the road all over again."

"That's not gonna happen while I'm here."

"What's the big deal about the road?" said Porter.

"We're getting ready to leave," said Zodiac. "The road needs to be clear for our vehicles."

"Isn't this kind of sudden?" said Marta.

"Not really. I never had any intention of staying here. Now's as good a time as any to vamoose. And we got a mission ahead of us. We're going back east."

"Where's my gun?" said Box.

"No pieces," said Zodiac. "Like last time, you use hammers, crowbars, and whatever else you can scrounge up."

"You want us to get close to them?"

"How else can you kill them? That's why they call it CQB."

"We'll be breathing their spores when we get close to them."

"Why do you care? Remember what the doc said. You three are already infected with the zombie plague."

"What if he made a mistake about us? What if the bloodwork results prove nothing?"

"Wear your masks and gloves."

Box shot him a baleful look.

"Go over there and choose your weapons," said Zodiac, pointing to a pile of tools and gardening equipment the camp members had discarded after their first pitched battle with the invading ghouls.

Box ambled over to the heap of tools. He rooted through it and selected a crowbar. Marta and Porter followed him. Marta brushed aside a couple of tools and selected a spade with a red square metal blade. Porter found a sledgehammer with a short foot-long handle and a peen on one end of its head. The three of them selected and donned work gloves that had been left in a pile by camp members beside the hugger-mugger of tools.

"Why do you always send us out there to do your dirty work?" Porter asked Zodiac.

"Because you're already infected."

"If those things bite us, it's not gonna matter if we're carriers or not. The plague will get into our blood and we'll turn. Everyone that gets bit turns. I never seen any exception to that rule. A ghoul's bite is a thousand times worse than any of their spores."

"That's why you're going out there armed. If I wanted you to die, I wouldn't give you any weapons. Get out there and keep the road clear. Tyler's getting our vehicles ready for us now."

Overhearing them, Hilda approached Zodiac. "Did I hear you right? You're leaving?"

"You heard right," said Zodiac. "The camp's all yours—unless you want to pull up stakes with us."

"We're not gonna be able to defend ourselves against a shitload of ghouls, especially if you guys desert us, and you know it."

"I never said I was gonna stay here forever."

"You picked a fine time to split—leaving us in the lurch. Thousands of ghouls out there are coming in for the kill."

"I said you could come with us. What more do you want?"

Hilda surveyed the compound. "I don't want to leave my people behind. This is a second home to me."

"Then die with them. I don't care."

"At least leave weapons for us."

"I can't spare any. We need all the guns and ammo for ourselves. I'll leave all the tools and gardening equipment for you guys. And you can keep your crossbow."

"We need guns, damn it."

Zodiac scanned the swarm of ghouls advancing on the gate, a massive cloud of flies hovering over them.

"Those ghouls are getting too close," he said. "You carriers get out there and keep them off the road."

Crowbar in hand, Box led the sortie out the gate, which the guard swung open.

Chapter 82

Outside the compound, Box got an eyeful of the corpses blanketing the road. Or so he thought—until one of the "corpses" reached up and snagged his trouser leg. Stunned, he reared up his crowbar and thrust it into the female ghoul's head, fracturing her skull and pulverizing her brain. Glop oozed out between the cracks in her skull.

"Some of these things might still be alive," said Box, scoping out the bodies strewn on the road. "Make sure they're dead before you try to move them off the road."

Box latched onto the ankles of the ghoul he had just killed and dragged her out of the road, leaving a wake of brain paste smeared on the tarmac. Due to her emaciated condition she weighed less than a hundred pounds.

Warily, Porter eyed the advancing mob of ghouls.

"Their vanguard will be here soon," he said. "Why don't I go meet them and give them something to think about while you two clear the road?"

"Sounds good," said Box.

He kicked a male teenage corpse clad in a grey hoodie in the head. When the stiff didn't move, he seized its wrist and hauled the creature off the road.

Marta shoved her spade into a groaning, squirming supine middle-aged male ghoul's forehead, cleaving it and the brain inside the skull in half. The ghoul stopped squirming and groaning. Marta snagged its wrist and dragged it off the tarmac.

Holding his sledgehammer raised above his head, Porter charged one of the ghouls in the vanguard, a short male teenager with a maggot-infested necrotic hatchet face, and hammered the ghoul on the top of its head, crushing its skull and brain. The ghoul collapsed.

"Want some?" he said to the other ghouls, brandishing his sledgehammer above his head like he was Thor.

Box and Marta rushed to clear the road of cadavers.

"Why do we have to do this?" she said, breathing hard after hauling away a heavy female corpse with a protuberant belly clad in a bikini. "Can't he just run over these things with the SUV?"

"They might get stuck in the wheel wells or tangled up on the axles," said Box, dragging the middle-aged female corpse of a lawyer wearing a black pin-striped suit by her long brown hair off the tarmac. "There are just too many of them. In some places there are stacks of them. Let's deal with those first."

Marta worked on a stack of corpses, pulling the top one off by the foot and dragging it after her. It was a fiftysomething male ghoul with even features and a high brow. She thought he might have been handsome before he came down with the plague. As she was dragging the creature on its back, it sat up. Her heart in her mouth, she dropped the thing's foot and sliced its head off at the neck with the edge of her spade's blade.

"Don't these things ever die?" she said, gasping.

"Only when their brain is dead," said Box.

"What if you cut their heads off?"

"The brain's still alive."

Marta chased the head that was rolling across the street, caught up to it, and waited for it to come to a halt. The ghoul's decomposing face stared up at her, its face sloughing rotting worm-eaten skin. Shivering with consternation, Marta wondered if the flakes of skin were infested with contagious spores.

The face blinked and glowered up at her with pale eyes. Disgusted, she lifted the spade with two hands, thrust down, and buried the blade between the creature's white eyes. The spade sliced the creature's brain in two, killing the ghoul.

Marta made a point of staying away from the creature's shed skin that lay smeared on the tarmac like rubber from a skidding tire. She kicked the head off the road.

"The invaders are getting closer," said Marta, eying the vanguard surging toward them, which Porter was wading into wielding his sledgehammer with feral abandon. "We're not gonna be able to clear the entire road before they get here."

Box gazed into the compound searching for any sign of Zodiac's SUVs near the gate. He didn't see them.

"As long as there's no more than one layer of ghouls on the road, the SUVs should be able to drive over them. It's when there are two or more layers that the ghouls' corpses can get wedged inside the wheel wells by rotating wheels pushing them up. With one layer, not so much. The wheels are able to find traction on the tarmac and go."

Marta dragged a maggot-faced nurse ghoul's corpse by the wrist off the tarmac, her back starting to get sore. She deposited the nurse on the road's shoulder, straightened, and, wincing, massaged her lower back.

Out of the corner of his eye, Box caught sight of a blonde ghoul who could have been in her thirties but it was hard to tell because of the advanced putrescence of her face. She was schlepping toward him, having slipped past Porter. Despite its advanced decay, there was something about her face that nonplussed Box.

Adrenaline coursed through his body as he watched her approach. His heartbeat exploded into a thunderous out-of-control rataplan.

He recognized her.

Chapter 83

Was it possible that he knew her? Box wondered. He had not seen anyone he had recognized since finding himself alone in the desert, dying of thirst, where Porter and Danny had happened upon him.

Images flashed through his mind as he beheld her face. It was the same blonde in a white dress he had seen gliding along the beach in his dreams. It was her face. He saw Vegas. A mushroom cloud looming over the neon-lit strip. Radioactive air. A bunker in the desert. Transhumanists hiding inside it. Plotting a conspiracy for world takeover. He and the woman burning rubber trying to escape the bunker. A door in the bunker lowering. The door coming down. The car crashing—

Victoria. Her name was Victoria.

How he could recognize her now with her face half eaten by pestilence was beyond him. Maybe it was her eyes. Even though they were mantled with a milky veneer thanks to her disease, he could see they used to be blue.

She kept trudging toward him.

He stood rooted to the spot. He could not bring himself to kill her.

"Victoria," he managed to say through a dry throat.

She showed no reaction to her name. Why would she? he decided. She was already dead. And infected. And she was coming for him.

She bared her yellow teeth, snarling at him.

"What are you doing?" cried Marta, alarmed by his paralysis. "Kill her."

It was Victoria, he told himself. He couldn't kill Victoria. They had been through so much together, surviving the unforgiving plague. So many times they had cheated death together, battling the ghouls. And now . . . and now she was one of them.

"Kill her," said Marta, worried because she didn't think she could reach him in time to kill the thing. "She's not human. Snap out of it. You gotta kill her."

How could he kill her? he wondered. He had to. Marta was right. It might have looked like Victoria, but it wasn't her anymore. It was a walking corpse, infected with a plague that had wiped out most of the world's population. This thing standing before him was a flesh-eating ghoul that would tear apart his flesh and gorge on him as soon as look at him. It had no memory. It didn't recognize him. All it saw when it looked at him was food, a tasty treat waiting to be scarfed down.

"Get a grip, man," cried Porter, taking in Box's funk. "Waste it."

At that moment, Box knew for certain as he watched Victoria that he was Chad Halverson, black-ops agent for the Central Intelligence Agency. What Pataki had told him was true, as Halverson had suspected, but couldn't be sure. Now, as the memories of his calamities and breathtaking escapes, many with Victoria, came flooding back to him, he was sure. He *was* Halverson.

Mushroom clouds, flesh-eating ghouls roaming the earth, pestilence, apocalypse, death, and destruction. No wonder his mind didn't want to remember any of it and had blocked his memory. His mind couldn't grasp the magnitude of the wretchedness he had suffered along with other survivors.

And yet they couldn't give in. Marta, Porter, and him. They had to keep fighting.

The ghoul was so close to him he could smell the miasma of its festering flesh and wanted to vomit. Was he so close to the thing that he was breathing spores emanating from the creature? He would end up like her if he let her teeth pierce his flesh, tear a chunk out, and gobble it down, relishing it like it was filet mignon.

As Victoria jutted her head toward his throat to take a bite, he jerked the crowbar in his hand upward, driving its tapered edge through the bottom of her mouth, through her decomposing tongue and palate, and into her brain, destroying her. Her head skewered on the crowbar, she stood before him, motionless, her white eyes staring into infinity.

He couldn't stand seeing her in such a gruesome condition, her once-beautiful face now a gorgon's inches away from his.

Aghast, he flipped the crowbar over, let her head slide down its shank, and yanked the crowbar out of her brain. She slid to the road in a lifeless heap.

Tears welled in his eyes. He couldn't separate the ghoul at his feet from the living breathing woman he had known. Alive, she had almost always been at his side as they fought the ghouls together. And now she lay dead at his feet. What the hell had he done? He couldn't come to grips with it. All of the suffering they had experienced ended just like that—and by his hand. She was gone forever. How could this be?

Breathlessly, Marta sprang up to him. "I thought you were a goner."

She saw the tears in his eyes.

"What happened?" she said, horrified, taking in his body searching for a wound. "Did it bite you? Are you infected?"

"No," he muttered.

"Then what's wrong?"

Halverson didn't want to talk about it at first, but then decided it might help.

"I knew her," he said, gazing morosely at Victoria's corpse. "We went through a lot together."

"How awful," said Marta. "I know what you're going through. I lost people close to me, too. My mother, my sister."

"I know. We all have. That's the worst of this plague. Knowing people who are suddenly torn from your life, leaving you alone in the empty chaos."

Porter charged over to them. "I can't hold these things off much longer. There are too many of them. We gotta vamoose."

Halverson scoped out the juggernaut of attacking legions of ghouls and saw the truth in Porter's words.

"Let's get back to the gate," he said. He scanned the road, still cluttered with corpses, but not as many as before. "We did our best. We're out of time."

Chapter 84

Hilda heard the constant din of the ghouls' myriad feet trudging across the ground toward the compound drumming in her ears, as she stalked up to Zodiac near the gate.

"What you did to Diego was reprehensible," she said.

"What are you talking about?" said Zodiac, sickle in hand.

"I heard you tell him to kill himself. That's—"

"Wait a minute," said Zodiac, cutting her off. "There was a reason I said that. I don't know how much of our conversation you heard—"

"I can't believe you told him—"

Zodiac held up his hand. "Hear me out. The holy man told me we had to sacrifice someone. That's the only way we could come to peace with the ghouls. So I told him to sacrifice himself. He refused, of course, because these holy men have no desire to save mankind. What they desire is to line their pockets like those megamillionaire televangelists. I was exposing him as the fraud he is."

"To tell him to commit suicide is unconscionable, whatever your reasons."

"He didn't kill himself, so why are you throwing a fit?"

"Through no fault of yours."

"Look, he's a threat to the community. He's against violence. How are we supposed to defeat the ghouls without violence? Survival is all about fighting. He doesn't get it. If we don't fight the ghouls, they'll kill and devour all of us."

"He's entitled to his opinion."

"And I am to mine. If he wants to make a sacrifice, let him sacrifice himself. He's dead weight. He's useless to us, since he refuses to whack the ghouls."

"Telling him to kill himself is the same as murdering him."

"There are too many of these holy men and monks in this country. Monks and holy men everywhere I look. They're sapping the lifeblood from the human race with their peacenik, meek-as-a-lamb notions. They all should be burned at the stake before they suck the very blood out of us and destroy us. The reason they wear a black robe is because they represent death, and black is the color of death. They are harbingers of death. We can't let them destroy us."

Hilda shook her head at him in disapproval. "You read too many comic books."

"I'm gonna rescind my invitation to you to come along with us, if you keep chattering like a magpie. How about I kneecap you instead?"

"You're the one that's gonna end up destroying all of us."

"Fine. You can stay here with the holy man and not defend yourself from the ghouls and see how that works out."

"If you take all our guns, how can we take on the ghouls?"

"Make a sacrifice like the holy man said," said Zodiac, his face smug.

"You're sentencing us to death."

Zodiac made a show of mulling it over. "Maybe not. Maybe the fence will hold."

"Open the gate," said Halverson, appearing at the gate with Marta and Porter.

Zodiac angled to the gate and peered through the chain links past Halverson at the road.

"You haven't finished your job," said Zodiac. "There are carcasses on the road."

"We cleared off as many as we could. The ghouls are closing in."

"Go back and keep clearing off the road."

Porter caught sight of a tall female ghoul in a grimy marmalade dress shambling toward him, a knife sticking out of her throat, her mouth open, exposing her jagged, rotten teeth, as she moved in for the kill. Wheeling around, Porter crashed his sledgehammer into her temple, fracturing her skull, and atomizing half of her brain. Her knees buckled.

"Let us in, damn it," Marta told Zodiac, as the dead ghoul collapsed behind her.

Glancing over her shoulder, she picked up on a thirtysomething bespectacled Chinese ghoul in a black suit and aqua tie lurching toward her, maggots squirming out of his nostrils, strips of his skin hanging from his cheekbones. She whirled around and thrust her spade into the ghoul's head, shearing off the top of his skull and brain, dropping the creature in his tracks.

Her face glistening with sweat, she pirouetted to confront Zodiac. "What are you waiting for? Do you want us to die first?"

"Don't tempt me," said Zodiac.

He started and slewed around at the cacophony behind him, wondering what the source of the commotion was.

Zodiac's black Lincoln Navigator, Tyler at the wheel, rocketed to the gate and came to a screeching halt, laying down rubber.

Zodiac ordered the guard to open the gate.

Halverson, Marta, and Porter rushed into the complex, six ghouls shambling in their wake.

"Let's load up and beat it," Zodiac called to his men.

He plugged the first three ghouls in their heads with his Glock, felling them.

Halverson took out another one, an old gap-toothed guy with shaggy pewter grey hair, jamming his crowbar through the creature's glazed white eye, transfixing the brain. Halverson yanked the crowbar out of the ghoul's head, brains dripping from the high-tensile steel, while the ghoul fell to its knees and onto its punctured face, a hole through the back of its skull where the tip of the crowbar had burst out.

Tyler leapt out of the SUV's driver's seat, wielded his AR-15, and blasted the two ghouls remaining in the road six feet away from Halverson, bursting their rotting heads into shards of skull and gouts of brain matter.

"Load up, load up," cried Zodiac, beckoning with his arm over his head.

His men piled into the SUVs queued up at the gate.

Zodiac clambered into his Navigator, riding shotgun with Tyler at the wheel.

"Halverson, drop your crowbar and get in here with me," said Zodiac. "You're my guide."

Ditching the crowbar Halverson climbed into the Navigator's backseat.

"You two in the backseat, too," Zodiac told Marta and Porter.

They piled in after Halverson.

"Floor it," Zodiac told Tyler. "Run over anyone that gets in our way."

Tyler crushed the accelerator. The Navigator blasted through the open gate with a convoy of SUVs trailing it.

"Mount Weather, here we come," said Zodiac.

Chapter 85

Inside the Mount Weather bunker, wearing gas masks, three SEAL Team Six members were preparing to open the bombproof door and blast their way through the ghouls surrounding the complex.

Forty-year-old SEAL Ben Strider was leading the attack. A senior chief petty officer sporting three days' growth of stubble on his face, he stood six three with a bent aquiline nose and blazing blue eyes. In his hand he gripped a grenade. In his rear trouser pocket he carried a miniature Bible.

He pressed the red plastic button that opened the bunker's steel door electronically. The door whooshed open.

At the sight of the opening door, hundreds of ghouls that were milling in front of it headed for the doorway.

Strider lobbed a grenade into the closest creatures, pressed the red button, and shut the door, which was solid steel and thick enough to withstand a nuclear blast. Even with the protection of the door, he covered his ears and opened his mouth as the grenade exploded a few feet from the door.

He opened the door again to reveal a smoking pile of dead ghouls, most of them dismembered. For good measure he unclipped a grenade from his belt, lobbed it into the smoking carnage, and shut the door. Again he covered his ears and opened his mouth.

The ensuing blast rattled the steel door. After the shaking stopped, Strider opened the door.

"Give me the flamethrower, Johnny," he told the SEAL behind him.

A stocky, bull-necked five-nine African American pushing thirty handed a flamethrower to Strider. "Why not let me do it, Senior?"

"I'll do it. I want to make sure those things are dead. Stand back."

Strider aimed the flamethrower at the clusters of corpses strewn in front of the door. He squeezed the trigger. A tongue of flame lashed thirty feet out of the flamethrower's muzzle, incinerating everything in its path. Strider waved the flamethrower to and fro, laying down fire, making sure he smoked every ghoul anywhere near the bunker exit.

"Now let me have the RPG-7," said Strider, leaning the hot flamethrower against the cinderblock wall.

Johnny handed the RPG-7 to him. "Why do you get to have all the fun, Senior?"

"Stand clear of the blowback," said Strider, waving his arm behind him.

Johnny and the other SEAL backed fifteen feet away and off to the side so they wouldn't be standing directly behind the RPG-7 in the way of the blowback that could burn off their faces.

Strider brought the RPG-7 to his shoulder, aimed it through the dissipating smoke into the nearest mob of ghouls, and fired. A cloud of smoke erupted from the RPG-7's muzzle, while another cloud of smoke mixed with flaring flames burst from the rear. Thirty-six feet from the muzzle, the rocket ignited boosting the grenade to maximum velocity. The rocket-propelled grenade blasted through a knot of ghouls at a hundred and sixty feet, taking with it other ghouls slogging behind them as it tore through all of them, catapulting severed body parts and decapitated heads helter-skelter.

"Let's clean the first air duct," said Strider, scoping out the corpses smoking outside and seeing no movement in the immediate vicinity. "And get it done before they regroup."

He leaned the RPG-7 against the wall and gripped his Brügger & Thomet MP9, set on full auto, loaded with 9 mm Parabellum rounds, which was slung over his shoulder on a leather strap. He shrugged the leather strap off his shoulder and strode out the door.

"Johnny, you're on my six," he said. "Shoot anything that moves."

Armed with another B&T MP9, Johnny followed, keeping his eyes peeled.

"Joon-ho, watch our rear," Strider told the third SEAL, "and make sure none of them sneak around behind us and cut us off."

The man known as Joon-ho was a wiry, twenty-seven-year-old, five-eight Korean American armed with an MP9.

"Nothing gets by me unless it's filled with my lead," he said.

Cradling his B&T Strider trotted out the door among the smoking ghoul corpses strewn on the ground, watching for any movement. Johnny and Joon-ho followed in tandem on the qui vive.

Strider halted and unleashed a burst at a female ghoul with no arms and wearing flaky scarlet lipstick worming her way over a cadaver, her jaws snapping. Sickened by the sight, he kept firing till the ghoul's head disintegrated into bone fragments and gobbets of brain.

"That's no way to treat a lady," said Johnny.

"That ain't no lady," said Strider.

Johnny grinned.

Chapter 86

Strider jogged through the wafting smoke on his way across the battleground to the HVAC duct.

He almost missed the duct because the area around it was so congested with converging ghouls that he couldn't see the aperture. He opened up on them with his B&T, peppering them with 9 mm Parabellum slugs that detonated their heads.

Johnny and Joon-ho came up blasting, wiping out the rest of the ghouls that were standing around the duct. The shambling ghouls stopped dead in their tracks with lead in their brains and toppled to the ground, deceased for good this time.

Strider, Johnny, and Joon-ho commenced hauling the moldering corpses out of the way to clear a path to the duct.

Strider approached the duct, which was clogged with ghouls writhing in it eager to enter the bunker, their feet struggling to find purchase as they crawled over each other in a kind of danse macabre that turned his stomach.

Behind him, Johnny fired a burst from his B&T. Strider whipped around, gun at the ready.

"One of those things was still alive," said Johnny, nodding at a now-inert ghoul lying prostrate at his feet, a fresh bullet hole in the back of its head.

Strider nodded. "We gotta haul those stinking things out of the duct. Best do it one at a time. Johnny, you drag them out of there by their feet, and me and Joon-ho will make mincemeat of their heads."

"I hate touching those things," said Johnny, pulling a face. "They're packed in there like sardines."

"Where are your gloves, man? Put on your gloves. You don't want their infectious spores getting on you."

Johnny withdrew a pair of work gloves from a cargo pocket on his trousers and slipped them on. He set to work latching onto the kicking feet of the nearest ghoul and pulling the creature out of the crammed duct.

"No wonder we can't breathe inside with all these scumbags stuffed in there," said Joon-ho.

Johnny dragged the ghoul out of the duct. Flailing its arms and trying to bite him, a male ghoul in his twenties jackknifed and tried to take a bite out of Johnny's arm. Strider shot the ghoul with a brief well-aimed burst that atomized the creature's necrotic head, which was swarming with flies.

Johnny set to work on the next nearest ghoul wedged in the duct.

"There must be hundreds of them jammed in there," he said, struggling to peer through the duct. "How many HVAC units does the bunker have?"

"Five," said Strider.

"This could take a week if they're all as clogged as this one."

"Shake the lead out. I see another mob of ghouls gathering in the distance for an attack."

"A volley of lead in their brains will change their minds," said Joon-ho.

"There are too many of them for us to make a dent in their numbers. When their main force gets here we'll have to retreat and clear them out with the flamethrower and the RPG-7."

Johnny snagged another pair of ghoul feet, attached to a thirtyish convict with tattoos of spiders on his shaved head wearing an orange jumpsuit. Johnny tugged the feet's owner out of the congested vent.

"What's to prevent the attacking ghouls from crawling into the air duct to take the place of the ones we remove?" said Johnny, grunting as he pulled on the ghoul feet.

"Every time they clog the duct we'll have to come out and unclog it."

"But there are millions of those things, and they just keep coming," said Joon-ho, surveying the advancing horde of ghouls raising clouds of dust as they plodded up the sloping ground and emitted guttural growls that charged the air with an eerie din.

"Would you rather suffocate to death in the bunker?" said Strider.

"We got the best army in the world," said Johnny, dragging a weltering, beetle-browed, thickset, swarthy male ghoul out of the conduit. "You would think we could wipe these scumbags off the face of the earth easy-peasy."

The ghoul managed to turn itself over so it lay on its back, snarling. It reached up to grab Johnny with its clawing dirty fingers.

"Stop bitchin', Johnny," said Strider, and fired a short burst from his B&T MP9 that obliterated the ghoul's decrepit head.

The ghoul lay on its back motionless, half of its skull missing.

"Next," said Strider.

Johnny went back to work hauling ghouls out of the vent.

Chapter 87

What ordinarily would have taken thirty-three hours took Zodiac's convoy of twelve SUVs the better part of three days to reach Bluemont, Virginia, from their camp in Arizona via I-40E and I-64E on account of having to clear away the raft of motor vehicles abandoned on the interstate by people fleeing the ghouls, running out of gas, and running out of luck. Most of these hapless skedaddlers ended up dead, their corpses either decorating the tarmac or the highway shoulders. They hadn't reanimated because their brains had been scooped out of their heads like poi and devoured by marauding ghouls.

Zodiac, who was in a hurry to reach Mount Weather, didn't even bother to remove the bodies from the highways. He told his men to run over the scattered corpses whenever the SUVs encountered them in the way.

When they encountered scrums of ghouls roaming on the interstate, the SUVs mowed them down and kept going—unless there were too many of the creatures, in which case, the SUVs detoured and got back onto the interstate elsewhere.

Two of the SUVs broke down during one of their detours over rough terrain and had to be abandoned. One of them broke its drive shaft, rendering it inoperable. The other, a Ford Explorer, crashed into an oak tree smashing its left front fender so badly that the damaged fender prevented the wheel from spinning.

Zodiac left the passengers to fend for themselves, since he had no room for them to fit into his remaining SUVs. All but four of the passengers, anyway. The four who had smashed the Explorer into the oak protested his decision to leave them, declaring he was abandoning them to die at the hands of the ghouls. They demanded to be taken with him.

"We have no room for you," said Zodiac, standing near the Explorer taken out by the oak tree. "Our SUVs are full."

"Throw out some of your weapons and make room for us," said the Explorer's driver, Morgan, a short thirtysomething guy in jeans and cowboy boots with a big mouth and a Zapata mustache standing facing Zodiac. "You need us. You need manpower to fight the ghouls."

"I need firepower to fight them."

"You're condemning us to death if you leave us. The ghouls will kill us. There's only four of us, and you took our guns. How can we fight thousands of ghouls without guns?"

"Necessity is the mother of invention," said Zodiac, unconcerned.

"Why are you punishing us for your poor planning?"

"You're the one who plowed your Explorer into a tree. Don't blame it on me."

Zodiac returned to his Navigator.

"What if we sit on your tailgates and hitch a ride with you?" said Morgan. "You won't have to make room for us inside the vehicles."

Zodiac reached for the leather panel on the interior of the Navigator's passenger-side door and withdrew an AR-15 braced on it.

"What if I shoot you so you stop shooting off your mouth?" he said, and unleashed a burst into Morgan and the two men and one woman with him, stitching a crimson swath of bullets across their chests.

They collapsed on the dirt and lay in motionless heaps.

"Guy doesn't know when to shut up," said Zodiac, climbing into the passenger seat and shutting the door behind him. "Drive, Tyler."

Grim-faced, Halverson, Marta, and Porter sat in the backseat, their wrists bound behind their backs by black plastic zip ties.

"Asshole," muttered Porter, shooting a dirty look at the back of Zodiac's head. "What kind of a leader kills his own men?"

"Did someone say something?" said Zodiac.

Nobody answered.

"Drive, Tyler," said Zodiac.

"You got it, boss," said Tyler.

He fired the Navigator's engine and peeled off.

Chapter 88

Halverson's directions were accurate, as his memory had resolved into crystal clarity since his confrontation with Victoria. The convoy had no trouble finding Mount Weather. Once they reached the bunker, Halverson would have to find a way to escape Zodiac so he could contact the president and warn him about Zodiac's intentions to overthrow the government.

They drove into a bosky area that led up to Mount Weather.

Zodiac watched Halverson's every move, having no intention of letting Halverson escape.

"There's a secret code to enter the bunker, isn't there?" said Zodiac. "And you know it. You're the one that's gonna let us inside the president's bunker."

Halverson said nothing.

There was no way he was going to help Zodiac enter the high-security Area B.

"Things will go better for you if you cooperate," said Zodiac, craning around his neck from the front seat to check out Halverson. "I didn't bring you here to enjoy the scenery."

"Don't tell him," Porter told Halverson.

Zodiac glowered at Porter. "You best keep your mouth shut."

"Aren't you afraid of riding in a car with us carriers?" said Porter. "You could end up infected, breathing our spores."

"Let me worry about that. You worry about how long I'm gonna let you live once we get to the president's bunker."

Tyler slammed on the brakes, whiplashing Zodiac forward.

"What the hell?" said Zodiac.

"Ghouls up ahead," said Tyler, his face sweaty, peering through the Navigator's windshield. "Millions of them."

Zodiac faced forward, taking in the scene from hell of thousands of corpses marching through the piney forest in the same direction he was headed, their backs to the Navigator.

"Are they all making for the bunker?" he said.

"They're heading somewhere. They're not foraging."

"Could they know our government is holed up in the bunker?"

"The dweebs? They're too stupid."

Zodiac chewed it over. "Maybe they can smell living humans in the bunker."

"Then it's lucky we're downwind of them."

"We're gonna have a fight on our hands. Not just the government, but the ghouls, if there are more of these things at the bunker."

As the ghouls kept shambling away, they revealed, like curtains parting, a grisly sight. A black woman in her thirties with thick features was lying on her back on the road, her dress and stomach ripped open and a good ten feet of her intestines unwound and grasped in the hands of four ghouls that were gripping the intestines and eating them with relish like they were chewing corn on the cob.

"Help me," the woman screamed in anguish, her body racked with pain.

"Ohmigod," said Marta, watching from the backseat of Zodiac's Navigator. "Do something."

"I don't see how she's still alive," said Zodiac.

"She won't be much longer," said Tyler. "She's bleeding out and gonna turn any minute."

"Not anything we can do."

"The poor woman," said Marta, her gaze riveted in horror on the ghouls consuming the woman's entrails. "There must be something we can do."

"At least, put her out of her misery," said Halverson.

"If I shoot her, the ghouls will know we're here, turn around, and lay into us," said Zodiac.

"Those four ghouls already know we're here and aren't attacking us."

"Because they're feeding. Nothing interrupts suppertime for those things. As long as their buddies don't see us, we're OK."

One of the ghouls, a fiftyish woman with black hair, wearing black plastic butterfly-framed spectacles, her hair in a ponytail, let go of her segment of the entrails and reached into the victim's open stomach under the rib cage groping around in search of her heart.

The downed woman emitted a heart-wrenching yelp.

"I can't stand listening to her scream," said Marta.

"Then don't listen," said Zodiac. "We need to get off this road and find another route that leads to the bunker." He looked over his shoulder toward the backseat. "How about it, Halverson?"

"There's another road about a mile south of here," said Halverson.

"Tyler, double back and take the first road that heads south till we hit the road he's talking about."

The woman being mauled by the ghouls became silent and lay motionless, as the pony-tailed ghoul latched onto the woman's heart, tore it out of the rib cage, raised it triumphantly, and without ceremony crammed it into her gaping mouth, which dripped with fresh blood as she commenced tucking into her lip-smacking meal.

"Jesus Christ," said Tyler, the color draining from his face.

He couldn't get out of there fast enough. He executed a U-turn and drove back the way they came with the convoy in pursuit.

Chapter 89

When Tyler reached the nearest intersection, he turned south and kept going till he reached the auxiliary road that led to the bunker, where he hung a left. He drove along the winding road under the canopy of pines.

"How far, Halverson?" said Zodiac.

"Any minute now," said Halverson.

Tyler eased off the Navigator's gas. "It's not any better here, boss."

"I see that," said Zodiac, eying the thousands of ghouls slogging up the mountain toward the bunker.

"What do we do?"

"How many miles away is the bunker?" Zodiac asked Halverson.

Halverson scoped out the mountain's woods. "It's hard to tell. I'm not sure exactly where we are."

"Give me a guesstimate. Ten miles, twenty, a hundred?"

Halverson scrutinized the area. He made out a clearing up ahead.

"Keep on driving," he said. "I think that clearing is where the chain-link fence should be."

"Keep going," Zodiac told Tyler.

"I don't want those things to see us," said Tyler.

"Just keep going."

Halverson leaned forward peering past the front seat through the windshield.

"That clearing is where the fence should be," he said.

"I don't see any fence."

"A fifteen-foot-high chain-link fence should be there with a gate across the road marking the perimeter of the Emergency Operations Center complex."

"So where's the fence?"

"Keep driving," said Halverson.

"You heard him," Zodiac told Tyler.

"I don't want to get too close to the dweebs. They'll hear our engine."

"Just a little farther," said Halverson, squinting through the windshield.

Tyler drove forward at twenty miles an hour.

"I see," said Halverson. "Look. The ghouls trampled down the gate and the fence."

Ghouls were marching over the gate that lay flat across the road up ahead. They had trampled the entire perimeter of the chain-link fence that surrounded the complex.

"Nothing can stop those things," said Tyler with awe. "There are just too many of them. Look at them. I never seen so many. How will we get by them?"

Thousands of the creatures were traipsing across the clearing heading up the mountain, where the agency had cleared away the trees, to the bunker. The narrow road was chockablock with ghouls.

"Stop," said Zodiac. "We need to think this out." He turned to Halverson. "How far is it from here to the bunker entrance?"

"About a mile, more or less," said Halverson.

"We could try to cut a swath through them," said Zodiac, rubbing his chin. "But as soon as they know we're here, they're gonna converge on us."

"We can't take on all of them," said Tyler, scoping out the mass of dead flesh ascending the mountain like an undulating carpet. "We'll run out of ammo."

"Is there some other way to reach the bunker entrance?" Zodiac asked Halverson.

"No," answered Halverson. "It's either this road or the other, which we know is no better than this."

Zodiac shook his head. "We'll never be able to run over all of them for a mile. You got any bright ideas?"

Halverson agreed with Zodiac's assessment. "No."

Zodiac thought about it. "Maybe the holy man was right."

"Boss?" said Tyler, eying Zodiac in confusion.

"He told me we need to make a sacrifice to defeat the ghouls."

"What good does that do us?"

"A diversion."

"What kind of sacrifice are you talking about?"

"Human."

Zodiac craned around and stared at Halverson. "I know just the guy. The CIA agent."

Halverson didn't know what Zodiac was talking about and figured he was better off not knowing. In any case, he would find out soon. He stared back at Zodiac.

"But first tell us the code to the door," said Zodiac.

"You don't have security clearance," said Halverson.

"You'd rather be the holy man's sacrifice?"

"Why do you need the code? We're nowhere near the bunker door, and there's no way to get there."

"There will be after you're sacrificed."

Halverson said nothing. Zodiac's plan was no clearer to him. There was no way Halverson was going to let Zodiac into the bunker, where the maniac would slaughter President Cole and his cabinet—and, no doubt, any other officials left of the current administration.

Zodiac turned to Tyler. "Get me two large branches in the woods."

"How large?" said Tyler, wondering what they would be used for.

"How tall are you, Halverson?"

"Six two," said Halverson.

"One needs to be at least . . . uh, eight feet long," Zodiac told Tyler. "And it needs to be thick and strong. At least six inches thick. And no rotten wood. It needs to be fresh."

"If it's lying on the ground, it's probably gonna be rotten, since it's dead."

"Then break it off a tree." Zodiac paused. "No, get the saw out of the toolbox and take it with you."

"How big do you want the other branch?"

"Six or seven feet should do it. Same thickness. Cut off any extraneous branches sticking out of them."

Tyler retrieved a crosscut saw from the Chevy Suburban in the convoy, took three other soldiers with him, and set off to find the branches.

Chapter 90

A half hour later Tyler returned with his men with the two branches to Zodiac. Two men carried each branch between them.

Zodiac and Tyler stood next to the Navigator.

"Good job," said Zodiac. "I've been thinking about what the holy man told me. I'm thinking if one sacrifice is good, two would be even better. What do you think?"

"Makes sense," said Tyler, unsure what Zodiac was getting at.

"Rig the catapult for firing."

"At what?"

"At the ghouls. Take Porter with you."

"For what?"

"Ammo for the catapult."

"You bastards," said Porter, who had overheard them from the backseat of the Navigator.

"Don't blame me," said Zodiac. "It was the holy man's idea."

"Diego's not even here."

"What distance?" said Tyler.

"About three hundred feet toward the bunker," said Zodiac.

"He won't reach the bunker."

"He's not supposed to reach it."

"How am I supposed to get past the ghouls to the bunker after I land?" said Porter.

"Don't worry about it," said Zodiac. "The fall will probably kill you."

Porter gave him a look. "Even if I make it to the bunker, I don't know the code to the door."

"You worry too much."

Tyler hauled Porter out of the backseat. "Let's go."

"You're killing me," Porter told Zodiac, outraged.

"You should be thankful you're not getting Halverson's treatment."

"What's that supposed to mean?" said Porter, struggling to break free from Tyler despite his bound wrists.

Tyler set off frog-marching Porter to the catapult at the end of the convoy.

"Never mind. Bon voyage," said Zodiac, waving good-bye.

"You son of a bitch," said Porter.

He stumbled forward as Tyler gave him a vicious shove from behind.

"Don't do this," said Halverson in the backseat of the Navigator. "What's the point?"

"Haven't you been listening?" said Zodiac. "I'm making a sacrifice. The holy man said it's the only way we can survive."

"Killing Porter serves no purpose."

"He's getting off easy compared to you."

Halverson had no idea what Zodiac meant. "The less people you have to fight the ghouls, the less chance you have of beating them. Killing Porter diminishes your forces."

"Ready, boss," cried Tyler from the catapult, waving his hand above his head.

Zodiac nodded in acknowledgment.

"Please let him go," said Marta, sitting beside Halverson, her voice urgent.

"Porter's a good fighter," said Halverson. "You said so yourself."

"We need diversions and sacrifices," said Zodiac, raising his arm, extending his forefinger deliberately above his head, and looking at Tyler.

"What kind of a diversion is this? Porter won't last five minutes out there. They'll be all over him in seconds."

"I'll be your girlfriend if you let him go," Marta told Zodiac, desperate to save Porter's life.

Zodiac looked amused for a moment then became serious. "You had your chance. You blew it."

"Wait a minute," said Halverson. "I'll tell you the bunker code if you let him live."

Zodiac paused, considering Halverson's offer. "All right. What's the code?"

"Are you sure you should do this?" Marta asked Halverson.

"I can't stand by and let Porter die," answered Halverson.

"What's the code?" said Zodiac. "I'm not waiting any longer."

"Boss?" said Tyler from the catapult, awaiting the signal.

Halverson decided he had no choice. He gave Zodiac the pass code to the bunker door.

"Thank you," said Zodiac. "Fire," he told Tyler, raising his voice, and bringing down his hand.

"No," said Halverson, his heart in his throat.

Tyler fired the catapult.

His wrists bound behind him, his face a mask of horror, Porter soared through the air for the best part of three hundred feet and crashed into the churning horde of ghouls encompassing the bunker. Seconds before he landed he screamed. He crash-landed onto three ghouls, helping break his fall. Nevertheless, he broke several ribs and knew he must have sustained injury to internal organs on account of the shooting pain he felt. The ghouls converged on him as he lay squirming on his back cursing them.

From the Navigator Halverson watched in misery as Porter's severed arms yanked out of their shoulder sockets trailing streams of his blood soared out of the mob of ghouls that tore him apart and devoured him in a feeding frenzy. Other ghouls in the serried mob, incited by the metallic odor of fresh blood charging the air, reached out, snagged the bleeding arms in midflight, and shoved them into their mouths.

Tears welled in Marta's eyes at the revolting spectacle.

Seething hatred for Zodiac superseded Halverson's sorrow at Porter's dying as the murderous ghouls drowned out Porter's screams by killing him.

"You goddamn liar," said Halverson. "I gave you the code and you still killed him."

"Everybody lies," said Zodiac, calmly watching the throng of ghouls make short work of Porter's remains. "Look at the bright side. At least, he's not gonna turn. There's not gonna be anything left of him when they're done feeding."

"I'm sure that makes him feel a lot better."

Zodiac ignored Halverson's sarcasm. "Anyway, how do I know you're not lying about the code till I try it on the door?"

"You're sick in the head," Marta told Zodiac. "You're worse than a ghoul. They don't even know what they're doing. You do."

"Shut up," said Zodiac, "or you're next in the catapult. Wanna join your buddy Porter?"

"Not much of a diversion," said Halverson, watching the creatures. "They've already resumed trying to break into the bunker."

"Another sacrifice is necessary. And you're elected, CIA sociopath working for the corrupt government that's turning our country into a wasteland."

Chapter 91

"Tyler, get some rope and tie those two branches together in the shape of a cross," said Zodiac. "And get some tenpenny nails and a hammer out of the tool chest." He turned to Halverson. "Get the idea, Halverson?"

Halverson's heartbeat raced. He had to find some way for him and Marta to escape. He knew whatever Zodiac had in store for them wasn't good.

"Get out of the car," said Zodiac.

"Come and get me," said Halverson.

"Sammy, pull him out of there."

"You got it, boss," said Sammy.

Sammy opened the Navigator's rear door, reached into the back, grabbed Halverson by the arm, dragged him out of the backseat, and threw him on the road, where Halverson landed on his side, smashing his elbow and ribs.

"Get up," said Zodiac, staring down at Halverson.

"How am I supposed to get up with my wrists tied?" said Halverson.

"Just do it."

Halverson tried, but no soap. He managed to get on his knees, and that was as far as he got.

"You're helpless," said Zodiac. "What would you do without me? Sammy, get him up on his feet."

"Give me your hand," Sammy told Halverson, extending his hand.

"Very funny," said Halverson.

"Then we'll do it the hard way."

Sammy stood behind Halverson, looped his arm around Halverson's neck, wedged it in the crook of his arm, and lifted Halverson up. Halverson managed to get his feet under him and extend his legs. Sammy released his hold.

"Tyler, did you finish making the cross?" said Zodiac.

"All set," said Tyler, finishing tying knots in the rope securing the two limbs together in the shape of a cross.

"Good. Now nail Halverson to the cross."

"You're insane," said Halverson.

"I'm saner than all of you and smarter, too. How do you think I got to be number one, even though the system is rigged against me?"

"By lacking a conscience."

"What good is a conscience? Why do I want something that's unnecessary? Something that is, in reality, a ball and chain?"

"Like I said, you're insane."

Zodiac laughed. "I may be insane, but you're gonna be crucified. How's that grab you?"

"You really think the ghouls are gonna let you into the bunker if you give them me on a cross?"

"They want a sacrifice, according to the holy man, and you're it. Take him to the cross, Sammy."

Sammy frog-marched Halverson to the cross, which was lying on the road in front of Zodiac's Navigator.

"Are we taking him to the ghouls on a cross, boss?" said Tyler, standing near the base of the cross.

"He's taking himself," said Zodiac.

Tyler scratched his head. "But how can he walk?"

"Nail his hands to the crossbeam, but leave his feet alone. Untie his wrists and start hammering."

Sammy released the plastic zip ties that bound Halverson's wrists.

Halverson wheeled around and slammed a right cross into Sammy's jaw, rocking Sammy back on his heels. Groaning, Sammy rubbed his aching jaw. Halverson was about to grab Marta and make a dash for the woods when Zodiac whipped out his Glock and trained it on him.

"I don't want to shoot you," said Zodiac. "You're more valuable to me alive than dead. On the other hand, if I have to, I'm not gonna spill any tears."

Breaking into a sweat, Halverson didn't like his chances either way. Getting shot would mean a quicker death than getting crucified and fed to the ghouls. Cold comfort, he decided. He would die either way. He would never make the cover of the woods if he cut and ran. Zodiac would shoot him in the back.

Halverson stood his ground.

He felt crippling pain in his lower back and groaned. Sammy had sneaked up behind him and jabbed a fist into Halverson's kidney.

"You didn't think I was gonna let you get away with sucker-punching me, did you?" said Sammy.

"That's enough fun," said Zodiac. "Lay him on his back on the cross and nail his hands to it."

Sammy grabbed Halverson by the arm and shoved him to the cross.

"You heard the boss," said Sammy. "Lie down on the cross."

Wincing from the blow to his kidney, Halverson didn't see any way out. Zodiac was still training his Glock on him.

"If you shoot me, the ghouls will know you're here and attack," said Halverson.

"But you'll be dead. So why should you care?" said Zodiac. "Lie down now. It's time for your funeral procession up the mountain."

Chapter 92

Grudgingly, Halverson stooped down and lay supine on the longest limb, which dug into his spine. Sammy snatched Halverson's right wrist and tied it to the crossbeam with a zip tie. Tyler did the same with Halverson's left. Tyler picked up the hammer and a tenpenny nail that he had retrieved from the toolbox, which he had set on the tarmac. Crouching beside Halverson, he placed the point of the nail on Halverson's hand and raised the hammer.

"Make sure you don't hit any arteries," said Zodiac. "I don't want him bleeding out before the ghouls get to him."

"Where are the arteries?" said Tyler, looking uncertain, as he held the hammer poised above the nail head.

"Put the nail in the exact middle of the hand."

"No problem."

Halverson eyed the hammer suspended over his hand, his face sweaty.

Tyler glanced at Halverson's face. "I'm glad I'm not you."

Tyler returned his gaze to Halverson's hand and hammered the nail into the middle of Halverson's palm. He missed the nail head a couple of times, smashing Halverson's palm with the hammer.

"Oops, sorry," said Tyler, grinning at Halverson's pain as bones fractured in his hand under the hammer's blows.

Halverson didn't want to give Zodiac the pleasure of seeing him in pain. He tried to put the kibosh on his emotions. Nevertheless, he ground his teeth and winced.

Tyler hammered the nail all the way through Halverson's hand and deep into the limb. Hammer in one hand and a new nail in in the other, Tyler strode over to the other end of the crossbeam, hunkered down, and nailed down Halverson's other hand.

"Now get him up," said Zodiac.

"Boss?" said Tyler, baffled.

"I want him to stand with that thing on his back. He's gonna carry it into the ghouls."

Tyler and Sammy stood on either side of the crossbeam, lifted the cross, and proceeded to flip it over so Halverson stood beneath it.

"Walk into the ghouls, Halverson," said Zodiac.

Halverson had enough trouble standing, let alone walking. The base of the cross wasn't flush with the ground, causing him to bend slightly forward, putting additional stress on his back, which was already burdened with the weight of the cross.

"Stop it," said Marta from the Navigator.

Zodiac holstered his Glock, angled to the Navigator's backseat, and hauled Marta roughly onto the road.

"Do you want to join him?" he said.

"Anything's better than being with you," she said, standing in the road, her wrists bound.

"You got your wish."

He shoved her over to Halverson. She stumbled forward and almost fell.

"At least, untie me," she said.

"You ingrate. You should be thankful I'm not nailing you to a cross like your boyfriend."

"He's not my boyfriend."

"Oh yeah. That's right. You said I'm your boyfriend now."

"Only if you let Porter go. And you didn't. The offer is revoked."

"Are you willing to make the same deal to save your own life?"

"Why should I trust anything you say? You lied about letting Porter go. Why should I believe you're leveling with me now?"

Zodiac thought about it. "Even if you offered yourself to me, I wouldn't accept."

Marta laughed at the idea. "In your dreams."

"The only way I might accept you is if you get down on your knees, crawl to Halverson, crawl back to me, and beg me to be your boyfriend."

Marta shook her head in disgust at him.

"That's too bad," he said. "You know what the Bible says. Pride goeth before a fall."

"What would *you* know about the Bible?"

"My hippie mom used to read it to me once in a while after she'd dropped Owsley acid."

"She wasted her breath."

"Then good luck," he said. "And rest in pieces after the ghouls get their hands on you. You saw what they did to Porter."

Marta walked toward Halverson.

Zodiac followed her to send them off. "You two losers deserve each other. Take a hike."

He placed his foot against Marta's buttocks and gave her a shove.

Yelping in surprise she stumbled forward.

"I'm gonna kill that guy, so help me," she told Halverson, who shambled after her, grimacing, carrying the cross on his back straight toward the hordes of ghouls surrounding the emergency operations bunker, his impaled palms dripping blood on the road.

"It's a little late in the game to be plotting against me now," said Zodiac, and guffawed.

Chapter 93

His back aching from the weight of the cross, Halverson figured he was heading for certain death. The ghouls would butcher him when he reached them and there was no way out of it. His clothes were soaked with the sweat of fear.

How could he defend himself with his hands nailed to the cross? He supposed he could thrust the top of the cross at the ghouls like a battering ram. But he had no maneuverability. The cross on his back was unwieldy to say the least.

He considered turning back toward Zodiac. What good would that do? Instead of being devoured by the ghouls, Zodiac would blow him away.

Halverson would take his chances with the ghouls. If he got lucky, maybe he could reach the bunker door and let himself in. *Ha*, he thought. *Oh, sure, that'll happen.*

He plodded up the mountain, getting closer to the ghouls, able to smell their putrid stench and hear the din of their shambling feet. So far, they hadn't picked up on him, as he was behind them. It was only a matter of time.

"Do you have some CIA gadget to get us out of this?" said Marta, terrified as she walked in front of Halverson under the shelter of the top of the cross.

Halverson gave a hollow laugh.

When the ghouls spotted him, they gave him a strange look. He couldn't decide what kind of a look it was. They weren't looking at him like he was their next meal, nor were they drooling or baring their teeth. Maybe the wooden cross on his back had them confused. After all, it altered his shape. And yet, it didn't alter his smell. He was under the impression ghouls could smell humans.

The bottom line was, they weren't laying into him. Not yet, anyway. They could change their mood with a shift in the wind, for all he knew.

"Why aren't they attacking?" said Marta, her voice fraught.

"Beats me. They're gathering around us and following us. They could tear us to pieces in a New York minute."

"They stink something bad," said Marta, wrinkling her nose. "There are so many of them, it sounds like a stampede when they walk. Are they herding us somewhere?"

"It's more like they're following us. They haven't made any attempt to block or alter my course to the bunker entrance."

"It's creeping me out."

"Stay under the cross with me. The only thing I can figure is, the cross on my back changes my shape. Maybe they're not seeing a human when they look at us."

"They're too damn close," said Marta, cringing.

"Can you see what Zodiac's doing?"

Marta craned around and looked down the mountain slope. She couldn't see past the ghouls swarming behind them.

"I can't see past the things," she said. "Why do you want to know?"

"He might decide to attack, since he can see the ghouls aren't devouring us. He might think they won't attack him, either, and that he can make his way safely to the bunker door."

"I don't trust the ghouls."

"We got another problem."

"What?"

"They could still infect us if we breathe their spores."

"Zodiac said we're asymptomatic carriers. So the spores can't infect us."

"I don't trust Zodiac. He could've rigged the bloodwork tests to make us look like carriers when we're not. The only thing he cares about is power, and he wanted us out of his hair. What better way to demonize us than by claiming we're carriers and getting everyone to turn against us?"

"You're freaking me out. That means the spores can infect us."

"We can't rule it out."

"With them this close to us we're bound to get infected by the spores."

"It's not like we have a lot of choices. We need to reach the bunker."

Chapter 94

President Cole was sitting behind his desk in his office, while his personal physician Dr. Albert Morrow sat across from him. Wearing round rimless spectacles and a white smock, pushing sixty, Morrow was five nine and bald with a paunch. He had a brown fiberboard clipboard with Cole's medical records on it resting in his lap.

Morrow's Doctor of Medicine degree from Johns Hopkins had given him an inside track to a job at the White House as the president's physician, but hadn't prepared him for anything remotely like the zombie plague.

"I'm having difficulty breathing," said Cole.

"All of us in the bunker are, Mr. President," said Morrow. "The oxygen level is down because of the clogged air ducts."

"The ghouls are clogging the ducts and so far we've been unable to remove the filthy creatures. As soon as we do, more ghouls crawl in there and take their place."

"This isn't a medical problem, Mr. President. I don't see how I can help."

Cole got up from his seat and took a brief walk, his head bowed in thought, gripping the football chained to his wrist.

"I'm planning to leave the bunker," he said.

"We're surrounded by infected ghouls," said Morrow in surprise.

Cole looked at Morrow. "That's why I need something to prevent the ghouls' spores from infecting me. Do you have something for that?"

"I don't have anything to protect you from their bites. Once they bite you, you're infected. Nobody's immune to their bites."

"I'm not talking about bites. I'm talking about inhaling their contagious spores."

Morrow flipped through Cole's medical records on the clipboard on his lap. "You're in good physical condition."

"I could go ten rounds with Mohammad Ali," said Cole, sucking in a deep breath and beating his chest with his fist.

"You aren't taking many medications," said Morrow, glancing down at his clipboard. "Just something for your cholesterol level and your blood pressure."

"Hardly any."

"Nothing that would contraindicate my prescription."

"In plain English, Doctor."

"I have a steroid that might be of use. It was used with some success during the Covid-19 pandemic. It hindered that virus from spreading. We believe it has the same effect on the zombie plague spores."

"Will it make me immune from infection?"

"It's not a vaccine. It's a therapeutic. It reduces inflammation and will hinder the spread of the plague, if you inhale some of the spores."

"All right. Give me a shot of it," said Cole, offering his arm to Morrow.

"I would be derelict in my duty as a physician if I didn't tell you this particular steroid, like any steroid, has its risks."

"What steroid are we talking about?"

"Dexamethasone."

"Never heard of it. Is it dangerous?"

"It could have adverse effects."

"Such as?"

"Steroids affect moods. Dexamethasone could cause you to go insane."

Cole withdrew his arm and harrumphed, thinking.

"A lot of my opponents think I'm already insane," he said.

Morrow smiled.

"If it's a choice between dying from the spores or going mad, give me the shot," said Cole, offering his arm to Morrow again.

"I don't have any on me. I'll have to get some from the pharmacy. When do you plan on leaving?"

"Very soon. The musty air in this bunker is making me sick," said Cole, pulling a face. "I won't be able to stand it much longer." He coughed.

"How do you plan on solving the problem of ventilating the bunker?"

"I don't know yet. I need to get some fresh air so I can figure it out. The poisonous air is giving me headaches."

"Who's going with you?"

"General Pabst. Give him a shot of this steroid, too."

"When do you plan on coming back?"

"Hmm. Uh, as soon as Strider and his men get the HVAC ducts cleaned out. They'll notify me, and I'll return to the bunker. Get me that steroid shot now. I can't think straight in this toxic air we're breathing."

Morrow didn't like the sound of this. Somehow he doubted Cole was going to return, in which case he would be left to fend for himself in a bunker that would be devoid of oxygen in the foreseeable future. He hoped he was wrong about Cole.

"Yes, Mr. President," he said, and left to retrieve the steroid.

Chapter 95

Standing with Tyler and Sammy twenty feet from his Navigator, bewildered, Zodiac watched Halverson, nailed to the cross, trudge up the mountainside seething with ghouls. The ghouls weren't attacking him. Zodiac couldn't believe his eyes. Not only were they not attacking Halverson, they were following him, as though he was their leader.

"What the hell?" said Zodiac.

"What's wrong, boss?" said Tyler.

"Look at those stupid ghouls. They're not ripping Halverson apart."

Tyler dropped his jaw. "Maybe that cross is protecting him. The ghouls can't get to him because he's carrying that thing on his back."

"That's ridiculous. They could surround him, stop him, crawl under him, and rip his ribs out. Or they could knock him down, flip him over, and feast on his face. They could tear Marta to shreds, too, but they're not. They're letting the two of them go to the bunker."

"I never seen anything like it."

"Maybe these ghouls are different," said Sammy. "Maybe they don't attack humans."

"You're wrong," said Zodiac. "You saw what they did to Porter."

"Maybe their plan is to let Halverson get into the bunker so they can follow him inside," said Tyler.

"Those things can't think. They can't make plans. They're things, not humans anymore."

"What's their problem?"

Zodiac mulled it over. "Maybe this means they're accepting our sacrifice, like the holy man said. Which means they'll let us pass in peace."

"Do you really think that, boss?"

"If they're leaving Halverson alone, why shouldn't they leave us alone? We're the ones that gave them the sacrifice."

"I guess that makes sense, but—"

"I don't know what to think. The ghouls aren't reacting normally for some reason. It has to be our sacrifice of Halverson. What other explanation is there?"

"So what do we do?"

"We go up the mountain behind Halverson and let ourselves into the bunker after him."

"They'll kill all of us. There are too many of them. We can't blow all of them away without running out of ammo."

Zodiac surveyed the thousands upon thousands of ghouls flocking around the bunker trying to get inside.

"We need to get inside the bunker and get the president's football," he said in frustration. "We can't take over the country without that football. Whoever possesses the football is president."

"Do we walk up?"

"No, let's use the Navigator. If they turn on us, the SUV will protect us."

They strode back to the Navigator. Tyler climbed into the driver's seat. Zodiac rode shotgun. Sammy clambered into the backseat.

Zodiac pumped his fist. "Move it."

He turned on the dashboard CD player. Wagner's "Ride of the Valkyries" blared in the Navigator.

"Yeah," he screamed, invigorated by the music, his eyes glowing.

Tyler drove forward up the mountain into the throbbing mass of resurrected dead flesh.

The ghouls heard the booming music approaching and turned around to find out what was behind them. As the Navigator approached them, a phalanx of thousands of ghouls broke off from the main swarm and swept down on the Navigator and the convoy of SUVs behind it. Ravens appeared in the sky and swooped down to take a closer look at the impending strife.

"Why are the dweebs attacking us, boss?" said Tyler, straining to be heard above the music.

"Fuck 'em," said Zodiac. "Blow 'em all to hell."

He snagged an AR-15 from its mount on the side of his door, racked the first round into the chamber, aimed the muzzle out the window, and strafed the advancing ghouls with a thirty-round burst. Heads of the first line of attackers blew apart.

The bolt locked back. Zodiac swapped magazines and fired another burst, cutting down a scrum of ghouls with devastating headshots. The rising crescendo of "Valkyries" vibrated in his ears and inflamed him as the AR-15 blasted away, cutting a swath of death across the closest ghouls.

But for every ghoul that died, hundreds more took their places and plowed toward the SUV in a wave of imminent death.

Tyler and Sammy joined the fracas, opening up on the ghouls with their AR-15s, scything the ghouls with bullets.

"They just keep coming," said Tyler, jacked up with adrenaline, his face bathed in sweat.

"We need more mags," said Zodiac, swapping magazines. "One of you has to go outside and get mags from the SUV behind us."

Neither Tyler nor Sammy volunteered.

"Those things are too close," said Tyler. "We'll never make it. I'm out," he said, his bolt locking back after he squeezed off a final burst.

"Club them with your rifle stock," said Zodiac.

"They're so close now I can smell them."

"Sammy, what about you?"

"I'm down to my last mag," said Sammy.

"All right. Go outside and get ammo from the next vehicle."

Sammy widened his eyes with fear, watching the ghouls advancing in a ragged, lurching mob toward the Navigator.

"I—uh—I—I—"

"Do it now. That's an order."

Chapter 96

Grinding his teeth Sammy flung open the back door and stepped out of the Navigator. A quartet of ghouls slogged after him.

"Shut the door," cried Zodiac.

Sammy slammed the door shut behind him.

He cut down two of the ghouls with shots to their heads before his magazine emptied. He bolted for the next SUV, a black Chevy Suburban, where soldiers in the front seat were firing from their open windows blasting the ghouls with their automatic rifles.

"The boss needs more mags, Hank," Sammy yelled at them, clubbing an attacking buck-toothed female brunette ghoul with collagen-swollen lips in the head with his AR-15's stock.

"We're almost out," said a short twentysomething black man with a round face and a flat nose wearing a white T in the driver's seat, the veins in his muscular arms standing out like primer cord.

"Gimme what you got."

Hank reached into the foot well and dredged up three thirty-round magazines.

"Here," he said.

"That's it?" said Sammy in exasperation.

Hank shrugged. "Maybe the guys behind us got more."

Sammy took the magazines and stuffed them into his trouser cargo pockets.

He felt rather than saw ghouls converging on him from behind. Wheeling around with his AR-15 raised, he swung at the nearest head, connecting with bone and shattering the longhaired teenage male ghoul's skull. The skull split open. The ghoul's brain fell out and plunked down next to Sammy's feet. Revolted, Sammy stamped it into the ground, flattening it.

He sprang back to Zodiac's Navigator. Three ghouls trudged in front of him, blocking his path. Holding his AR-15 horizontally in front of him with two hands, he shoved them out of his way. He withdrew the magazines from his trouser pockets and tossed them through Tyler's open window.

A grey-haired female ghoul with a wizened face and a hunched back bit Sammy in the wrist.

Sammy screamed in pain and ripped his wrist out of the ghoul's blood-filled mouth, the radial artery in his wrist torn and jetting blood. Dropping his rifle he tried to open the Navigator's back door with his good hand. Zodiac craned around and aimed his Glock at Sammy's head.

"Boss, no, no," hollered Sammy, his face twisted with fear, his bitten wrist spurting blood.

"You're infected," said Zodiac.

He shot Sammy in the head. Sammy crumpled on the tarmac.

Zodiac unloaded on the two ghouls nearest Sammy's door, blasting their heads into bone chips and dollops of brain matter.

"Power up Sammy's window," Zodiac told Tyler. "I don't want any of those things crawling in here."

Tyler obeyed. "They're surrounding us. I don't get it. How come they left Halverson alone, but they're attacking us?"

"Shoot first. Ask questions later."

Zodiac holstered his Glock, scoffed up his AR-15, and aimed out his window at two thirtysomething male ghouls that looked like twins. He fired a brief burst. Hollow point slugs exploded their heads. His AR-15's bolt locked back.

"Toss me one of those new mags," he said.

Tyler leaned down into the foot well, snagged one of the fresh magazines that Sammy had brought back, and tossed it to Zodiac. Zodiac caught it and swapped magazines. Tyler slapped one of the other magazines into his AR-15.

"Only one mag left, boss. There are too many of those things out there."

Zodiac scoped out the battlefield. Thousands of ghouls were trampling the bullet-riddled dead ghouls on the ground making their way to the convoy. The first line of attackers was no more than ten feet away. Ghouls engulfed the Navigator like a boa constrictor squeezing its prey to death.

"Close the windows," said Zodiac. "I don't want those things getting in here."

They powered their windows up.

"Now we can't shoot them," said Tyler, watching them with apprehension as they converged on the Navigator.

"It is what it is."

Zodiac heard gunfire rattling behind him, emanating from the convoy of SUVs in tandem. He unclipped his walkie-talkie from his belt.

"Vehicle number two, how much ammo do you have left?" he said. "Over."

"None. We gave you our last three mags. Over."

"Copy that. Cease fire and power up your windows. Tell the other vehicles to do the same. Over."

"Roger. Over."

Hundreds of bloodthirsty ghouls swarmed around Zodiac's Navigator shoving their faces against the windows trying to bite through the safety glass. Some of the ghouls set to pounding their fists against the windows trying to break them.

"The windows. Are they gonna hold?" said Tyler.

"Those things are feeble. They can't punch through bulletproof glass."

"I hope you're right," said Tyler, unconvinced, his face lined with worry.

Unable to break the windows, the creatures commenced rocking the Navigator side to side trying to tip it over.

"Drive forward," said Zodiac, bracing his hands against the dash.

Tyler fired the engine. He shifted into drive and crashed into the ghouls huddled in front of the Navigator.

"Now what?" said Tyler.

"Run 'em over."

Tyler ran over several rows of ghouls before the Navigator came to a halt.

"Keep going," said Zodiac.

Tyler gunned the engine. The Navigator didn't move.

"No soap," said Tyler.

"What's wrong?"

"There must be bodies wedged in the wheel wells."

The ghouls ganging around the Navigator renewed their attempts to tip it over, rocking it from side to side.

Zodiac craned around and peered through the rear window. They couldn't reverse the Navigator without running into the vehicle behind them.

He cursed.

"Go out there and remove the stiffs from the wheel wells," he said.

"Those things'll kill me," said Tyler, eyes wide with fear.

"Take your gun."

"There are too many of them."

"What other choice do we have? We need to go forward. We need to attack. Attack. Always attack."

Breaking into a cold sweat, Tyler gulped and tried to open his door as countless ghouls pressed against it and rocked the Navigator to and fro.

"I can't open the door, boss."

"Keep trying."

"I'm dead meat if I go out there."

"I'll fire you if you don't get us the hell out of here," cried Zodiac.

Tyler stepped on the gas.

The Navigator didn't move forward. Even when some of its tires were able to spin, they failed to gain purchase, like they were stuck in mud. But it wasn't mud, it was layers of prostrate ghouls—some of them still living—whose decomposing slimy flesh provided no traction for the tires.

Annoyed at its rumbling engine and the blaring Wagner, the ghouls shoved the Navigator even harder, trying to tip it over.

"Boss?" said Tyler, still stepping on the gas, his eyes pleading.

"Don't fail me," said Zodiac. "Attack. Attack. You're not worthy of me, if you fail."

He turned "Valkyries" on full blast on the CD player.

His mouth working, Tyler floored the gas, cutting no ice.

Chapter 97

President Cole in his navy blue suit and General Pabst in his full dress uniform were sitting in the backseat of an electric golf cart that hummed along through a long, deserted, green ceramic-walled, arched tunnel in the bunker. Driving the cart was a Secret Service agent with a bull neck, wearing a black suit, a flesh-colored wire trailing down his neck from an earbud plugged in his ear. Cole had the football beside him chained to his wrist.

"Shouldn't we be wearing gas masks, Mr. President?" said Pabst. "The air's bad in here."

"The air's sickening is what it is," said Cole. "And wearing a gas mask makes me even sicker."

"When we go outside with the ghouls, they might infect us with their spores when we breathe the air around them."

"That's why I told Dr. Morrow to give you a steroid shot. Dexa—something or other. Did he give you your injection?"

"Yes, Mr. President."

"Good. Morrow says it fights off infection from the spores."

"Are you sure we should leave the bunker?"

Cole coughed. "What other choice do we have? There's no fucking oxygen here. It's only a matter of time before we all suffocate."

"Mind if I smoke?" said Pabst, reaching for a pack of cigarettes in his breast pocket.

"Yes, I do mind. We're already short of air. Tobacco smoke won't help matters. And your match's fire will consume our oxygen."

Pabst left the cigarette pack in his pocket, sliding his empty hand down the front of his uniform jacket, feeling jittery without his hit of nicotine.

"Marine One is ready and waiting for us at the helipad," he said.

"How do we get from here to the helipad with all those creatures surrounding the bunker? Are we taking Cadillac One?"

"The Secret Service and I agree that an SUV would be a better bet. We're taking their Roadrunner."

"Roadrunner?"

"It's the SUV they drive in presidential motorcades. It's a black Chevy Suburban tricked out for communications. Satellites on the roof and all that."

"Why are we taking that?"

"I'll show you when we get there. We're almost there now."

The golf cart careened around a corner and sped down another ceramic-tiled corridor that reminded Cole of a subway station, except it was deserted.

At the end of the corridor they reached the Suburban, which was parked in front of the closed nuke-resistant steel door that led outside.

He got out of the cart and pointed at a CCTV screen mounted near the top right corner of the door that showed the ghouls massing in the driveway.

"How are we supposed to get past those things?" said Cole, climbing out of the golf cart, lugging the football with him.

Pabst approached the black Suburban.

"Look how we modified the Roadrunner," he said, pointing. "We jury-rigged a snowplow on the front of the bumper to clear the ghouls out of the road."

"Why can't we just steamroller them?"

"The Suburban doesn't act like a steamroller, Mr. President. The corpses will stack up in front of the vehicle's wheels until we can't go forward. We've experienced the problem before. There are just too many of those things out there, and more keep coming."

Cole and Pabst clambered into the Suburban. Rudy, the Secret Service agent with a taurine neck, took the driver's seat.

"Is this car gonna hold up when the ghouls attack?" said Cole, inspecting the interior of the Roadrunner.

"Have no worries, Mr. President. It's armor-plated. Not that those creatures can fire arms. But they can't break through the windows either. The windows are bulletproof."

"What are we waiting for? I'm having trouble breathing," said Cole, coughing, tugging at the turquoise silk moiré tie collaring his neck.

Rudy used a remote fob to raise the electronic door, which led to a vestibule, where he drove the Suburban and stopped in front of another nukeproof steel door. He pressed the fob and lowered the steel door shut behind them.

"We don't want any of those ghouls getting inside the bunker when we exit," explained Pabst. "They'll rush into the vestibule when the front door opens and we leave. They'll get trapped when the door lowers behind us. Then our men inside will spray them with lighter fluid and set them on fire."

Behind them the vestibule's steel door lowered with a thud.

"We're ready to rock and roll," said Pabst.

Cole tugged at his tie, yanked it out of his collar, tossed it to the floor, and unbuttoned the top of his shirt so he could breathe.

"None too soon," he said.

"Are you ready, Mr. President?"

"Ready, General. Let's plow those suckers into an early grave."

"Greenlight, Rudy."

"Yes, *sir*," said Rudy.

He pressed the red button on the fob that activated the front door.

The heavy steel door rumbled, vibrating the entire vestibule, and slowly rose.

"Buckle your seat belt, Mr. President," said Pabst. "We could be in for a helluva rough ride."

"I wish my wife was still alive," said Cole, somber at her memory. "If only the damn zombie plague didn't infect her in DC."

"My family's holed up in a remote cabin in West Virginia. My wife and three kids. I hope they're all right. I haven't been able to contact them."

"Three kids?"

Pabst nodded yes. "George, Frederick, and Morgana."

"How old are they?"

"George is twenty. Fred is—um—nineteen. He's gonna kill me if he finds out I couldn't remember his age. And Morgana is seventeen."

"Whoever thought it would come to this?" said Cole, shaking his head.

"One question, Mr. President."

"Yes?"

"Where are we going?"

"Anywhere we can make a safe landing and breathe fresh air. As long as I have the football, I'm still the president," said Cole, glancing at the football beside him on his seat. "Maybe an island in the Caribbean that doesn't have any ghouls on it."

"The Virgin Islands."

"What about Epstein's Island?"

"He certainly isn't using it."

"And then we can regroup the government."

"Here they come."

The ghouls ducked under the door as it lumbered upward. They crowded around the Suburban pressing against it, peering inside, baring their teeth and drooling, clawing at the vehicle's locked doors trying to open them.

"Any time now, Rudy," said Pabst, cringing at the proximity of the ghouls, their faces plastered against his window, their noses flattened against the bulletproof glass, their gaping mouths slobbering.

As soon as the door rose high enough to allow the Suburban's roof to clear it, Rudy slammed the gas. The Suburban bucked forward, smashing ghouls out of its way with the snowplow, and roared onto the ghoul-jammed driveway.

Hindered by the dense rows of writhing ghouls, the Suburban ground forward plowing ghouls out of the road, making progress, however slow. The ghouls knew no fear. Despite the punishing impact of the steel plow with their festering flesh, they never retreated and continued their onslaught against the SUV.

"I hope the helipad's not going through anything like this," said Cole, taking in the throngs of ghouls surrounding the Suburban.

"The last I heard the helipad is clear for takeoff," said Pabst.

Chapter 98

Halverson trudged up the mountain to the bunker entrance
with the crushing weight of the cross on his back bearing down on
him. The longer he carried the cross the heavier it felt. Marta
stayed under the cross with him, defenseless with her wrists bound.
To Halverson's continued amazement, the hordes of ghouls parted
for them, watching them with something akin to reverence.

"We're almost there," said Marta, eying the bunker door
teeming with ghouls in front of it.

"With any luck they'll move away from us when we arrive,
like their pals who are following us did," said Halverson. "Then
I'll punch in the code on the door."

As expected, the ghouls constellated around the door cleared a
path for him when they saw him carrying the cross toward them.

Grimacing from carrying the cross, his hands bleeding,
Halverson approached the steel door. Marta sidestepped out of his
way. When he extended his hand to reach the code lock, his
fingers came up short thanks to the top of the cross that projected
over his head and blocked him from getting near enough to punch
in the code. In any case, his fingers were going numb from loss of
blood in his hands nailed to the crossbeam.

"I can't reach it," he said. "You'll have to do it."

"How can I with my wrists tied?"

Halverson thought about it. There had to be a way. They had
come so close. He couldn't let anything stand in their way now.

"Can you punch the code in with your nose?" he asked Marta.

She shrugged. "I can try."

Marta angled to the door. "What's the code?"

He gave her the numbers. She pecked at them with her beak.

Nothing happened.

"Are you sure you punched in the correct numbers?" he said.

"I can't press very hard with my nose. I'm sure I hit the right
numbers. Maybe the buttons didn't go down all the way. I'll do it
again to make sure."

She punched in the numbers again.

The door didn't budge.

"Maybe your memory's playing tricks on you again," she said.

"I don't think so. That's the correct code—unless—"

"Unless what?"

"Unless they changed it. Which easily could have happened, since I haven't been here in over ten years."

"Now what do we do?" said Marta, slouching in defeat, worried the ghouls that were shambling mere inches away from them awed by them might decide to turn on them in a trice.

Halverson caught sight of the CCTV camera mounted above the steel door jamb. He peered into the lens. Maybe they would let him in when they saw he wasn't a ghoul. On the other hand, seeing a guy nailed to a cross would make them suspicious, to say the least.

"We're being attacked," he said to the camera. "Let us in."

"Do they even know we're out here?" said Marta.

"There's gotta be a guard manning their CCTV." He paused. "On the other hand . . . I don't want to think about it."

"Stop teasing me. Think about what?" she said, and pressed her lips together in a tight white line.

"Everyone inside could be dead," he said, his tone bleak.

"How could they be dead? The bunker hasn't been breached. The door is locked."

"I don't want to bum you out, but maybe someone inside the bunker caught the plague and infected everybody inside."

"I thought you didn't want to bum me out. You're too cynical. Is there another way inside?"

"The garage door."

"Let's check it out."

Halverson pricked up his ears as he heard a squeak and saw the steel door commence to rise.

Chapter 99

Armed with their B&T MP9s and wearing gas masks, Strider, Johnny, and Joon-ho watched the bunker door rise after Strider pressed the button on the control panel that activated it.

When the door had risen far enough, Strider and his men strafed the ghouls outside the entrance with bursts from their B&Ts shattering heads and providing cover fire for Halverson and Marta to enter the bunker. Halverson had to wait for the door to fully open before he could fit the cross underneath the steel lintel. Fortunately, the bunker had a wide door or he never would have been able to fit the cross through it.

Strider and his men swapped magazines and kept smoking the ghouls, preventing any of them from entering with Halverson and Marta.

Halverson carried the cross all the way inside the bunker, Marta with him.

Strider closed the door. He and his men kept laying down fire to prevent the ghouls from sneaking under the door as it lowered.

The heavy steel door thudded shut.

"I can't believe it," said Strider, his voice muffled by his gas mask, staring at Halverson. "Halverson, is that you?"

"Strider?" said Halverson, straining to discern Strider's face through the gas mask's glass eye shields.

"Do you guys know each other?" said Marta with amazement.

"We took SERE training together at Fort Bragg," said Strider. "I wasn't sure it was you with that beard and hair."

"Yeah," said Halverson.

"Why weren't the ghouls trying to bite you? They kept walking up the slope with you like you were their leader."

"I wish I knew. *Can you get this damn thing off my back?*"

"What the hell is it? It looks like a cross. You're bleeding, man," said Strider, watching blood drip from Halverson's hands.

"That maniac out there did this to me."

"We saw the SUVs trying to get up here. The ghouls aren't letting them pass. And yet the ghouls gave *you* an escort. What's that all about?"

"Do you mind? I'm bleeding to death."

"Johnny, get a claw hammer and get those nails out of Halverson's hands."

Johnny scooted down the bunker tunnel to retrieve a claw hammer.

Halverson picked up on the flamethrower and the RPG-7 leaning against the wall.

Strider went over to the desk with a computer console on it, pulled out the top drawer, and withdrew a bottle of Johnny Walker Black Label.

"Want a drink?" he said, offering the bottle to Halverson.

"You got a straw?" said Halverson. "I can't drink anything in this condition. I can't tilt my head back."

"Do you mind telling me how you got nailed to a cross?"

"Zodiac."

"Come again?"

"The guy in charge of that convoy of SUVs coming up the road. He's coming up here to take over the government."

"I saw them on the CCTV. I wondered who they were."

"They're the enemy. Zodiac's their boss. He's the one that nailed me to the cross."

"Why?"

"As a sacrifice. He thought if he made a sacrifice, the ghouls would leave him alone."

"I can tell you, it's not working. Those things are all over his convoy. They're trying to tip over the SUVs."

"For some reason the ghouls left me and Marta alone."

Strider eyed Marta.

"You always got a woman with you. But it's never the same one," he said with a brief laugh.

"I can barely breathe in here," said Marta, screwing up her face and coughing. "Can someone untie me?"

Strider untied her wrists.

She massaged them.

"I noticed the same thing," said Halverson. "The air smells bad. What happened in here?"

"The air ducts are clogged," said Strider. "We're trying to clear them, but the ghouls clog them up as soon as we clear them out. We're losing oxygen. That's why we're wearing these gas masks."

"Is the president OK?"

"He's alive, if that's what you mean. Whether he's lost a couple of screws, your guess is as good as mine. He declared a national emergency and proclaimed himself president for life."

"I heard. Pataki told me."

"Pataki? Pataki found you? Where the hell is he? That guy owes me twenty bucks on a bet we made about you."

"About me?"

"I bet you were dead. He bet you were still alive."

Halverson grunted. "Thanks for the vote of confidence."

"Our SERE training didn't take into account a zombie apocalypse."

Halverson paused, not looking forward to breaking the news to Strider. "Pataki's out front."

"Where?" said Strider with concern. "He's not gonna last five minutes with those ghouls outside—"

"He's dead, Ben. Zodiac killed him."

"Pataki?" said Strider, disconcerted. "He always joked he was immortal," he muttered. "Poor bastard. How?"

Halverson decided to spare Strider the gruesome details of how Pataki had met his end at the hands of Zodiac.

"Zodiac shot him," said Halverson.

"He's not the only one Zodiac killed," said Marta.

"This Zodiac character sounds like a piece of work," said Strider. "I can't wait to meet him." He slapped his B&T's magazine for emphasis.

"I need to talk to the president," said Halverson. "Armed insurrectionists led by Zodiac are scheming to overthrow the government."

Chapter 100

Johnny returned with a hammer.

"Untie those zip ties around his wrists and yank those nails out of his palms," said Strider.

Johnny unfastened the zip ties and discarded them on the floor. He eased the hammer's claw between the tenpenny's head and Halverson's palm.

"This might hurt a bit," he said.

"It's not giving me a ton of pleasure now."

Johnny held Halverson's arm with his left hand and tugged on the nail head with the hammer in his right.

Halverson gritted his teeth in pain.

At first, Johnny worked the nail out slowly. When he had enough of the nail out that the claw had a good grip on it, he pulled the rest of it out with one jerk.

Halverson groaned through his gritted teeth.

"Next one," he said, dropping his free arm down at his side, feeling his blood resume circulating.

Johnny repeated the procedure clawing out the nail, freeing Halverson from the cross. Johnny lifted the cross off Halverson's back and threw it on the ground.

"Hold your palms up," said Strider.

Straightening up now that the cross was off his back, puzzled, Halverson did as Strider requested.

Strider unscrewed the cap from the whisky bottle and doused Halverson's wounded hands with whisky.

Halverson winced at the stinging sensation of the alcohol on his open wounds.

"We don't want your hands to get infected," said Strider.

"Now it's my turn," said Halverson. "Give me the bottle."

Strider handed it to him, baffled.

Halverson took a long pull on the scotch.

"Leave some for me, you hog," said Strider with a grin.

Halverson gave him back the bottle.

"Open the door," said Halverson.

"You crazy? Those things are out there."

"I know."

Despite his aching hands, Halverson snatched up the flamethrower.

"Wanna barbecue some ghouls?" said Strider.

"Just open the door."

Strider complied with a shrug.

Halverson aimed the flamethrower at the opening door. When the nearest ghouls tried to crowd inside, he let them have it. The flame shot out and torched them.

The door opened completely.

Halverson waved the flamethrower from side to side frying ghouls' heads until they exploded, their brains splattering out like seeds out of a burst cantaloupe. Strider gave him help by firing bursts from his B&T MP9, filling the ghouls with lead, blowing apart skulls, ejecting a steady cascade of brass shell casings onto the bunker floor. Johnny and Joon-ho joined in with their MP9s blazing away until the path to the door was a battlefield of fire and lead strewn with dead ghouls.

With the living ghouls cleared from the doorway, Halverson lowered the flamethrower and waited for the smoke to clear.

"Cease fire," said Strider.

Johnny and Joon-ho obeyed.

Halverson exchanged the flamethrower for the RPG-7.

"Now what?" said Strider, watching him.

As the smoke dissipated, Halverson could make out Zodiac's Navigator farther down the road. Hundreds of ghouls had surrounded it and were rocking it back and forth trying to overturn it.

"Stand back, everyone," said Halverson, glancing behind him to make sure nobody was standing close enough to get in the way of the RPG-7's blowback.

Halverson trained the RPG-7 on the Navigator, steadying the grenade launcher on his shoulder, breathing slow, calming his nerves, as he acquired the Navigator in the red dot reflex sight, and fired. The rocket shot out of the muzzle, streaked through the air, and slammed into the Navigator's fuel tank. The Navigator bucked and burst into a fireball. A pillar of black smoke spouted from the burning wreckage.

"I need another rocket," said Halverson.

Johnny collected another rocket and gave it to him. Halverson loaded it into the RPG-7's muzzle.

He aimed and fired. The rocket streaked through the air and took out the second SUV. It burst into flames and bounced high on its tires.

"Is that necessary?" said Strider.

"Maybe not," said Halverson, lowering the RPG-7. "Without their leader they might call off their assault on the bunker. On the other hand, they're seeking shelter from the ghouls, and this is the closest place for them to take refuge."

"Aren't you taking this personally?"

"The slime bucket nailed me to a cross. Of course, it's personal."

"Why bother with the rockets? The ghouls have those guys trapped. There's no way for them to escape. The ghouls are gonna knock the SUVs over, smash the windows, break into the interiors, and feast on whoever's inside."

"You're probably right. I don't see how Zodiac's gang can shoot their way out. They don't have enough ammo to waste all those ghouls."

Strider lifted a pair of binocs that was hanging from his neck to his eyes and glassed the convoy. "Looks like eight SUVs left."

"We had two more, but they broke down on the trip from Arizona."

"Arizona?" said Strider, lowering his binocs. "You were in Arizona? We thought you were in California."

"It's a long story."

Halverson surveyed the mountainside, which was infested with ghouls. As thousands of them converged on the convoy of SUVs, thousands more were massing toward the bunker entrance, plodding inexorably toward it.

"Time to batten down the hatches," said Strider.

He pressed the button that lowered the steel door.

"I need to brief the president about Zodiac," said Halverson, coughing and feeling lightheaded. "If I don't pass out first from breathing the toxic air in here."

Chapter 101

The Roadrunner plowed along the road pullulating with shambling ghouls.

Reaching the helipad's tarmac, which, for the moment, had a smattering of ghouls on it, the Roadrunner was able to put on speed, plowing a half dozen ghouls aside, and blasted across it to Marine One, a Sikorsky VH-60N White Hawk, which awaited President Cole and General Pabst. In no time hordes of ghouls on the outskirts of the landing zone were traipsing across the helipad's tarmac toward the helo until they were a mere fifteen feet away from the aircraft and about to converge on it.

The Roadrunner screeched to a halt.

"We have to get inside the helo before the ghouls reach it," said Pabst, clambering out of the backseat.

A knot of ghouls gathered around the helo.

Rudy bolted to the helo, shoving two ghouls out of his way, sprang into the cockpit, and claimed the pilot's seat.

Lugging the football with him Cole ducked out the Suburban and scanned the area. As far as the eye could see, there were hordes of ghouls shambling across the landscape, kicking up dust with their feet and suffusing the air with the eerie drone of their growling.

"They're everywhere," said Cole, dismayed.

A cloud of ravens flew in front of the sun and blocked it, darkening the sky.

"Hurry, Mr. President," said Pabst. "We need to take off before those cursed things reach the helo."

Rudy found a B&T MP9 in the helo and fired at the nearest mob of ghouls.

"This football isn't light," said Cole, straining to walk faster with it, his gait stiff.

Rudy fired the engine activating the rotors to commence whirling.

One of the ghouls lunged at Pabst. It was a male fortysomething ghoul with a receding hairline and his eyelids chewed off. Pabst whipped his Glock 17 out of his holster and blew away the ghoul's head.

"Come on, Mr. President," said Pabst, his face oozing sweat as he stood near the helo, its rotors whumping above him. "We have no time."

Cole trotted awkwardly toward the helo with the heavy football chained to his wrist weighing him down and straining his back. The downdraft from the rotors whipped his hair and face. He squinted in the racketing wind.

Pabst blew away the skull of a fourteen-year-old freckle-faced female ghoul with pigtails who was wearing red tights striated with multiple runs. Her hand was touching Cole's wrist, as her head exploded and her brains splattered Cole's arm. She crumpled on the tarmac with half a head left on her neck split vertically down her forehead.

Cole grimaced in disgust at the brains pasted on his arm. He felt the urge to wipe them off, but he dreaded touching them. He needed a rag or paper towel.

"Hurry, Mr. President," said Pabst, standing on the tarmac near the hatch, his hair whipped by the helo's churning rotors, motioning to Cole with his hand.

"My arm," said Cole in revulsion, leering at the brain matter coating his arm.

Standing and leaning out of the hatch, Rudy extended his hand.

"Take my hand, Mr. President," he said.

Cole mounted the steps and grasped it. Rudy helped Cole into the helo. Cole fought the downdraft and climbed the rest of the steps into the craft with Rudy's help, the thunderous rotors deafening him. Rudy reached down and gave Pabst a helping hand into the helo after Cole.

A half dozen ghouls waylaid the helo.

Rudy darted back into the pilot's seat, grabbed the collective, and attempted liftoff. A gaggle of ghouls converged on the White Hawk, grasping the wheels and clutching the open hatch, scrambling to get in.

"Knock those things off," said Rudy. "I can't take off with them hanging on the helo."

Pabst stamped on the ghouls' fingers trying to get them to loosen their grips and fall off.

More ghouls crawled over the bodies of the ghouls hanging from the hatch and struggled to make their way up into the helo cabin, clawing clothing and anything else they could use to gain access to the fresh meat inside the aircraft.

Pabst snatched Rudy's MP9 and emptied the magazine into the nearest ghouls, brass cartridges arcing from the MP9. Three heads—two male and one female—exploded in the hail of lead he unleashed. Their bodies fell limp to the tarmac.

Rudy fought to gain control of the collective and retain the helo's balance. Under the weight of the chain of ghouls hanging from the door, the helo was threatening to tip over and crash.

A whirling rotor dipped and beheaded a male fortyish ghoul in scarlet suspenders who was climbing on top of the other ghouls toward the helo. His head spun end over end sailing through the air.

His magazine empty, Pabst stamped on the fingers of ghouls hanging on the hatch's metal threshold.

"Don't worry, General," said Cole. "I have the football. If push comes to shove, I can wipe those things out with one press of a button."

"You can't authorize a nuclear strike without the approval of the secretary of defense, Mr. President," said Pabst, crushing a female ghoul's hand with his black oxford's leather heel.

"The secretary of defense died of a heart attack. You know that."

"Then you have to go through COCOM."

"Do I look like I have time to contact COCOM?" said Cole, straining to hold onto the hatch's jamb and keep his balance in the shuddering, listing helo, as the football hung from his wrist.

"The combatant commanders are next in the chain of command after the secretary of defense as per the Goldwater-Nichols Act."

"Fuck the Goldwater-Nichols Act. I'm appointing you next in command. We're the de facto government now. Man up and accept your responsibility, General."

As the helo rocked, Cole dug the "biscuit" out of his trouser pocket. The biscuit was a plastic card similar in size to a credit card that listed the Gold Codes, the codes for a nuclear launch. Cole consulted the biscuit and entered the code on the football for a nuclear strike on Mount Weather.

"You need to step up and take the secretary of defense's place and verify the launch code for me, General."

"COCOM does that."

"COCOM's not here. It's up to you, General. I'm the commander in chief, and I'm ordering you to do your job."

"We'll all die," said Pabst, aghast.

"Would you rather die eaten by those things or get nuked? I don't know about you, but I'm not gonna let those filthy things eat me. Put your finger on the football's fingerprint reader."

Pabst hung fire, appalled at the consequences.

"Let me remind you, General. You *cannot* veto my order. Not even the secretary of defense, if he was here, could do that."

Still, Pabst hesitated.

"When the ghouls see that I've pressed the button, they'll retreat," said Cole. "Then I'll hit the kill switch, and we're out of here."

Pabst wasn't convinced.

Before Pabst knew what was happening, Cole snatched Pabst's hand and pressed the general's forefinger on the football's print reader.

Cole pressed the fire button, whose red light commenced flashing.

"You're insane," said Pabst.

"I can hit the kill switch and countermand the order to fire within sixty seconds. If we're not out of here by then, we'll never get out of here, and I won't touch it."

Yanked halfway out of the hatch by a ghoul's hand that had grabbed his ankle, Pabst kicked off the ghoul's hand and clung to the jamb with one hand.

A tall female ghoul pushing thirty, wearing a lime green tank top, with carmine lipstick smeared haphazardly on her lips, scrabbled up the living bridge of ghouls, reached up, snagged Pabst's free hand, and yanked him out of the helo.

Losing his balance Pabst screamed in terror as he lost his grip on the jamb and toppled into the writhing chain of ghouls that were suspended from the shuddering helo. Ghouls fell to chewing his face, ripping chunks of flesh from his cheeks and jaw. He struggled to free himself from their clutches, grappling with them, as they held him above them like they were slam dancing in a mosh pit, ripping his uniform off so they could devour his flesh.

Pabst screamed in pain as a ghoul's jaws tore a grapefruit-sized chunk of flesh out of his stomach.

"Pabst," cried Cole, framed in the helo hatch, football in hand.

Pabst screamed again as another ghoul's rotting teeth tore out his carotid artery, sending blood jetting ten feet into the air, spraying the frenzied creatures, who were transported by the fresh steaming blood that showered down on them.

"I'm losing equilibrium, Mr. President," said Rudy, wrestling with the collective to level out the tilting overhead rotors and working the foot pedals to change the pitch angle of the tail rotor. "I can't keep her steady much longer. Clear the hatch of all excess weight. Or we're gonna crash."

The helo rocked to starboard, its tilting rotors slicing the air and decapitating a tall twentysomething ponytailed male ghoul who was climbing over a mob of ghouls to reach the helo hatch.

Pabst stopped screaming and died, as the creatures fed off his corpse.

Cole raised the football in his hand and brandished it at the ladder of ghouls hanging from the hatch. The red light on the football flashed insistently.

"Let go of the helo," he cried, the tendons in his neck straining, sweat popping out of his face. "I have the football. I'll blow us all to kingdom come if you don't let go. I will . . . I will . . . I will. I swear I will. Do you hear me? Listen. If I don't press this kill switch in ten seconds, we all get nuked. Do you hear me, you fucking idiots?"

Bucking wildly the helo was on the verge of tipping over and jettisoning Cole, who clung to the hatch jamb for dear life, the weight of the football threatening to throw him off balance.

Ignoring his words the ghouls kept climbing over each other toward him in the open hatch.

Chapter 102

As the twisted metal wreckage of Zodiac's Navigator burned, and smoke plumed above it, Wagner's "Valkyries" continued to blare from the CD player.

Countless ghouls flocked over the wreckage seeking body parts that had been flung haphazardly by the impact of the rocket Halverson had fired from the RPG-7 and the subsequent explosion of the SUV's fuel tank. The creatures pawed through the burnt-out husk of the SUV rooting through debris and scooping chunks of bloody roasted human flesh off the charred and contorted steel.

A short ghoul in a fireman's uniform, deep in concentration, scraped drying gouts of mouthwatering brain matter off the steering wheel with his fingernails and licked his fingers clean. Beside him a twentysomething female blonde ghoul with unkempt locks and clad in rags sat on the buckled chassis munching a man's naked foot in her hands. On the road a few feet from the chassis lay a scorched sickle.

A piercing whistle shrieked through the dark sky choked with gyring ravens and interrupted the ghouls' meal. Several of the ghouls looked up from their foraging seeking the nature of the cacophony overhead and spotted a coruscating LGM-30G Minuteman III ICBM fitted with a W78 thermonuclear warhead with a yield of 350 kilotons on its final leg of gravity's rainbow screaming down at Mach 23 from the clouds toward the Mount Weather Emergency Operations Center.

"Valkyries" reached a soaring climax.

A deafening explosion shook the ground as the ICBM collided with earth, followed by the eruption of a mushroom cloud unfurling into the sky and looming above a battlefield of mass carnage and mayhem.

Somehow, as if by a miracle, the music played on.

ABOUT THE AUTHOR

Bryan Cassiday writes horror fiction and thrillers. He wrote *Zombie Apocalypse: The Chad Halverson Series.* Books 1–5 are available as a boxed set. He lives in Southern California.